REDEEM ME

BECKETT BROTHERS

L A GALLAGHER

For those of you dreaming of a brooding Irish billionaire...

This one's for you.

Chapter One

CAELON

June

It's been seven hundred and eighty-four days since my wife died. Two years, one month, and twenty-four days of unescapable wrath, rage, and an unquenchable thirst for revenge. No amount of whiskey, wine, or nameless, faceless women have been able to provide an escape – believe me, I've tried.

Though truly, I don't deserve an escape.

I deserve to spend the rest of my life consumed by Isabella's death. If she hadn't married me, she wouldn't have been caught up in the violent feud between my family and the O'Connors, a feud that's spanned generations. She'd still be living, breathing, laughing, loving.

'Perhaps it's time you went home.' James, my older brother, pushes a crystal tumbler towards the redhead manning the black marble bar, but I snatch it, clutching it like a lifeline.

We're in the darkest corner of Elixir, Dublin's trendiest new bar. At thirty-four, I feel too old for trendy, but Dermot, my best friend, convinced me to meet him here. The place is wedged, the music's too loud, and the drink is overpriced, but it beats bumbling around a house that, no matter how many people visit, will always feel empty.

'I'm not going anywhere.' I raise my voice over the music. 'Dermot's on his way. I haven't seen him in weeks.'

Other than my four brothers, Dermot is my only friend. We met five years ago at an exclusive gentlemen's club. He's the friend I'd phone if I needed help hiding a body. The friend who would swear on the Bible I was with him any time and every time. The friend who consoled me through the guilt and shame the first time I fucked a woman after Isabella died. The only person, other than my brothers, who has a key to my house. He's my ride or die. And tonight, I'm in desperate need of a ride.

A short-lived lust-fuelled high. A hot body to press against my cold heart.

I lean in towards the barmaid. She's pretty. Curvy in all the right places. Big green eyes. She's no Isabella. No one is. But I could sink into the softness of her skin, shut my eyes, and pretend for a while.

A love like Isabella and I shared only comes around once in a lifetime. I'm not stupid enough to look for it again. The only thing I'm looking for is to kill the bastard responsible for her death. Not the pitiful excuse of the drunk, drugged-up human, Danny Bourke – the man lying in a coma after ploughing headfirst into Isabella's Range Rover so hard and fast that we had to have a closed coffin funeral. I want to kill Jack O'Connor–the man who put him up to it.

But first, I want to see him rolling on the ground, writhing in agony, pleading for his miserable life.

I want to torture him for days, weeks, maybe even years before I even contemplate ending his suffering, because my suffering will never end. And the prospect of violent vengeance is the only thing keeping my frozen heart beating.

That, and my two children, Owen and Orla. I do my best for them. It's nowhere near good enough, but I'm nowhere near the man I used to be.

Since Isabella died, we've been through eight nannies, nine goldfish, and approximately five hundred takeaways. I'm not proud, but we're alive to tell the tale.

James exhales heavily. He nods to the barmaid to fill up my glass with Beckett's Gold, our family's whiskey, and the original source of our family wealth. We've branched out since my grandfather's time, but the whiskey empire continues to generate the majority of the family fortune.

'I'll have one more, but that's it. Scarlett will string me up by the balls if I'm not home in time for the dream feed.'

'You have enough staff to start your own army,' I remind him.

'She insists on doing everything herself.' James rolls his eyes, but his lips curl upwards at the mere mention of his fiancée's name.

'Who the fuck even are you?' I turn to my brother, formerly the country's hottest billionaire, and the playboy starring at the centre of multiple sex scandals, which involved several company employees. Now he's with Scarlett, he's like a fucking teddy that Barbie put together in a Build-A-Bear factory—big wide smile, starry eyes, and a laugh that's almost infectious. Almost—unless you're the most miserable, grumpy, hateful bastard on the planet, which, in case you haven't gathered, I am.

James and Scarlett have had two babies in two years. The minute the first child vacated her vagina, he banged the next one in. The entire world knows my big brother can't leave his fiancée alone.

I remember what that was like. No matter how many times I had Isabella, it was never enough. Envy blooms in my chest, mingling with the wrath and rage, intensifying my need for revenge.

'I'm your older brother, and the man who promised our mother I'd get you home in one piece tonight. But if Dermot's on his way, I'll pass that responsibility onto him.' James tosses a hundred euro note on the counter and tells the barmaid to keep the change. 'Any luck finding a new nanny yet?'

'The agency's sending someone on Monday.' I snatch my drink up to my lips and down the contents in one mouthful, then hand it back for a refill. The redhead hesitates, glancing between James and me.

'Try not to terrify this one,' James sighs, nodding at the barmaid to pour.

A gaggle of giggling women flock towards our dark corner, nudging closer. James glowers in their direction and they simultaneously step back.

Cock block. Even a miserable man has needs.

I tear my eyes from the women and meet my brother's stare instead. 'I wouldn't have had to bite her head off if she was any good at her job.' Truthfully, none of the nannies were the right fit for our family. I doubt anyone ever will be.

'Look, I don't need to tell you that kids need stability. Especially after everything they've been through.' James's eyes fall to the floor. 'I'm so sorry for you, Caelon. For what happened to Isabella. I can't even imagine your pain, but your kids need the fun-loving father who chased them round the garden with the watering hose. The father who used to make forts under the dining room table and hide with them. The one who made them laugh so hard their stomachs hurt.'

His words pierce my chest like a knife. He's right. But that version of Caelon Beckett died with my wife. I'm not him anymore. And as much as I know I need to be more, to give more, I have nothing left *to* give. Nothing but the aforementioned wrath and rage and my relentless obsession with revenge.

'I'm trying.' I swallow the suffocating lump forming at the back of my throat. 'It's just fucking hard, man. It's hard waking up knowing I'll never see her again. Never touch her. Never hear her breathing beside me at night. And it's fucking unbearable knowing that the man who ordered the hit on her *is* still breathing, even if it is behind the bars of Ravenhill maximum-security prison.'

A thunderous expression clouds James's face. 'We still don't know it was him.'

'We do. You know it as well as I do. Jack O'Connor ordered the hit on Issy. And one day we'll prove it. And when we do, God fucking help him.' My molars clank together so hard they're in danger of crumbling. 'There isn't a man or beast capable of stopping me carving out his heart, the way he carved out mine. Even if I have to commit murder to become his cellmate to do it.'

James flinches. 'If there's a connection, Killian will find it.'

Our brother, Killian, owns the most sought-after security company in the country. He provides everything from state-of-the-art CCTV to lethally trained bodyguards. 'It's been two years and nothing.' I thrum my fingers on the marble counter.

James places his palm on the back of my hand, stilling the movement. 'Give him more time. We can't start another war with the O'Connors until we have proof.'

The O'Connors and the Becketts have been bitter rivals long before James and I were born. I don't need proof they were behind the 'accident' that killed my wife. Even if the timing didn't coincide with our last altercation, I feel it with every fibre of my body.

'Sit tight, brother. The truth always emerges in the end,'

James assures me. He signals to the barmaid for another round.

So much for 'just one more,' but conversations as morbid as this would send anyone searching for oblivion, either in the form of alcohol or sex.

Seeing as the alcohol isn't cutting it tonight, I need sex. Hot, meaningless, filthy sex.

I glance towards the door, watching as a short, striking blonde struts in. She's wearing a low cut, sequinned blush-coloured mini dress which stops several inches above her knees and shimmers with every step she takes.

Her glossy hair is tousled in casual-looking beach waves that cascade over the bare skin of her tanned, toned shoulders. Bright blue eyes glitter. She exudes sass and sexuality as she scans the busy bar. Cherry-red lips lift into a grin as her hips subtly shimmy in time to a sped-up remix of Taylor Swift's *You Need To Calm Down*.

I'll try not to judge her for that.

Sunshine emanates from her every pore. She's so young. So fresh. So flawless – basically everything that I'm not.

But her sharp eyes scan the room like she's on the prowl for something. Or someone.

So, perhaps we have something in common after all.

I take another sip of my drink without taking my eyes off her.

She shimmies towards us, well, towards the bar anyway, effortlessly graceful in silver, six-inch stilettos.

She's a knockout. No doubt about it. My dick stirs in my trousers.

Those huge sparkling eyes finally land on mine. Without a hint of hesitation, she strides towards us with more confidence than Beyonce. She bulldozes past the gaggle of women James scared away and squeezes into the space beside us. Dainty fingers pluck up a cocktail menu as her head flicks round. Her tongue dips out to wet her lower lip. Another cat-like grin reveals the perfect Hollywood smile.

I don't return the gesture. I'm incapable. I'm looking for a fuck, not a BFF.

Her pupils dart between James and me, then rove thoughtfully from my face to my torso, then back up again to lock eyes with mine again.

'Cheer up, for fuck's sake.' Her honeyed voice is just as sunny as the rest of her. 'Christ, you two look like someone died.'

Chapter Two

IVY

It was supposed to be a joke. An ice breaker. But now a thick tension swirls through the air—and not the sexual type that I picked up from the sullen but sexy guy from forty feet away.

Oh, I didn't miss the innate broodiness he oozes. In fact, it was one of the things that caught my eye, along with his sculpted, muscular shoulders encased in an expensively tailored ebony suit that fits so perfectly it had to have been made for him. Mr Tall, Dark, and Tortured has this repressed look in his big black eyes, like he's in pain and desperate to unleash himself on someone. His jaw is locked so tightly he reminds me of a firework waiting to go bang.

And after being babied by my big, burly, overprotective brother for the past three weeks, scratch that—for my entire life—I'm in need of a bang—one that makes *me* see fireworks.

If I have any hope of getting laid tonight, it's imperative I find a suitable candidate before my brother, Dermot, bull-dozes in with his size thirteen Burberry patent loafers and a warning look that would terrify an army of blood-thirsty gladiators.

I might be his little sister, but I'm a twenty-three-year-old woman with desires that need to be taken care of, preferably, before I start my new job. Things have been dry for too long down under. I'm determined to fix that tonight. Once I move into my new accommodation in the leafy suburbs of Dublin, opportunities to get to bars like this will be few and far between.

I try not to salivate over the men beside me. Both are beautifully masculine with shadowed jawlines and sharp, prominent bone structure. Mr Tall, Dark and Tortured's eyes are a deep espresso colour, but instead of that rich brown exuding a warmth, it exudes a chilling sorrow.

Maybe someone did die.

Maybe they stopped in here for a drink after a funeral.

Fuck.

'I'm sorry.' I raise my palms in apology. 'That was really insensitive of me.' I've never been one to think before I speak. My mouth has got me into plenty of trouble in the past. But right here, this isn't trouble, it's just downright awkward.

Tortured composes himself quicker than a nun caught with her knickers down. 'Don't sweat it.' He picks up his drink and drains it in one gulp. I watch as his Adam's apple bobs. He might be miserable and melancholy, but he is one hundred percent *male*. My pheromones kick-start into overdrive.

The barmaid flits towards us and I order a double whiskey neat. I like my alcohol the way I like my men—strong and sharp—and these two are exactly that. Shame I just sank my size six stilettos in it. I should probably have ordered a Sex on The Beach. It might be the closest thing I get to experiencing any action tonight given the way my mouth shoots off.

I pull out my phone to pay but before I can tap it, Tortured tosses a hundred euro note to the barmaid. 'Keep the change,' he says, taking my drink and handing it to me.

His voice is deep and gruff, like the rest of him. It does things to me. Things that ignite a heat in my belly.

'Another one, James?' He turns to his friend.

'No. I really have to go. Scarlett's waiting.' James pushes his glass away. 'I'll call you tomorrow. Have a good night.' He slaps a hand on Tortured's broad back, nods at me and abruptly leaves.

'And then there were two...' I edge closer to my new drinking buddy, wedging him further into the corner of the bar, flashing him my most seductive smile.

'You ought to have a licence for that smile. It's seriously blinding.' He cocks his head to the side. 'Are you always so sunny?'

'Are you always so sullen?' I retort, taking a mouthful of whiskey.

'I wasn't always this way.' He sighs, swirling his drink around the glass.

'What happened?' There goes my big mouth again.

'It's not exactly Saturday night chit-chat material when I'm trying to get into your knickers.' His face remains deadpan.

'How do you know I'm wearing any?' I'm going to make him smile if it kills me.

Torrid flames flicker in his irises. 'Careful, sweetheart, or I might be compelled to slip my hand under that indecent little dress to find out.'

A million butterflies sweep through my stomach. 'Careful, Tortured, or I might just let you.'

'Tortured?' he scoffs, 'What kind of nickname is that?'

'It was the best I could come up with on the spur of the moment.' I shrug.

'I've been called many things before, but that's new. Not to mention eerily accurate.' He leans casually on the bar.

'What's your name?' His cologne swirls through the air. It's expensive, unique and masculine.

'Does it matter?' I trace a finger up my glass and watch as his gaze follows the movement before flicking back to my face.

'Oh, you're one of those girls, are you?' The flames in his irises intensify, bleeding into his pupils.

'Tell me what "one of those girls" is and I'll tell you if I am one.' I bring the glass to my lips and drink without breaking our stare. The air crackles like a live wire and I am here for it.

He leans closer until his hot breath brushes my lips, mingling with mine. 'One of "those girls" who knows what they want and aren't afraid to grab it by the balls.'

He's partially right. I'm sort of one of "those girls".

When it comes to men, I know what I want. Which is more than I can say for every other aspect of my life. Much to my parents' dismay, I took a gap year to work as a nanny in the States. It was only supposed to be until I figured out what I want to do with my life. Five years later, the only thing I've actually figured out is that I want to be a mother myself one day. Not that Tortured needs to know that.

'I'm not afraid to grab anything, or anyone, by the balls, as you've probably gathered,' I shrug, 'but you have one thing wrong.'

'What's that?' His mouth twitches.

'I'm not a girl.' I step forward and rest my hips against his. The bass thumps through my ears, but not nearly as loudly as the blood pounding through my pulse. 'I'm all woman.'

'Is that right?' He shifts his own hips in the slightest, subtlest movement, but it's enough for me to feel something rock solid stirring in his trousers.

'Yes. And I need a man to remind me. And fast.'

'What's the hurry?'

'Because it's been over three months since I had sex. I

haven't even had peace to enjoy some time alone with my vibrator. I have about half-an-hour before my overbearing big brother rocks up and if I don't get laid sometime soon, I might spontaneously combust.'

'Whoa.' He rubs a thumb over the stubble dotting his square jaw. 'You really are one of those girls, I mean women.'

'If you really want to find out, I suggest we leave now.' I want him. Even if he is tortured and repressed. *Especially* because he's tortured and repressed. I want him to take every single ounce of whatever made him like that out on me. I'm sick of being treated like I'm fragile. I want to be fucked, royally and thoroughly, to the point where I won't be able to walk without being reminded of it for at least three days. Is that too much to ask?

'If I were to leave with you now, where would you take me?' He dips his face closer and lifts a thick finger to my collarbone, barely skimming the skin. Goosebumps ripple in its wake.

'You'd have to take me to your place. I'm crashing with my aforementioned overbearing big brother.'

A low tut slips from his lips. 'My place is miles away. And I never take women there.'

Disappointment snakes through my stomach. It was too good to hope that the hottest man in the bar had an apartment around the corner.

'Oh well,' I feign nonchalance, 'if you see an explosion, it's just me spontaneously combusting.'

'Just because I can't take you home doesn't mean we can't have some fun.'

'Do you even know the meaning of the word, Tortured?' I joke, but there's nothing funny about the throbbing sensation stirring in my panties—yes, I am wearing some, not that Tortured will ever find out either way, worse luck.

'You'd be surprised.' His lips brush over my ear. 'Switch places with me.'

My eyes widen. Fuck, this guy is insane as well as every-thing else. 'You want to fuck me in the bar? Here? In front of everyone?' I scan the crowd, a mix of young, glamorous women and suited men. No one is paying any attention to us. Everyone is immersed in their own unique bubble, chatting, drinking, flirting, dancing. But seriously, not so much that they wouldn't notice two patrons going at it like rabbits spiked with Viagra. The lighting is low, but not that low.

'Believe me, sweetheart, if I thought I could get away with it, I would.' His hand slides over my waist to grip my hip as he guides me into position into the dark corner he was occu-pying. I'm sandwiched between the hard, hot planes of his torso and the marble counter, with the wood-panelled wall to my side.

The sheer size of his physique blocks anyone from even seeing I'm there, let alone seeing the hand that slides up my thigh and dips beneath my dress.

'What are you doing?'

'We've already established you're one of "those women," but I'm about to show you I'm one of those guys.'

'What guys?' Nimble fingers skim higher until they meet lace. My pulse thunders through my ears. I swallow back the saliva flooding my tongue.

'The type that knows what he wants and isn't afraid to grab it by the...' gleaming eyes bore into mine. He yanks my lingerie to the side and sinks his fingers into my slickness, 'pussy.'

I gasp and his lips curl in satisfaction. It's not exactly the smile I was aiming for, but he definitely looks slightly less tortured.

I part my legs, scanning the bar to check if anyone has noticed a dark stranger has two fingers inside me and is currently pumping them hard enough to rock not only my body, but my entire world.

'No one is watching, sweetheart. No one but me.'

'You didn't even kiss me first.' What kind of stupid line is that? I told you my mouth opens, and anything is liable to come out. In my defence, it's impossible to think about anything other than his fingers.

He laughs, but it's low and cruel. 'I don't do romance, sweetheart. But I will make you come hard enough to see stars.'

I believe him.

Someone jostles into the space next to us. Over Tortured's shoulder, I glimpse a guy ordering drinks. There's no way he can see I have a stranger's hand under my dress. Not with the way his body is shielding mine, but still, a ripple of anxiety whips through me, but the added danger only adds to the experience.

Tortured isn't anxious. His fingers don't stop. If anything, they quicken. My arousal drips all over them as I keep one eye on the guy beside us.

'Don't you dare look at another man while my fingers are inside you.' He lowers his face and drags his stubble over my cheek. 'Look at me while I make you come.' It's not a request, it's a demand, and it is hot as fuck.

He jerks his head back and our eyes collide. 'Is this what you came here for?'

I nod as my thighs tighten and tremble.

'Me too. I came looking to lose myself in someone. I imagined it would be my cock sinking into that wet heat, not my fingers. Though, watching you writhe is oddly satisfying.' His thumb pushes on my clit.

'Have you ever been finger-fucked in a bar before?' His gravelly voice will live rent free in my head forever, along with the memory of this night.

'No.'

'Good.' Electricity hums between us. 'I like that this is new to both of us. Now be a good girl and come on my hand before we get thrown out of here.'

White hot lust squeezes my core. The sheer naughtiness of this entire scenario is almost enough to get me off alone, so when he adds a third finger, I'm gone, catapulted into the most decadent, all-consuming oblivion.

Heat suffuses my skin. My breasts ache with a heavy longing. My core convulses around his fingers, and my limbs go taut before shaking and shuddering. A depraved, decadent pleasure pulses through my pussy as I shamelessly grind against his hand, wringing out every second of the most debilitating orgasm known to woman.

Tortured watches on with smug satisfaction, probably knowing he's just ruined me for any other sexual experience after this.

I wanted fireworks. I got a nuclear bomb.

When he's coaxed every ounce of pleasure from my body, he slides his fingers out, bringing them to his lips. His tongue slips out and he licks them without breaking eye contact.

It's the hottest thing I've ever seen. The bar is packed but I only have eyes for him.

'Caelon.' A familiar voice booms from behind Tortured's back, shattering my orgasm-induced bubble. 'There you are.'

'Dermot?' Tortured spins around to face my brother.

'How are you doing?' Dermot extends a hand.

Tortured—I mean *Caelon*—glances at his own hand. The very hand that's still slick with my arousal. The hand that's wearing a goddamn fucking wedding ring!

How did I not notice that before I let him slide it into my lingerie?

It's like watching a car crash in slow motion, but I can't tear my eyes away.

Caelon slaps Dermot's back with his other hand and pulls him in for a man hug.

'Are you getting soft in your old age or what?' Dermot laughs, his eyes falling to me, wedged into the corner. 'Ivy! I see you met Caelon.'

I smooth my dress down, praying I don't look as thoroughly fucked as I feel.

'She certainly did.' Caelon's gaze flits between Dermot and me, like he's trying to figure out the missing piece of the puzzle. 'Ivy is your... girlfriend?' Oval eyes narrow in my direction. Rich coming from the man who's wearing a wedding ring.

Dermot's laugh reverberates through the air over the music. 'Don't be ridiculous. Ivy is my sister.'

Caelon leaps away from me like he's been stabbed with a red-hot poker.

Chapter Three

CAELON

Fuck. My. Life. This cannot be happening. I just finger-fucked my best friend's little sister in a fucking bar. Worse still, I still have the proof of her pleasure on my hand and in my mouth. I swallow hard. If I wasn't already going to hell, I just bought myself a one-way ticket, first class.

'Your sister?' I repeat, running my fingers over my jaw. 'She didn't mention that part.' I turn to Ivy and shoot her a glare.

I've never met Dermot's kid sister. She'd just moved to the States when I met him. He talks about her all the fucking time, though. If he had his way, she'd be wrapped up in cotton wool at home with their parents.

'You didn't exactly give me much of an opportunity,' Ivy snaps. Her cheeks are flushed, her chest rises and falls in rapid waves as she fights to get her breath.

'You should have told me.' It's a battle to keep the anger from my voice. Everyone knows the bro code–never touch your best friend's sister. It's an unwritten rule of every friend- ship. If Dermot had any idea what I did, what just happened between us, he'd skin me alive. Hell, I'd do the same if the roles were reversed. My sister Zara is only twenty. The thought of her and Dermot... it doesn't even bear thinking about.

'Like I said, it wasn't the first thing that came up.' Ivy's eyes dart to my crotch.

Thankfully, realising you've made a major fuck-up is a quick way to kill a boner.

'It should have been.' I grab my glass from the counter.

'You seriously expect me to walk into a bar and tell every man I meet I'm Dermot Winter's little sister?' she scoffs.

'I'm not every man.' I grimace.

'We've already established what type of man you are, remember?' She juts her chin defiantly. Her glare could level a skyscraper. I don't know why; it should be me who's pissed. It'll be me Dermot murders if he so much as gets a hint of what happened.

Thankfully, he's too busy beckoning the barmaid over to notice our exchange.

'I thought you were in the States.' I remember Dermot going over to visit a couple of times.

'Well, I didn't think about you at all.' She shrugs, snatching up her whiskey.

'You will now, though,' I mutter. The image of Ivy's face lanced with animalistic pleasure will be forever etched into my brain. It took me eighteen months to work up to having sex with a woman that wasn't Isabella, but since then, there have been many.

But none of them memorable.

None of them as sassy, or as sexy as Ivy.

Fuck.

Dermot turns to us. 'Ivy got back from San Francisco three weeks ago. Her last boss turned out to be a total creep. Kept trying to put his filthy fingers all over her. I've a good mind to fly over there and snap them from his hand.'

I flinch as my eyelids squeeze shut. 'I have to go.'

Dermot's mouth pops open. 'What do you mean, you have to go? I only just got here.'

'I need to get back. Orla's not feeling great.' It's not entirely a lie. Orla hasn't been feeling great since Isabella died. Then again, none of us have.

'Who's Orla?' Ivy asks, her voice thick with suspicion.

'My daughter.' I slap Dermot's back. 'Sorry, man. I'll call you next week.'

'Make sure you do. We're long overdue a catch-up.' He rakes his fingers through his hair. It's the same shade of sunshine yellow as Ivy's. Now they're side by side, I can see the similarities, well except Dermot looks like a younger, sterner Jean-Claude Van Damme, where Ivy looks like Blake Lively, but even sexier.

'It was, er... nice to meet you.' I chance a glance at Ivy, who seems to have recovered from almost being caught with her panties down, or to the side, I should say.

'The pleasure was entirely mine.' She shrugs as her big blue eyes glare at my hand once again. I follow her gaze, trying to work out where her animosity has come from.

Ah. My wedding ring.

I haven't been able to take it off. It seemed too final. Too real.

Ivy flashes me another killer smile, turns her back and studies the cocktail menu like it's Dan Brown's latest thriller and she's just got to the twist.

What a brazen little madam! I've a good mind to bend her over the bar and slap her perfect peachy ass.

But she was wrong when she said the pleasure was entirely hers. She might have been the one to have come harder than a freight train, but watching her do exactly that was entirely *my* pleasure.

'See you.' Though truthfully, I won't see her. Next time

Dermot suggests a drink, I'll make certain it's just the two of us. No way am I putting myself within five miles of Ivy Winters ever again.

She's trouble.

And not because she's Dermot's little sister, but because she's the most interesting and attractive woman I've met since Isabella. A sliver of guilt snakes into my stomach even thinking that way.

Isabella.

What would she make of tonight's events?

You'll never find out, that inner voice reminds me. Isabella is gone. And so is the man she married.

All that's left is this hateful beast.

I stride across the bar, searching for my driver, Damon, as I weave through a throng of bodies. My head twists, something in my chest compels me to glance over my shoulder as I reach the exit.

Blue eyes blaze back at me from across the room. Something sharp stokes my sternum.

I tear my eyes away and march out into the night.

'You don't have to do this, you know.' Dermot loads my suitcase into the boot of the private hire car. 'You don't have to take this job. Stay with me for as long as you like. Why don't you take the summer to make a five-year plan? You could start college in September. Think about it.'

'You sound like our parents. Did they put you up to this?' I rock back on my heels and fold my arms across my chest.

The sun beats down on my face and I can literally feel more freckles sprouting on my nose and across my cheek-bones. I was told throughout my entire childhood they would fade as I got older, but every summer they come back with a bang. In the States, I had to carry my ID everywhere or risk being refused entry to bars and nightclubs. Here, I just have to say I'm Ivy Winters and there isn't an establishment in the country that would refuse me. My father is a famous judge, my mother one of the country's top paediatricians, and my brother has made millions on some sort of state-of-the-art IT software.

And me? Well, I'm a nanny.

My family wants more for me. A high-flying career. A big

house and an even bigger bank balance. And not because they want something to brag about at the golf club, but because they love me—in their own way. But that doesn't stop the irritation flaring in my chest.

The truth is, I like being a nanny. I'm brilliant at it. Kids are so much simpler than adults. If they think something they say it. Want something, then they ask. Spending time with them doesn't feel like work, it feels like fun. And the longer I do it, the less I want to do anything else. Even if admitting it to my overachieving family makes me a pariah.

'I love my job. I love kids.' I squint up at Dermot, shielding my face from the sun with my hand.

'So, why not follow Mother's footsteps and become a paediatrician?' He shuffles from foot to foot, indicating to the driver that we'll be another minute.

'Because I love *kids*. Not sick kids. I don't want to be a hero. I want to be the fun one who bakes cookies and bounces on the trampoline.'

'You could be so much more.' Dermot sighs.

'Am I not enough as I am?' It was supposed to be a joke, but the words come out more seriously than I intended.

Does not having a college degree, or a five-year plan make me less of a person?

Dermot pulls me against his chest and ruffles my hair. 'Course you're enough. We just want you to be fulfilled. Happy. Being a nanny was supposed to be a stopgap. Do you seriously see yourself in the same job at fifty?'

Truthfully, no. I see myself minding my own kids one day, but Dermot doesn't need to hear that right now. The thought of someone impregnating his baby sister is not one he's comfortable with. Or someone having sex with me at all. Which is why it's a damn good job he didn't walk into the bar five minutes earlier the other night.

The entire decadent scenario lasted about six minutes, but I've replayed it in my head six million times since.

It was wrong on so many levels, but it was hot AF.

His poor wife.

I tried my best to milk Dermot for information after Caelon left the other night, but he refused to tell me anything other than that his friend's had a rough couple of years. Ha, as if his tortured face and entire demeanour didn't already give that away.

'I haven't given it much thought.' I step away from my brother and turn to the car.

'Well, I'm asking you to think about it now, Ivy. Do you even know anything about this family? You're literally moving in with strangers. Again.' Dermot winces, throwing an exasperated hand into the air.

The only family that makes me feel like a stranger is my own. Not that I voice it out loud. I had a twin, Katie. She died of an asthma attack when we were five. Since then, my parents prefer to love me from a distance. It's almost like looking at me is too painful. Unfortunately, my brother went the other way, smothering me. The eleven-year age gap between us means I'll always be a baby to him, which is one of the reasons I put an ocean between us the second I turned eighteen.

'It's a job, Dermot. One I've been doing pretty damn well for years. It's perfectly safe. The agency does all the checks. Stop worrying about me.'

'You have a knack for attracting trouble.' Dermot shakes his head.

What I have is a knack for attracting troublesome men, unfortunately. Which is why my last position didn't work out. My previous employer's husband thought his wife was paying me to take care of his dick, as well as his children. It got ugly when I refused his advances. Which is when I got this mad notion about coming back to Ireland.

I'm regretting it already.

'How much trouble can I get into nannying in a mansion in Malahide?' I open the car door and hop in.

'Call me later. Let me know you're okay,' he urges.

'I'll call you at the weekend. Stop mollycoddling me.' I swat my hand in front of his face. 'Love you.'

'Love you too.' He smooths out the frown on his face. 'Be careful.'

I exhale a sigh of relief as the driver starts the engine.

Forty minutes later, we pull up outside my new home. High sand-coloured stone walls surround the property. A motorised gate prevents us from entering. A security guard, wearing a smart black suit and stoic expression, approaches the car. He's in his thirties. Not bad looking. He's no Tall, Dark and Tortured, but he might be up for the craic.

The driver winds down the window.

'Can I help you?'

'I'm the new nanny.' I pluck my phone from my pocket and tap into the email from the agency, holding the phone out to him.

'Nice to meet you. I'm Damon, head of security. He's expecting you.' His nostrils flare. 'Good luck.' He nods and steps back from the car.

He?

Does *he* have a name?

The agency sent me the kids' names, ages, and said the father works away a lot. I scanned the details all too quickly in my rush to escape Dermot's eagle eyes.

And good luck? Something in Damon's voice makes me think I'm going to need it. A shiver of apprehension streaks down my spine.

Who even has security in Dublin?

I don't have time to contemplate it as we crawl up the tree-lined driveway and the house comes into view. It is breathtaking. Built out of the same sand-coloured stone as the wall, it's modern, luxurious, with ginormous floor-to-ceiling windows that scream sophistication.

There's an elaborate water feature, row upon row of colourful planters lining the perimeter, an industrial-sized firepit, and best of all, a huge outdoor pool with thick, plush cushioned sunloungers flanking it. I've worked for some wealthy families, but this is something else.

The driver slows to a stop at the front steps. A solid sage-coloured front door swings open and a man appears. I'd put him in his mid-forties. His dark hair is peppered grey and he's wearing a suit almost identical to the guy at the gate. He descends the steps with speed and stealth.

He doesn't seem too intimidating. The apprehension eases a fraction as his thin lips stretch into a smile. 'Miss Winters, welcome.' He shakes my hand firmly, then heads to the trunk to fetch my luggage. 'I'm Samuel. It's a pleasure.'

My new boss is a gentleman.

Phew. Despite my bravado in front of Dermot, after my last boss put his hands on me, I admit, I was slightly apprehensive coming here today.

'I can do that.' I motion to my tightly packed suitcase. It contains pretty much everything I own, which is why it's almost ready to burst at the seams.

'It's my job,' Samuel says.

My stomach sinks. How many staff work here? I glance between the gate and the opulent entrance. I'm contemplating bailing out when a high-pitched wail comes from the open front door. 'She's dead! She's dead! She's dead!' The voice belongs to a child. An inconsolable one.

My head yanks round, the hairs on my neck pricking despite the summer sun warming my skin.

'It's okay,' a deep masculine voice booms from somewhere inside. 'It's okay, baby.'

'It's not okay. Everyone round here dies!' The anguish in the child's voice slices open my chest.

Instinctively, I stride towards the open door, following the sound of sobbing. I step inside the double-height hallway, barely taking in the opulent surroundings in my quest to find and console whoever is crying.

A broad-shouldered man crouches on the floor with his back to me. He's wearing dark designer jeans and a fitted white polo neck, which hugs his broad chest and muscular arms in a way that should be illegal. His arms are wrapped around a little girl, hugging her tightly to his chest. She has stunning dark curly hair, olive skin, and big chestnut brown eyes. She stares at me over his shoulder, tears streaming down her cheeks.

I part my lips into a wide, reassuring smile, lift a hand and wave, lowering myself to her level as I scoot closer towards them.

'Hi. You must be Orla.' I muster my brightest tone.

Orla.

The name hadn't meant anything to me when I read the email from the agency last week, but as it pops from my lips, something clicks. In the same heartbeat, the man crouching spins around.

Tall, Dark, and Tortured stares back at me with an expression of horror – one that mimics my own.

Chapter Five

CAELON

What the fuck is Ivy Winters doing in my hallway?

Her expression freezes, a picture of shock, but she recomposes herself in an instant, flashing that megawatt grin. It's just as blinding as it was on Saturday night.

Why is she smiling at my daughter like some sort of stalker psycho?

What the fuck is she playing at?

Did Dermot put her up to this?

Is it some sort of sick joke?

'What the actual—?'

Her sunny demeanour has no right being in my house. Neither do her sparkling blue eyes, her tempting curves, or her tousled sexy beach-wave hair, which I'd love to wrap around my hand and—

She cuts me off before I can finish speaking and thinking.

'I'm your new nanny.' Ivy wiggles her fingers, coaxing Orla over, like it's not the most fucked-up thing that she's standing in my hallway right now.

The new nanny?

Fuck. My. Life.

It's bad enough she's Dermot's sister. She can't be the new nanny as well. Someone somewhere is trying to punish me. As if I haven't endured enough in this lifetime.

'What happened, sweetie?' Ivy opens her arms to my daughter.

Orla won't go to her.

She's uncomfortable with strangers. With change. With anything and everything since Isabella died.

'Come here, sweetie,' Ivy coos. 'You and I are going to be great friends. We're going to have so much fun together.'

Actually, you're not.

There's no way she can stay. No way in hell. It's implausible. Nanny or not.

I scrape my nails over my scalp and blow out an indignant breath as she continues her attempt to win over my daughter.

'Come over here and let me wipe those tears away,' Ivy singsongs.

To my utmost surprise, Orla wiggles free from my arms and darts across the hallway, hovering in front of Ivy, hopping from foot to foot in her favourite pink Nike runners.

Unbelievable.

Ivy scoops her into her arms as if she's a six-month-old, instead of a six-year-old, and kisses her forehead. The air whooshes from my lungs.

'I'm Ivy. I've been so excited about meeting you.' She straightens her spine and runs a thumb over Orla's tear-streaked cheek. 'What happened, honey?'

'Jasmine died.' Orla hiccups another sob.

Ivy frowns at me, rubbing soothing circles on Orla's back. 'Who's Jasmine?'

'My fish,' Orla says, before I have the chance to intervene. 'It's the tenth one I've killed.'

'Ah, I'm so sorry, sweetie. Fish don't live long, I'm afraid. Not like humans,' Ivy continues.

I stiffen, bracing myself for what I already know Orla is going to say.

'Neither do humans,' she sniffs. 'Jasmine died and now she's with my Mammy and the other fish in Heaven. And it's not fair. I want to see them. But Daddy says I'm not going to Heaven for a very long time.'

Ivy's palm slows to a stop on Orla's back. Her eyes drift to my wedding ring. Realisation, then pity, clouds her eyes.

I don't need her pity.

I need a nanny.

Preferably not one I've finger-fucked in a bar.

The colour drains from Ivy's rose-hued cheeks and her smile fades into a sympathetic grimace. Thankfully, she keeps her focus on Orla. 'Oh, Orla, I'm so sorry. It must be so hard for you. I can only imagine.' She shifts my daughter from her right hip to her left. 'You know Heaven isn't that far away, though. I'm so sure your mammy is watching over you. I bet she's so proud of what a big girl you're growing into.'

Orla buries her face in Ivy's hair and lets out another heart-wrenching sob.

She's coped exceptionally well with her mother's death, with the help of an excellent play therapist, but every time one of those damn fish dies, it triggers her again, which naturally triggers me.

There's nothing worse than seeing your child in pain.

And as much as I hate to admit it, Ivy's soothing murmurs and gentle rocking motion are doing a surprisingly stellar job of easing Orla's pain or, at the very least, distracting her from it.

But that doesn't mean she's staying.

No way.

Samuel stalks in the front door laden down with a green leather suitcase that's about three stitches away from bursting all over the hall floor.

'I'll take this upstairs.' Samuel starts towards the wide, winding staircase.

'No need.' I hold a hand up to halt him. 'There's been a mix up at the agency. Miss Winters isn't staying.'

Ivy's head snaps up and her blue eyes blaze like twin flames. She opens her mouth to speak, but Orla beats her to it.

'What do you mean, Daddy? She just said she's my new nanny.' She sniffs again. 'I like her. I don't want her to go as well. Everyone dies or leaves.'

I flinch. Kids don't lie.

Pinching the bridge of my nose, I suck in a ragged breath.

Ivy can't stay.

Not now the image of her face as she came undone on my hand is seared into my brain.

Not now I know what she tastes like.

Not now I've beaten myself off thinking of her six times in the shower since.

It's too awkward.

Too weird.

It's just wrong.

'Why don't I stay for a while, and we can talk about this mix up later.' Ivy beams at Orla without sparing me a glance. 'Do you have any dolls? Or teddies? Or are you a Polly Pocket type of girl?'

Huh. I know exactly what type of girl–woman–Ivy Winters is, and even though she's doing a great job at calming my distraught daughter down, she's no fucking Mary Poppins. Mary Poppins would never have let a stranger get her off in public.

'I'll show you the playroom,' Orla exclaims. 'We have everything. Barbies. Lego. Even a tent with fairy lights. You need to see it!' She slides down Ivy's tight white vest top and ass-sculpted jeans, slips her hand into hers and drags her down the wide corridor.

Samuel stands in the hallway with a quizzical expression on his face. 'The luggage, Mr Beckett?'

'Leave it there. She's not staying,' I repeat.

'Very well.' Samuel raises his bushy eyebrows but doesn't linger.

My son, Owen, trundles down the stairs with his favourite stuffed animal, Patches, tucked under his arm. Patches is an oversized, tatty teddy bear who's seen better days, like the rest of us. His stuffing is falling out, he's lost an eye, and he's in desperate need of a wash, but Owen won't part with him for a second, let alone the hour it would take to put him through the washing machine.

'New nanny?' he scowls.

Owen has hated every nanny we've had. It's not their fault they're not Isabella. He was only three when she died, but he talks about her every day. Though he doesn't have that many memories of her, he likes to go over the ones he does, which is endearing, but brutal, for me.

There's no escaping the reminders of her. I know I don't deserve to escape, but sometimes to do so is a relief.

Owen refuses to let another woman close to him. Is it possible that he feels the same sense of disloyalty I felt the first time I had sex with another woman?

'Yep. But this one isn't staying.'

'Good.' He reaches the bottom step. 'Dad, I have to fess something.' His huge chocolate eyes fall to the floor. Both kids inherited my colouring, but they both have their mother's soft features.

'What is it, buddy?' I cross the hall and crouch to his level. The scent of pee clings to him and his 'fession' is suddenly obvious. He's been bed-wetting most nights since Isabella's death.

'I —'He swallows thickly and tugs at Patches' one eye.

'It's okay, buddy.' I pull him against my chest, feeling his heart thud against mine. 'I'll take care of it, don't worry.'

We have a housekeeper, Liz, but Owen would rather I put his sheets in the wash than tell the staff about his accident. Liz is a firm but fair type of woman, but the kids find her a little intimidating.

'Come on up. I'll put you in the bath while I strip the bed.' I hoist him up and carry him up the stairs.

I have a million things I need to do today, but at least I'd arranged to work from the home office this week. It usually takes a few days to get the new nanny settled. I should know. I've done it way too many times now.

And now Ivy showing up has tossed a brand-new spanner in the works.

I don't have time to spend weeks settling in new nannies while trying to run the Beckett chain of boutique hotels. I'm bang in the middle of acquiring six more properties in several countries. Some of the older hotels are undergoing extensive refurbishment, and I'm busting my balls trying to help push through planning for a brand-new luxury flagship on a piece of land my brother, Sean, has acquired in Galway.

Time is money.

I run the bath, place Owen into it with plenty of toys, then strip his bed, all the while trying to work out what the fuck I'm going to do about the woman playing snakes and ladders with my daughter. My daughter, who is usually inconsolable for days when one of her fishes dies but is now laughing like a hyena on helium. The sound travels up the stairs and seeps through my sternum.

I pull my phone out of my jeans pocket and dial the agency that supplies the nannies.

'Hello, Tatiana speaking, how may I help you?' The manager always answers with the same cheery tone. Who are these people who can muster enthusiasm on a whim? Do they have coffee on an IV drip? A pocketful of Haribos? Two lines of cocaine with their breakfast? How are they always so fucking cheerful?

'It's Caelon Beckett. You sent me the wrong nanny.' I stalk towards the big window overlooking the pristine front lawn. Not that I can take any credit for it. It's all down to my gardener, Jared, who comes four times a week. His man vests are tighter than mankinis, and he often reeks of weed, but he gets the job done.

'Ah, Mr Beckett, give me a second.' I hear the tap tapping of fingernails on a keyboard.

'We sent Ivy Winters. Did she not arrive?'

'Oh, she "arrived".' *Right over my hand on Saturday night.* 'But there's been a mix up. She's completely and utterly unsuitable for the position.'

'Did she do something wrong?' Tatiana's voice hitches with surprise. 'She came with excellent references.'

'I specifically requested someone who has five years' experience with children, is trained in CPR, and is a competent swimmer.' *And preferably someone who doesn't look like a fucking supermodel would be really fucking helpful.*

'Miss Winters meets all the criteria. She has buckets of experience, excellent references, and her mother is one of the top paediatricians in the country,' Tatiana boasts.

I know. Mainly because that top paediatrician also birthed my best friend too.

'Look, she's just not a fit for this family. Can you please send someone else?' I lean against the door frame, watching as Orla and Ivy stroll across the grass hand in hand. Something sharp twists in my chest as they stop by the water fountain and peer at the lily pads. Ivy says something to Orla, and she laughs.

Tatiana clears her throat, 'I'm afraid there isn't anyone

else. I lost four of my girls to a charity dig in Africa. Two have accepted "real jobs", their words not mine, and the others are all settled with families. There's a possibility I might have someone in a few weeks, but the background checks take a while, as you know.'

For fuck's sake.

'How about you keep Miss Winters for the summer and get back to me in September if things don't settle?' Tatiana suggests. 'How does that sound?'

I could try another agency, but Tatiana's is the best in the city.

I sigh sharply. We're at the start of the summer holidays. Orla's school has finished up for ten weeks. Owen's just graduated from playschool and is about to start big school in September. I need someone now. I can't be here all the time.

'It sounds like I don't have a choice.'

Chapter Six

IVY

Orla is one of the sweetest, cutest kids I've ever worked with. My heart breaks for what she's endured in her short life. Dead fish and multiple nannies clearly aren't helping.

I could help though. I'd love to try at least. Try to bring some happiness back into this beautiful little girl's life. I've always been compelled to help people, kids especially. Perhaps because I couldn't help my own sister. My mother begged me to study medicine. She's convinced I'm a 'fixer'. I think that's just wishful thinking.

It's not ideal that Orla's father is the tall, dark and tortured stranger who got me over the line faster than a Formula One car, but I can get over that happy accident, if he can. Especially now I know he's a widow, not a cheater. Though, given the way he's been simultaneously scowling and spying on me all morning, and the fact my suitcase is still at the bottom of the stairs, him "getting over it" isn't looking likely.

Is he worried I'm going to spontaneously jump him?

Or say to his kids, "Hey guys, guess what Daddy did the other night."

As if.

We're both adults. Professionals. We can forget it ever happened. Well, okay, I'll probably never forget, but I can pretend. It doesn't have to be an issue unless he makes it one. We both know it can never happen again.

'I'm hungry,' Orla whines, tugging me towards the opulent kitchen. The back wall is entirely made of glass and opens out onto a dark, polished wooden decking area with a rustic - looking table and six chairs.

A woman in her late fifties is washing lettuce over a white porcelain sink. She's wearing a white short-sleeved blouse and smart navy slacks. Her greying hair is scraped back into a tight bun. She tilts her weathered face to us as we approach, her eyes flicking between Orla and me. 'Hello, who do we have here?'

'This is Ivy. She's my new nanny,' Orla announces proudly.

'Dad says she's not staying,' a voice squeaks from behind us.

'Oh, hi Owen.' I turn to find a little boy with the same cold eyes and surly frown as his father. He has a tattered teddy under his arm and a defiant expression on his face. 'Where have you been hiding all morning?'

I'd hoped he might join Orla and me in the garden. I'd hoped to get the chance to prove to Caelon that I'm the right woman for the job, because the last thing I want is to have to go back to Dermot's with my tail between my legs and admit I got fired on my first day. By his friend, no less.

'She *is* staying.' Orla stamps her pink Nike runner on the tiles.

'Is not.' Owen barely even looks my way.

Tall, Dark and Tortured chooses this moment to strut into the kitchen. He ignores the bickering erupting between his children and simply scoops his son up into his arms.

It's a good job he's so crabby or I'd be at serious risk of

crushing on him, whether it's professional or not. Mind you, the man has plenty of reasons to be crabby, given he lost his wife. Orla didn't mention what happened to her mother, but she did let slip that they've had eight nannies in that time.

Damn Dermot for not telling me more the other night. As soon as I get a free second, I'm going to google the shit out of Caelon Beckett.

'Is it lunch time, Liz?' Caelon refuses to look my way.

'It'll be ready in five minutes, Mr Beckett. I set the table outside.' She nods to the open back doors.

Am I supposed to sit with them or make myself scarce? In my previous placements, I've been the cook as well as the nanny, eating only after I'd served the family.

But I can't sit down with the Becketts and pretend I'm one of them. That would be weird. What did the other nannies do?

'Come on.' Orla tugs my hand, guiding me to where a cool summer breeze brushes in through the kitchen.

My feet remain rigid. I crouch to my knees and untangle my fingers from hers. It's clear Caelon doesn't want me here. I could crash in a hotel for a few nights, sign up to a few more agencies until I find another position. Somewhere sunny. Somewhere the father doesn't despise me. Somewhere far away from my overbearing brother. 'Orla, I've had the best morning playing with you.'

'Don't.' Orla slaps her palm over my mouth. 'Don't say you're leaving too!'

I prise her fingers away and give them a gentle squeeze. Tears well in her eyes and my chest cracks open. 'You heard your daddy. There was a mix up at the agency. I'm sure they're going to send you someone really nice.'

'But you're really nice!' she wails. 'Daddy, please don't let her leave.'

Caelon sighs, a pained expression settling on his face as he focuses on his daughter. 'Relax, Orla, sweetheart.' He crosses the room and ruffles her hair affectionately. 'Ivy can stay, for the summer anyway.'

I swallow my surprise and lock eyes with my new boss. 'I can?'

He holds my stare, sporting that same tortured expression. 'If it suits you?'

'Absolutely.' It'll give me time to get something else lined up, and time to hang out with Orla. It's obvious how much she craves affection, attention and security, and while I'm here, I'm going to smother her with all the above. I'm also going to make it my personal mission to win over Owen. After everything this family's been through, these kids need some fun. I'm the right woman for this job, even if Caelon doesn't want to admit it.

'Yessss!' Orla fist pumps the air and drags me outside to the table. Silver cutlery sparkles in the sunlight. 'You're sitting next to me.'

I look to my new boss, checking if he's okay with me eating with them. He shrugs. 'I'm not usually around for mealtimes.'

Well, that should make things easier, at least.

Though tell that to the sharp stab of disappointment in my sternum.

I brush it off, taking the seat next to Orla. Caelon and Owen take their seats across the table. My gaze sweeps over the lush landscape. It's so peaceful. So tranquil. The lawn could double up as a golf course. Boxes of lavender line the decking and a stone pathway leads to another outdoor area where a swimming pool glitters invitingly from forty feet away.

This house, these grounds, are heavenly.

What a setting to spend the summer.

'Owen, do you want to play "floor is lava" with me and Ivy

after lunch?' Orla picks up her knife and instinctively I take it from her hand and place it down again.

'No.' Owen doesn't even pause to think about it.

'Do you want to play tag?' I venture.

'He doesn't like running,' Orla informs me, while Caelon watches on silently.

'What do you like?' I lean forwards, but Owen refuses to meet my eye. 'I'm not great at football, but I can be the goalie if you want to play penalties?'

Owen glances at his father, then towards the pool sparkling at the far side of the house. 'I like swimming, but we're not allowed unless Dad's with us. He worries we're going to die like Mammy did.'

Caelon winces.

Did his wife drown? I open my mouth to say I'm a competent swimmer, but Caelon speaks first.

'I'll take you to the pool later, buddy.' He lifts a glass of water from the table and raises it to his lips. 'It'll give Ivy time to unpack.'

Owen's face lights up and he looks like a different child. 'Yes! Thanks, Daddy. You're the best.' Caelon pats his head affectionately. 'Do you remember the time Mammy jumped into the pool and soaked you in your work suit?'

Caelon's teeth sink into his lip. 'Course I do.'

'And when you told her off, she got out and pretended to say sorry, but then she pushed you in with all your clothes still on.' Owen hoots as his tiny hand slaps the table. 'And the two of you laughed for ages after that.'

My eyebrows rocket skywards. So, Mr Tall, Dark, and Tortured wasn't always this way. His wife's death must have hit him horrendously hard. He must have loved her so much. I can't imagine what he's been through. No wonder he's miserable, sullen, and cold.

He might not want me here, but he needs me. These kids

need to laugh again. And so does he, whether he wants to
or not.

Chapter Seven

CAELON

'Your room is upstairs. Fifth door on the right,' I tell Ivy, without adding that it's not the usual nanny room, it's the most opulent guest bedroom in the house and, coincidentally, the furthest room away from mine. 'Samuel will take your luggage up shortly.'

I must be mad letting her stay, but how could I say no when Orla has latched onto her like a vine clinging to an oak tree?

'Thank you.' she flicks her golden hair from her shoulders and my focus is drawn to the bare skin of her chest. Her vest does nothing to conceal the perky tits straining beneath, or the faint outline of the lace pattern of her bra.

Where is Nanny McPhee when I need her?

Instead, I'm stuck with Nanny McSexy. Nanny McSunshine. Nanny McBestFriend's FuckingSister.

All the work I have on at the moment suddenly seems like a blessing. Manual labour in ninety-degree heat would be less work than keeping my eyes off my newest employee.

And that's the crux of the problem.

I don't date. I fuck. There's a reason I don't bring women

home. I don't let women near my house or my kids. And now, suddenly, the woman I've spent the weekend wanking myself stupid over is my new roommate.

Even if I *was* looking for something, which I'm not, other than revenge, of course, Ivy is completely and utterly off limits for a million different reasons.

Liz steps out into the sunshine carrying two plates of pasta bake for the kids, places them on the table and returns to the kitchen.

'You should have most of the information you require in the contract, but I'll run over it quickly, anyway.' Ground rules. That's what we need. Firm, rigid, unwavering ground rules, for my benefit, as much as for hers.

'Great.' Her tongue darts out to wet her lower lip and I imagine it darting over my cock.

Fuck's sake, Caelon. Get a grip.

I blink hard, forcing the image away.

Orla stabs a piece of penne with her fork, gazing at Ivy like she's some sort of goddess. Ivy winks at her and pats her forearm affectionately. She really is a natural with children. At least her sunny, sassy warmth is good for something.

'I work long hours. I travel frequently. It's easier during term time when the kids are in school, but summers are hard. I need someone who is prepared to be here when I can't be. Having said that, I always try to be home on Friday night to put the kids to bed myself. If I am, you can take the night off. Saturday nights I usually go out.' I avert my eyes as the memories of last Saturday night crash back through my brain. 'And all my employees have Sundays off.'

'That's very generous,' Ivy says, and I can't work out if she's being sarcastic or not.

'The nights I am home, we eat together as a family. You're welcome to join us.' I clear my throat. 'We have a gym, a cinema room, and you can see the pool. Use them as you like.

I'd like you to spend half an hour each day helping the kids with their reading. Other than that, you're free to entertain them any way you like.'

'Ah, Daddy! I hate reading,' Owen complains.

'I know, buddy, but you hate it because it's hard. Sometimes the things we find the hardest are the most important things to master.'

Isn't that the truth?

Liz returns with two giant bowls of Caesar salad topped with parmesan. The scent of smoked bacon wafts through the air.

'I can cook, if you want me to,' Ivy offers.

'You most certainly can't!' Liz exclaims, her thin lips purse into a tight line. 'That's my department.'

'Oh,' Ivy startles, 'I didn't mean to step on anyone's toes. I'm just saying I can help in other ways if you need me to. Use me any way you like.'

I cough to cover my gasp.

'Oh God, that came out wrong. I didn't mean...' Her fingers fly to her luscious lips as her cheeks flush to a hot pink.

'Uncle James told Daddy it's okay to use women, as long as they understand up front that's all it will ever be,' Orla announces with a mouth full of penne. 'I heard them talking at Granny's house last weekend.'

Liz's jaw almost hits the floor. She spins on her sensible flat shoes and stalks back to the kitchen.

Oh my God.

Now it's my cheeks flushing red.

Ivy splutters and thumps her chest with a fist before reaching for a glass of water.

I clear my throat. 'Thank you, Orla, but that was a private conversation between grown-ups. You mustn't eavesdrop on adult conversations.'

'Oh, you mean like the time I heard—'

'That's enough. Thank you.' I cut her off before she can say anything to lower Ivy's opinion of me further.

Not that I care what she thinks, of course.

'There's an SUV in the garage. It's yours while you work for this family. I'll get you the keys, along with a set of house keys, and I'll get you a credit card. Take the kids out. Buy them things. Spoil them. They've been through enough. I want them to be happy.'

'Perfect. Is there anything else I should know?' Ivy spears a chunk of chicken and pops it into her mouth.

Not unless you want to know how many times I've thought about your slippery wet cunt in the last thirty-six hours.

'The kids go to bed at seven-thirty. When I'm here, I prefer to read their stories myself.'

'Okay dokey.' Her mouth moves as she chews and it's a struggle to tear my gaze away.

'What will Dermot think of you working for me?' Truthfully, it's the least of my worries, but I am aware it might cause some tension.

'I'm sure he'll be happy knowing I'm in safe hands.' She smirks and I scowl. 'Better the devil you know, right?'

She has no idea.

We both reach for the salt at the same time and our fingers meet. A sharp shock sears my skin.

'Sorry,' she stammers, yanking her hand back.

So am I.

Sorry that she stirs something in my trousers.

Sorry that I know how fucking sweet she tastes.

And sorry that I can never taste her again.

Chapter Eight

IVY

Caelon's house is grander than any hotel I've ever stayed in. My bedroom is the size of a small apartment. Decorated in warm shades of blush pinks and magnolia, it's luxurious and inviting. It boasts an enormous ensuite, a power shower with mood lighting, and a walk-in wardrobe that's bigger than my bedroom at Dermot's, and that wasn't small by any means.

French doors open onto a balcony overlooking the stunning lawns and pool below. Two wrought-iron chairs and a small table are flanked by flowerpots overflowing with pretty pink peonies.

I lug my case onto the soft silk sheets and unzip it. Other than a few "Saturday night outfits", my clothing collection consists of comfort pieces; vests, yoga pants, denim shorts, and casual summer dresses. If I'd have known I was coming somewhere so opulent, I might have gone shopping.

But then again, I'm not here to look good. My hot new, brooding boss barely glanced at me all day, anyway. Is he repulsed that the new nanny is naughty enough to let him get her off in a bar? Or that he was naughty enough to do it in the first place? Regardless, I should be grateful he's not looking for a repeat. Tall, Dark and Tortured has more baggage than a conveyor belt at Dublin Airport in August.

Mind you, I would too if I'd been widowed with two young kids.

I grab my phone from my back pocket and type Caelon Beckett into Google. My screen is flooded with articles and images about my new boss, the hotel chain he runs, and his family's billion-euro whiskey empire. I scroll down until I find what I'm looking for and tap on a news article published two years ago.

Isabella Beckett, wife of Caelon Beckett, CEO of Beckett Boutique Hotels, was tragically killed in a road traffic accident earlier today. Two cars collided head on. Two people were fatally injured at the scene. Another is reported to be seriously injured.

Fuck.

A memory of Saturday night catapults into my brain - and not a good one.

Christ, you two look like someone died.

Oh. My. Fucking. God. Could I have been more insensitive?

Nausea rises in my stomach. I've put my foot in it a million times in my life, but this is like jumping into an open wound with six-inch stilettos. No wonder the man can barely look at me. The second I get the chance to apologise, I will. Profusely.

Until then, it's nose clean, head down.

I hang my dresses in the wardrobe, lay out my toiletries on the ivory marble bathroom countertop, and set my Kindle next to my bed, plugging it in to charge. I'm addicted to mafia romance novels. I plough through four of them most weeks, the darker the better. The more the hero needs love, the more I fall in love with him.

What can I say? I have terrible taste in broody bad boys. Is it any wonder out of a bar filled with men, I was drawn to Tall, Dark and Tortured?

But life isn't a book. Caelon's issues are real, and I am not the heroine in this story.

My phone rings as I'm stowing my case away.

Dermot.

I blow out an exasperated breath and roll my eyes to the heavens. I've barely been out of his sight for a couple of hours.

I snatch the phone to my ear. 'Sorry, I can't talk right now. I'm mid orgy with the two hot dads who hired me to mind their kids. We've been at it three times already since I left your house, but you know, some guys are just insatiable.'

'Not funny, Ivy,' Dermot bites out. 'Where are you?'

'I told you, a mansion in Malahide.'

'What are the family like? Who are they? Do I know them?' Dermot fires question after question without pausing for an answer. 'Caelon lives in Malahide. I bet he'd know them.'

'Yeah, about that...' I twist a long strand of hair around my index finger and tug it hard enough to pull on my scalp.

'What?' Dermot's voice sharpens.

'Funny story.' Or not, given what occurred the other night. Better to just come out with it. He's going to find out I'm living with his best friend sooner or later. 'It's actually Caelon.'

'What do you mean, it's Caelon? What's Caelon?' Dermot demands.

'I'm nannying for Caelon. Well, Orla and Owen.' Though Caelon could clearly do with some TLC himself. 'Apparently, he can't keep a nanny for more than a few months, so yours truly is stuck with him for the foreseeable future...' I trail off.

Silence greets me at the other end of the phone. Seconds

pass. Then raucous, booming laughter. Dermot's guffaws echo through my ears.

'Ha! Talk about baptism of fire,' he snorts.

'For him or me?' I stare at the phone open-mouthed.

'Well, both of you now you come to mention it. Caelon's just so...'

'Sullen? Snappy? Short-tempered?' I finish for him.

'Exactly. And you're just so...' he trails off.

'Cheery, patient and empathetic,' I prompt.

'Exactly,' he sighs. 'And there was me worrying you'd get stuck with another creepy boss who can't keep his hands off you.'

I wish.

No, Ivy. Nose clean, head down. And not down in my boss's crotch, no matter how much I keep imagining what he's packing down there.

'You don't need to worry about that at least.' *Worse luck.* 'You could have told me about his wife, though.' I exhale heavily.

'I would have done, if I'd have known you were going to start working for him,' Dermot says. 'Bad business. Really bad. It was a terrible car crash, but Caelon is convinced there's more at play.'

'In what way?' I pad across the plush ivory carpet to stare out over the gardens.

'The Becketts and the O'Connors have been enemies for years. The families run rival whiskey empires. Weeks after the Beckett brothers helped put Declan O'Connor behind bars, Isabella was killed in an "accident" that makes no sense whatsoever.'

'But it was a car crash...' I feel my eyebrows furrow.

'The guy driving owed the O'Connors a serious debt. The rumour is the debt would be wiped out and his family taken care of if he did this last job.' Dermot's voice drops to a husky low.

'But that's crazy.' I rest my palm over my heart.

'It's a crazy world we live in,' Dermot concedes. 'Caelon has made it his life's mission to find out the truth, but the only surviving passenger, the man driving the other car, is still in a coma over two years later.'

'Shit.' It explains everything about Caelon. It's bad enough his wife was killed, but to be deliberately taken from him by his family's rivals, well, that's a different type of burden to bear.

'Don't say I mentioned anything. Caelon is a private person. He hides his anguish behind a mad quest for revenge. God help the O'Connors if that driver ever wakes up, or if Caelon finds any other form of proof.'

A cold shiver ripples over my spine.

'I'm glad he has you to take care of the kids, Ivy. But more importantly, I'm glad he values the importance of family. You're safe with Caelon. He'd never lay a finger on my little sister,' Dermot scoffs. 'He knows better.'

I cough to cover the hiss that slips from my lips.

'I'll catch up with you soon. Call me if there's anything you want or need,' Dermot says.

'Will do,' I promise.

But truthfully, there's only one thing I want—to comfort Caelon Beckett. To put my arms around him and to take his misery away, if only for a few minutes.

Chapter Nine

CAELON

Knowing Ivy is under my roof is a special type of torture, one that has left me tossing and turning every night for the past two weeks. One that had me in my home gym at five o'clock this morning just to work off some of the tension tightening my muscles. One that has me wondering what she wears to bed. I could look, this place has more security cameras than Buckingham Palace, but I wouldn't invade Ivy's privacy no matter how many times I've thought about it.

Since she took the position, I've been working from home most days, and today is no different. I glance at the framed photograph of Isabella on my desk.

'You'd like her,' I mutter. 'She's sunny and warm, and she's great with the kids.'

I used to be sunny and warm once, before this eternal blackness set in to my soul. Now all I can think about is revenge.

I skim through my emails to find there's been a delay in construction starting on the Monaco hotel. The company we hired has gone bust, and it's taking an age to secure a new one. There are endless issues with permits and planning, but time is money. I fire off a message to Stephanie, my PA, to chase up the planning application and then call Killian.

Although each of my brothers runs a different division of the family empire, we all operate under the same global corporation. Killian's security company provides everything from world-class CCTV to trained bodyguards and his services have become the most sought-after in Europe.

'Caelon,' Killian answers in his usual gruff tone. Out of all four of my brothers, Killian is the most taciturn. He's the first brother I'd call in a crisis, and the last I'd call if I wanted a drinking buddy.

'Any update?' I cut to the chase. Every week without fail, I call him for a report on the O'Connor situation. Killian has men inside the prison. His guys are overqualified to work as prison guards, but get paid well to pretend. They're our eyes and ears in there. James suggested Killian's men should simply take out our enemies quietly, make it look like an accident, or a suicide, but I want the O'Connors to suffer like I am.

He sighs. 'Not yet, but I'm working on it.'

'It's been over two years. To say I'm beginning to get impatient is an understatement.'

'You think I don't know that, brother?' Killian says grimly. 'You think I don't want to punish the person who ordered the hit on my sister-in-law?'

'Sorry. It's just frustrating.'

'Look,' he pauses for a long beat, 'I don't want to get your hopes up, but I might have something.'

'Seriously?' I shoot forward in my seat. My eyes home in on the picture of my wife again. I *will* avenge Isabella if it's the last thing I do.

'Don't get excited now, I've yet to prove anything, but Danny Bourke's wife, Stacy, has been mouthing off about how her old man set her up for life with "one last job." I can't find a paper trail of money, but she could be using a foreign bank account. I won't give up until I find out.'

'The fucking audacity!' Rage ripples over my skin. 'Bragging about her useless waste of space husband who ploughed a car into my fucking wife! Doesn't she realise the only reason I pay his medical bills is because I want to be the one to kill him myself after I've found out who put him up to it? I swear if she knows anything about it, I'll burn her and Danny's world down, as well as Declan O'Connor's.'

'And I will help you, brother, believe me. Just sit tight for a while longer,' Killian promises.

'If only Danny would wake up.' I would drag the truth out of him, even if it meant sawing off every one of his limbs.

'Don't do anything irrational. You've got two kids relying on you,' Killian says, like I need reminding.

'Call me the second you know more.'

'Obviously.' Killian disconnects the call without so much as a goodbye.

I pace my office like a caged lion, hungry for action or distraction. Seeing as I'm not in a position for action, I opt for the latter.

I pull up the mansion's elaborate CCTV system on my computer screen and scan the cameras until I find what I'm looking for. Ivy. Though I haven't stooped to snooping on her in her bedroom, the communal quarters are fair game. Spying on her is something I've been doing way more than is healthy over the past couple of weeks. I could pretend I'm checking on her abilities as a nanny, but truthfully, I'm checking out which ass-sculpting pair of yoga pants she's wearing.

Her sheer proximity is driving me demented with lust, which is why I've been hiding out in my office until past ten every night since she moved in, just to avoid being alone with her.

This morning, she's in the playroom with Orla and Owen.

Her blonde hair is tied up in a high ponytail that reveals a long, slender neck. She's wearing a fitted white t-shirt, and a pair of faded denim cut-off shorts that show off her tanned, toned legs. The very same legs that had me gawping like a fucking horny teenager in the bar a few weeks ago.

Orla's snuggled onto her knees, listening to whatever story she's reading. I crank up the volume to hear which one.

'Will you teach me your roar?' Ivy singsongs the story, her honeyed voice flooding my office.

Owen is curled up on a beanbag in the corner with Patches tucked under his arm. He's forcing an expression of boredom, but I know he's listening because this story, The Lion Inside, is one of his favourites. Ivy seems to be making progress with him, slowly but surely, but he's not making things easy for her.

She readjusts Orla on her lap, using one hand to turn the page and the other hand to stroke through Orla's dark curly hair. I swallow back the emotion pricking my throat.

'Yep, you'd love her,' I look at Isabella's photograph again. 'She's perfect for the kids.' Which is why I need to stop perving on her on the cameras and get on with my fucking work.

I switch off my computer just before one and head for the kitchen in search of lunch. The house is unusually quiet.

'Where is everyone?' I ask Liz, swiping a chunk of cheese from the ploughman's platter she's preparing. It looks delicious.

She slaps my hand away and tsks. 'Who knows where those hands have been!'

I know exactly where those hands have been. The memory is branded into my brain like a tattoo.

'Wash them before you start plucking at my pretty plat- ter.' She nods towards the sink and lifts the wooden tray.

Liz is the only member of my staff who would dare to speak to me like that, but she's practically family. She pretends she's gruff and grumpy, but beneath it all she has a huge heart. When Isabella died, Liz single-handedly kept the house running. I simply wasn't capable.

'I'll carry that out,' I tell her. 'It looks heavy. Give me a second.' I cross the kitchen to the sink, turn the tap on and pump the soap dispenser.

As I scrub my hands, I glance out the window, and my eyes are drawn to Ivy. Specifically, her ass in those shorts. She's running round the lawn chasing the kids. Owen's clutching a water gun, firing it at Ivy and Orla. The distant sound of his laughter carries on the breeze and for the first time in a long time, my lips lift into a genuine smile.

But it freezes on my face when I spot Jared, my tight-vested gardener, meandering towards Ivy.

It's impossible to hear what he's saying to her. It's also impossible to miss the way his beady eyes are roving over her torso like she's a brand-new shiny toy. He stops, leaving barely a foot between them, and says something. She turns to him, throws her head back and laughs.

Who the fuck does he think he is?

I'm paying him to work, not to hit on my nanny.

And what's so fucking funny?

Ivy runs her fingers through her hair and beams at him. It's his turn to laugh. The urge to put my fist through his face is suddenly overwhelming.

'Lunch is ready.' Liz stands at the open patio doors, beckoning Ivy and the kids over.

Impeccable timing. My molars clank together as Jared reaches out and touches Ivy's arm before backing away.

Clearly, I'm going to have to watch this newfound friendship.

'I set the table outside again,' Liz calls to me, obliviously.

'Got to make the most of this weather while it lasts.' She tilts her face up to the sky and closes her eyes with a gentle exhale.

I dry my hands and lift the platter. 'This looks amazing,' I tell her as I pass. Even if my stomach is twisted to the point I might not be able to eat any of it.

'Huh, flattery will get you nowhere with me, Mr Beckett,' Liz snips, but there's a hint of humour in her tone. I place the platter in the centre of the table and slide into my seat, dragging the summer air into my nose to calm down.

Why should I care if my gardener is flirting with my nanny?

Why?

Because she's barely been here two weeks and she's already got under your skin, a little voice shouts inside my head.

'Daddy, did you see me?' Owen shouts, jogging towards me. 'I got the girls good.' He thrusts the now-empty water gun in the air triumphantly.

'I saw you, buddy. Looked like a lot of fun. Go wash your hands before lunch.' I prise the water gun from his hands and place it on the ground behind me. 'You too, Orla.' She's close on his heels, with Ivy tight on her tail.

Ivy in her wet, tight white t-shirt.

Fucking. Hell.

No wonder Jared was staring. I almost wouldn't blame the guy—almost.

The thin white cotton is completely transparent over her fabulous, full tits. Dark rosy nipples are almost visible through the lace outline of her bra. It's impossible not to stare. My cock thickens in my shorts.

'Owen seems to be coming out of himself a bit,' Ivy says, sliding into the seat opposite me, grabbing a grape from the centre of the table.

'He's not the only one.' I tear my eyes from her chest and scowl at Jared's retreating back. 'You should get changed.'

'Me?' She laughs, then glances down. 'Oh, gosh.' She swipes a napkin from the table and tucks it over her t-shirt. 'Sorry, I didn't realise.'

'It's a spectacular sight, but one I'd prefer you didn't treat my gardener to.' My tone is thick with disapproval.

Her mouth drops open, but the kids trundle back to the table before she can articulate a reply. Thankfully, they keep a steady stream of conversation flowing because I have no idea what to say to the woman opposite me. The woman I can't stop stealing glances at. The woman I'm imagining bending over this table and fucking into next week.

'Can we swim this afternoon?' Owen asks, his eyes bright for once.

Ivy cocks her head at me. 'If your dad says it's okay, I'll take you into the pool.'

Ivy in a swimsuit. Fuck.

'I'll keep them safe, I promise. I'm no Pamela Anderson,' she laughs, glancing down at her chest, 'but I'm a pretty good swimmer.'

The napkin is soaked and is also now completely transparent. Someone is testing my restraint.

'I'd say you could give her a pretty good run for her money.' I force my focus from her breasts to her face in time to see her look of surprise, followed shortly by a sliver of a smirk. Our eyes lock and electricity crackles in the air, tethering us together with an invisible thread.

'Can we, Daddy, please?' Owen begs.

'Sure, I don't see why not.' I ruffle his hair, and he holds his hand up for a fist bump.

I need to get out of here. Time to go to my office in the city. Ivy in a swimsuit is not a sight me or my dick need imprinted into my sex-starved subconscious.

Chapter Ten

IVY

July

In the three weeks I've been living with Caelon Beckett, I've learnt three things about him. One, he's a workaholic. He spends every night in his office while I sit on his insanely comfortable couch reading or binge-watching *Love Island*. Two, he is ridiculously good with his children when he does emerge from his office. Three, he gets up at the crack of dawn to work out. That's how he maintains his mouth-watering physique.

Perving on my hot new boss in his home gym is my favourite morning pastime, closely followed by googling the ever-living shit out of him.

I've got into a routine of waking before six and this morning is no different. The summer sun leaks in through the cracks on either side of the curtains. I pull the bed covers back and creep down to the kitchen to make coffee before the kids wake up, and before Liz comes in to make breakfast for everyone.

As I creep down the thick-carpeted stairs, bare foot, the faint sound of the radio radiates from the gym at the far end of the house. Feeling like the Pink Panther, I follow the noise along the corridor until I reach the gym. The laundry room is next door, so if I get busted, I can pretend that's where I'm heading. So far, Caelon's always been too engrossed in his weights to notice me. I'm hoping this morning is no different.

I peep inside, hoping to steal a glimpse of my hot boss, but it's empty. I must have missed him.

Caelon has been mostly avoiding me. We've shared a few mealtimes, which would have been awkward if it weren't for Orla's incessant stream of conversation. Sometimes I think I feel the weight of his stare, but every time I dare to look up, he whips his eyes away.

The tension is palpable. I wish he'd just chill out. He must have realised by now it's not like I'm going to leap on him. Even if I fantasise about doing precisely that each night in bed, knowing he's only along the corridor from me. I'm only human, and he is spank-bank perfection personified. Throw in the tortured edge, and the big soulless eyes, and he's my own personal type of kryptonite.

There are two pictures of his late wife in the house; a family photo on the mantelpiece in the sitting room and a wedding photo in the grand drawing room. Isabella Beckett was a beautiful woman. It's easy to see where the kids get their stunning looks. Both their mother and father could front a Hugo Boss modelling campaign. Which, given I'm forced to live with their widowed dad, isn't helpful for my ovaries or my unruly hormones. Especially when I know what his hands are capable of. I've tried my best not to imagine the rest of him.

Tried.

I'm not even going to pretend that was successful.

But bar these sneaky perving sessions, I've managed to keep my head down. I'm doing my best to provide a stable routine for two adorable kids who have clearly had little stability over the past couple of years. Owen's still taking his time warming to me. Though, the recent swims in the pool are gaining me a few brownie points. So are the yoga poses I've been teaching them. Down dog is Owen's favourite. It's not a lot, but it's a start. As are the regular trips to the park and the ice cream parlour. Samuel always accompanies us. Either Caelon is paranoid about the rivalry Dermot mentioned, or he's paranoid about my abilities to take care of his children. I'm not sure which is worse, but I don't mind Samuel's company. He's funny, easy to get along with, and he always drives, something I'm eternally grateful for because the SUV Caelon mentioned is actually a brand-new Mercedes. I'm almost as afraid of denting it as I am of leaving it unlocked.

I retrace my steps in search of coffee, beating down the silly disappointment swirling in my stomach. There's always tomorrow. I step into the kitchen and almost jump out of my skin when I see Caelon already there, wearing nothing but a tiny pair of running shorts that sculpt the globes of his ass cheeks to perfection.

He stands in front of the open fridge, peering in with his head cocked thoughtfully to the side. His broad back is bare, revealing an enormous tattoo of a phoenix rising from the flames. It's shockingly colourful, intricate, and immensely detailed. The urge to run my hands over every line and curve sets the tips of my fingers tingling.

And don't get me started on the smooth display of skin, the taut defined shoulder muscles, and the strong muscular biceps which shift and tense as he reaches up for a carton of orange juice.

Holy fuck. He looked hot in a suit in the club. He looks smoking in jeans and a polo shirt; he looks savage in his training gear, but fuck me, half naked, he looks fit to be devoured like an all-you-can-eat buffet.

'Morning.' I lick my lips.

He startles. The carton of orange slips through his fingers and hits the ground, spilling all over the tiles.

'Shit,' he hisses.

'Sorry, I didn't mean to startle you.' I cross the floor and tear a huge wad of kitchen paper from where the mount is on the wall. 'Let me get that.'

'No,' he snaps. 'I'm perfectly capable of cleaning up my own mess.' He grabs a tea towel and tosses it on the ground.

I stand back, watching as it soaks up most of the juice. When I look up, Caelon's gaze is focused firmly on my nightie, a white silk slip from Victoria's Secret. It has tiny straps, dips low in a V at the front, and stops mid-thigh. Basically, it leaves nothing to the imagination. Not that he needs to imagine much. He knows exactly what's hiding beneath.

I lean on a kitchen unit and fold my arms across my chest in a feeble attempt to conceal my bullet-shaped nipples.

'I was in the gym.' He points to his torso in explanation.

'I came down looking for...' What did I come down looking for again?

'Coffee?' He heads towards the fancy machine in the corner.

'Exactly. I need a coffee.' *But I'll take anything else that's on offer too...*

He examines the row of capsules and snatches up a white china cup. 'How do you like it?'

Heat flushes my neck. Does he realise what he just said? Is he trying to give me heart failure? Or is he oblivious to the fact I'm more attracted to him than I've been to any other man in my life?

When I don't answer, he turns his attention from the coffee pods to me. Dark, bottomless pools dart over my thighs, roving up over my chest, before meeting my gaze.

'Strong? Steaming hot? Sweet?' he probes, and I swear he's biting back a smirk.

For a second, I see a glimmer of the man I met in the bar that Saturday. That surliness is still there, but there's a hint of fun beneath his cold exterior just dying to burst out.

I shrug, forcing nonchalance even though my mouth is watering at the sight of him. 'Strong, always. And I'm sweet enough already,'

'Don't I know it,' he mutters under his breath. 'How are you settling in? Orla adores you.' His tone is almost begrudging.

'Okay, I guess.' I shrug. 'It was quite a shock, realising you were my new boss.'

'You don't say.' He loads a capsule into the machine and hits the start button. 'I never bring women home, ever. Then suddenly you turn up with a smile the size of the sun, and your suitcase.' He skims his hand over his stubble. 'I thought Dermot put you up to it as payback for me coming on to you.'

'It was just a mad coincidence.' Though, I don't believe in coincidence. 'As if I'd admit to my overprotective big brother what went down seconds before he arrived.'

'Good job. He'd probably cut my cock off and shove it where the sun doesn't shine,' Caelon murmurs grimly. The coffee machine begins to spurt, and a delicious aroma floats through the air.

'Yep. Then he'd cut you into tiny pieces and feed you to the sharks.' I'm not joking.

Dermot insisted I join him for dinner the last two Sundays, once at a fancy à la carte, and once at our parents' house. His weekly interrogations are grating on me. Have I thought about college? What am I going to do with my life? Blah blah blah. The list goes on.

'Good job it'll never happen again then,' Caelon says gruffly.

'Good job.' My mouth agrees, but my lady parts scream otherwise.

Of all the men in the world, why does the hottest guy to lay his hands on me have to be my new boss and my brother's best friend? And if that wasn't enough, he also happens to have more issues than Playboy magazine.

The coffee machine stops. Caelon picks up the espresso and hands it to me. My fingers graze his. The heat of the cup has nothing on the hot, prickling sensation of our skin touching. He jumps back like he's been scalded. Good to know I'm not the only one suffering.

He turns his back to me, studying the coffee capsules like they're the morse code. 'You're good with them, you know.'

'Orla yes. Owen's still making his mind up.'

'He's never warmed to any woman other than his mother,' Caelon admits.

I pause for a second, unsure whether to comment or not. As usual, my mouth wins the battle against my brain. 'I'm so sorry about your wife. And I'm sorry I was so fucking insensitive in the bar the first night.'

'Don't be. I don't need your pity.' His shoulders go rigid as he shoves another capsule into the machine and slams the lid down hard.

I flinch. 'I didn't mean to...'

He sighs and his back relaxes slightly. 'Look, it is what it is. We do the best we can without her.'

'Want to join me on the patio for a few minutes?' I gesture towards the sun streaming through the window. I'm dying to get to know him a bit better. It might be overstepping, given that he's my boss, but considering we live together, and we're already sort of intimately acquainted, maybe it's okay?

His jaw sets in a fine line. Shit. I *did* overstep. My fucking mouth again. I'm his employee, not his friend.

'Sorry, Tranquil, no can do.' He shakes his head.

'Tranquil?' I squeak.

He's given me a nickname. Surprise rises in my chest.

'You nicknamed me Tortured, so I nicknamed you Tranquil. You brought the kids tranquillity. I see you teaching them yoga. You're a good influence on them. There have been fewer meltdowns. They're more Zen or whatever.'

He's teasing me. 'Zen? You think I'm some sort of hippy or something? Yoga reduces cortisol levels, therefore reduces anxiety.'

'Relax, I didn't mean to insult you. If anything, I'm grateful.' He pats my arm in what I think is supposed to be a reassuring gesture, but in reality, it sets my skin on fire. 'I'd better clean up the orange juice before Liz comes in and kicks my ass into next week.'

'Okay.' I take my coffee outside and sit on one of the plush wicker armchairs overlooking the pool. The cool air does nothing to help the fire blazing over my skin.

Tranquil. Huh. I suppose I've been called worse.

The following evening, Caelon swans into the dining room with a bottle of red wine in one hand and two glasses in the other. He places them on the table between us. Things are looking up. I haven't had a drink since that night at the bar and the prospect of one tonight, amongst other things, has me salivating.

Given that it's Friday, I gather he's going to put the kids to bed, which means I have the night off and I have every intention of using my free time wisely.

I've had an itch brewing for weeks. And living with Tortured is doing nothing to take the edge off. In fact, it's exacerbating it. Smelling his cologne wafting through the corridors, watching the strong but gentle way he interacts with his kids. And don't get me started on that pornographic tattoo I glimpsed in the kitchen yesterday.

I need to get out, let off some steam, get sexually sated, and then maybe I won't ruin my panties every time he walks into the room.

'Daddy!' Owen and Orla both jump from their seats and

run to Caelon, whose biceps flex as he pulls them into his arms.

What is it about single dads that is so freaking hot?

'Hi guys, did you have a good day?' He kisses their foreheads, then ushers them back into their seats and uncorks the bottle.

'If I recall correctly, whiskey is your preferred tipple,' his lips quirk like he's biting back a smirk, 'but Liz is cooking steak tonight. This will pair perfectly with it.' He pours it into the two glasses without waiting for my response. It's the first time he's referenced that night in such a casual way.

'Steak sounds fabulous.' My stomach rumbles in response.

'No, it doesn't. It sounds gross,' Orla pipes up from my right, fiddling with her fork. She's barely let me out of her sight since I moved in. The poor pet is probably terrified I'll leave, given that's what every other nanny seems to have done. What did Caelon do to them that was so bad?

'Don't worry, Liz is making you chicken goujons.' Caelon slides into the seat opposite me. His finger traces the elegant stem of his wine glass as his heated eyes flit to mine. I force my gaze to Owen, who's sitting beside him, opposite Orla, with that teddy under his arm again. I've offered to wash it fifty times since I moved in, but he's point-blank refused to part with it.

'Can we go to the beach tomorrow, Ivy?' Orla blinks at me like a puppy.

'Of course we can.' I glance out of the window. Irish weather is notoriously unpredictable, but the forecast is promised fine for the weekend. 'We'll pack a picnic and some buckets and spades. It'll be so much fun.'

'Can I come?' Owen asks in a small voice. 'I wanna jump in the waves.'

'Absolutely! I love wave jumping.' Progress, at last. It's the first time I haven't had to coerce him into doing something fun with me.

I lift my glass from the table and put it to my lips. The wine is rich and fruity, and probably costs more than my weekly wage, which is ridiculously generous. It hits my taste buds, and it's a battle not to moan out my appreciation. With any luck, the alcohol might dull the hypersensitive awareness I perpetually experience around Caelon.

'Can you manage both of them at the beach?' Caelon's concerned eyes catch mine.

'I've been minding kids way wilder than these two for years,' I laugh.

'It might be dangerous,' he muses, rubbing a thumb over his lower lip. 'The tide is strong round here.' He takes three large mouthfuls of wine, and I wonder if he, too, is trying to dull the sharp sting of electricity between us.

'It'll be fine. I'll hold each of them by the hand and we'll jump the waves together. We won't go deeper than their waists, I promise.'

The man is obsessed with keeping his kids from danger, which I get, given what happened to his wife, but they need to live a little too. Wrapping them in cotton wool won't help them. They need a childhood filled with fun and carefree laughter, not to be mollycoddled at home.

'Take Samuel with you,' Caelon says. It's not a request.

'Or you could come, Dad.' Owen's little face lights up like a beacon. It's so rare he smiles, just like his father. How could anyone refuse him?

Caelon's features furrow. 'I don't think so, buddy.'

'Why not?' Owen is like a dog with a bone.

'Can we go to the ice-cream parlour on the way home?' Orla licks her lips, as if she can already taste the sugar.

I raise my eyes to Caelon's. 'Go on, it'll be fun.' And it'll be another excuse to get an eyeful of that panty destroying tattoo.

'Fun?' he scoffs. 'I'm trying to run a business, oversee a multimillion-euro hotel restoration project, and keep this family together. I don't have time for fun.'

'Perhaps you should make time. After all, you manage to find time for other types of "fun".' I press my thighs together as memories of the bar bombard me for the millionth time.

'Just because I can't bring you home doesn't mean we can't have some fun.'

'Do you even know the meaning of the word, Tortured?'

So much for the wine dulling that crackling tension between us. Caelon's pupils blaze and his shoulders stiffen. Oh, he's definitely getting the same flashbacks. He inhales deeply and blows out a long, slow breath.

Has he had anyone else since I moved in?

Or has he been wanking himself senseless like me?

Orla and Owen stare at each other wide-eyed, and the room falls eerily silent.

I hold my breath.

'Fine,' he says with forced joviality. 'Let's all go to the beach tomorrow. It'll be so much *fun*.'

'Wonderful. Speaking of fun, seeing as you're here to put the kids to bed, I'm going out later.' I lean back in my chair and swirl the wine around my glass.

'Look! A rabbit!' Orla exclaims, pointing to the open patio doors before dashing out into the evening sun. Owen is on her heels and the two of them speed across the lawn.

Caelon's expression is thunderous. 'Absolutely not.' His tone leaves no room for debate.

'Excuse me?' I thought he'd have been pleased at the reprieve from the weirdness between us.

'I said no.' His black eyes blaze. 'You're not going out tonight.'

'You're not my father.' Though, I wouldn't be averse to calling him daddy, especially if he did that thing to me again...

'No, I'm not your father. I'm your boss. And you're needed here tonight.' He grits his teeth.

'But on Fridays you said you like to...' I swat a hand towards the kids, who are still searching for a rabbit that's long bolted. If I had any sense, I'd do the same. Because the man in front of me is glowering at me like he's dreaming up ways to punish me.

'Not every Friday.' He places his glass on the table and folds his arms across his chest. 'There's no way you're going out to get laid tonight. No fucking way.' His eyes are cold, but I sense a blazing inferno behind his steely front.

'Who said anything about getting laid?' Anyone with an iota of sense would get up and leave the table right now. Instead, I'm egging him on, calling him out on his bullshit. 'But if I want to, what's it got to do with you, anyway?'

'If I can't have you, you can be damned fucking sure no one else is going to. Not while you work for me, at least.'

I should be horrified. I should be outraged. But no, my Caelon-sabotaged-vagina is positively preening.

So much for Tranquil.

We're both tortured, because this thing can never happen between us, but tell that to my vagina because she didn't receive the memo.

No, she glimpsed a radiant neon-green light.

And now she's intent on driving us all the way to Dickville, even if the road is narrow, winding and entirely uphill.

Chapter Twelve

CAELON

Something about the woman drives me so crazy, I barely recognise myself.

Who the fuck do I think I am?

I know who I'm not.

I know who I can never be.

What I can never be. But being around Ivy does things to me. Stirs sensations in my stomach that I haven't felt for a long time.

The thought of her going out to a bar, of another man touching her, kissing her, makes me nauseated. I've no right to stop her going out. I've no claim on her. I'm so fucked up, and she's so flawless, I can offer her nothing. I could pretend I'm protecting her the way I promised Dermot I would when he heard his sister was working for me, but this has fuck all to do with Dermot, and everything to do with the way I can't stop staring at her. Can't stop thinking about her.

Knowing she's down the corridor every night is a fresh brand of torture. I've never been interested in another woman. Not before Isabella. Not after Isabella. Not until *her*.

'You don't want anyone else to have me...' she processes out loud, her pearly white teeth digging into her lower lip.

I hold her gaze as the air thickens between us. Now I've basically banned her from going out, there's no point tiptoeing around the fact she's driving me insane with lust. 'The attraction between us is painful.'

'But you've been actively avoiding me since I moved in. You've been colder than ice.' Confusion colours her tone.

'Because I'm so fucking hot for you, I'm walking around with a permanent semi in my pants,' I hiss. 'Because every time I look at you, the urge to tear your clothes off consumes me, and because none of that is okay, for a hundred different reasons, not least because you're too young, you're my best friend's sister, you're the nanny, and we're living together in the house where my children sleep.'

She shifts in her seat, arching forwards like she's about to challenge me. The simple summer dress she's wearing is so thin it's practically see through and it's not helping my resolve.

Thankfully, Orla and Owen race back into the room before either of us says something we'll regret.

I'll be lucky if she doesn't resign with immediate effect.

And if she doesn't, what does that say?

'Daddy, we lost it.' Orla slips her hand into mine and squeezes to get my attention. 'Will you buy me a rabbit? It might live longer than a fish. Or even better, what about a dog?'

'I'll think about it.' Every parent's universal answer for 'no', without causing a scene.

Liz strides in with a tray full of delicious-smelling food. 'Steaks are medium rare, served with potato gratin. I'll bring the veg now.'

'Is my dinner ready?' Owen sniffs the air and thankfully all talk of a pet rabbit or dog is forgotten, for now.

But it will be a very long time before I forget my confession to Ivy, specifically, the look in her eyes when I admitted how badly I want her. The way they flared with a hope that had no right to be there.

We finish the steaks and the wine, and when the kids go in search of the damned rabbit again, it feels like a great idea to open another bottle of red.

'Is this okay?' Ivy's eyes drift from my face to my chest as I refill her glass. 'I mean drinking with someone who's too young, your best friend's sister, the nanny, and someone you live with in the house where your children sleep?'

'Are you always so insolent?' My gaze lingers on her full, luscious lips.

'Are you always so uptight?' Amusement laces her tone.

'Believe me, it's better this way.' I blow out a breath.

'Better for who?' She arches forwards to pick up her wine glass again and I get another glimpse of her spectacular cleavage.

'Don't push me, Ivy.' I drink in her smooth, flawless skin. 'It won't end well–for either of us.'

The kids reappear, knees covered in grass stains.

'Let's get you guys bathed and ready for bed.' I take two large mouthfuls of wine and stand.

'Can Ivy come?' Orla pleads.

'I'd love to.' Her blazing blue eyes hold mine as she pushes her chair back from the table.

Her smart mouth is testing every bit of my willpower.

Ivy runs the kids a bath. I read them a story. She tucks Orla in, while I tuck Owen in.

When his soft snores echo through the room and his face relaxes into a peaceful expression, I back out of his bedroom. Slowly, gently, I close the door.

Ivy is on the landing, closing Orla's door.

'Is she asleep?'

'She is.' Ivy makes a point of checking the tiny silver watch on her wrist. 'So, seeing as I'm not "allowed" to go out tonight,' she uses her fingers to make quotation marks, 'what am I supposed to do now?'

My eyes roam over her dress. It would be so easy to slip my hand beneath it, or better yet, tear it from her body to see all of her.

But I can't.

I won't.

She's Dermot's sister. I'd do well to remember it. Especially as he hasn't stopped harping on about how grateful he is that she's been placed under my roof. Under my protection.

In reality, the only person she needs protecting from is me. Everything about her has me imagining ripping the clothes off her and making her mine. Tonight's outfit is doing nothing to alleviate that. I'm not sure what's worse, Ivy in a dress, or in those yoga pants.

'You're supposed to behave yourself,' I growl, 'and stop fucking tempting your boss with dresses that show the swell of your perfect tits.'

'Is that any way to speak to your employee?' Her rosy lips twist like she's biting back a smirk. We're way beyond the simplicity of a working relationship.

'Is that any way to dress for work?' My fingers itch to touch her.

'Technically, I'm off the clock.' She juts her chin out defiantly.

Brat. I've a good mind to put her over my knee.

'You seem determined to drag me off the straight and narrow.' I step closer, against my better judgement, and get a whiff of her feminine scent – pomegranate perfume and whatever lotion she puts on her flawless, satiny skin.

'I'm not the one who put *my* hand in your underwear,' she

reminds me, sending my mind straight back to the memory of her sweet, dripping heat.

'More's the pity.' My cock strains against my pants. The wine. I can only blame the wine.

'Let me.' She places a hand on my chest. It sears my skin even through my shirt.

'It's never going to happen.' I reach up and grip her wrist, but can't quite bring myself to drag her hand away. Not when it feels so fucking good to be touched.

'You know why I wanted to go out tonight?' Fire dances in her pupils.

'I got the general idea.' I scowl. Jealousy leaks into my stomach. What is this woman doing to me? Still. I don't let her wrist go.

'I wanted someone to take the edge off because I've got this insanely hot boss, who I'm stuck sharing a house with, and every time he walks in the room, I ruin my lingerie.'

She swallows, and my eyes are drawn to her long, elegant neck. What I wouldn't do to run my tongue over it. To sink my teeth into her skin and mark her as mine, to Jared and to every other man out there. But she's not mine. And she never can be.

She thought I was tortured before; telling me she's wet for me just made it a million times worse. She's driving me insane.

'*Every* time he walks into the room?' I'm playing with matches in a mansion made of wood and yet I still can't stop myself. I lean into her, inhaling her scent deep into my lungs.

'Every. Single. Time.' She punctuates each word for effect.

'Are you wet for me right now?' The words are out before I can stop them.

'Yes,' she whispers, inching closer.

Our faces are millimetres apart. Her breath is my breath.

'Show me,' I demand, hating myself, but unable to help myself. The air crackles. Let's see how brazen she is now.

She hesitates for a beat, then that boldness kicks in again. She keeps one hand on my chest, while the other one disappears beneath her dress. Her eyelids drift close for a split second, and she hisses out a tiny breath that transforms my blood to molten lava.

Shifting on her feet, she reopens her eyes and raises her hand up like she's about to take an oath. The glistening slickness on the tip of her middle finger is enough to make me break one.

I lean forwards and run my tongue over her finger, tasting her arousal. She pulls in a sharp breath as I take it in my mouth and suck it clean. She tastes like the world's most decadent dessert, and I'm starving for her.

I need more.

'I'm going to take that edge off for you, once and once only.'

What the fuck am I doing?

'Thank God, or I'll be forced to sneak out of the bedroom window later.' She wets her lips, and my gaze drops to that criminally enticing mouth. That perfect Cupid's bow that's begging to be licked.

I don't kiss her, though. This isn't about romance. It's about satiating her need.

'Don't thank God, thank me. And as for the window, I dare you to try.' I pin her against the wall with my hips and she gasps.

'Or perhaps I could sneak someone in.' Her tone is provoking. 'Jared made it clear he's more than willing.'

Oh, she knows exactly how to push my buttons.

'Do that, Ivy, if you can live with passing a death sentence. Because if I find a man in my house, I'll be forced to assume the worst and put a bullet in him. Maybe ten, just to be sure the threat is eliminated.'

'Shut up and put something in me.' Her eyes dart towards my bedroom door.

No way.

I'll never allow another woman in my bed. It would give the wrong idea.

'My office, now,' I grit out, tearing my hips from hers. I nudge her down the stairs, towards my office door. At least if any of the staff notice us disappearing, I can say it's work related. And my office is one of the few rooms in the house without cameras. 'Don't mistake this for something it's not, though. I already told you I don't do romance, sweetheart.'

'But you will make me come hard enough to see stars.' Ivy tosses my own line back in my face, word for word.

I open the office door and drag her in by her dress. My cock is leaking precum and I haven't even touched her yet.

'On my desk.' I shove the pile of paperwork onto the floor.

Ivy hops up without hesitation, lifting her dress up over her head and tossing it to the floor. A strapless, white lace bra supports perfect, round breasts which heave with her ragged inhales. Inch after inch of creamy skin tempts me all the way down to a flimsy ivory thong. Very virginal. But I already know there's nothing innocent about Ivy Winters. There's nothing innocent about the way her body responds to mine.

'Remove your lingerie. It looks sexy as fuck, but it'll look better on my floor.'

'What if someone walks in?' She glances at the door.

'Then they'll see my head buried between your thighs, lapping at your pussy like a man who hasn't had a drink in a week.'

She hisses out a breath, reaching around to unhook her bra. It falls to the floor with a soft, satisfying thud. She's even more beautiful than I imagined. Her rosebud nipples stand to attention, begging to be worshipped.

'And the rest.' My eyes fall to the lace triangle between her legs. I've felt her slick, softness. Tasted it twice now. But I haven't seen it.

I hold my breath as she slides the thin material down her trembling thighs and onto my floor. She stares at me almost challengingly as she inches her ass back onto my desk and spreads herself wide for me like a goddamn fucking dessert.

'Like what you see?' Her eyes lock on mine. I love her confidence. Her brazenness. The way she is utterly unashamed of her body and what it wants. It's so fucking sexy.

'You're fucking flawless, Ivy.' I prowl towards her, taking my time. If it's only going to be one time, I'm going to make the most of it. 'I've wanked myself stupid, remembering the feel of your tight little cunt, and the taste of the mess you made all over my fingers.'

I stand between her legs, towering over her.

'There's something so fucking hot about being naked in your office,' she admits. 'Maybe I should say I'm going out more often.'

'Don't even think about it. This is a onetime thing.' I trace a finger along her inner thigh and watch as goosebumps ripple across her flesh.

'Better make it memorable then,' she goads me.

She actually *goads* me.

My fingers skim higher, lingering at her groin. She squirms, and I laugh. 'Patience, Ivy. All good things come to those who wait.' I slide through her slickness once, then tear my fingers away. An animalistic cry leaks from her lip as I bring my finger to my mouth and suck. 'Why do bad ideas taste so good?'

I reach for her again. I couldn't stop if I tried. Her eyes

latch on mine, staring at me as I slide from her clit to her slit with slow, deliberate strokes.

It's my turn to goad. I dip my face lower, but I still don't kiss her. Instead, my lips capture a nipple and suck, as I sink two fingers into her centre, wishing they were my cock. But this isn't about me. It's about her. 'How's that edge doing?'

'I'm about to fall off it sometime really fucking soon,' she pants, her head lolling back as her eyes roll to the ceiling. 'Catapult might be a more accurate description.' Her core clenches around my fingers and I slide them out.

'Don't even think about coming.' I tilt her head up, forcing her eyes back to me. 'I'm nowhere near finished with you yet. Up on your knees. On all fours.' I step back from the desk, watching as she hoists herself round and lifts her smooth, peachy ass cheeks into the air. Fucking hell, I could come from that sight alone.

'Like this?' She glances at me over her shoulder, her glossy blonde hair falling over her eyes.

'Exactly like that.' I pause for a second, committing every inch of her to memory before burying my nose in her ass and my tongue in her pussy, reminding myself with every single stroke of my tongue that this will be the *only* time.

Chapter Thirteen

IVY

Caelon's lips and tongue devour me like he's enjoying this as much as I am. However good he is with his fingers, his oral skills are sublime.

'Do you do this to all your nannies?' I pant, my legs trembling.

His tongue pauses and I curse my big mouth for talking once again. 'No.' His voice is low and guttural.

I grip the edge of his desk, my head inches away from his computer screen, his keyboard between my knees. I hope to fuck it's waterproof because I am saturated.

'I'm so close,' I hiss, bucking my ass back against his face. His fingers grab my hips and still them as his tongue slows to almost a stop.

'You don't come until I say you can.' Every word causes his lips to brush over my clit, sending shock waves radiating down my thighs.

'I won't be able to help myself,' I whisper.

'Now you know how I feel, faced with this sight all damn day.' He slaps my ass with the palm of his hand, hard enough to sting in the sexiest way, while his other hand reaches for my breast, squeezing and kneading.

'Let me take the edge off for you.' I buck my hips backwards again.

'No.' His fingers still my hips and his mouth returns to my pussy. He offers one long, slow lick that sets my legs shaking again. 'Next time you think about going out and getting fucked, I want you to think about this. Be a good girl and go up to your room and play with yourself instead. Got it?'

'Yes.' I'd agree to absolutely anything right now. Anything. The need to come is overriding all rationale.

'Good girl,' he purrs, slipping two fingers into my core and pumping as his lips capture my clit. 'Now that's settled, you can come now, Ivy, darling. Come all over my face,' he commands, and I'm gone, spiralling into an earth-shattering release that shakes every cell. Explosives detonate from my core, sending shock waves in every direction. White hot pleasure bursts through my entire body, and as he continues to lap at me, I shake and shatter on him.

Even when I stop shuddering, his tongue still works me, licking, savouring, cleaning. Eventually, he stills, gives my ass another playful slap and then turns me over until I'm sitting, legs spread on his desk again.

He inspects my pussy carefully. Another woman might feel shy, but after having him tiptoe around me, barely looking at me for three weeks, being the focus of his unwavering perusal is hot as fuck.

'I did mention I'm more than capable of cleaning up my own messes.' He sounds oddly satisfied.

'If you keep looking at me like that, there will be another one really fucking soon.' My breath is ragged from my release.

His low chuckle resounds through the air. 'Greedy girl. Now get out of here before I do something I'll regret.'

'Like what?' I challenge him, parting my legs wider in a less than subtle invitation.

'Like fuck my best friend's sister.'

'I won't tell if you don't,' I promise.

'It's never going to happen, Ivy.' His dark eyes fall to something beside his computer. I turn my head to see what he's staring at. My gaze lands on a picture of his wife.

I swallow thickly, slide off his desk, pick my dress up from the floor and pull it over my head. The cold sting of rejection rapidly replaces my post-orgasm glow. Tall, Dark and Tortured is obviously not over Isabella.

It shouldn't matter.

He's my boss, not my boyfriend, for God's sake.

This was supposed to be a release and nothing more.

The problem is, I want more. I've been crushing on him ever since I arrived. I want him inside me so badly it hurts.

And it's never going to happen.

I need to put it, and him, out of my head once and for all.

'You know, I might go out, after all...'

He glowers. 'That wasn't the deal, Ivy.'

'Deals are broken and renegotiated all the time.' I shrug, strutting out of his office, leaving my lingerie lying on his floor.

Before the door clicks behind me, I hear him mutter, 'She's going to be the actual death of me...' To whom, I can only imagine.

An hour later, I tiptoe out of my room. The sun has set, and the sky is an eclectic mix of deep pinks and purple hues.

My Uber should arrive any minute. I'm not going out to find a man, but Caelon doesn't need to know that. I can't just sit around here and wait to see if he'll throw me a bone – pun intended. After what just happened in his office, it's better if I put some distance between us, for a few hours at least.

I can't think straight when he's near.

It's not natural. I've never known attraction like it. It's so visceral. So primal. So animalistic. Hell, I don't even particularly like the guy, yet every bone in my body longs to jump his. The way my body responds to his touch is like nothing I've ever experienced before, nor am ever likely to again, unfortunately. Which is why I *need* to get out of here.

I felt used by the way he dismissed me after such soul-shattering intimacy. Even though I wanted that intimacy more than I wanted anything before. He warned me that was all it would be. I thought I could handle it. But I thought wrong.

Which is why he's right. It can never happen again.

I smooth a hand over my black silk dress. It's a short number that I picked up in Macy's last summer. I don't particularly miss the States, but I miss the shopping. I miss hanging out with my nanny friends at Union Square. I miss Saturday nights drinking in Irish bars with other Irish people who are living away from home. I miss adult company. I've been away so long, I don't have any real friends in Dublin. Maybe it's time I made some new ones.

I check on the kids briefly. Orla is asleep with her hands thrown above her head and Owen is clinging onto his favourite teddy, unable to part with it even in his dreams. I creep down the stairs, listening for any movement, but I'm greeted with silence.

'Going somewhere?' Caelon's low, velvety voice greets me through the twilight. He steps forwards from the shadows.

I jump. Has he been waiting here, on guard, this entire time?

'Yes, I am, as a matter of fact.' I straighten my spine. I'm only five foot five, but with these five-inch stilettos, I don't have to crane my neck to meet his glare.

'And where would that be, exactly?' He positions his body between mine and the exit.

'For a drink in the city, not that it's any of your business. I'll be back long before the kids wake up.' The scent of his cologne wafts through the air, deep and rich and sensual.

'And how do you plan on getting to the city?' Gold flecks light his irises as he inches his body closer to mine.

'I called an Uber. It'll be here any minute.'

He places a palm on my lower back and guides me towards the front door. Tingles shoot up my spine. My treacherous nipples stiffen at his touch. He eyes my dress and smirks. He fights dirty, and he doesn't even try to hide it.

He opens the front door for me, and I inhale a lungful of balmy, fresh air. Headlights swing up to the gate, but when I step out onto the step, Caelon catches my wrist. Heat sizzles over my skin. His eyes lock on mine.

'Don't go,' he bites out, and I glimpse a rare flash of vulnerability.

'What?' The man all but kicked me out of his office an hour earlier after I offered myself to him naked.

'Don't go,' he repeats, slightly softer this time. That tortured look flashes in his eyes.

My anger melts. I'm still a sucker for a tortured bad boy. 'On one condition.'

'I can't have sex with you.' He shakes his head briskly.

'I wasn't going to ask you to,' I huff. One rejection today is enough. 'Have a drink with me.'

'A drink? Haven't we had enough?'

'One more, for the road.'

'We've already established you're not hitting the road. You're not going anywhere, Ivy.'

'Which is why you should have a nightcap with me.' My shoulders sag, the fight falling from them. 'I like spending time with your kids, but I could do with some adult conversation from time to time. I don't have many friends. I've been away so long, they've all moved on, formed new friendship groups. Have a drink with me, please.'

His shoulders relax a fraction and his lips curl up into a half-smirk. 'I suppose it's easier than tying you to your bedposts.'

I press my thighs together. What a visual. Another set of underwear ruined. Not fucking helpful. 'That's my ultimate fantasy,' I hiss.

His eyelids squeeze shut like he's forcing away the image. 'Why am I not surprised?'

'I'll speak to the driver.' I start towards the driveway.

'No need. I already told Damon to send him away with a tip.' There's a smug edge to his voice.

My mouth falls open. 'But what if I'd said no?'

'Then I would have tied you to the bedposts. Wine? Whiskey? Beer?'

This man is giving me whiplash.

'Whiskey. I have a feeling I'm going to need it.' I ditch my handbag at the bottom of the stairs as we pass, and head for the patio as Caelon fetches the drinks.

Crickets chirp in the distance. The scent of freshly cut grass and lavender lingers in the air. I kick off my shoes and get comfortable on the L-shaped couch overlooking the pool.

Caelon appears with two tumblers of whiskey. He hands me one, then sits on the other end of the couch like he's worried I might throw myself at him or something.

'I don't get you,' I blurt. 'You say you don't want me, but you don't want me to go out either.'

He taps his index finger against the side of his glass. 'I want you, but I shouldn't want you. In case you haven't already gathered, I'm fifty shades of fucked up.'

'Really?' I tease. 'I hadn't noticed.'

Caelon gazes out across the shimmering pool. 'It took me

eighteen months after Isabella died to even look at another woman. Then it took me another month on top of that to take one to bed.' He pauses to sip his drink.

For once, I manage to keep my big mouth shut and wait for him to continue.

'I felt guilty, you know? But then, after the first few times, I kind of let loose. I liked losing myself in someone else, for a while at least.'

'We're human. It's what we were put here to do. Our purpose is to procreate.' That's what I tell myself on the days that I feel bad for wanting kids instead of a high-flying career, anyway.

'I have a different purpose.' His face darkens.

My curiosity piques. Work? His kids? Both? The revenge Dermot hinted at? The more I get to know Caelon, the less I'd put it past him. He has a dangerous edge to him. Like he's got nothing left to lose, which isn't true. He has his kids.

He pauses for a beat before continuing. 'Which is why I can't get involved with anyone. Even if their mere presence in my house is sending me demented enough to do things I'd never have dreamt of.'

I swallow. 'Do you want me to go?'

'Hell, no!' His gaze snaps to mine. 'Was it not obvious when I sent the Uber away? I want you to stay. You're great with the kids. You're... just great. But I need you to stop walking around my house looking like this, okay?' He flicks a hand towards my dress. 'You're a distraction I don't need right now.'

'So, where does that leave us?' My teeth dig into my lower lip. I can't work him out. More like five hundred shades of fucked up.

'Well, the second you walked in the front door, we were already more than employer/employee. I know what you taste like. Know how you shudder when you come.' Our eyes meet with an intensity that could start a fire. 'The chemistry between us is insane, but we can't act on it again. But maybe we could... I don't know, try to be friends?'

Warmth flares in my chest. 'You know, I was only thinking earlier that I could do with some new friends.' I reach across the couch and clink my glass against his. 'Cheers to that.'

'That doesn't mean I'll stop wanking over you, though,' Caelon quips, and his lips stretch into an actual grin. However handsome he is when he's brooding, he's beautiful when he lets his guard down. The effect is devastating. 'Thanks for the lingerie, by the way.'

I snort. 'You know, this is the first time I've seen you really smile.'

'It doesn't happen often,' he says, as his lips return to their usual grimace.

And just like that, it becomes my mission in life to make sure it does.

But there's no way I'm going to stop walking around his house in tiny outfits. If I have to endure this chemistry between us, I have no intention of making it easier on him.

Quite the contrary, in fact.

Chapter Fourteen

CAELON

I wake up feeling slightly lighter than I've felt all week. Admittedly, I fucked up yesterday. Tongue fucking Ivy on my desk was not on my to-do list, but at least we've agreed it will never happen again. Last night seemed to clear some of the tension between us.

I throw on a pair of running shorts and hit my home gym before Owen and Orla wake up. I do a full upper body workout and run ten kilometres before eight. By the time I reach the kitchen, Liz is dishing up breakfast for the kids. I scan the room until I find what I'm looking for. Or rather, *who* I'm looking for.

My molars clank together as I take in the tiny, faded denim shorts barely flirting with her full, round ass cheeks, and I kid you not, a fucking bikini top, secured by tiny strings that I could snap with my teeth.

Did she not hear a fucking word I said last night?

Does she want me to bend her over the kitchen counter and fuck her into next week?

She's barefoot, stretching up on her tiptoes to reach a coffee cup.

'Daddy,' Orla squeals.

Owen jumps from his seat and runs towards me, wrapping his arms around my legs.

I lift him up and balance him on my hip. 'Morning, buddy. How did you sleep?'

'Okay,' he says quietly, his gaze falling to the floor.

I place my hand on the back of his head and whisper into his ear. 'Do you want me to change your bed sheets?'

He nods, nibbling on his lower lip. 'Sorry, Daddy.'

'Don't be sorry, buddy. Everything's okay,' I whisper. Changing the sheets gives me the perfect excuse to escape my half-naked nanny.

'Can we still go to the beach today?' Hope lights his eyes.

'Sure. Give me an hour to get sorted and shower and grab something to eat.'

'Morning,' Ivy calls over her shoulder as she hits the button on the coffee machine. 'You want a cup?'

'No,' I say gruffly, before remembering we're supposed to be friends. Though if she can't hold up her end of the bargain by dressing appropriately, why should I hold up mine?

She spins to face me with a questioning look. My eyes fall to her breasts, supported by two red triangular scraps of Lycra tied at the nape of her neck.

She arches a single eyebrow.

'No, *thank you*.' I force the words out and tear my eyes from her tits.

'Scrambled eggs?' Liz calls across the kitchen.

'I'm not hungry.' Not for food, anyway. I slide Owen down my legs until his feet meet the floor. 'Eat your breakfast, buddy. You'll need energy for the beach.'

How am I going to survive a trip to the beach with Ivy looking like that?

There's only one thing for it. We'll go early, swim, then come straight home. I'll invent a meeting. Something urgent.

A crisis at one of the hotels. A construction disaster. A severe bout of highly contagious stomach flu. I drag my fingers through my cropped hair, running my nails over my scalp.

'I packed you a picnic.' Liz nods towards a huge wicker basket with a folding lid. 'It's great you're having a beach day.' Her tone is overflowing with approval.

'Oh, I...' Fuck. 'It's just for an hour.'

'Daddy, you promised!' Owen's face falls.

Orla inhales sharply.

Ivy's head whips around.

'Or two, maybe.' I exhale a huge breath and accept my fate.

An hour later, I load the kids into Ivy's Mercedes, strapping them in carefully.

Ivy hovers nervously by the driver's side.

'I'll drive. Get in.' I pack the picnic in the boot along with buckets, spades and way too many inflatables, then strap myself in.

The only reason we're taking her car is because I don't want a driver hanging around all day. It's rare I go out without security, but how dangerous can the beach be? I'm certainly not going to bump into Jack O'Connor there. But if I did, I'd have no qualms about drowning him. Slowly.

No, Damon and the others can wait here, man the house. I don't want any eyes other than mine on Ivy in that bikini. Which is why we're going to the smallest, quietest beach in Dublin. The same beach I spent my childhood on. It's a stone's throw from my parents' house. The only way to access it is via a short, woodland trail at the back of their land. And seeing as my parents are on holiday touring Europe right now, there's no chance of running into them on one of their daily walks.

'Which beach are we going to?' Ivy asks, as I start the engine.

'It's a surprise.'

'Oh, I love surprises!' She rubs her hands together gleefully.

'Why doesn't that surprise me?' I say wryly.

Ivy spends the entire journey singing Taylor Swift songs to Orla, teaching her the words to *Love Story* until it's stuck in all of our fucking heads.

Even Owen is singing along.

I can't cope.

When we finally reach the woodland trail, I park the car in a shady spot beneath some sycamore trees and unload the stuff from the boot.

'We're at Nanny and Grandad's beach!' Orla announces, bounding from one pink sandalled foot to the other. 'Can we go see them?'

'They're not here. They're on holiday.' Thankfully. Because if my mother knew I was at the beach with my kids' nanny, she'd get all sorts of stupid notions. Notions that have no right being in anyone's head—especially mine.

'This is your parents' land?' Ivy's hand sweeps over the vast horizon.

'Yes.' I nod, looking anywhere but at her again. I suppose I should be grateful she threw on a tiny vest top over the bikini, but those legs should be illegal in public.

'You grew up here?' Awe taints her tone.

'Yes.' I don't mean to be short with her, but I can't help it.

Just when I think things can't get any worse, I hear a familiar engine rumbling in the distance. There's only one person who drives a Porsche who would be on my parents' land.

My brother, Rian.

Rian is the baby of the family. James is the oldest, then

me, Killian, Sean, and Rian. Plus, there's my sister, Zara, who is just finishing college. Rian pretends to run a chain of exclusive bars and nightclubs, but in reality, he mostly parties in them, prowling for his next shag. James was a playboy in his day, but he had nothing on Rian. Our youngest brother has more 'swifties' than Taylor herself.

And fucking *Love Story* is still stuck on repeat in my head.

Ivy's eyes flick towards mine. 'Do we have company?'

'It would appear so, unfortunately.' I close my eyes and will for a tornado to sweep me as far the fuck away from here as possible. Rian's probably brought some chick down here to woo and bang on the beach.

But no, it gets worse.

It's not some random woman in the passenger seat. It's my brother, Sean.

Ivy grabs the kids' hands as the Porsche skids to a stop and my brothers hop out.

'What do we have here?' Rian lifts his Raybans from his eyes, balancing them on his head as he lets out a low whistle. His beady eyes rove over the length of Ivy's body before finally reaching her face.

'Uncle Rian!' Owen launches at him, as Orla reaches for Sean.

'What a lovely surprise.' Rian lifts Owen up without taking his eyes off my nanny. I don't think the surprise is seeing his niece and nephew.

'Guys, this is Ivy, our nanny.' My words are steeped with a clear warning. 'Ivy, this is Sean, my middle brother, and Rian, my littlest.'

'Huh,' Rian scoffs, 'I might be the youngest, but any woman who knows me doesn't call me little.' He waggles his eyebrows at Ivy, a dirty laugh tumbling from his lips. I thump his bicep hard enough to make him yelp.

'What was that for?' he says with wide eyes. The little fucker.

'Behave yourself in front of the kids,' I warn gruffly.

Sean extends a hand to shake Ivy's. Thankfully, he's a little more reserved than Rian, who's bounding around like a dog with two dicks. 'It's nice to meet you, Ivy,' Sean says warmly.

Apparently, I should have punched Rian harder, because he didn't get the memo. He takes Ivy's hand and lifts it to his lips, pressing a kiss against the back of it. 'Ivy, it's a pleasure.' He jerks a thumb towards me. 'I hope he's treating you better than the other nannies.'

Girlish laughter peals from Ivy's luscious lips as her eyes lock with mine. 'He's certainly treating me differently, by all accounts.'

Oh, I've a good mind to bend her over, smack her ass and tease her with my tongue again for that smart remark.

But no. I'm on my best behaviour.

I cut to the chase. 'What are you doing here?'

'Same as you, by the look of it.' Rian nods towards the picnic basket. 'Thought we'd make the most of the day. James is on his way down with Scarlett and the babies,' Rian gloats gleefully. 'They'll be here any minute. We couldn't have planned it any better if we'd tried! I'm going to call Killian. Maybe he's free to come down too.'

Could this outing get any worse?

Chapter Fifteen

IVY

James and his fiancée, Scarlett, arrive with their baby daughters, Harper and Halle, minutes after Rian and Sean. Caelon makes the introductions, and we stroll along the short woodland path to the beach together.

'What are the chances?' James slaps Caelon on the back. 'It's great to see you out in the daylight. I was beginning to think you were a vampire.'

'I'm still waiting for my fill of blood,' he grunts, exchanging a look with James that sets a shiver down my spine.

'Do we have to be so morbid?' I tilt my face to the sky. 'The sun is shining. We have a basket full of food and drink, and the kids are getting an impromptu playdate with their cousins. Life is good.'

'Is she always this cheerful?' James's pupils flit between Caelon and me with mild curiosity. If he recognises me from the bar, he doesn't mention it.

'Unfortunately, yes.' Caelon gives me the side-eye. 'I'm going to have to put a clause in her contract.'

'Huh, I might add a few clauses in myself.' I nudge his ribs with my elbow. All eyes turn to us. Mouths open wide enough to swallow the Titanic.

'Holy shit! He's fucking the nanny,' Rian whisper shouts. Thankfully, Orla and Owen, who are running ahead, are out of earshot.

'I am not fucking the nanny.' Caelon's face is grim. 'But if I was, it would be none of your business.'

'Oh, they're definitely fucking,' Rian says gleefully to Sean, who's ambling along the path next to him.

'I'll fuck up your face if you don't watch your mouth, little brother.' Caelon's eyes glint.

'Whatever. Ivy, if you're not fucking Caelon, would you like to go out with me tonight?' Rian winks at me.

Does the man have a death wish? I mean, it is kind of funny, but Caelon's clenched fists look primed to swing at any point.

'You know, I can't tonight, with the kids and everything,' I sing sweetly. Caelon's fists relax a fraction, and the temptation to wind him up trumps all rationale. 'But tomorrow's my day off.'

'Ivy,' Caelon growls, his feet slowing to a stop. All eyes remain on us. 'Do I need to put you on my desk again?'

'Told you! He's fucking the nanny.' Rian winks again and dramatically thrusts his hips back and forth. Everyone except Caelon dissolves into laughter. Everyone, including me.

'Details about what went down on the desk!' Scarlett squeals. 'Or who, should I say?'

'Ivy and I are friends, that's all.' Caelon's haughty tone convinces nobody as he starts walking again.

'You don't have any friends apart from us,' Rian argues.

'Not true. I have Dermot,' Caelon reminds him. 'Who also happens to be Ivy's brother, so watch your mouth, okay?'

'The plot thickens!' Rian says. 'Does Dermot know you're fucking his little sister?'

'Rian!' James's voice is low, his tone final.

The trees thin and open into a large, white sandy clearing. Gentle waves lap against the shore, the water so turquoise it's hard to believe we're in Ireland.

'This is so tranquil,' Scarlett beams, soaking it all in.

Caelon and I exchange a smirk. Technically, I'm Tranquil, but he won't keep calling me that if I keep joking about dating his brother. Caelon might not be willing to act on this attraction between us, but he's made it damn clear he doesn't want me getting it anywhere else. And while that is ridiculously unfair, there's something really fucking hot about it. And now I know it galls him enough to send him–*ahem*–south, I plan to use that fact to my full advantage.

'Who's up for a game of volleyball?' Rian eyes his brothers. 'Unless you decrepit old fuckers can't keep up with me.' He puffs his chest out in an unspoken challenge.

Caelon and James exchange a look. 'Time to teach the little punk a lesson.'

For a bunch of panty-melting billionaires, Caelon's brothers are hilarious. Not to mention ridiculously down to earth.

Scarlett and I set up blankets and towels in a semi-circle and sit side by side facing the sea, the scent of seaweed and summer wafting on a gentle breeze.

Orla and Owen lunge for their buckets and spades and start digging a hole. I reach for the picnic basket, helping myself to a can of Diet Coke. I offer one to Scarlett, but she shakes her head, watching as her toddler, Harper, runs to Orla to join in the fun.

'How old is she?' I peep at the beautiful bundle in Scarlett's arms.

'Eight weeks.' Scarlett runs a finger over the child's fluffy shock of dark hair. 'She wasn't exactly planned.' Scarlett points to her toddler. 'Harper was eight weeks when Halle was conceived, so I'm keeping James at arm's length this time round.' She laughs. 'Well, trying to, at least.'

It's my turn to laugh. 'You know what they say. If you can't be good, be careful.'

'How long have you been with Caelon?' she asks.

'Oh, I'm not with him!' I blurt, clutching my chest. 'We're not... I'm not...'

Scarlett's eyes snap to mine. 'Oh my God, Rian was right, you guys *are* sleeping together!' she hisses. 'This is so exciting! Caelon hasn't dated since Isabella and, you know, it's about time.'

I hold my hand up. 'We're not. We only...' Me and my fucking mouth! I only met the woman a few minutes ago and somehow I've managed to big a digger hole than the one the kids are carving in the sand.

'Only what?' Scarlett wiggles her eyebrows conspicuously. 'Spill the beans, Ivy. I can already tell we're going to be great friends.'

I glance at the Beckett brothers, engrossed in their highly competitive game, then back at Scarlett.

'We're not sleeping together. I only started working for him a few weeks ago.' I pop the can open and take a drink.

'I'm sensing a but here,' she coaxes. 'Is there any wine in that basket? That might loosen your lips.'

'Believe me, these lips are loose enough! There's no but.' Not unless you count his nose being buried in my *butt* as he ate me out yesterday.

'He's never been anywhere with a nanny before,' Scarlett muses. 'In fact, he hated every single one of them. They were all terrified of him. Which is hilarious really because beneath his grouchy exterior, he's an absolute teddy bear.'

'You heard what Caelon said. He's friends with my brother, Dermot.' I shrug, conveniently skipping over the finger fuck in the bar. 'That's probably why he's different with me.'

Scarlett scoffs. 'It might have something to do with it, but I'm telling you, the way he bit Rian's head off was territorial. He wants you.'

'He doesn't.' I swat my hand in front of my face, dismissing the notion. The memories of him staring at the picture of his wife just seconds after I came on his face surge through my mind.

'It was so awful what happened to Isabella.' Scarlett's voice drops.

'Were you guys close?'

'No. I only met her a handful of times. James and I got together just before the accident.' Scarlett strokes a thumb over her baby's cheek. 'She was lovely, though. She and Caelon were childhood sweethearts. They were so happy together. Just goes to show, you've got to make the most of every day. Live for the moment.'

Which is precisely what I did last night, even though it was wrong on so many levels.

A loud thwack from the volleyball game prevents me from asking any further questions.

'Ow, mother fucker!' Rian clutches his nose, glaring at Caelon.

'Oops, sorry.' Caelon shrugs, a half-smile flirting with his lips.

'You did that on purpose!' Rian sinks to the sand.

'Time out.' Sean raises a hand in the air. 'You two need to cool off before someone gets hurt.'

'Is there any beer in that basket?' James eyes the picnic Liz prepared.

'It's eleven am,' Scarlett says pointedly.

'Yeah, but it feels like four o'clock given we've been up half the night.' James winks at her and she flushes.

'With the baby,' Scarlett says to me.

'Arms' length, hey?' I snort.

'I said I was trying, not succeeding.' She grins.

'No judgement here. We're going to be great friends, remember?'

Caelon strides over to where the kids are digging, ruffling Owen's hair. 'You okay, buddy?'

'Yep.' Owen barely glances up. He's so engrossed.

The sun beats down on my shoulders, scorching my skin. 'I feel like I'm burning.' I reach for my beach bag, patting around for the sun cream I packed this morning. I flip open the lid and squeeze a dollop onto my palm, massaging it into my shoulders.

'Need a hand, Ivy?' Rian calls, dusting sand from his knees as he rises from the ground.

Caelon snarls at his brother and lunges for me, snatching the bottle out of my hand. He sits on the towel behind me, positioning one leg either side of mine, so I'm sitting between his thighs.

I wish he was sitting between mine.

We should spend more time with Rian. I like the effect his flirting has on Caelon. It makes him positively primal.

'She doesn't want your filthy hands anywhere near her,' Caelon snaps.

Scarlett chuckles. 'Ivy, how does it feel to be the shiny new toy everyone's fighting over?'

Caelon's hands land on my shoulders, kneading and massaging the cream into my skin. Electricity dances down my spine. 'It feels so good,' I sigh, happily.

'We don't have to fight, brother.' Rian smirks at Caelon. 'We could share.'

'I swear to fuck I'm going to murder you one of these days.' Caelon's voice is dangerously low. Rian guffaws and does the hip thrust thing again.

'Someone phone Killian,' James says, prising the baby from Scarlett's arms and beaming at his fiancée lovingly. 'Tell him to bring beer and pizzas.'

'You should probably take your top off, Ivy.' Rian smirks, pulling his phone from the pocket of his shorts. 'It would be awful if you got tan lines.'

A growl rumbles in Caelon's throat, and I feel him inch closer to me. The sun has nothing on the heat radiating from his body. Skilful fingers continue sliding over my skin long after the sun cream is well and truly rubbed in. His hot breath skims my neck. 'If you take your top off, I'll take you right here on this beach in front of my entire fucking family.'

'Is that a promise?' I think it was supposed to be a threat.

'And to think I mistook you for a good girl.' His fingers dip to my collarbones and my nipples go rigid. 'But I think you might actually be as bad as me.'

Given half the chance, I could be. If I could be sure he wasn't imagining I'm someone else while he's buried inside of me.

I can't compete with that.

Chapter Sixteen

CAELON

She works for me, I remind myself over and over again.

She works for me.

She works for me.

So why does hanging out at the beach with Ivy feel like a date? One that I accidentally brought my super annoying family on.

Killian arrives with pizzas, beer, and champagne for Scarlett and Ivy. His expression doesn't falter when he spots me sitting with my legs either side of my new nanny, but I'd bet my life his eagle eyes are taking in every minute detail.

I tear myself from Ivy's towel to greet him.

'Do I look like a fucking pizza delivery boy?' he says gruffly, handing out boxes from Juliana's, the most exclusive Italian in Dublin. 'How many staff do you guys have between you? Next time, call one of them to do the food run.'

'Any update on the O'Connors?' I ask in a low voice.

'I found the money trail.' His voice is grim.

'You did?' Finally. The proof we've been looking for.

'I sent two female security agents to interrogate Stacy

Bourke. She didn't deny receiving money, but she claimed it came from an anonymous source.'

'That's ridiculous. Does she think we're fucking stupid?'

'We need Danny to wake up. When he does, you can extract every detail from his body, painfully. Hang tight.'

'My patience is wearing thin.' It's the understatement of the century. Any patience I had died along with my wife. Now all I have left is a thirst for blood, oh, and a highly inappropriate desire to devour the nanny.

Ivy was right. Even when it's sunny, I feel morbid. Restless. There's a beast beneath my skin just bursting to break free.

'The other problem is that we took or froze all the O'Connor assets. Which begs the question, if it was them, where did they get the money from to pay Stacy, anyway?' Killian's voice is grim. 'They must have at least one remaining affluent friend.'

'Fuck,' I spit.

'Is it okay if I drink this?' Ivy calls to me, holding up the plastic flute of bubbles Scarlett handed to her.

'You don't need my permission. You said it last night. I'm not your father.'

'No, but you are my boss.' She sucks the inside of her cheek.

I empty my lungs in a long, slow exhale. 'Don't stop until you get to the bottom of this,' I tell my brother before turning my back on him to rejoin Ivy. She is possibly the only person capable of distracting me from my rage.

I might have "taken the edge off" for her, but truthfully, something about her takes the edge off me. I feel slightly less irritable when she's beside me. Her warmth will never be enough to penetrate my frozen heart, but it does take the chill from my skin.

'I think we've already established it's not as clear cut as that. Last time I checked, we were trying to be friends.'

I should have suggested friends with benefits. That way there's no promise of a future, no pretending I'll ever be able to give her anything more than my fingers, mouth and cock. But I could give her orgasms. Lots of them. 'Drink, relax, I'm driving anyway.'

In fairness, she's worked damned hard with my kids since she started. Chasing them around playing tag. Taking them to the park and the pool. The yoga in the garden. Some nannies do the bare minimum, but Ivy goes above and beyond, her enthusiasm for her job is obvious. She deserves a bit of down time. Just not on a Friday night in a bar where there are men out to prey on vulnerable, sexy-ass women like her.

'Cheers to that.' Ivy raises her glass and takes a mouthful.

'Can we go in the sea now, Dad?' Owen comes running across the sand with his armbands and goggles already on. Traces of pizza sauce line the corners of his mouth.

'Come here, sweetheart.' Ivy beckons him over and swipes the sauce away with her fingers. He doesn't even flinch. 'Were you saving that tomato sauce for later?' she teases, pressing his nose playfully.

He laughs. *Laughs.* My serious little son is smiling.

It appears Ivy has us all under her sunny, sassy spell.

Fuck.

Another reason why I can't fuck things up, no matter how badly I want to sink my cock into her.

'Mary Poppins has got nothing on you,' Scarlett says wistfully. 'How much is Caelon paying you? We'll double it if you come and work for us.'

Ivy laughs, but Owen's face falls.

Thankfully, Ivy spots the change immediately. 'Don't worry, buddy, Scarlett's only joking. I'm not going anywhere.'

'I'm not,' Scarlett mutters, low enough that I can hear, but

Owen can't. 'She's a keeper,' she says, and I'm pretty sure my future sister-in-law isn't referring to Ivy's employment status.

'Come on then, let's go wave jumping,' Ivy says, handing Scarlett back the glass of champagne. 'Will you look after this for me?'

'Sure.' Scarlett puts it on top of the pizza boxes beside her.

Ivy beams at me. 'Are you coming, Daddy?'

I'd like to. All over your tits if you keep calling me Daddy.

'Sure.' I kick off my Nikes, pull my t-shirt over my head and toss it on Ivy's towel.

Her mouth opens, but words don't come. She's staring at my torso like she's never seen a shirtless man before. Her tongue dips over her lower lip in a feline gesture. 'What a gene pool,' she finally mutters.

'What's a gene pool?' Owen asks. 'Is it like a rock pool?'

'Not exactly, buddy.' I bite back the grin that's threatening my lips. I don't grin. Not anymore. Well, apart from last night with Ivy, when I thanked her for the lingerie, but that was a slip up.

I extend a hand to help Ivy up. The second she takes it, a fizzing warmth sears my skin. She kicks off her flip-flops, her fingers reaching for the hem of her top.

The polite thing would be to look away.

I never claimed to be polite, though.

I'm torn between a desperate urge to see her in that bikini again and the urge to cover her up so my brothers can't see her. Mind you, James wouldn't notice if Ivy got naked. He only has eyes for Scarlett. Killian and Sean are probably too gentlemanly to stare, but Rian, well, I wouldn't put it past him to dry hump Ivy's leg like a mangey rabid dog.

'Orla, we're going in the sea now.' Owen runs towards his sister, who is still digging.

'Am I safe taking this off?' Ivy glances at her top. 'Or will you really "take me in front of your entire family?"' she whispers with a giggle.

'I'm still contemplating it,' I mutter. My cock is already stirring in my swimming shorts. I need to get in the water fast, or risk embarrassing myself in front of my brothers.

'I'll take my chances.' A smirk touches her lips before she yanks her top over her head and stares at me defiantly.

'That bikini top is nothing more than a couple of Post-it Notes covering your tits,' I grumble. 'Are you trying to torment me?'

'Maybe,' she shrugs, her blue eyes sparkling with mischief.

'We talked about this last night.'

'We did a lot of things last night,' she reminds me. As if I could forget.

An ear-splitting wolf whistle pierces the air. Rian. I catch Ivy's wrist and pull her towards the water. 'Don't make me drown my brother. My parents would probably be cross.'

'What time will I pick you up tomorrow, Ivy?' Rian shouts.

'Oh, leave him alone, Rian!' Scarlett chides.

'The only thing you'll be picking up is your ass from the floor after I knock you on it.' I glare at him, and he chortles.

'I needed some fresh material for the spank bank!' Rian grabs his crotch and laughs.

'I will kill him.' I shake my head as I mentally commit every inch of Ivy's body to my own personal vault.

Owen slips his hand in mine and Ivy takes his other one. Orla grabs Ivy's free arm until the four of us are joined physically for safety. Mentally, I'm not sure how safe any of us are. The kids are already forming attachments with Ivy, and they aren't the only ones.

'On the count of three, we run in together, okay?' Ivy says, swinging the kids' arms back and forth.

'It looks cold.' I stare at the waves cascading in front of us.

'Says the ice king himself,' Ivy quips. 'One. Two.' She glances between my kids, checking they're ready. Their little faces are lit up with glee and my heart thaws a fraction.

'Three!' Ivy calls, pulling me forwards until the cold water slaps my skin.

'Fuck! It's freezing!'

'Daddy! That's a bad word!' Ivy scolds jovially. The kids are too busy shrieking with laughter to pay any attention.

'I'm a bad man, Ivy.' If I'm not thinking about torturing and murdering the entire O'Connor family, I'm thinking about fucking my best friend's little sister.

Bad doesn't cut it.

'I don't think you are.' Her head turns towards mine. 'I think you're a good man who's been through a really awful time.'

Oh Ivy, you have no idea.

Ignorance really is bliss, I suppose.

Chapter Seventeen

IVY

Whoever came up with the saying, "red sky in the morning, shepherd's warning," was wrong. Shades of pink and purple tint the sky, and the forecast promises another corker of a day. I sit on the plush, padded outdoor sofa, gazing out over the pool with my coffee, waiting for the kids to wake up. It's supposed to be my day off, but it feels weird not helping with breakfast. Plus, it's another excuse to ogle my tortured boss.

After our day at the beach yesterday, we came home and put the kids to bed together before he disappeared into his office. I spent the evening binge-watching Love Island, nursing a tumbler of his family's whiskey, hoping Caelon would emerge and join me, while simultaneously hating myself for hoping for anything.

He's clearly still grieving. I thought he didn't want me, but it took until midnight to remember he fought Rian over me. That has to mean something, doesn't it?

An incoming text pings on my phone.

Dermot: Won't make lunch today, something came up.

Urgh, please tell me it wasn't your dick. What's her name?

While Dermot is super obsessed with preserving my virtue (he has no idea I don't have any), he has no such concerns for his own. Women flock to him and he laps it up.

Dermot: Wash your mouth out, young lady. I've a good mind to forward your message to Mother.

I dare you. I'm a grown woman. When will any of you accept that?

Dermot: Maybe when you get a real job and start acting like one.

A flicker of irritation burns in my chest.

Shall I tell your best friend you don't consider me minding his kids to be a real job?

Dermot: Caelon gets it. He has a little sister too. Which is why I know you're safe with him.

I snort. Sated, yes. Safe, no. Watching him with his kids makes my ovaries weep.

I'm still trying to think of a reply when I hear the soft thud of approaching feet.

Caelon.

A million hummingbirds swoop through my stomach at the sight of him. He's barefoot, wearing a pair of low-hanging grey sweatpants and a tight black t-shirt that clings to his torso like a super-seductive second skin. His dark hair is tousled, and there are crinkle marks on his cheeks from his pillow. My fingers itch to smooth over them.

'What are you doing up?' He saunters over and drops to the other end of the couch.

'I'm an early riser. Always have been.' I shrug.

His gaze flicks over my shorts and vest top before settling on my face. 'It's your day off. You should relax, stay in bed.'

'It's no fun alone.' There goes my big mouth again.

His lips press tightly together, tension lines his jaw. He's so serious all the time. What I wouldn't give to see him loosen up a little.

'I had fun yesterday at the beach.' I take a sip of my coffee. 'You have an amazing family.'

'They're okay, I guess, apart from Rian, who I could cheerfully choke,' he says, but there's no missing the affectionate taint to his tone. 'Your family is pretty cool too,' he adds. 'Dermot is one of the few people I'd call if I needed help to bury a body.'

'Ha ha.'

'I'm not even joking.'

He is. He has to be. The alternative doesn't bear contemplating. 'Dermot is sound, but we don't share the banter you have with your brothers. Dermot has always babied me. He means well, but it can be suffocating. It was one of the reasons I went to the States.'

'What about your parents?' Caelon asks, staring over the horizon. 'Your mother is one of the top paediatricians in the country. That's impressive. Do you have a good relationship with her?'

'I exasperate her!' I laugh, though it's not funny. My perceived lack of ambition is a bone of contention with both my parents. 'She keeps asking when I'm going to get a "real job"' I scoff.

'Should I be worried?' Caelon's gaze cuts to mine. 'About you leaving us? I do have a habit of driving nannies away.'

'No!' I sit straighter. 'I enjoy my work. And I consider my job to be just as important as what my parents do. Raising children is a privilege. My parents were gone so much when I was small. I was passed from childminder to childminder. It wasn't fun. I vowed if I had kids, I'd be at home with them, play with them, make sure they felt wanted.'

'Did you feel unwanted?' Caelon's eyes darken.

'It wasn't that I didn't feel loved. If anything, my family smothered me. They still treat me like I'm fragile, weak, incapable of making my own decisions and of knowing my own mind.' I pause and take another sip of my coffee. 'I had a sister. She died. I suppose that's why they're the way they are with me.'

'Jesus, Ivy, I had no idea.' Caelon inches closer. 'Dermot never mentioned it in all the years we've been friends. That is rough.'

'It was a long time ago.' I sigh. 'My parents threw themselves into their work, and just like Orla and Owen, I had a lot of nannies. I shouldn't judge, but I like to think if I lost a child, I'd lavish love on the ones who survived.'

'Do you want your own kids?' he pries, blurring the boss/employee/friend line even further.

I don't hesitate. 'Yes. Four of them.'

He swipes a hand over his stubble. 'Why am I not surprised?'

'So, if I'm going to stay here on a long-term basis, you're probably going to have to reconsider your stance on me going out on a Friday night, because I'm not going to find a man here. Eventually, I'm going to start dating.' I sweep my hand over the pristine grounds just as Jared comes into view. He's wearing a tight vest and khaki shorts and holding a watering hose. 'Unless...'

'Oh, please. He's so doped up with weed, I doubt he could get it up,' Caelon scoffs, a frown creasing his already sullen face. 'And Dermot definitely wouldn't approve.'

'Dermot doesn't approve of anyone.' I drain the remainder of my coffee, and we sit quietly for a few minutes, both staring out over the water.

'I need to ask you something.' Caelon swallows and I watch as his Adam's apple bobs in his throat.

The man is a walking red flag, yet I'm still stupidly hoping he's going to reconsider our unusual situationship, because the more time I spend with him, the more I want him. Tall, dark and tortured is my jam, and I'd do anything to have him spread all over me.

'Ask me anything. I mean, you already know me better than any other boss I've had.'

Translation: you've already made me come twice and I wouldn't be averse to a third time.

Anticipation swells in my chest like a helium balloon.

Did he spend the night stewing over Rian's outrageous flirtation?

Did the day at the beach yesterday stir something in him?

'Will you be okay with the kids for a few nights next week? There are some complications with one of the hotel refurbs in Monaco. I need to meet with the architect in person.'

The balloon in my chest bursts like it's been poked with a pin. I thought for a second there we bonded, but no, I'm the nanny, not his friend, or anything else significant.

'Of course.' I plaster on my widest smile. 'That's what you pay me for. They'll be fine, I promise.'

'Thanks, Ivy.' He stands, hovering for a second. 'What are your plans for the day? Are you going for dinner with Dermot again?'

'No.' I swallow hard and straighten my shoulders. If Caelon doesn't want me, I know a man who does. Rian slipped me his card yesterday and I'm damn well going to use it. 'I'm going on a date,' I announce.

His head snaps up. 'With who?'

'Your brother.'

'You've got to be joking.' Caelon's expression is positively murderous.

'Like you said, it's my day off.' I stalk towards the back door, deliberately sashaying my denim-clad ass.

I take it back. Whoever said, 'red sky in the morning, shepherds warning' was right. I am about to do something dangerous.

Chapter Eighteen

CAELON

My blood pressure is higher than the Empire State Building, my stomach twisted tighter than a tornado, and a thick lump in my throat threatens to choke me.

What is it about Ivy fucking Winters that has me in knots?

She defies me at every turn.

Challenges me.

Now she's going on a date with my fucking brother.

I should sack her with immediate effect. But that would mean not seeing her sexy little ass swaggering around my house, which is probably marginally worse than seeing it, wanting her, and hating myself for it.

I want her more than is good for either of us.

But I don't date.

I fuck.

And I really shouldn't fuck her, no matter how badly I want to. I'm no good for her. I certainly can't give her what she wants – not in the long term, anyway. Orla and Owen traipse out into the garden, where I'm still reeling from Ivy's revelation. Owen has that damn teddy under his arm again. 'Dad, I have a 'fession.'

'It's okay, buddy. I'll go sort the sheets, don't worry.'

'Thanks, Daddy. I'm sorry.' He hugs my legs.

'Don't be sorry, it's an accident. Accidents happen.' Like accidentally plotting to murder my kid brother and locking my nanny in her bedroom. She did say being tied up is her favourite fantasy.

Rian might be closer in age to Ivy, but that does not make him more suitable. He's a blatant manwhore. If Ivy wants to settle down and find a husband, she's wasting her time with him. 'Come on, let's get some breakfast.' I ruffle Owen's hair.

The house is always peaceful on Sundays. The only staff are the security at the front gate. I prefer it this way, but I can't manage the kids on my own and hold down my business.

'Where's Ivy?' Orla glances round the kitchen.

'It's her day off,' I remind her.

'Do you think she'll want to come with us today?' Orla asks hopefully.

On Sundays, we usually lay flowers on Isabella's grave before going to my parents' for dinner, although mine are out of the country, so I guess we'll be eating out. My parents idolise Owen and Orla, as do Isabella's. Every few weeks, the kids go to Isabella's parents for the night.

'No, sweetie, she has plans.' Even if she wasn't going on a date with my brother, I'm pretty sure she would rather do anything in the world than visit my wife's grave.

I can't stop her going out with Rian, or anyone else. I shouldn't try. The other night was a one-off. I can't keep getting her off to stop her from getting it elsewhere.

Can I?

'Daddy, can we watch TV?' Owen pleads. They're only allowed TV in the mornings at weekends.

'Okay, buddy. Just for half an hour.' That should give me enough time to persuade Ivy not to go out with my brother.

I switch on the big TV in the lounge and get the kids a second bowl of cereal. 'I'm just going upstairs to get dressed. Shout if you need me, okay?'

Neither Owen nor Orla reply, both already engrossed in a high-pitched cartoon.

I stalk up the stairs and head straight to Ivy's room. Her exotic pomegranate scent lingers in the air, luring me in, as the sound of her tinkling laughter travels through the thick oak door.

'Great, I'll see you then,' she says. It's enough to send me charging in like a two-thousand-pound Charolais bull.

Ivy's hair is wet from her shower. She's wearing nothing but a tiny white towel tucked around her torso. Her eyes widen as I stride across the room. Without heels on, she's tiny compared to my six feet four. I want to scoop her up into my arms and keep her there, but I can't.

'You can't be serious.' My voice is cold enough to send goosebumps scattering up her arms.

'I've never been more serious.' Her wide lips part and all I can think about is slamming my mouth over them. But I won't. Because while I've kissed between her legs, kissing another woman's mouth feels too intimate. Too meaningful. Less like a transaction of pleasure and more like a sign of genuine affection. Because the last mouth I kissed was Isabella's. And because, while I'm a wealthy man, when it comes to intimacy and affection, I have nothing. I give nothing and I expect nothing. I don't deserve it, and I don't want it.

Yet with Ivy, somehow, a part of me does. I want to kiss her. I want to wrap my arms around her. I want to drag her into my bed and keep her there.

'Get on the bed,' I growl.

'No,' she shakes her head vehemently. 'You can't just make me come and tell me not to go out.'

'But I'm so good at it.' I trace a finger over her exposed collar bone, dipping it beneath her towel and tearing it from her body. It falls to the floor along with my jaw.

Ivy's body is pure perfection. Silky soft skin. Curves carved in all the right places. Rosy peaked nipples. The way it reacts to mine is magnetic.

'You're beautiful,' I tell her honestly.

She stares at me with unashamed longing. This attraction between us is feral. It sucks the oxygen from the room until I can hardly breathe. She wants me as much as I want her. I feel it with every fibre of my being.

'Call Rian and tell him you've changed your mind, and I'll lick your pretty little pussy until you come all over my face.'

'No.' She stares at me with a defiance. I'd love to fuck it out of her and then kiss every inch of her better.

'I bet you're wet for me already.' I skim my palms over her nipples and she hisses. 'Let me take care of that ache for you.'

'No.' Her protest is weaker this time.

'All you have to do is pick up the phone,' I coax, running my hand lower over her stomach.

Even if she doesn't call Rian, I'm going to devour her, anyway. The memory of her sweetness is all too fresh from Friday. The sound of my name on her lips as she cries out is more addictive than heroin.

'I won't do it,' she says.

'Let me see if I can persuade you.' I slide my fingers lower and slip them through the slickness between her legs. She is saturated.

'Is it the prospect of your date with my brother that has you wet enough to hydrate an army?' I brush my lips over her ear.

'You're not playing fair,' she hisses.

'I never claimed I would.' My fingers skim her clit, and she moans.

'Call him,' I insist, pressing my erection into her hip.

'No.' Her eyes fall shut. 'I need more.'

'Oh, baby, why didn't you say so?' I guide her backwards until the back of her legs hit the bed. I give her a gentle nudge, and she falls to the mattress.

'I didn't mean...'

I'm on my knees with my head buried between her legs before she can finish her sentence.

'Fuck, what are you doing to me?' she pants.

'I'm making you come so hard that even if you do go on a date with my brother, all you'll be able to think about is this.'

I'm not doing this for her. I'm doing it for myself. Because it's all I can think about every fucking time she's near me.

Last night, it took all my willpower to stay in my office, knowing she was sitting there in my sitting room, probably waiting for me. Probably hoping for this. I don't want to give into this thing between us. Don't want to develop an obsession with Ivy Winters, yet here we are. I can't stay away from her.

I need more time to get my head around the idea of fucking another woman in this house. Of fucking my nanny. Of fucking my best friend's little sister. Of fucking up everything.

This is all I can give her right now, so I'm going to give it to her regardless of whether she goes out with Rian or not.

'As much as I loved eating you out from behind, I'm going to enjoy watching your face as you lose it on my tongue.' Our eyes lock as I sink my lips over her hot centre.

'I'm still going on a date with your brother,' she pants.

'You little witch.' I suck her clit and sink two fingers inside her. 'What are you doing to me?'

'I know what I'd like to do to you.' Her fingers thread

through my hair, halting me. 'But for some reason, you seem determined to keep me away from your cock. Do you think Dermot will mind you licking my pussy less than if you fucked me?'

'I never want to find out,' I mutter, shaking my head free of her grasp and catching her clit with my lips again.

Her hips buck, her back arches, and her thighs tremble. I watch her the entire time as she breaks and shatters on my tongue. Ivy's mews and moans are my favourite Sunday morning soundtrack. She stares straight back at me with a wondrous look in her eyes.

She thinks there's hope for me yet.

The only hope I have is that I don't embarrass myself by coming in my pants. Because Ivy Winters is fire and I am ice. And I can't afford to melt in a puddle.

Chapter Nineteen

CAELON

Ivy tugs my hair as she comes on my face, but worse than that, she tugs something in my chest. Something I thought was frozen so solid it was untouchable.

I crawl up the bed, blazing a trail of tiny kisses over the smooth plane of her stomach, between her breasts, up her neck and over her jawline. Her limbs are languid, but her eyes are sharply aware. I'd swear she's holding her breath, waiting for me to kiss her mouth.

My lips hover over hers. Her chin dips in a clear invitation.

I can't do it.

I can't kiss her. No matter how badly I want to. Kissing changes everything.

I press my lips to her cheek and leave Ivy's room without another word. If she wants to go out with Rian, I can't stop her.

The kids are thankfully still engrossed in their cartoon show, so I head up for a shower. It takes all of an embarrassing ten strokes of my cock before I come harder than a hurricane all over the glossy, ivory tiles, imagining my hand was Ivy's tight hot channel.

Maybe if I give into this thing between us, I could get her out of my system? Then she can go on her merry quest for a husband, and I can continue my quest for revenge.

No.

We can't.

She'll want more, and I'm not capable of that. Someone will get hurt. And we've all had enough pain for one lifetime.

By the time I leave my bedroom, dressed and ready for the day, I've vowed, once again, to leave Ivy alone. Stripping my son's urine-soaked bedsheets is a swift reality check. My life is complicated.

Ivy has no place in it other than in a professional capacity.

When I stroll into the living room to switch the TV off, I find Orla sucking on a lollipop.

'Where did you get that?' I tut, glancing at the clock. It's way too early for a sugar high and the inevitable crash that will follow.

'Uncle Rian gave it to us,' Orla and Owen exclaim unanimously.

Of course he did. A tightness weaves into my torso. I scan the gardens, looking for his car. 'Where is he?'

'He's gone. He took Ivy out for a spin. We asked if we could go, but he said he only had two seats.' Orla pulls a puppy-dog look.

'Go and get dressed. I'll take you for a spin, princess.' I smooth her hair back from her eyes.

'And me?' Owen bounces on the couch like it's a trampoline and not a fifty-thousand-euro Italian custom-made piece.

'Of course.' I clear up the discarded cereal bowls. 'Get dressed. We'll go visit Mammy, then head somewhere nice for dinner.'

'Can I order a chocolate brownie?' Orla's eyes light up.

I nod. 'Only if you eat your dinner.'

'Did you think any more about if we could get a dog?' she asks.

'Sorry guys, a dog is a huge commitment. I'm not here enough to take care of one. They need a lot of attention. They shed hair everywhere. They need to be toilet trained. Walked.'

'But Ivy's here now. She could help.' Owen jumps from the couch to the floor like he's a superhero. 'Do you remember the time Mammy doggy sat Aunty Jenny's puppy and it dug up the plants?'

'I do.' A flicker of warmth flares in my chest at the memory. 'It's a hard no, guys.' Bad enough these two treat the couch like a trampoline. I refuse to have a furry beast slobbering all over it as well.

I cross the open plan room to the kitchen with the empty bowls. 'Right, get dressed. Let's see who is quickest. Timer starts now.' The two of them scramble out of the room and up the stairs.

The scent of Ivy's pomegranate perfume lingers in the kitchen. I force away the image of her sitting in the passenger seat of Rian's car. Of his hand dropping to her thigh. Of him flirting with her. Making her laugh. The house is enormous, but suddenly, the walls are closing in on me. I need to get out of here. 'Hurry up, guys!' I call up the stairs.

We pile into the Bentley, and I drive slowly down the driveway.

'You sure you don't want me to accompany you?' Damon checks as he opens the gate.

'No, we're fine, thanks.' Security is important, but so is my sanity. Sometimes I just need to feel normal for a while.

We stop by the florist on the way to the graveyard and pick up a lavish bouquet of Isabella's favourite blush pink peonies. The kids race up the narrow stone pathway to their mother's marble headstone, laughing and chatting about one of the characters on the TV show they were watching. Visiting their mother's grave is normal for them, but it will never feel normal to me.

I lay the flowers, then run a hand over the top of the white shiny marble, while the kids skip between the tombstones.

'Hi Issy.' I pause, feeling the usual stir of guilt in my sternum, though this time, it's for a different reason.

I blame myself for Isabella's death. I hold Jack O'Connor responsible, more so than that fucking druggie, Danny Bourke, but I have to accept some of the blame. If Isabella hadn't married me, she wouldn't have been caught in the crossfire of the feud between the O'Connors and the Becketts. As long as I live, I'll never forgive them for taking her from us. But I'll never forgive myself either.

Today, I'm also shouldering the weight of my newfound feelings—I mean attraction—to another woman.

'Caelon,' a familiar voice calls, and I twist on my heels to see Isabella's mother, Jocelyn, ambling towards us with a smile the size of Switzerland on her weathered face. She aged twenty years after her daughter's death. Then again, so did I.

'I thought I might meet you here.' A slow smile stretches her mouth open.

'Nanny!' Orla and Owen run to their maternal grandmother. I should make more of an effort with Jocelyn. Even though the kids visit one weekend a month, I usually ask my parents or the nanny to drop them over.

Seeing my in-laws is hard. They've only ever been lovely to me, but again, I don't want, need, or deserve their sympathy or affection. What I need is to avenge their daughter. To make someone pay for the huge gaping hole in our lives.

'Hey you guys! You've grown in a matter of weeks! Are you coming to visit me soon?' Jocelyn crouches and hugs the kids.

'Can we come today?' Orla and Owen bound around Jocelyn's legs like a couple of excited labradors.

'Of course you can,' she coos, at the same time as I say, 'Not today.'

'Ahh, Daddy, Nanny said it's okay. Please!' Owen tugs at the hem of my polo shirt.

Jocelyn turns her focus on me. 'I'd love to take them for a few hours if it suits you. I don't want to intrude if you have plans, though.'

'The plan is to eat a chocolate brownie,' Orla announces, before beckoning Owen over to sniff a batch of giant wild daisies.

'Maybe you'd like a few hours to yourself?' Jocelyn whispers. 'Or maybe there's someone you'd like to spend a couple of hours with?'

It's not the first time my mother-in-law has tiptoed around the notion of me moving on. The problem is, I don't know how to. Not in the way that someone like Ivy wants or needs.

Ivy.

She's with my brother.

If the kids go with Jocelyn, I could gatecrash their date. Because I know my brother. I know how his tiny little brain works. Where he'll take her to impress her. But he doesn't know Ivy at all.

I've only known her a couple of weeks, but she's spent the entire time under my roof, and when I haven't had my tongue buried inside her, I've been watching her—even when I shouldn't have been.

I know what she likes, what she's interested in, and it's not being wined and dined in an overpriced, pretentious restaurant, which is undoubtably where Rian will take her. He thinks throwing money at women is enough to get into their panties. Sometimes he's right. But not with Ivy.

She comes from an ambitious, affluent family, yet instead of studying at a pretentious college and pursuing a high-flying career she's not passionate about, she unashamedly admits her life goals are to have a family.

People are what matter to Ivy. Not places. She was happier than a pig in shit with the pizzas on the beach yesterday. The quiet coffee we shared in the garden. That's more her thing. The little things are the big things to her.

I hesitate, biting the lining of my cheek. Jocelyn steps closer, placing a hand on my forearm. 'Oh, Caelon, I hate seeing you like this. Isabella would hate to see you like this. You used to be so vibrant, so full of life. Now you look so...' she fumbles for the right word before settling on, 'tortured.'

I cough to cover my snort.

'You need to move on. It doesn't mean you love Isabella any less. You could have another fifty, sixty, maybe even seventy years on this planet. Do you really want to spend them alone?'

'I never thought about it,' I admit truthfully. I've been so consumed with rage and a thirst for revenge, I've never thought past those things. And while I don't want to embark on a relationship with Ivy, I definitely don't want her as a sister-in-law.

'Let me take the kids today, please,' Jocelyn urges.

'If you're sure.' I blow out a breath. 'I'll collect them this evening, around six.'

'Perfect.'

Rian gatecrashed my day with Ivy yesterday.

Today, I'm going to gatecrash his.

Chapter Twenty

IVY

Where Caelon is dark and tortured, Rian is a ray of sunshine. His easy banter and blatant flirtations are a balm to my soul, but they don't set it alight the way that Caelon does. The second I met Caelon, something inside of him sparked something inside of me, and it hasn't stopped burning since. Living in his house, I'm almost as tortured as he is, knowing he's so physically near, yet so out of reach.

'We'll take a bottle of the 1971 Dom Perignon Plenitude, please,' Rian tells the waiter, without bothering to ask me what I'd like.

I glance around the restaurant, an opulent Thai where it's notoriously difficult to make a reservation. It's frequently mentioned in the society pages and the trashier gossip blogs. There's always some celebrity being papped here.

Everything is pristine white, so much so it's almost blinding. The cutlery gleams. The crystal glasses send rainbow colours cascading in every direction. Floor-to-ceiling windows overlook St. Stephens Green below. I watch as people stroll through the lavish grounds, tilting their faces up towards the sun, revelling in the rays. My feet itch to be outside. This is lovely but yesterday was so much better.

I squirm in my seat as the memory of this morning shoots through my brain like a torpedo.

'So, Ivy, tell me about yourself,' Rian says, his huge oval eyes flick over every inch of my face before darting to my chest then back again. I picked out a simple summer dress which is probably way too casual for a restaurant like this, but I'm comfortable and it's cute.

Each of the Beckett brothers is drop-dead gorgeous, but while they all share the same shocking dark hair, enviable bone structure and strong physique, they're all unique in their own subtle ways. Rian has a playfulness to him that the others lack. Mischief dances in his dark irises, lighting him up from the inside out.

'What do you want to know?' I skim my finger over my fork for something to do with my fidgety hands. We spent the morning driving through the Wicklow countryside making small talk about the scenery before heading into the city for lunch. The weight of his full attention is making me question what I'm doing here.

Although, deep down, I know exactly what I'm doing. I'm giving Caelon–Can-Make–You–Come-Hard–Enough–To–See–Stars the proverbial middle finger. Which probably isn't fair on Rian, though I'm pretty sure when it comes to the opposite sex, he doesn't play fair either.

'Favourite sexual position,' he smirks.

I shake my head with a snigger. 'So, you want to play this game, do you?'

'I always find it's better to cut to the chase.' He shrugs. 'Saves a lot of messing around.'

'Okay, well, in that case, let *me* cut to the chase. My favourite sexual position is irrelevant because you won't get past first base.' I mimic his playful tone, although I'm deadly serious.

'Never say never, Ivy. You're not my nanny, or my best friend's sister. If you looked at me the way you looked at Caelon yesterday, I'd have pinned you to the sand and taken your lingerie off then and there.' He arches his eyebrows. 'But he didn't... and you're pissed because you're into him, which is why you called me,' he surmises.

'You're not just a pretty face,' I admit, raising my palms in the air. 'But you still came on a date with me. Why?'

'I have my own reasons.' He taps the side of his nose.

'Like?'

'Firstly, it's fun pissing Caelon off. It's too easy. He used to be so relaxed and easy-going. Nothing riled him. Now, he's like a nuclear weapon waiting to go off.' Rian sits back as the waiter returns with the champagne and pours two glasses.

'And secondly?'

I take the crystal flute the waiter hands me. I'd have preferred a whiskey, but alcohol is alcohol and I could do with a little this afternoon.

'Secondly, you're not the only one pining for someone they can't have,' he sighs, tapping his fingers on the table.

I scoff. 'I'm pretty sure there isn't a woman in the world who'd turn you down.' I raise the glass to my lips and pause, 'Well, apart from me.' I grin.

'You'd be surprised. It's a long story. One for another day.' His thick eyelashes blink hard. 'Let's get back to the fun questions. Best shag you've ever had?' He winks.

Laughter bursts from my throat, echoing around the restaurant loudly enough to attract attention.

'The right answer, in case you're wondering,' he grins at me across the table, 'is that it hasn't happened yet, but to ask you again in a couple of hours.'

'You've just told me you're into someone else. And I didn't deny being into your brother!'

'Yep, and as neither is happening, we could always get our kicks with each other in the meantime.' He runs a thumb over his baby smooth jawline, and I have no idea if he's serious or joking. 'Tell me, what did my brother do to you on that desk, Ivy? I bet I could top it. I bet I could make you scream.'

A dark shadow appears from nowhere, clouding the sunlight streaming in the window. 'The only person screaming will be you, little brother, if you continue to flirt with what's mine.' Caelon booms thunderously and slides into the seat beside me.

I swallow hard, not sure if I'm elated he's here or exasperated. Judging by the heat pooling in my core, it's the former.

'Yours, is she?' Rian sits forward, interlacing his fingers on the table. His glee is apparent with every fleeting micro facial expression.

'She was this morning when she came on my face, and she will be again later,' Caelon says casually.

Heat flushes my cheeks. I pick up my drink and take a huge mouthful. 'Is nothing sacred?'

Caelon shrugs, then signals to the waiter. 'Whiskey. Beckett's Gold,' he barks.

'Hitting the hard stuff early?' Rian folds his arms.

'It's not for me. It's for Ivy.'

He's been paying attention. Beckett's Gold is my favourite. I take another mouthful of champagne, just for something to do.

'You swallow fantastically,' Rian teases, and I almost spray the liquid through my teeth.

'You'll never find out,' Caelon growls. 'Fuck this. Come on Ivy, let's get out of here.'

'Oh, what!' Rian exclaims. 'Things were just getting interesting!'

'Not nearly as interesting as they will be when I get Ivy home.' Caelon pushes his chair back with his legs.

'I'm not going anywhere with you,' I say defiantly. Although it's hot as fuck that he's come in here all alpha and possessive, I have more respect for myself than that. His hot/cold behaviour is giving me whiplash. I thought this morning, I'd finally cracked his hard outer shell, first outside, then in my bedroom, but he couldn't even bring himself to kiss me on the mouth.

'What?' Caelon's eyes flit to mine. 'You wanted my attention, you got it.'

'I want to be wanted *all* the time, not just when you feel threatened by someone else wanting me.'

'Ivy,' he mutters, 'you have my attention all the damn time, whether I want to give it to you or not. You steal it every time you're in the vicinity. And when you're not, I find myself watching you on the cameras. You've ploughed into my house, and into my head and there's not a damn thing I can do about it.'

'You watch me on the cameras?' It should be creepy, but I'm oddly flattered.

'Every damn day.' He shrugs again, accepting the whiskey from the waiter and passing it to me.

'How do I know you're not just saying that to get me away from my date?' I take the glass from his hand. 'I refuse to be some little fuck-toy you like to wind up and walk away from. I want to touch you. I want you to kiss me.'

Rian watches our exchange like he's watching a tennis ball pinging back and forth. All he's missing is a punnet of strawberries and some clotted cream.

'You want to touch me?' Caelon slides back into his seat and tucks his legs under the table. 'Touch this.' He grabs my hand and places it on his crotch. Thank God for the table-cloth covering his lap because there's no missing the thick length pressing against his dress shorts. Fuck. My mouth waters. But it doesn't escape my notice that his lips didn't seek out mine.

It's Rian's turn to stand. 'My job here is done. As much as I wouldn't mind seeing Ivy get eaten out on the table, there's not a hope in hell I want to see your hairy cock.'

'You orchestrated this on purpose?' Caelon glares at Rian without releasing my hand.

'You looked like you needed a nudge.' He shrugs. 'If you need another one, I'm happy to take Ivy out any time.' He presses a gentle kiss to my cheek and stalks towards the exit.

'Now what?' I press my thighs together.

'Now, I guess I'll have to take you on a real date,' Caelon says.

Chapter Twenty-One

CAELON

I don't date. Fucking is one thing; dating is an entirely different ball game. But when I walked into that restaurant and saw Ivy with Rian, I wanted, no needed, to be the one sitting with her. The one commanding her undivided attention. The one to make her laugh loud enough to attract an audience. Even if it means my best friend is liable to cut my dick off and shove it up my arse.

'Where are we going?' Ivy asks, glancing out of the passenger window of my Bentley as we leave the city behind.

'Somewhere you'll like.' I indicate to take the exit off the dual carriageway for Dun Laoghaire, a coastal town east of Dublin.

'You think you know me?' she teases. 'Have you really been watching me on the nanny cam?' Her lips slant upwards. 'If I'd known I had an audience, I'd have given you a show.'

'You give me a show every time you swagger around my house, whether it's in those indecent ass-sculpting yoga pants or those dresses.' I cock my head to hers. 'Besides, you're not too late. I told you I'm away next week. I'll be keeping an eye on things.'

She forms an expression of mock horror. 'Mr Beckett, are you suggesting what I think?'

'I believe you were the one being suggestive.' My lips twitch. Despite my permanent rage, it's impossible not to feel lighter around Ivy. She has a habit of taking everything dark and making it brighter.

'Do you really want to take me on a date? Or did you barge into that restaurant just to spite Rian?' Ivy flicks her hair from her shoulder. It's loosely styled in blonde beach waves, understated and sexy as fuck, just like the rest of her.

'No, I don't *want* to take you on a date.' My eyes roll skywards. 'I don't want to take any woman on a date. Dating's not on my agenda. But you pushed buttons I didn't even know existed, and the thought of my brother putting his hands on you drove me demented.' I inhale a lungful of air before blowing it out slowly. 'Selfishly, I want you more than is healthy for either of us. You've been clear about what you want out of life, and I will never be the man to give you those things.'

'I said I wanted kids one day, not necessarily right now. I'm only twenty-three-years-old!' she exclaims.

As if being my best friend's little sister wasn't bad enough, Ivy is also closer in age to my own sister than she is to me. 'As if I could forget.'

'I want a family, a home of my own, filled with love and laughter, but I don't necessarily need it now. When that day does come, I want to know I've lived a full life. In case you hadn't noticed, I'm not exactly saving myself for marriage,' she snorts.

The thought of Ivy with another man turns my stomach. Which is precisely why my kids are with their maternal grandmother and I'm driving the nanny for a romantic stroll and a fucking ice cream. What the hell is wrong with me?

'Have there been many men?' I'd like Killian to track

every single one of them down and wipe them from the face of this earth.

'No one memorable.' She shrugs.

I clear my throat pointedly and glare at her.

'Well, up until I met this really tortured-looking hot old guy in a bar recently.' A wicked smile spreads across her face.

'I'm thirty-four, not eighty-four!' I thrum my fingers on the steering wheel. 'Didn't anyone ever teach you to respect your elders? Any more of your cheek and I'll pull over, bend you over the bonnet of this car and slap your ass so hard you won't be able to sit down for a week,' I growl.

'Is that a promise?' she sings in a sultry tone, 'because I quite like it rough.'

My cock thickens further in my pants. 'I've a good mind to call your brother and tell him what a bad girl you are.'

'And I'll tell him exactly how you found out,' she chirps gleefully. 'Lighten up, let's have some fun. I just want to feel your cock inside me. It'll be our little secret.'

'There's nothing little about it.'

'Your cock or the secret?' she chuckles.

I shake my head. 'Your filthy mouth wasn't listed on your résumé,' I grunt, glancing across at her again. Like a fucking magnet, she keeps drawing me in.

'Neither was my ability to suck dick, but I'm pretty good at that, too.' Her blue eyes glint with mischief and I almost choke on my own saliva. 'I'm surprised you even looked at my résumé by the way.'

I didn't look at it until after she moved in, then I pored over it, memorising every detail. And not because I was concerned for my kids; the agency's background checks are rigorous. I scoured it, desperate to learn everything about the woman I'm obsessed with.

'Did you speak to your previous bosses the same way you speak to me?'

'My previous boss was a creep. If I spoke to him the way I spoke to you, he'd have dropped his trousers already, which is more than I can say for you...'

'Ivy...' My tone is weighted with warning and now it's her turn to roll her eyes.

'Okay, okay!' She brandishes upturned palms in the air. 'I've never spoken to any man the way I speak to you.' She crosses one lean leg over the other and my gaze is drawn to six inches of exposed thigh. 'What can I say? You bring out the best in me.'

'Or the worst,' I sigh, shaking my head. Dermot would murder me if he had any idea what I'm contemplating doing to his little sister—what I've already done to his little sister.

'Don't let me be another thing to beat yourself up about, Tortured,' she pats my knee. 'I'm a big girl. I know what I'm doing.'

'That makes one of us then,' I mutter.

She flicks her hair from her shoulder. 'I want your body, not a marriage proposal.'

'The kids adore you. I don't want to fuck that up. And Dermot will fuck me up if he so much as suspects I'm sniffing around his little sister.' Everyone knows the bro code. Although, the temptation of doing something forbidden only makes it so much more, well, tempting. Ivy was wrong. I *am* a bad man.

'It's just sex. Well, it would be, if you'd get over yourself,' Ivy teases.

'You are determined to drag me straight to Hell.' Though, realistically, I resigned myself to it a long time ago.

'I have needs. Besides, we established the first night we met what type of *woman* I am.' She slaps my thigh playfully and I snatch her hand up and bring it to my lips.

'You're like no type I ever met before, which is why I will at least try to, how did you put it, "get over myself?"'

'What is the problem? Do you have some daddy-dom kink where you prefer giving pleasure to taking it? Are you afraid of losing control? Or is it something else entirely?' Her stare burns the side of my face. I keep my attention focussed on the road.

'Do we have to dissect my sexual preferences? Why do you try to drag every quirk or kink into the conversation like you're asking which flavour of ice cream I prefer? I like making you come. What's wrong with that?'

'I want to make *you* come.' She pouts.

'You already have, more times than you'll know, in my shower.'

'You *have* had sex with someone other than Isabella?' Ivy frowns. It's not a question technically, but the way she accentuates the word *have*, makes it one.

'Yes, plenty, but not someone I actually liked.' God, it's like this woman is wielding a hundred-megawatt torch into my darkest corners and dragging my deepest truths into the light.

Her grin is so wide, her teeth blind me. 'You like me,' she squeals.

'Fuck's sake, Ivy, we're not a couple of high schoolers,' I tut. 'If barging in on your date with my brother and claiming you as mine doesn't scream "I like you," then nothing does.'

'So, let me get this straight.' She inclines her head thoughtfully. 'You like me, which is why you haven't had sex with me, because you feel... guilty? Because of Isabella?'

'Amongst other things. Like I'm your boss. And your brother's best friend.'

'Don't worry about Dermot. He'll never find out.' She puffs out a breath. 'As for Isabella, I can't even begin to imagine what you've been through and how you feel, but you can't live in this permanent state of dark and tortured forever. It's not good for you, and it's not good for the kids. You need to live while you can. I know nothing about your wife, but I do know that she wouldn't want you to live in a permanent state of misery.'

Ivy's words are an uncanny echo of Jocelyn's. *'Isabella would hate to see you like this.'*

'I told you already, I don't want a proposal, I want your penis. Don't panic. Don't overthink this. We both know where we stand. It's one summer in both of our lives. It doesn't have to be complicated. You can use me as a practice run for when you find a woman you really do want to date.'

I can't think of any woman in the world I'd rather date than Ivy.

I suppose that's why they say opposites attract.

'Life is short, and everything can change in the blink of an eye. You know it better than anyone. Let's live for today,' Ivy says, patting my knee.

For a horny twenty-three-year-old who chose not to pursue a formal college education, she's the smartest woman I know.

Chapter Twenty-Two

IVY

Tortured *likes* me. It's enough to give me the warm and fuzzies.

I wasn't lying when I told him I wanted his penis, rather than a proposal, but I have a feeling if he were to lose the armour (along with his underwear), I could fall hard and fast for a man like him. A man who's strong and self-assured. Successful and confident. Which is why *I* need to erect some defences.

'You're like the blazing sun, bright, blinding and flaming hot.' His hand lands on top of mine on his knee and electricity bolts between us again.

'It's a life choice. You should try it sometime,' I tease to lighten the tone.

His onyx-like eyes land on mine, burning hot enough to melt me into a puddle. 'What did Rian say that was so hilarious?'

'He asked me what my favourite position is.' I bite back a smirk.

'That little prick.' He shakes his head and his jaw clenches. 'Did you tell him?'

'No, I'm more of a show than tell type of woman.' I squeeze his knee. 'Whenever you're ready.'

'I'm trying. I just need a bit of time.' He rubs a hand over his dark stubble, and the memory of it grazing my inner thigh has me drooling. 'You already know my cock is utterly invested in the idea.'

'In the meantime, buy me an ice cream and I guess I'll settle for being Daddy Pleasure Dom's fuck toy.'

Ten minutes later, Caelon pulls up in the Royal Marine Hotel car park, a stone's throw from Dun Laoghaire East Pier.

'Oh, my God! Can we go to Teddy's Ice Cream Parlour? I haven't been here since I was a kid!' I hop out of the car, scanning all the smiling faces surrounding us.

'And there was me thinking I'd got rid of the kids for the day,' he says drily.

My head whips round. 'Did you just make a joke? Next thing you know, you'll be cracking a smile.'

'I blame you,' he says, falling into step beside me. The pier stretches out ahead of us, long and inviting. The Irish Sea glitters under the sunlight, the waves gently lapping against the stone pier. Boats and yachts are lazily anchored in the harbour, their sails fluttering like languid summer butterflies. A group of kids are fishing off the edge, their excitement almost as bright as their neon shorts.

Colourful buildings and lively cafés are dotted all along the shoreline. The smell of fresh coffee and pastries wafts over us, mixing with the sea breeze. People lounge on benches, soaking up the sun, and a few couples are having picnics on the grassy patches nearby. Caelon is quiet, thoughtful, or perhaps he's just soaking in the scenery, like me. The silence between us is anything but awkward. It's comfortable, especially given the hustle and bustle around us. We pass a busker strumming away on a guitar, adding a soulful soundtrack to our walk. I toss a coin into his case, because good vibes deserve a little appreciation.

As we near the end of the pier, we're treated to a gorgeous panoramic view of Dublin Bay, stretching all the way to Howth and beyond. The horizon expands like an endless promise.

I pause, taking it all in. The sound of the waves, the distant chatter, the seagulls caw-cawing overhead—it's like the perfect symphony of summer.

'You hungry?' The tips of Caelon's fingers brush against mine, and he twists his head to face me with a rare half smile. Our eyes connect and it feels more intimate than when I was on all fours on his desk.

'Always.' I beam at him. 'I never met a calorie I didn't like.'

'You want that ice cream? Or something else?' he asks, flames licking the edges of his ebony irises.

'Something else.' I tilt my face upwards. 'I know you don't do romance, but if this was a real date, this would be the perfect place for a first kiss.'

'I've kissed you before, Tranquil.' His gaze falls to my mouth.

'Not here, you haven't.' I press a finger to my lips, a million butterflies soaring through my stomach as I wait.

Seconds pass and he doesn't move. A pained expression crosses his face. That guilt again.

It's okay.

I sidestep, closing my eyes and tilting my face up to be kissed by the sun instead. Within seconds, a shadow looms over me, though the chill that swoops over my spine isn't a cold one. It's sizzling hot and full of promise. My eyelids snap open to find Caelon towering over me, the pained expression on his face replaced with a promising one.

'I suppose I'm going to hell anyway...' He shrugs, then his

hard, hot lips crash onto mine, hungrily parting my mouth with his tongue, demanding entry, deep and hot and urgent.

I submit to his kiss, grabbing his polo shirt, twisting it in my fist. His arms reach around my back, yanking me against his taut torso until our bodies are flush, hip to hip, toe to toe. My skin fizzes. My legs are weak. I could kiss this man all damn day and it wouldn't be long enough. My soul is on fire. The rest of the world melts away as his tongue dances with mine, exploring, capturing, claiming.

All too soon, he pulls his mouth from mine and I feel bereft.

'How badly do you want that ice cream?' he demands.

'It depends on what else you're offering.' I shimmy against him.

'I'm offering you exactly what you wanted.' He dips his face to my ear, nibbling on the sensitive skin of my lobe. 'My penis, not a proposal.'

Excitement fizzes through me in dizzying waves. 'In that case, what are we waiting for?' I slip my hand in his and drag him back towards the car before he changes his mind.

The drive home is silent, the air thick with tension. I'm frightened to open my mouth in case he has second thoughts.

When we reach the house, Damon is manning the gate. He glances curiously between us, greeting us with a curt nod.

The gate slides open, and it feels like it takes forever to glide up the driveway. Caelon abandons the Bentley at the front door, not even bothering to lock it.

I follow him out of the car, a split second behind. He pauses at the top step.

'Are you sure this is what you want?' His velvety voice low and guttural. 'Because once I start, I won't be able to stop.'

'I want it.' More than I've wanted anything in my life. I want him to unleash himself on me.

'Let's go.' I push him through the front door.

Chapter Twenty-Three

CAELON

The door slams shut behind us, and I pounce on Ivy before she changes her mind. If she had any idea of how truly fucked-up I am, she wouldn't want me near her, so it's imperative we do this before she realises that, when I'm not imagining burying myself in her, I'm imagining burying bodies in the ground. She's so sunny, so perfect and so damn positive with her *let's just live for today* spiel, and I'm so dark, so troubled, and yes—she has it right—tortured.

My lips fuse with hers, and my hips pin her against the wall. It's a good job there are no housekeeping staff in today because I wouldn't be able to stop myself taking her right here, right now.

I've held back for long enough. There's no going back. I've kissed her and I'm doing my damn best not to overthink it. Not to spiral. Ivy's only here for the summer. There's a time limit on this thing. There's no need to panic.

She melts into me, her body writhing against mine. Eager hands grapple my neck, dragging me further into her like she's silently willing me to devour her. My cock is rock solid between us, nudging the junction between her parted legs. I grab a handful of her pert tits and squeeze. She bucks against my pelvis in response.

Tearing my lips from hers, I run my tongue over her jawline and along the column of her throat. My fingers circle her wrists and pin them against the wall over her head. 'I can't believe you went out with my brother. Did he make you writhe like this? Do you wish it was him pinning you against this wall? His cock pushing at your entrance?'

'No,' she pants.

I pull my pelvis back and slam it against hers. 'I should slap your ass for getting in his car.'

'I want you.' She grinds against me and slips a hand beneath my polo shirt, tracing the indentations between my pecs. 'I nearly came on the spot when I saw your tattoo the other morning. It took me less than two minutes to get myself off thinking about it.'

The thought of her touching herself, thinking of me, makes my cock even harder. I slip my hand beneath her dress and tear her lingerie from her body with an abrupt tug. 'No one gets you off but me from now on, okay?'

She swallows thickly, wide-eyed and wanting.

'Do you understand, Ivy? While you are mine – and you are now – until this thing between us runs its course, I am the only one to make you come, understood? If you need a release, you come to me.' I slide my fingers through her slickness, and she moans, nodding as her head rolls back against the wall.

She'd agree to pretty much anything right now. She's so greedy for my cock. 'If anyone lays a finger on what's mine, they will be punished. And that includes you.'

I want all of her pleasure. I need it like I need oxygen. Because I know once I take her, no matter how many times I pleasure myself thinking of her, of this, it will never compare.

So, if I can't reach ecstasy without her, there's no way I'm going to allow her the same privilege.

I drag my hand from between her legs and she moans in protest. 'Take me to bed.'

'Absolutely not.' I pull her dress over her head and drop it to the floor. 'I'm going to fuck you where you stand.'

Taking her to bed would feel like making love, and I'm nowhere near ready for that kind of intimacy. Plus, I have an ulterior motive for taking her right here in the hall. I point to the tiny security camera in the corner of the room. 'Smile for the camera, baby.'

Her pupils dilate to the size of dinner plates. 'Is that thing recording?'

'Always.' And when I'm away next week, I'm going to enjoy watching this particular home movie on repeat.

I reach around her back, unhook her silky bra, and toss it to the floor. Her pink nipples are like bullets. My lips latch on, sucking and nipping, until she gasps. Impatient fingers drag over my scalp.

'Do you know what you do to me, Ivy?' I straighten myself, grab her hand, and shove it inside the waistband of my shorts. She grips the base of my cock and pumps without hesitation.

'The only woman I've ever fucked in this house is my wife. I promised myself I would never bring a woman here, but you and your perfect tits and tight little cunt are my weakness. I hate myself for it, but I can't stop. I can't stay away from you, and I want to punish you for that.'

Though truly, the only person that deserves to be punished is me. But I've spent the past two years beating myself up, and it's got me absolutely nowhere. So, I'm trading it for decadent oblivion inside Ivy's sweet little pussy. Sleeping with her is wrong on so many levels, but it feels so fucking right.

'So, do it.' She pumps my cock faster and it weeps precum for her. 'Punish me. I can take it.'

'You have no idea what you're asking for. I want to slam my cock into you so hard, fill you up so good that you won't be able to think about anything but me for a week.' I pull my shirt over my head and toss it aside. Her eyes drink in every inch of my torso before falling to my crotch. She stares like she can't quite believe her hand is wrapped around it.

'I want you, Tortured. Why do you think I picked you in the bar that night? My whole life I've been treated like I'm fragile. For once, I want to be treated like the woman that I am. I know what I want, so give it to me. And don't you dare hold back.' Her blue eyes blaze and she shifts her feet further apart.

Lust claws through every vein and artery. 'Have you been tested?'

'Yes. And I'm on the pill.'

Before she's even finished the sentence, I've popped the buttons on my shorts, allowing my dick to spring free. It's like a metal detector homing in on precious treasure, butting at Ivy's slit like a charging bull. I grab her ass cheeks, slide my hands beneath them and lift her off the floor in one swift movement, thrusting my cock into her hot, slippery channel.

My eyes roll back in my head. She's so tight, so wet, so fucking responsive. I moan, sinking my teeth into her slender neck and suck her pomegranate-scented skin. Her legs wrap around my waist, locking me in position. As if I'd ever willingly leave.

I pump into her, hard enough to make her cry out, but all she does is lock her legs tighter around me.

'You feel so fucking good on my cock.' My fingers dig into her hips, slamming her up and down as I sink deep into her core, giving her every inch of me.

Her hands grip my shoulders, nails clawing at my back like a wild animal. 'Don't stop,' she pants. 'Harder.'

'You weren't lying,' I dip my face to suck on her nipple, 'you do like it rough.' I slam my cock into her over and over again in a relentless rhythm that sends my heart pounding. Her cheeks flush and sweat mingles on our skin as we slide against each other.

'I'd like it any way with you,' she pants, digging her fingers into my shoulders, holding on for dear life.

'Good, girl,' I murmur into her tits, licking a tiny glistening droplet of sweat from between them. 'I'm going to take you on every surface in this house. I'm going to take you everywhere and anywhere I feel like it. Because you're mine, Ivy. You made me break every single one of my own damn rules for you, and now you're going to have to live with the consequences.'

'Rules are made to be broken.' Her fingers sink deeper into my skin, piercing hard enough to draw blood as her core clenches around my cock. 'I welcome those consequences,' she pants.

Ivy takes my cock like she was made for it. My release builds and I pray to fuck she's close because my dick has mistaken itself for a teenager's.

'Kiss me,' she demands from under a dark veil of eyelashes. Her irises burn into mine like she sees me, really sees me. But she can't do, because if she did, she'd know I'm not just tortured, I'm broken.

My lips crash onto hers, my tongue invading her mouth, tasting, conquering and claiming, and her body goes rigid for about three seconds before she's shuddering and shaking and moaning through her release. Moans which I swallow directly from her resplendent, responsive lips. Moans which seep beneath my skin and spark something in my soul that I forgot existed.

Fire dances down my spine, heat builds in my core, and my own cataclysmic orgasm rips through me, tearing me wide open as I spill myself into the woman I've been obsessed with since the moment I laid eyes on her. My moans mingle with hers like a god damn fucking melody, and for the first time in a long time, I feel weightless.

When the last wave of pleasure ebbs away, I tear my lips from Ivy's mouth and place my forehead against hers. Our eyes meet in an exchange more meaningful than any spoken words.

I deliberately didn't take her to bed because I didn't want this to feel intimate. I wanted it to be animalistic. It turned out to be both. And there's no going back. Cold guilt dances with hot, giddy elation in my chest.

As if Ivy senses my dichotomy, she cradles my cheeks with her palms, her eyes softening, her fingertips gently grazing over the fine hairs at the nape of my neck with a tenderness I don't deserve.

When I think she's about to say something meaningful, something profound, she says, 'You know, for an old guy, you fuck like a sex-starved teenager.' Her laughter lightens the rare moment of happiness. 'I think I should go out with your brother more often.'

A growl rumbles in my throat. 'I dare you to try.'

Chapter Twenty-Four

IVY

My back glides gently along the smooth, cool wall as Caelon slowly lowers me to the ground, until my feet are firmly planted on the floor. I'm without a stitch of clothing, yet I don't feel naked until his hands leave my body.

'Stay there,' he orders, buttoning up his shorts. As he stalks towards the downstairs bathroom, I admire the view. The strong supple muscles of his back, the bold, dark patterns of ink on his sweat-sheened skin, the smooth globes of his ass in those shorts. His release is still dripping from me and I'm already wondering when I can get my next shot. I glance at the tiny blue light in the corner of the room and wink, just in case he really does watch this again.

Sex with Tortured is anything but torture. It's devastating, in the most deliciously debilitating way.

For a hot minute afterwards, I thought he was about to freak out. I know he doesn't like the idea of taking a woman in his family home, and I get that, but does he plan on staying single forever? It would be such a damn waste to womankind.

He wears his guilt like a badge—a badge I need to strip from him. He's broken, and the need to fix him consumes me.

But who will fix me afterwards?

I've never met a man like Caelon Beckett before. I'm never likely to again. If I was smart, I'd end this between us right now, before one of us—*me*—gets hurt. But I already know I'm incapable of walking away from him, or his children, even if it means I'll be the one who's broken at the end of whatever this is.

He returns moments later with a hot washcloth and a bottle of still water. I reach for the cloth, but he hands me the water instead.

'Are you sore?' he asks, his voice both rough and gentle at the same time. He places the cloth between my legs and gently washes me down with a tenderness he doesn't look capable of.

'I—I can do that.' I place my hand over his, attempting to prise the cloth away.

'I want to do it.' His black eyes bore into mine as he swats my hand away. 'I told you before, I clean up my own mess.'

'I like this mess.' Heat pools in my stomach. His repetitive movements with the cloth over my clit aren't helping. Yeah, there's no way I can walk away from this chemistry between us. 'In fact, if you keep stroking me like that, there could be another one really soon.'

He tuts, but his lips lift into a rare grin. 'I knew you were trouble when you walked in.'

'And there was me thinking *I* was the Taylor Swift fan.' I arch my eyebrows. 'Next you'll be singing *Love Story*.'

The smile freezes on his face, and I realise what I've said. Me and my big mouth again.

'This isn't going to be a love story, Ivy.' His voice is low but firm.

'It was a joke.' I wince internally.

'You said you want a husband, a house filled with love and

laughter. I'm not a love and laughter type of guy.' His fingers still.

'But—'

He raises a hand in a stop gesture. Normally, I'd never allow a man to silence me, but it's the pleading look in his pained eyes rather than his hand that renders me quiet.

'No *buts*, Ivy,' he resumes stroking with the cloth. 'We both know what we signed up for. You promised me you wanted my penis, not a proposal. Please don't tell me you've changed your mind.'

'You're a good ride, but you're not that good.' It's a lie. He's the best I've ever had. Or am likely to again. I've got it bad for him, but if he gets even a whiff of that, it'll be game over.

'Is that right?' He tosses the cloth to the floor and drops to his knees, his face in line with my crotch. 'Let me remind you exactly how good I am.'

I suck in a breath and use my hands to steady myself against the wall as he sweeps his tongue languidly over my centre before taking it away again.

'Don't make me call Rian,' I joke.

'Don't make me bend you over the kitchen table,' he warns.

'Pass my phone,' I goad, and he springs to his feet. I shriek as he scoops me into his strong arms and carries me towards the dining room.

'By all means, call Rian,' he says smugly, placing me on the table. 'He can watch while I fuck that smart mouth of yours.'

'Now we're talking.' I reach for his cock again.

By the time Caelon leaves to collect the kids, we've had sex four times. First in the hall, then on the table. Then on the plush Italian imported rug on the living room floor, which left me with carpet burns as a souvenir. Then on the kitchen counter. He insisted on pouring me a glass of Beckett's Gold, which I drank while he went down on me again. I swear Daddy Caelon is a pleasure dom and I am so here for it. I might not be able to walk tomorrow, but who needs to walk when you can float?

I help myself to a glass of water and wander aimlessly around the house, taking it all in. My eyes stray to a framed family photo on the marble mantelpiece. In the picture, Caelon's eyes are bright and his smile wide enough to see his molars. His arms are wrapped around Isabella in a loving embrace, while Orla and Owen sit on their knees.

'I'm sorry,' I whisper to Isabella, even though she can't hear me. 'I hope you don't mind me taking care of him. Of all of them.'

The front door opens and slams with a bang that makes me jump out of my skin. I leap away from the mantelpiece like a kid caught with her hand in the sweet jar.

'Ivy!' Orla calls. 'Ivy, where are you?' The pitter-patter of tiny feet approach from the hall.

'In the sitting room,' I call, snatching up the remote. 'I was just looking to see if there's a movie we can watch before bed.' I open the Disney app as she runs in and wraps her arms around my legs. Heat spreads through my chest. She looks adorable in a pink summer dress and pink Nike runners.

'We met Nanny at the graveyard, and she took us to her house,' Orla beams up at me. 'We baked brownies. I had two!'

The graveyard.

So that's where they go every Sunday.

'They were so yummy.' Owen speeds in with his teddy tucked under his arm. 'I put coloured sprinkles on mine.'

'They sound delicious, guys! Do you want some supper? Cereal? French toast?'

'Cereal,' they both yell, running towards the kitchen.

I swivel to see Caelon leaning on the doorframe, watching from a distance. 'It's your day off,' he reminds me. 'I'll take care of them.'

'I want to.' I cross the room, following the noise. 'I missed them today.'

His lips curl upwards in a small but significant smile. 'Could have fooled me.' He slaps my ass as I pass by, and I bite back a yelp.

As soon as the kids have eaten, I send them up to get their pyjamas on. Caelon disappears into his office and a sinking sense of gloom sets into my stomach.

Is he freaking out again? Avoiding me?

I set up a movie, a new Pixar one about emotions. Out of all of us, Caelon is the one who could benefit from watching it, but I won't hold my breath.

'You guys got your pyjamas on?' I jog up the stairs, feeling the stiffness creeping into my legs that only multiple mammoth sex sessions or running a marathon can inflict.

'Nearly,' Orla cries as Owen appears from his bedroom wearing spiderman pjs and clutching his teddy.

I grab a throw from my bedroom and head to the couch with the kids. It's far from cold but I want to wrap it around me like a hug.

'Snuggle in.' I pat the space on either side of me and hit play on the TV remote. As the opening credits roll, Caelon appears. 'Room for another one?' He's changed into a pair of grey, indecently decent sweatpants and a tight, white t-shirt, his hair still damp from the shower.

'Yessss!' Owen squeals. You'd swear Caelon had offered him a trip *to* Disney, not to *watch* Disney.

Orla scoots up onto my knee to make room and Caelon slips into her spot right beside me. I lift the corner of the blanket, offering him some. He stares at me, his huge, bottomless orbs boring into mine. Just when I think he's about to shake his head, he shrugs and slips it over him. Owen dives onto his father's lap, settling beneath the fleece throw.

I exhale a huge, contented breath. However satisfying this afternoon was, this sates another type of need in me.

Chapter Twenty-Five

IVY

The click of my door handle startles me awake. I lurch up in bed, clutching the bed clothes to my chest, half expecting to see one of the kids in the doorway, but it's their utterly delectable-looking father. He's wearing a navy fitted suit that sculpts his body like it was made for it and a white shirt, open at the neck. A chunky silver watch on his left wrist glints in the dim, early morning light.

'What is it?' I squint, rubbing the sleep from my eyes. 'Are the kids okay?

We put them to bed together last night after the movie and Caelon excused himself to pack for his business trip while I opted for a long Epsom-salted soak in the clawfoot tub, half hoping he'd join me.

Sadly, he didn't.

He stalks towards me with a predatory look and my stomach flips.

My boss looks every bit the billionaire CEO of an international chain of boutique hotels. Even without the designer suits and six-figure watch, he drips dominance. His sheer presence sucks the oxygen out of my lungs.

'I spent the night fighting the urge to creep down the corridor to your room,' he hisses. 'Now I have a jet waiting to take me to Monaco for four days and I'm wondering why.'

'Right. And there was me thinking something serious was up.' I fling back the duvet in an unspoken invitation. I'm wearing the Victoria's Secret night dress again, the one he couldn't take his eyes off in the kitchen last week. I'm still sore from yesterday, but not as sore as I'll feel if he leaves without getting us both off again.

'So. Fucking. Sexy,' he hisses, wrapping his strong hands around my slender ankles. I bite back a squeal as he yanks me down the bed until my ass is on the edge. My silk slip ruffles around my midriff, leaving me exposed.

He's on his knees between my thighs before I've even properly opened my eyes. Hot palms press my knees wider apart and he buries his tongue in my centre.

'Fuck.' I arch off the bed, zinging sensations cascading in every direction.

'Yes, we're going to do that, too.' I hear the smile in his voice. 'But only when you've come on my fingers and face first.'

'You should have done this to all the nannies,' I pant, drowning in my pleasure. 'None of them would have left. Fuck it. I'd work for you for free, even if you are a broody bastard.'

His low chuckle reverberates over my sex, eliciting another moan from my big mouth. 'The other nannies didn't drive me demented with lust.'

His lips roll over my clit as he sinks two fingers inside of me. He pumps and sucks and savours me like I'm his favourite snack. My legs tremble as my release looms like a skyscraper in the distance, big and bright and powerful. Everything pales in comparison. It's all I can see. That, and the God-like creature on his knees for me.

Hot pleasure claims every inch of my body. Blood pounds through my ears and my breath comes in ragged gasps as he continues the assault with his mouth and tongue and fingers.

'Come for me, Tranquil,' he demands. 'I want to turn your world upside down, the way you've done to mine.'

When he adds a third finger, I'm gone. My core clenches, pulsating as hot waves crash over me. My legs jerk and jolt, fingers scraping through his thick cropped hair as he pushes me all the way to my own self-indulgent heaven.

'Good girl,' he murmurs when he finally finishes lapping at my core. 'But I'm nowhere near finished with you yet. On your knees.' He stands, unbuckling his belt as he crosses the room towards the balcony.

'Where are you going?' I flip on to my front like he demanded and raise my ass in the air, giving it an inviting wiggle.

'Opening the curtains.' As he yanks back the lilac velvet drapes, sunlight spills across the plush carpet. 'I want to watch as I slam my cock into you.' He slides open the glass doors and the scent of freshly cut grass floods the room.

He stalks towards me, discards his jacket on the floor and unbuttons his trousers, freeing himself. My mouth waters at the sight of his erection with its bulging veins. It's powerful, demanding and fucking delectable.

'You're right. Everything is not okay.' I lick my lips in anticipation. 'You've wasted weeks working from home. Now you've finally remembered what your dick is for, you're leaving the country.'

He shoots me a wicked smile, placing his hands on my hips, nudging his rock-solid cock against my slit. 'Don't worry, baby girl. Daddy will be home soon. If you're good while I'm away, I might even bring you back a present.' He drives himself deep inside of me, filling me, consuming me. His thick fingers grip my hips tightly enough to leave marks.

I arch my back to meet his relentless thrusts. 'The only present I want is your penis.'

'And you will have it,' he promises, pummelling into me, before dragging himself out to the very tip and railing in hard again, hitting a sensitive spot deep inside my centre again and again. The angle is flawless, so deep, so decadent.

Another orgasm builds, this one even more debilitating than the first. There's something so carnal about him driving into me from behind.

When his fingers dance over my skin to my stomach and skirt down over that sensitive bundle of nerves, I don't stand a chance. The cry that leaves my lips is animalistic, and loud enough to wake the neighbours over a kilometre away.

My core clenches his thick length in a vice-like grip, dragging him into oblivion with me. He calls my name like a fucking curse as his hot release mingles with mine.

'That should do it,' he says, peppering tiny delicate kisses over the back of my shoulder.

'Do what?' I gasp, glancing over my shoulder at his smug smirk.

His head whips towards the open balcony doors. Jared is standing with his mouth open, staring up at us like he's just witnessed the second coming, which, technically, he did.

My face falls into my hands as Caelon slides himself out of me. 'You knew he was watching!'

Caelon shrugs, tucking his shirt into his trousers. 'What kind of man would I be if I didn't mark my territory?'

'A shameless one.' I don't know if I'm horrified or horny again.

'Short of tattooing my name on your pretty pussy, it was the best I could do.' He shrugs as he shoots me a wolfish smile. 'If he so much as looks at you while I'm away, I won't just fire him. I'll fire a twelve-gauge gun at his balls.'

His possessiveness should be disturbing. Should be, but

I've been dreaming about him claiming me since the first night he slipped his fingers in me.

I rise from the bed, smoothing down my hair. Caelon yanks me into his arms, hot lips capturing mine, and I melt into his embrace. His tongue invades my mouth, hands sliding over the small of my back, pressing me further into him. When he finally breaks away, a tiny mew slides from my mouth.

'I should wash you down, but I like the thought of leaving my mark all over you.' His dark eyes bore into mine and he cups my chin, tilting my face upwards. 'Be good while I'm away. Remember, no one touches what's mine. Not even you.'

'Safe travels.' I brush the tips of my fingers over his sharp jawline.

'I'll call you later,' he promises before spinning on his heels.

I collapse back onto the bed. A quick glance at my watch shows it's not quite five thirty. The kids won't be awake for another hour at least. My eyelids flutter shut, the image of Caelon burned into the back of them forever more.

When I wake, it's almost seven. I shower, dress, and get the kids up and ready for the day. I shove Owen's bedsheets in the wash and grab a coffee while Liz makes the kids pancakes for breakfast. She hums a chirpy tune under her breath. She's in a good mood this morning. Mind you, after multiple orgasms, she's not the only one. Maybe she's getting railed by some hot daddy, too. It's always the quiet ones, well, apart from me.

Samuel strides in with a smirk on his lips.

'What's so funny?' I demand as he hovers at the back door.

'Nothing.' He straightens his impeccable suit and puts a

finger to the Bluetooth in his ear. 'I just came in to see if you need a ride this morning.' He emphasises the word ride.

Heat stains my cheeks. He couldn't know, could he?

'Yes, actually, we do, if you don't mind. The kids asked to go into the city this morning, so if you feel like accompanying us, I won't say no.' Finding a parking space anywhere is Dublin is like finding a four-leaf clover in a desert.

'How was your day off yesterday?' His lips lift into another smirk.

'Very satisfactory, thank you,' I snap, and he actually laughs.

'I thought as much.' He waggles his thick, bushy eyebrows.

I close my eyes and will the world to disappear.

'Mr Beckett isn't the only one with access to the security system.'

'Oh. My. God.'

'Don't worry, Mr Beckett runs a tight ship. Everyone who works here is required to sign a non-disclosure agreement, so your secret is safe.' He taps the side of his nose.

'I'm going to kill him,' I hiss.

Samuel guffaws. 'Actually, I think you're going to bring him back to life.'

'Huh.' I flick my hair from my shoulders in a nonchalant gesture, trying and failing to ignore the warm fuzzy feeling swelling in my stomach.

I drain my coffee. 'We leave in ten minutes, guys,' I say to everyone and no one. The need to escape Samuel's scrutiny, however playful, is overwhelming. I'm not shy by any means, but even I find it hard to wrap my head around the entire house watching the home movie Caelon and I shot yesterday.

Seven minutes later, Owen sits at the bottom of the stairs in the hallway, struggling to get his shoes on. I bend over to help him, smoothing a hand over the back of my dress so I don't give the staff an eyeful. Although, it's a bit late for that.

My phone vibrates in my pocket with a text.

Caelon.

I open it to find ten fire emojis in a neat little line.

I want to be pissed off with him for not taking me somewhere private yesterday, yet I can't bring myself to regret it.

Another messages pings on my phone.

> Caelon: Bend over again. This time don't smooth your hand over your ass. I want to see you.

I shake my head and swallow my huff.

> Your children are here. Have you no shame?

> Caelon: None.

> I gathered that when Samuel came in with a smirk on his face ten minutes ago.

> Caelon: Relax. I limited access to the indoor cameras yesterday afternoon. They didn't actually see anything, which says enough in itself.

I sigh with relief.

> Caelon: They're my security team. I need them to know you're important to me. That way they'll take the best care of you while I'm away.

> You sound like my brother. I'm not fragile.

Speaking of my big brother, I've had two missed calls from him already this morning. If I don't call him back in the next half an hour, he'll have a SWAT team here and my face plastered over every milk bottle in the country.

> Caelon: Oh, believe me, there's nothing brotherly about my plans for you.

Butterflies whirl through my stomach as I shove my phone in my pocket and return my attention to the kids.

'Can we do the open-top bus tour?' Orla asks, hopping over the lines in the floor tiling.

'Can we go to the Lego store?' Owen pleads.

'I'll do you a deal, buddy.' I eye the teddy under his arm. 'If you let me put Patches in the wash, I'll take you to the Lego Store.'

Owen eyes his favourite stuffed animal like he's a forty-carat diamond.

'I'll even sew a new eye on him afterwards.' I brush

Owen's hair from his forehead. He's a miniature Caelon, gorgeous, stubborn and determined.

He shakes his head. 'I don't need any more Lego.'

My heart melts.

'How about we wash Patches in the sink together?' I'll get laundry detergent on that thing one way or another.

Owen's head snaps up. 'If I say yes, then can we go to the Lego Store?'

Orla rolls her eyes. 'But it'll take ages for him to dry and everything will be closed before we get there,' she complains.

'We'll dry him with a hairdryer,' I announce. 'That can be your job, Orla. We can pretend it's a salon.'

Orla perks up. Playing salon is one of her favourite games. It usually involves her dragging a brush through my hair hard enough to rip it from the roots, but it keeps her happy.

'Fine, you have a deal.' Owen sticks his hand out to shake on it. Oh yes, he's a mini-Caelon alright.

'While Orla is drying him, I'll stitch his eye on.'

My phone buzzes again.

> Caelon: You have a habit of getting your way with Beckett boys. Impressive.

> Stop spying on me.

> Caelon: It's my favourite pastime.

> Get some work done so you can come home.

> Caelon: And there was me thinking I was your boss, but I like your thinking. Call you later. X

That single kiss sets a fresh bout of butterflies swooping through my stomach. Fuck's sake, I'm like a schoolgirl with a crush.

I wink at the camera. When another text doesn't immediately ping in, I gather Caelon's getting on with his day. And I need to get on with mine. Easier said than done when every time I move a muscle, it feels like I've run a marathon.

I know I promised no one would touch me but him, but with yesterday on repeat on my brain, it will be easier said than done.

Besides, I quite like the idea of seeing how he'll punish me.

How much could it really hurt?

Chapter Twenty-Six

CAELON

'I don't give a flying fuck who you need to bribe or blackmail. Just get that fucking planning approved.' I bang the phone down, glancing around my office in Beckett's Monaco Bliss Boutique Hotel. It's anything but bliss for me. However tortured I was before, I'm a million times worse now. Knowing Ivy is in my house, wandering around in yet another low-cut sundress, while I'm stuck here under an avalanche of administration, is driving my dick demented.

I've already been here two nights and there isn't a hope of hell I can get back for at least another two. I have meetings lined up with investors tomorrow, a new team of architects the following day, and a charity event, brushing shoulders with Monaco's elite in the evening. Networking, James calls it. I call it a waste of my fucking time. The organisers should save everyone an evening of ass-kissing and let me get home.

Stephanie, my PA, sticks her head around the door with a grim look. Whatever she's about to say, I already don't like it. 'Sorry to interrupt, Mr Beckett, but there's an article I think you'll want to read. I forwarded it to you, but when I saw you hadn't opened it, I thought I'd better pop in.'

It must be urgent because Stephanie never "pops in". No one does.

'Thanks, Stephanie.' I wave her out the door. She's been with me for two years, and travels everywhere with me, but I know no more about her than when I hired her–other than that she's efficient, discreet and reliable.

I find the email and click on the attachment with a clenched jaw. Probably another damn hoop to jump over with some bullshit architect with a stick up his ass, pointing out some obscure planning regulation. Honestly, I have to deal with so many anal quibbles. My hotel brings so much trade to the area, to the surrounding restaurants, and a hundred other tourist-dependent businesses, yet it seems I'm constantly faced with red tape.

But it's not more red tape. It's a giant red flag.

The article is from Tattler's Tale, Dublin's trashiest blog and includes a photo of Ivy and me on the pier two days ago, lip locked in the most sensual kiss of my life. My hands are on her hips, holding her tight and her fingers gripping my neck like she's afraid I'm going to pull back. The headline reads, 'Money Can't Buy Privacy: Caelon Beckett caught kissing on camera with mystery woman.'

Fuck. I scan the article with a sinking sense of dread. Thankfully, Ivy isn't identified, but if Dermot sees this, he will rip my head off and shit down my neck.

I snatch up my phone and dial my brother, James. He answers immediately.

'I see you got papped with your hand in the honey pot,' he chuckles. 'I knew you were fucking the nanny!'

'I wasn't then, but I am now.' I swipe a hand over my forehead. 'Can you get it taken down?'

'It's already done, little brother.' James says smugly. 'Money *can* buy privacy, and it can also buy pain.'

'Thank you,' I sigh. 'Dermot will not take kindly to me defiling his little sister, even if she enjoyed every second.'

His low chuckle rumbles through the phone. 'I like her. She's got sass.'

'By the bucket load,' I agree. A warmth heats my chest.

'She's good for you, you know,' James says. 'Scarlett adored her. They swapped numbers and they're planning to meet up.'

I don't know how I feel about that, so I don't answer. I click the link again, but the article's no longer accessible. Looks like my head might remain on my neck for another day. Unless Dermot has already seen it.

But I don't think so. If he had, he'd have been at my house by now and dragged Ivy home with him. I've been keeping a close eye on the cameras and that hasn't happened.

'Oh, by the way, I'm sending a driver around this evening to collect the kids for a sleepover. Harper is desperate for her cousins to stay, and that way you can have some alone time with Ivy.'

I blink hard. 'I'm in Monaco.'

'Well, leave Monaco,' he says, like it's that simple.

'I can't. I have meetings.'

'Are you sure you're not just avoiding the nanny now that you've fucked her?'

'I'm not avoiding anyone.'

'You know Isabella wouldn't want you to be alone forever,' James continues wistfully.

'Yeah, so everyone keeps telling me.' I purse my lips.

'But can I make a small suggestion?' There's a cautioning note in his tone.

'Go on.' I hate it already.

'If you're serious about Ivy, you should probably tell your best friend you're shagging his kid sister. Imagine it was Dermot and Zara. We'd line up to tear his limbs off.'

'It's not serious,' I lie. I've broken all my own rules for Ivy.

I've kissed her on the mouth. Fucked her in my house. And I think about her all-damn day. I have done from the night she walked into that bar. It's about as serious as it gets, whether I like it or not.

'Whatever you say, bro.' James chortles.

'I've got to go.' I'm not ready to get into a deep and meaningful conversation with my brother about Ivy when I'm still processing what it all means.

It's after eleven when I get back to my hotel suite. I shower, then crash on the bed, opening the home camera app on my iPad. The kids are at James's house and I'm keen to see how my new nanny is spending her night off.

Now I've seen her naked, I have zero qualms about clicking on the camera in her bedroom. It's not like I'm looking at something I haven't already seen. Something I haven't already licked, kissed and fucked.

Ivy's sitting up in bed, squinting at her Kindle, tapping the screen every thirty seconds or so. Her legs are beneath the duvet, which is tucked around her waist. Her thin strappy top does nothing to conceal the pert swell of her breasts, or the outline of her nipples. Her wavy hair cascades over her tanned shoulders, wafting slightly from the breeze coming in from her open balcony doors.

I dial her number, watching as she pats around the bed for her phone.

A small smile flickers over her face as she peers at the screen.

'Hello?'

'What are you reading?'

Her head snaps up as she scans the room for the camera, homing in on the tiny circle above the balcony doors. 'Are you spying on me?'

'I'm admiring you.'

'If you wanted to see me, you could video call like a

normal person,' she complains, but her smile doesn't waver. 'Were you hoping for a show?' I watch on the iPad as she tosses her Kindle on the table next to the bed.

'No. I told you; no one touches you but me.'

I watch as her chin juts out. 'Remind me how far away you are again.'

A low growl reverberates in the back of my throat. 'You promised. We had a deal. I'm the only one who gets to make you come.'

'Why?' Ivy taps the screen of her phone, placing me on speaker before tossing it next to her Kindle. Her fingers skim over the tops of her shoulders, sliding down each of the thin straps of her top, one by one.

'Because I want you to be so desperate for a release by the time I get home, your slickness is sliding down your legs and your pussy is weeping for me.'

'It always is,' Ivy murmurs. 'No matter how many times I get myself off, it doesn't compare to having your mouth, your fingers, or your cock.' Her fingers skim lower over her chest, tugging off her top and flinging it to the floor. Her big, beautiful breasts are on full display. I'm tempted to lick the screen.

'Ivy,' I warn her, as her palms brush over each pert nipple.

'Let me show you what I do to myself when I think about you,' she pants.

My cock thickens in my boxers. 'No fucking way, Ivy. That's cheating.'

'It's not,' she argues.

'I want all your pleasure. Every single drop of it.'

'There's plenty more.' Her hand sinks lower, and she flips back the duvet. 'I want you to see.' The little brat hasn't got any lingerie on and all I can see is inch after inch of creamy, flawless skin.

'Are you trying to torture me?' I hiss, torn between

wanting to watch her get herself off and an irrational need to be the *only* one to get her off.

'You're already tortured, remember? I'm just trying to tease. Call it foreplay for when you get home.' Her legs fall open and her hand sinks between them. She stares at the camera defiantly before her eyes roll up in pleasure. Pleasure which I would be giving her, if I wasn't stuck here. 'If you don't want to watch me come hard, imagining it's your hand between my legs, then I suggest you turn off the camera.'

'Ivy,' I bite out. This wasn't the deal and as much as I want to watch her, I'm still going to punish her for this. Punish her for turning me on when I can't touch her.

'Touch yourself, Tortured,' she urges. 'Pretend it's my hand wrapped around the base of your big, beautiful cock, and in a few days, it will be.'

'Horny little brat. Have you got no sense of control?' I hiss.

'Not when it comes to you.' Her hand moves up and down in languid strokes.

'You are in so much trouble,' I mutter, even as I slide my hand inside the waistband of my underwear. 'I'm going to punish you for breaking our agreement.'

'I prefer the term "negotiating" rather than "breaking",' she says with a smirk, rolling a nipple between her fingers with her left hand, while her right hand slides inside herself.

I pump my cock, watching her as tiny cat-like mews slip from her lips. 'How wet are you?'

'Soaking,' she rasps. 'I wish you were here.'

'So do I.' I watch as her eyelids close and the strokes of her fingers get faster.

'Stop there, Ivy,' I demand, jealous of her hand.

'Make me,' she pants, her pelvis jerking from the bed as she cries out in pure primal pleasure.

Chapter Twenty-Seven

IVY

The second I wake, I know something is wrong. The duvet weighs a tonne. I can't move. I'm spread out like a starfish and there's something tight around my wrists, securing them above my head. My legs are tied wide open.

What the actual...? I blink hard as a ball of panic forms in my stomach.

I wiggle my feet and yank my ankles, but they don't budge. Whatever is restraining me isn't sharp. It's soft like silk, but strong like steel.

I try to rock up on my back, but the restraints are too tight.

Am I dreaming? Is this some sort of nightmare?

Then I hear a low, rasping chuckle.

Caelon.

'Hello, beautiful,' he sings through the darkness. The balcony door is open, and a crescent moon hangs low in the sky, nestled amongst a hundred stars.

The panic that stirred inside me is replaced by a depraved, electric anticipation. 'What are you doing here?'

'You invited me,' he purrs. His shadow prowls towards the

bed ominously. '"Make me", I believe were your exact words. If that isn't an open invitation, I'm not sure what is.'

'Is that why I'm tied to the bed and spread out like a starfish?' Blood pounds through my ears like a war drum, but arousal pools in my stomach and lower.

'Spread out like a banquet, you mean?' Bright eyes glint dangerously from the bottom of the bed. Through the shadows, I make out those damn grey sweats hanging low on his waist, but his top half is naked. I squint, my eyes eating up the smooth contours of his chest and the hard planes of muscles. He is perfection personified. Is it any wonder I touch myself thinking about him?

'You broke the rules, and now there are consequences. I told you no one touches what is mine and now you must pay the price.'

'And that is what, exactly?' My teeth sink into my bottom lip. 'You've tied me up to what? Tease me to the brink and then take it all away?'

His devilish laughter seeps into the air as he rips the duvet from my body with a sharp, swift wrench. I'm completely naked. With no one else in the house tonight, there was no need for pyjamas.

He drops to his knees between my legs and the mattress dips. 'Maybe. But I will make you come so many times you'll be begging me for a break.'

'That doesn't sound like much of a punishment to me.' I glance upward at the headboard and realise my restraints are actually his work ties.

'We'll see.' He shrugs, running his tongue up my inner thigh, sending shivers in its wake.

'How did you get home so fast?' I yank against the tie, but it doesn't budge.

'That's what you care about right now?' He quirks a brow. 'I have a private jet at my disposal. The second your fingers touched what was mine, I decided to commandeer it.'

'What about your meetings?' I pant, unsure whether to be flattered or frightened.

'A more important one came up.' His hand reaches for his bulging crotch. 'By the time I've finished with you, you're going to understand exactly how it feels to be able to look but not touch. How it feels to be a slave to someone else's urges. To want something so badly but know it's out of your reach.'

My stomach flips and fire spreads through my body at an alarming rate. My nipples are like twin peaks on my rapidly rising and falling breasts.

He halts his tongue, then licks the crease of my groin languidly. I buck and squirm, begging him to move with my body.

The hot breath from his laughter only adds fuel to the already scorching fire. 'I said I was going to make you come so many times you wouldn't be able to take anymore,' rough stubble skims the sensitive skin on my inner thigh, 'but I didn't say I'd be quick about it. In fact,' he makes a show of checking his watch, 'I'm free for the next thirty-six hours and I plan on using them wisely.'

His lips are so close to where I need them, yet so far.

'I'm sorry,' I pant, lifting my pelvis.

'I'm not,' he laughs. 'I've been praying for an excuse to tie you to these bedposts.' He peppers a trail of tiny kisses down my thigh, his lips a soft contrast to the stubble dusting his square jawline. When he reaches my knee, he switches to the other leg and works his way back up, pausing occasionally to suck hard enough to mark me.

Finally, his tongue sweeps over my swollen bud and I moan in pleasure as he licks and flicks, before dipping lower to my centre. I don't need to see to know my arousal coats his lips and chin. A deep masculine groan rumbles against me like he's enjoying this as much as I am. When he places a finger on either side of my clit and rubs, I'm about three seconds from coming all over his face. But just as my release shimmers tantalisingly close, he snatches it away, halting his tongue.

'Caelon,' I scream, squirming against the mattress.

'Yes,' he arches an eyebrow and offers one more languid lick before stopping again.

'Please,' I pant.

'Who do you belong to?' Black eyes bore into mine. The sight of him between my legs and the restraints are almost enough to get me off on their own.

'You.' I arch my ass from the bed.

'Good girl,' he purrs. 'And who is allowed to touch you?'

'You.' My entire body vibrates with a raw, carnal need.

'Don't forget it, okay?' Our eyes lock, and I watch as he plunges his tongue inside me, catapulting me over the edge in the most violent, soul shattering explosion. White hot plea- sure sizzles through every cell in my body, electricity crack- ling through the depths of my core.

If this is his way of punishing me, I'm tempted to misbe- have more often.

As the fireworks behind my eyelids subside, I attempt to wriggle free, but given he has me tied tighter than a rabbit in a trap, I'm going nowhere fast.

'Caelon,' I plead, squirming, as his tongue captures my sensitive clit. 'It's too soon.'

'Tough. This is your punishment, baby.' He sinks his teeth into my inner thigh. 'Now take it like a good girl, because I'm not about to stop anytime soon. Maybe next time you'll think twice about touching what's mine.'

It's so sensitive, it's borderline sore. 'Caelon, I can't. Give me a minute.'

'No. The only reprieve is while I'm talking to you.' He sucks hard enough to make me squeal. 'You wanted to come, and you're going to come. Again and again until *I* decide you've had enough.'

My treacherous vagina blooms like a fucking flower and blood floods below. His filthy, talented mouth is my undoing. A familiar throbbing starts below.

'You know, some people would call this assault,' I pant, pulling on the ties binding my wrists and ankles.

'So, shout for help.' He runs his tongue from my clit to my slit. 'Maybe Jared will hear you and burst through the balcony doors wielding one of his gardening tools.' His snigger reverberates through my core.

'You're a bad man,' I hiss, surrendering to the inevitable.

'That's what I've been trying to tell you.' Another long, languid lick sets shivers down my spine and goosebumps rippling over my skin.

'I need your cock.'

'Maybe for the next round.' He slides a finger inside my centre, gliding over that sensitive spot buried deep in my inner wall.

'The next round?' I feel my eyes widen.

'Yes, the next round, and the next, and the next.'

Daddy Caelon is definitely a pleasure dom. And as much as I protest, I fucking love it. Being tied up and teased is my ultimate fantasy and he knows it. He takes me to the brink, backs off, then does it again. And again. And again.

The sun has risen by the time I shudder my way through a second debilitating orgasm. He gives me a small reprieve, crawling up the bed to latch onto my nipple, circling it with his tongue, before moving to the other.

His erection presses against my legs through his sweatpants and damn, despite the orgasms, I'm still not fully sated. I need his cock inside me, filling me up, stretching me, completing me, and I'd bet my life he knows it.

This man is a god in the bedroom.

'Caelon, please...' His kisses trail over my collar bones and up my neck, where he sucks hard enough to mark me. As if he hasn't already marked every inch of my body as his.

'Please what?' His eyes glint as he towers above me, placing a knee on the outside of each of my thighs.

'I need you to fill me up.'

'My greedy girl still hasn't had enough.' He shakes his head in mock horror, his finger gravitating back towards my clit.

'I need you inside me.'

His hands reach for the waistband of his pants, and he yanks them down, setting his huge angry length free. 'Is this what you want?'

Saliva floods my mouth. He's so big. So fucking beautiful. 'Yes.'

I try to reach for him and hiss out my frustration as the tie holds my arm tightly.

'Have you learnt your lesson yet?' He nudges his tip at my entrance but doesn't push it in.

'Yes,' I grit out.

He runs the tip up my slit and I cry out in protest. I need him inside me, and he knows it. I grind against him, and he laughs, repeating his strokes on the outside.

'You're mine, Ivy.' His Adam's apple bobs.

'Okay. Untie me, I need to touch,' I beg.

'No can do, baby.' He winks. 'I'm still punishing you here. Can't let you off the hook too easily.'

'But I need to run my hands over your body.' My gaze roams over the squares of solid muscle of his six-pack.

'Now you know how I felt last night, watching you on the camera.' Fire dances in his irises as he thrusts his tip into me.

'More!' I drive back against him. He laughs, but gives me another inch.

'You take my cock so well, Ivy. It's like you were made for

it.' He sinks himself into me and my eyes roll back into my head.

'Open your eyes,' he demands. 'Watch me, like I had to watch you last night.'

I drink him in as he rails into me in a soul-shattering rhythm that has us both panting and cursing. When he finally spills himself into me, I come for the third time, milking him dry.

He collapses onto my clammy chest, slick with a thin layer of sex-induced sweat as his release drips out of me.

A bang from downstairs sets us both jumping.

'What was that?' I lift my head from the pillow, one of the few body parts I *can* move.

'The front door,' Caelon says grimly. 'It's probably Samuel.'

'He always uses the back door,' I remind him.

Caelon freezes. 'The only person to use the front door is Dermot.'

'He has a key?' I whisper shout in outrage.

Caelon leaps off the bed, yanking up his sweatpants with a panic-stricken face. 'He's my best friend.'

'Ivy!' My brother's voice booms from below as I remember I haven't returned his calls this week. Fuck.

My eyes dart to the restraints above my head and I waggle my feet like they're miraculously going to burst free.

Heavy footsteps pound below until they reach the bottom of the stairs. 'Ivy,' Dermot calls again. This time, there's a tinge of panic to his tone.

I can't call him. Jesus, if he finds me like this, or finds Caelon anywhere near me, he will murder both of us.

The footsteps get closer until they're almost outside the door.

I close my eyes and brace myself for the inevitable.

Chapter Twenty-Eight

CAELON

'I'll stall him.' I back away from the bed. 'He doesn't know which room is yours.'

I jog towards the door, reaching it as the handle turns. I place a hand and a foot against it, preventing it opening more than a couple of inches.

Dermot appears through the narrow gap. 'Caelon,' he says, as his brows knit together. 'I thought you were in Monaco.'

'I got back last night. Something came up.' I squeeze my eyes shut for a second, blinking away the guilt.

'Where's Ivy? I've been trying to get hold of her all week. I know she's probably tied up.'

I splutter and he fires me a weird look.

'You know, with the kids and all, but she usually returns my calls in the evening. I'm worried about her.'

She was too busy tormenting me to call Dermot.

'She's around somewhere. I think I heard the shower. Let's grab a coffee. I'm sure she'll be down when she's free.' I glance over my shoulder towards Ivy, still tied to the bedposts, spread-legged and dripping come. It might be the most beautiful thing I've ever seen. I could happily spend all day going to town on her pert heaving tits, but if I don't get Dermot away from here, the only place I'll be going to is hospital.

'Okay.' Dermot backs away from the door and I step out of the bedroom. I follow him down the stairs and when we reach the kitchen, Dermot's beady gaze rakes over my sweaty torso. 'Were you working out?'

'Yeah.' It's not exactly a lie. 'I'm just gonna go grab a top.' *And untie your little sister from the bedposts.* 'Stick a capsule in the machine and I'll meet you out the back. Liz is around somewhere. She'll be starting breakfast any minute.' I nod towards the decking outside the French doors.

'I've eaten, thanks,' he looks at me quizzically, but I back away before he can ask any awkward questions.

I jog up the stairs, and slip into Ivy's bedroom, closing the door quietly behind me.

'Untie me, quickly,' Ivy pleads, pulling at the ties around her wrists.

'You're lucky your big brother showed up.' I press a kiss to her lips before working on the knots. 'I had planned on fucking you all day.'

'Lucky?' she scoffs, flexing her hands as I free her. 'One, I'd have happily let you fuck me all day, and two, I saw my entire life flash before me when I heard Dermot's voice. It's one thing wanting him to know I'm a grown woman, and another for him to see it.'

'You're telling me.' I scoot to the bottom of the bed and free her ankles.

'Did you learn your lesson?' I dangle the ties in front of her face as she rocks upright.

'Yes.' Her full lips curve upwards. 'I learnt that I need to misbehave more often.'

'Brat.' I shake my head. 'Have a shower and I'll make you

a coffee.' I slip out of the room, grab a hoody from my bedroom as I pass, and head back downstairs. Dermot is outside sipping an espresso, staring out over the pool.

'Where are the kids?'

'With Scarlett and James for a couple of nights.' I opt for the furthest seat away so he won't detect the scent of sex that clings to my skin.

'So, Ivy had last night off?' His thick eyebrows furrow. 'I thought she might have called. She doesn't have many friends in Dublin anymore.'

'You know, I think she's become friendly with James's fiancée, Scarlett. They met with the kids at the beach and hit it off.'

'James is one lucky son of a bitch.' Dermot grins at me. 'Scarlett is stunning, smart, and a pole dancer. What a combination.'

James would murder Dermot for even mentioning his fiancée's past, but Dermot witnessed Scarlett in action at the Luxor Lounge. We all did—before James stole her away from there with a lucrative proposition. 'What is she? Seven years younger than him?'

'Ten,' I admit, keeping my eyes focused forwards.

'Can you imagine?' Dermot waggles his eyebrows at me.

I don't have to. The age gap between Ivy and me is the same—more, actually.

'Did you hear the Luxor Lounge has reopened under new ownership? We should go. It's been ages.' The Luxor was the country's most exclusive gentlemen's club before it was shut down suddenly.

My jaw relaxes at the change in the direction of conversation. 'Did you hear who bought it?'

'Who?' Dermot cocks his head.

'My littlest brother.' I roll my eyes. Rian started a chain of bars and nightclubs a couple of years ago. As part of his acquisitions, he purchased the Luxor Lounge to hang out with naked women all day and tell our father it's "work".

'No way, man.' Dermot straightens his spine. 'Well, now we definitely have to go. Got to support your brother's business, right? Did anyone hear what happened to Cole?'

Cole, the previous owner, is the same creep who tried it on with Scarlett, which didn't exactly go down well with my brother. Possessiveness runs in our blood. I have no idea where Cole is now, but I'd bet my life my brother has a good idea. And the fewer questions asked, the better.

I shrug, nonchalantly. 'Probably crawled back under his rock.'

'How is Ivy working out for you?' Dermot peers at me over the rim of his coffee cup.

I swallow my guilt. 'Great. The kids love her.'

Dermot crosses his ankle over his knee. 'She's a very loveable girl.'

'She's twenty-three. More woman than girl,' I say tentatively.

Dermot scoffs. 'She should start acting like one.'

An image of her tied to the bed forces itself to the forefront of my mind. 'What do you mean?'

'She needs to start thinking about the future.'

Somehow, in the whirlwind of my infatuation with Ivy, I'd forgotten she's only supposed to be here for the summer. It was me who insisted on it.

'I'm grateful to you, though.' Dermot's tone is sincere. 'Her last boss was a sleaze. It's one of the reason's she finally came home. She's my kid sister, you know. I hate the thought of her living with a strange family. At least here, with you, I know she's in safe hands.'

'I won't let anything happen to her,' I grit out. Not because she's Dermot's little sister, but because I'm obsessed with her. Obsessed with the tiny mews she makes when I slide my cock into her. With her tousled blonde beach waves. With her smart mouth and the way she lights up when she laughs. The way she looks at me as if I'm some sort of god, although little does she know, I have more in common with the devil.

'I know you probably think I'm crazy being so protective of her, but I can't help it.'

'She isn't a kid anymore. You should cut her some slack.'

'It's hard, you know. You have a sister. You know what it's like.'

'I am protective of Zara, but she's not some wilting virgin. I don't mind her dating, as long as she's treated well, and she's happy.'

'I know I'm probably hard on her. It's not her fault.' Dermot's knee bounces with a nervous tick. 'Ivy was a twin. Katie, our sister, died when we were just kids.' Dermot sighs.

'I'm so sorry. Why didn't you mention it before?' And why didn't Ivy mention her sister who died was actually her twin? Losing a twin must be like losing part of yourself. She probably understands my pain better than most.

'It's not something we talk about.' He rests a hand on his knee and the jerking stops. 'Talking about it won't bring her back.' He tuts. 'I couldn't save Katie, none of us could, but I'll do everything in my power to protect Ivy.'

Ivy chooses that moment to stroll out, bare foot and wearing a pastel pink cotton dress that stops three inches above her knees and dips low at the front. 'Dermot, what are you doing here?'

Her hair hangs loosely over her sun-kissed shoulders, damp from the shower. Her flawless complexion is devoid of make-up, but she has the telltale flush of a woman who has been thoroughly pleasured.

'I was visiting a client in Malahide. I thought I'd check on you on my way.' He stands, crosses the deck, and plants a kiss on her cheek.

I hold my breath, scanning her ankles and her wrists for any signs she'd been tied to her bed only a few minutes ago. The silk ties were a good call. There isn't a single mark on her.

'I don't need checking up on,' she huffs, her frustration creeping into her tone. 'As you can see, I'm fine.' She sweeps her hands over her body in an exaggerated motion.

Dermot steps back, scrutinising his sister from head to toe. 'Well, maybe return my phone calls every now and again and I won't have to worry. You're my kid sister. I can't help it.'

Ivy rolls her big blue eyes dramatically. 'The only thing you should be worried about is that I haven't had my caffeine fix today and I didn't get a lot of sleep last night.' Her eyes cut to mine, devilment dancing in her irises.

'I'll fix that for you.' I leap to my feet, eager to escape the awkward atmosphere that comes from shagging your best friend's sister—and being in punching distance of both of them.

'Another espresso?'

'No thanks,' Dermot says. 'I'd better go. It was a flying visit.' He drains his coffee and hands me the cup. 'Are you free for lunch next Sunday?' he asks Ivy. 'I can't do this week. I'm golfing with the guys, but I could do the following Sunday?'

Ivy's not free. The kids are going to Jocelyn's and while she won't be working per se, I have plans for her. Plans which I spent concocting while I was cooped up in the hotel in Monaco.

'Maybe, if you promise not to spend the entire duration asking me what I'm going to do with my life.' She folds her arms across her chest.

'Ivy, I hate to spoil your Sunday fun, but the kids have *that thing* on next weekend. I know it's your day off but...'

Ivy's eyes flare with understanding. 'Oh, course, I forgot.'

I swear she's relieved to be handed an excuse. 'Maybe Dermot can take me out for a drink instead.' She arches a defiant eyebrow.

Brat.

If she thinks she's escaping to a bar without me, she's wrong. It's not that I don't trust her. It's the men I don't trust to keep their filthy hands off my woman. They can look, but if any of them so much as lays a finger on her, I'll rip their head from their neck.

'We were actually arranging to go out for a drink ourselves.' I can't pretend to be apologetic about it.

'Well, that's convenient,' Ivy splutters.

Dermot's beady eyes dart between us. 'Jesus, you two are like an old married couple.'

'Rian's bought a new club and we're going, right, Dermot?'

'What club?' Ivy perks up at the prospect.

If she is hoping for an invite, it's not going to happen. Women aren't allowed at the Luxor Lounge, unless they're topless on one of the podiums, which Ivy will never be because I don't share.

At the mention of the gentlemen's club, Dermot's gaze drops to the floor as if he's realised his hypocrisy. How can he stand there being so protective of his little sister, while planning on a trip to the Luxor to ogle what could be someone else's little sister? 'It's male members only. Sorry, Ivy.'

'Male members?' Ivy snorts. 'So, it's a strip club?'

'Rian prefers the term, *gentlemen's club*.' I interject.

'What's Rian got to do with it?' A tiny crease forms on her forehead.

I glance at my watch. 'As of six pm yesterday, he owns it.'

'Sounds like Rian.' Ivy chuckles. 'Don't worry, Dermot, I won't grass you up to our parents. This time.' She winks. 'We'll catch up soon.'

'Call me if you need anything.' Dermot's hand brushes Ivy's bicep.

She tilts her head upwards and rises on her tiptoes to kiss her brother's cheek. At that second, a gentle breeze blows across the lawn, wafting her wet, wavy hair back from her neck. The same neck that I sank my teeth into over and over again the past few hours.

Even from ten feet away, the hickey on her neck is unmissable.

Fuck.

Dermot's eyes narrow. He pulls back from his sister like he's been burned, his fingers sweeping her hair back as she tilts her head in a silent question. 'Is that a love bite on your neck?' His tone is thunderous.

Her hands reach for her throat, cupping it protectively. 'What if it is?' Her tone dares him to challenge her.

'Jesus Christ, Ivy.' He rakes his fingers through his hair and paces the decking, shaking his head violently.

'I'm a grown woman, Dermot. Deal with it,' she says cheerfully.

'Oh my God. Caelon goes out of town for two days and you manage to get into trouble.' He sounds irate.

'I wouldn't call it trouble, really.' She sings in an overly cheery voice, making a show of inspecting her cuticles.

'Who is he?' Dermot demands.

'None of your business. Enjoy your night at the gentlemen's club next week.' She wiggles her fingers in a sarcastic wave.

Dermot sighs and shoves his hands in his suit pockets. 'Don't let her out of your sight,' he begs.

'If you insist.' I shoot Ivy a small smirk as Dermot marches round to the front of the house.

Chapter Twenty-Nine

IVY

While the kids had a second sleepover at Scarlett and James's place, Caelon had one in my bed.

We've spent the past two days in a decadent limb-locked bubble, coming up only for air, to eat, to shower, and to crash on the couch, with me binge-watching Love Island, while he cites all the reasons why the couples won't last.

My boss is a tad cynical when it comes to love.

He's claimed it's not going to be a love story between us, but as one day bleeds into another, I'm increasingly certain of how easy it would be to fall hard for a man like Caelon. For the past couple of days, he's been a lot less tortured and a lot more tender. We're supposed to be living for today, having sex until one of us gets bored, but the chances of getting bored with his kinky pleasure dom routine are slim to not-a-fuck-ing-hope-in-hell.

I'm both curious and nervous to see how he behaves with the children at home. Will he sleep in my bed and creep out before they wake? Or was their presence in the house the reason he fought the urge to slink into my bed before his Monaco trip?

I guess I'll find out soon enough.

Scarlett and James drop a tired-looking Orla and Owen back late on Friday evening. James's driver, Tim, helps Scarlett out of the car while James helps the kids. Scarlett greets me with a kiss on each cheek, then proceeds to scrutinise me from head to toe with unconcealed glee.

'You're glowing,' she nudges my ribs playfully. 'Anything you want to tell me?'

I shake my head, fight the smirk pulling my lips, and turn my attention to the children.

'Hi guys! We missed you! Did you have a nice sleepover?' I hug both kids hard, then take Orla's Minnie Mouse backpack as Samuel takes Owen's Spiderman case.

Samuel shoots me a less-than-subtle wink.

All the staff know Caelon and I are sleeping together. If limited access to the interior cameras wasn't enough to give it away, Liz walked in on us going at it like rabbits on viagra in the kitchen yesterday. She squealed, made a show of covering her eyes and yelled at us to stop contaminating her workspace, but her usual stern tone was more akin to something that sounded like excitement.

While I'm not shy, it's hard being watched and whispered about twenty-four hours a day.

I've crossed a line. I'm not exactly staff anymore, but I'm not a Beckett either.

'It was so good. Scarlett had a fairy wigwam set up for a tea party and we had cupcakes,' Orla announces, rubbing her eyes as she traipses up the steps and into the hallway.

'That sounds amazing,' I usher Scarlett into the house before me. Caelon and James shake hands then follow us inside.

'Where are Harper and Halle?' Caelon asks, as Owen wraps himself around his legs and clings onto to his father like a koala. I watch on while my ovaries vibrate with pure longing. I've spent the last two days physically attached to my boss, and it has done nothing to alleviate the perpetual horn I have for him.

James and Scarlett exchange a significant look, like they're having an entire conversation with their eyes about Caelon and me. I glance guiltily at the spot on the wall where we first had sex, as if the outline of our slick, entwined bodies has stained the paintwork.

Scarlett's silver eyes continuously bounce between Caelon and me, and the right side of her lip curves upward. 'Harper and Halle are with their nanny. Owen and Orla aren't the only two who are exhausted.'

'Liz has supper ready. Go and get something to eat before bed.' Caelon kisses the kids' foreheads and ushers them into the kitchen. When they've disappeared along the hallway, he turns his attention back to his brother and future sister-in-law. 'Drink?'

'Yes, please.' Scarlett rubs her manicured hands together.

Caelon motions us into the drawing room and pours James a whiskey from the Hollywood custom-made drinks cabinet against the wood-panelled wall, then opens a side panel which doubles up as a fridge. Pausing, he examines an extensive and expensive collection of bottles and selects an extravagant champagne. It's clearly for Scarlett's benefit, but I'm not prepared to let my new friend drink something that fancy alone.

'Are we celebrating?' I lean closer to Caelon. My arm brushes against his, sending goosebumps skittering over my skin.

'Actually, we are,' Scarlett says. 'James and I have decided to get married.' She raises her left hand to show off a glittering platinum solitaire.

'The huge ring sort of gave that away.' Caelon pops the champagne cork and pours into two long-stemmed flutes, handing one to Scarlett and one to me. 'But congratulations again,' he says, reaching for his whiskey.

'No, we're actually doing it.' James drops an arm over Scarlett's shoulder. 'We've set a date.'

'That's fantastic,' I gush, instinctively reaching for Scarlett's hand and squeezing it. Her cheeks flush, her smile so bright, it's practically neon.

Caelon's lips purse into a grim line as his gaze flits towards the fireplace. A picture of him and Isabella on their wedding day stares back at him. They look stunning in their wedding finery, but the most attractive thing about them is their smiles.

An intricate web of emotions clogs my throat.

I knew what I was letting myself in for when I surrendered my body to Caelon. He made it clear he's not interested in anything serious, but it already feels as though I'm losing part of my heart.

Caelon drags his eyes back to his brother. 'Oh? When?'

'The second of November.' The words practically burst out of Scarlett's mouth.

'All Souls Day,' Caelon says darkly.

'I didn't have you pegged as the religious sort,' I tease, as my eyes rove over his torso.

'I'm not.' His pupils morph into his irises, his jaw setting in a hard line.

The conversation is taking a dark turn, and I don't like it one bit.

'Cheers!' I raise my glass, conscious that in a heartbeat, Caelon's flipped from my flirtatious, fucktacious boss back to tall, dark and tortured.

'Where will you get married?' I ask the blushing bride.

'Cheval Blanc, St-Barth. You should see it — white sandy coves, stunning scenery, plush little villas that back onto the beach. We planned to travel the world before we had kids, but life is what happens while you're busy having fun, right?' She elbows James in the ribs. 'So, we decided on a destination wedding with a month-long honeymoon.'

'What about the kids?' A month is a long time to be away from them. If I had kids, I'd hate to be away for more than a weekend.

'We'll bring the nannies.' Scarlett beams. 'You'll come too, right?'

Is she inviting me as a guest, or as the hired help?

I glance at Caelon. 'Of course Ivy will be there. She's our nanny.'

My cheeks sizzle.

'Technically, I might have finished by then,' I remind him. He was the one that said my position was only for the summer.

His eyes narrow, flit to the photo on the mantle again, then refocus on me. 'Clearly, we need to discuss that.'

'Clearly, now is not the time.' I feel the weight of everyone's eyes on me. 'I'm going to check on the kids. It's my job, after all,' I say, flouncing out of the room with my champagne, embarrassed and humiliated. At least the drink might numb the stinging burn in my chest.

'Ivy...' Caelon calls, but I ignore him. I don't know how to be his nanny and his... what? Fuck buddy? We've had one official date and a tonne of transcendent sex. That doesn't make me his girlfriend, no matter how increasingly blurred the lines have become.

I stalk along the corridor, my bare feet sinking into the plush carpet.

'Ivy,' Caelon calls again, hot on my heels.

'Can we talk about this later?' I force a cheery expression

as the kids come into view, blinking back the hot dam of tears threatening to burst out of my eyes.

I sit with Orla and Owen at the table, quizzing them about their day while they pick at their dinner. Their tired murmurs and complete lack of enthusiasm assure me they're approximately three minutes away from face-planting into their food.

'Come on, guys. Let's get you bathed and ready for bed.'

While Caelon entertains James and Scarlett, I might as well do the job he's paying me for. And by the time I get the kids tucked in and have read them a story, James and Scarlett have gone.

It's Friday night. Technically, I'm off the clock. I could go out. But there's nowhere I'd rather be than here—well, if Caelon hadn't gone all weird on me earlier.

I poke my head into the drawing room. He's sitting in one of the crushed velvet armchairs, staring across the room at his wedding photo again.

'Are you okay?' I ask tentatively.

He blinks hard and turns his head towards me. 'Yes. About earlier... I didn't mean to make you uncomfortable.' He raises his whiskey to his lips and drinks deeply. His subtle slur is the only giveaway that it's not his first.

I cross the room and perch on the arm of his chair. 'I don't need to put a label on us, but I do need to know what you expect of me when we're around your family. One minute you're asking me to share a glass of champagne with your sister-in-law and the next I'm back to being the hired help.'

If Caelon wasn't so serious, I'd crack a joke about going to the wedding as Rian's date, but clearly, something is bothering him. I wish he'd open up.

Caelon swallows hard, his dark eyes dilating. 'James cancelled their original wedding plans because of what happened to Isabella. Now they've made new plans, it's as if they've accepted she's gone, and I... I just can't.' He swipes a hand over his jaw.

'It's bound to take longer for you. She was the other half of you for so long. It would be weird if you were over it so quickly.'

'You would know, apparently.' He arches a brow. 'Why didn't you tell me you had a twin?'

I sigh. Dermot. Big mouths seem to run in the family. 'It was a long time ago. I don't think I'll ever get over her death, but I've accepted it.'

'But I can't accept Isabella's death, not until I've made someone pay.' He clutches my hand and pulls it to his lips. 'I just can't.'

'You will. You have to accept things are the way they are. And with or without me, you have to go to your brother's wedding and smile.'

'If I take a date, it's as good as announcing we're together. That I'm over Isabella.'

'And you're worried what your family will think? What Isabella's family will think?'

'No, my family, my brothers at least, adore you. And Isabella's mother is forever telling me I should move on.'

'What then?'

'The press.' He grimaces. 'They're bound to splash pictures of the big day all over the tabloids and everyone will see you and me together, our enemies included.'

'Enemies?' It sounds overly dramatic.

Dermot's words from my first night at the house ring through my ears.

The Becketts and the O'Connors have been enemies for years. Both families run rival whiskey empires. Weeks after the Beckett brothers helped put Declan O'Connor behind bars, Isabella is killed in an "accident" that makes no sense whatsoever.'

'The guy driving owed the O'Connors a serious debt. The rumour

is the debt would be wiped and his family would be taken care of if he did this last job.'

I've read enough articles to know Jack O'Connor and his oldest son, Declan, are behind bars, while the other brothers are missing. Even if they were responsible for Isabella's death, they're already serving time, even if it is for a different crime.

'Are you worried they'll attempt to sabotage the wedding?' I place my hand on Caelon's shoulder, silently urging him to open up to me.

Caelon snorts. 'I'm worried they'll think I've forgotten that they murdered my wife. I'm worried they'll sleep peacefully in their shitty prison cells because I've moved on, and I despise the thought of giving them even a minute's peace. I want them to live in fear–because I'm coming for them.'

'You can't be serious?' My jaw drops. This is crazy talk. Dermot was right.

'I've never been more serious in my life. I'm going to prove they were responsible for Isabella's death, and I'm going to make them pay–with their lives.'

A violent shudder skitters over my spine. He's so unbelievably hot, but could he really be that cold?

Could he really take a life?

No, it's the drink talking. It has to be.

'Shh, now, that's not the Caelon I know, and lo—' I catch myself before the 'l' word slips out. It might just be a turn of phrase, but anything is liable to tip him over the edge tonight.

'You need to focus on the here and now. Not the past. Life is a gift. We can waste it or use it wisely. Losing my sister taught me that.'

'I live for two things; my kids and revenge. I have no intention of leaving this earth until I've taken care of all of them. Losing my wife taught me that.'

'It won't bring her back,' I whisper.

'It might bring *me* back, though.' He eyes me darkly. 'Part of me died with her. And I *will* get my revenge for both of us.'

I prise the glass from his hand, down the contents, slip my arm through his and help him to bed. The darkness blanketing his room matches the darkness blanketing his soul.

Chapter Thirty

CAELON

Letting slip to Ivy that I plan to murder my enemies slowly and painfully doesn't seem to have put her off. She's let me creep into her bed every night this week.

Maybe she assumed it was the drink talking. Sure, it may have loosened my lips but my plans are cemented like concrete.

The second we have the confirmation that the O'Connors were involved in Isabella's death, Killian's men plan to isolate Jack and Declan while I personally deliver revenge. I'd have done it already, but Killian insists we wait until we have proof.

Of all my brothers, Killian says the least, but when it comes to experience of war, he has the most. He's spent years fighting someone else's battles serving our country. It changed him. He projects an air of disinterest, but nothing escapes his attention. He has a frightening, violent streak, tempered slightly by a deep sense of morality. I'd bet there isn't a shrink in the world who could work that fucker out.

'Where are we going?' Ivy asks, eagerly peering out of the

helicopter window as we speed over lush mountains and picturesque lakes. The excitement in her tone is infectious.

She's wearing another one of those goddamn summer dresses. It's taken all my willpower not to lift it up round her waist and admire what's underneath, but I'd hate to distract the pilot.

'You'll find out in about ten minutes.' The kids are with Jocelyn this weekend, and while I love shacking up for marathon sex sessions with Ivy, I'm aware I haven't had the chance to take her out properly. She deserves better. She deserves to be wined and dined and spoiled like a princess. While I'm not comfortable dating, I am comfortable with Ivy. Given we've been living together for weeks, and shared both deadly secrets and decadent secretions, we've got to know each other pretty damn well, skipping over dating milestones in a short space of time.

Now, I finally have the chance to take her out, I won't risk us getting papped again. I have enough enemies as it is, without adding Dermot to the list.

Rian is reopening the Luxor Lounge next week and my best friend is like a dog with two dicks. Obviously, I have to attend the grand opening night to support my little brother, though the prospect of being surrounded by naked women doesn't do nearly as much for me as being around his little sister.

The Donegal mountains crest on the horizon, rugged green caps piercing the clear blue skies.

'I've never been to Donegal before.' Ivy blows out a breath as she presses her nose against the glass like a child.

'We have a habit of not making the most of what's right in front of us.' I shrug.

'Is that an innuendo, Tortured?' Ivy spins to face me. My eyes fall to the freckles dusting her cheekbones.

'Take it any way you like.' I press a kiss to her temple, breathing in the scent of her familiar shampoo.

'Oh, I intend to,' she chuckles. 'I've never been flown away for a dirty weekend before.'

If I could, I'd whisk her away every weekend. I seriously need to get a new nanny. Not because I don't like this one, but because I need someone to take care of my children so I can monopolise her attention.

Eight minutes later, we land on a small circular helipad at a five-star lakeside hotel I've recently bought. The previous owners went bust and I snapped it up to add to the Beckett Bliss range. The location is priceless, but the building is majestic, too. I've had a construction crew working twenty-four-seven to get it ready for its reopening next month, but for this weekend, it's just Ivy and me, and a handful of staff.

'Wow,' she gasps, as an impeccably dressed porter greets us.

'Mr Beckett, welcome.' He nods and offers a welcoming smile.

I glance up at the building. It looks a hell of a lot better than the last time I was here. 'This is Ivy.'

I don't introduce her as my girlfriend. One word doesn't do justice to describe what she is to me. And we've already established she's not a girl; she's all woman.

My woman.

I thought the attraction between us might fizzle, crash, and burn, but the fire between us rages stronger with every passing day. It's unsettling, but undeniable. No matter how many times I have her, I crave my next hit like an addict.

So, what does that mean for the future?

Until I met Ivy, my future involved nothing but wreaking revenge on the O'Connors and raising my children.

Ivy is my twinkling glimmer of hope at the end of a long

and dark, suffocating tunnel. For the first time in a long time, I'm wondering what my life might look like after I've dealt with the O'Connors. I'm finally considering the possibility that I may actually have a life afterwards, even if I don't deserve one. Which is in equal parts enthralling and terrifying.

I shut my eyes, forcing away thoughts of anything other than the present.

'This is unbelievable,' Ivy gushes, rushing up the red-carpeted steps to explore, her eyes wide with wonder. 'Don't tell me you own this place as well?'

'Yep.' I follow her inside, my soles clicking over the black-and-white marble flooring. A brilliant white grand piano takes pride of place in a huge hallway. Gilded landscapes of the Donegal scenery line the walls. An impressive, glistening crystal chandelier hangs from the centre of the room, sending tiny rainbows in every direction.

Ivy runs a finger over the top of the piano and cocks her head. 'Where is everybody?'

'It's just you and me, Tranquil.' I wink. 'I figured we've given the staff enough to talk about for a while.'

'I am "the staff." Did you forget?' She winks back and takes a seat at the keyboard, tapping out what I've come to recognise as another damn Taylor Swift tune.

'Not this weekend, you're not.' I hover beside her, watching her slim fingers fly over the keys. 'This weekend, you're the queen of this castle and you know what queens do, right?'

Her fingers slow to a stop. 'They wear crowns?'

'They rule.' She's spent weeks taking orders from two four-foot-tall dictators. It's time she gave a few orders herself. 'Whatever you want, just say. Whatever you need, I'll make sure you get it. If you want to stay in the castle for the next two nights and not leave, we can. If you want to skinny-dip in the lake or climb the mountain, we can. This weekend is all about you.'

Her tongue darts out to wet her lower lip and I watch her throat as she swallows her surprise. 'Why?'

'Because you give so much of yourself to me and my kids every day, I want to do something for you.'

Her hands fall from the piano to her lap. 'Every time you touch me, you do something for me. You spend every free minute giving me pleasure. You don't need to do this as well.' Her bright eyes glisten. 'You know, for a man who claims not to do romance, this is pretty romantic.'

'I want to spend time with you without everyone watching.'

Ivy shrugs. 'It's kind of weird at home, isn't it? Like we're a cross between Love Island and Big Brother.'

'Which is why I've requested different staff, so you wouldn't feel like the nanny.'

'Like I said, it's romantic.' Her lips twist like she's suppressing a smirk. I pause, waiting for whatever line she's about to deliver. I know her well enough to know one is coming. 'Let's hope you can keep all the balls in the air.'

'Why?'

'I don't do romance, but I will make you come hard enough to see stars...' She tosses my line back at me.

'Oh, sweetheart, leave the balls to me.' I roll up the sleeves of my shirt. 'Get up on that piano now.'

'What?' Her eyebrows rocket upwards.

'Get up on the piano right now. You have a date with my tongue and some stars.'

She scans the room. 'What if someone sees us?'

'If they don't see us, they'll definitely hear us. Now get on the fucking piano. Or do I have to tie you to it?'

Chapter Thirty-One

IVY

Caelon wasn't joking. We spend the weekend at the hotel eating and drinking like royalty, then fucking everywhere and anywhere like carefree peasants. The place is bigger than the mansion in Malahide and every bit as opulent, inside and outside.

The hot tub is built into the ground at eye level with the lake, and is almost as big as the swimming pool, but twice as warm, which is why we're in it for the third time in two days.

Caelon is different away from Dublin. Maybe it's not having to worry about the kids. Or maybe it's because he hasn't bothered to look at his phone, let alone respond to any emails. Or maybe it's because he's away from the permanent reminders at home of all he's lost. There's a boyishness to him I haven't seen before. Maybe this is the Caelon Isabella fell in love with.

'I wish we could stay forever.' I rest my chin in my palms and prop my elbows on the side of the hot tub, memorising every meter of the horizon. I want to be able to summon this scene for the rest of my life.

'We could, you know.' He sidles closer, placing his hand on

the small of my back. 'We could keep this for ourselves as a holiday home instead of opening it up as a hotel.'

My stomach flips. He's talking like we have a future together.

Do we?

I know I'm the one who insists on not making plans, but given half the chance, I'd make plans with Caelon because I already can't imagine my life without him. Or without Owen and Orla.

'If only.' I turn to face him. However stunning the scenery, it has nothing on the man beside me. Droplets of water glisten on his sharp cheekbones and his eyes glitter like two onyx diamonds.

'You'd probably get bored after a while,' he teases, tugging at the string of my bikini top until it comes undone. 'I mean, you're young. You'd probably rather be in Elixir, dancing to Taylor fucking Swift and drinking cocktails than stuck here with me, right?' The glint in his pupils proves he knows he's talking utter bollocks.

'I'm sure you could find a way to entertain me.' I shrug. My bikini top flaps in the breeze, supported by only one thin string at the nape of my neck. 'Unless you're tired... Is keeping up with me depleting all your energy?'

He grasps my wrist under the water and drags my hand to his swimming shorts. 'Does this feel tired to you?'

'It feels like it needs some love.' The words are out before I think about them. My big mouth strikes again. I tense, waiting for him to pull away, but for once, Caelon doesn't flinch at the 'l' word.

'It can wait.' He releases his grip on my wrist and reaches for the remaining tied string, tugging it and tossing my top away. My nipples harden under his greedy stare.

'You're so fucking beautiful, Ivy.' His palms reach for my

breasts, kneading and squeezing while his thumbs circle my sensitive nubs.

'You're not too bad yourself.' I inch closer, resting my hips against his, searching for friction. His face dips and his lips catch mine with an unexpected tenderness. He moans into my mouth as I surrender to the sensation of his lips and tongue. Fizzing tingles blitz through my body.

His fingertips skim lower, setting goosebumps over my skin before dipping beneath the water to pull the strings either side of my bikini bottoms. They float to the surface as I sink deeper into Caelon's kiss, widening my feet as his hand travels between my legs. When I reach for his cock, he slaps my hand away.

'Patience, Ivy,' he murmurs. 'Let me take care of you.'

'No.' I squeeze my thighs together, halting his hand. 'Let me take care of you for once.'

'Later,' he whispers.

'Now.' I'm adamant, slipping my hand inside his waistband. 'I want to worship your body, the way you worship mine.' Our eyes lock and that tortured look creeps back.

'What is it?' I wish he'd open up to me. I've given him all of me, and he's still locking a part of himself away.

'I don't deserve to be worshipped. I told you already, I'm not a good man.' He shakes his head.

'I don't believe you.' I wrap my hand around his length and pump, watching as his eyes roll back in his head. 'You're a good man, Caelon. *My* man, and I want to make you feel good.'

'You already do.' He stills my hand with his. 'Just being with you makes me feel good—better than I deserve.'

It keeps coming back to that one word.

Deserve.

'Do you think you don't deserve to be happy? Is that what this is about?'

He shrugs. 'If only you could see the thoughts inside my head.'

'Everyone deserves to be happy. Do you think you were put on this earth to be miserable?' I reach up and cup the back of his neck, forcing his face to look at mine.

'I've had my fair share of misery.'

'And now you have me. We're supposed to be making the most of the here and now, remember? So, let's do it.'

He pauses for a second, a thoughtfulness clouding his ebony orbs. 'About that...'

A sinking sensation settles in my stomach. Is this the part where he calls it a day? Maybe the 'L' word did terrify him after all.

Or maybe he's got tired of fucking me six ways to Sunday.

He's a hot billionaire who could have any woman he wants. Did I really expect him to settle down with me, the nanny?

I'm not putting myself down. I know what I am and what I have to offer. I also know that it might not be enough for a man like Caelon Beckett.

We said we'd have some fun. I told him I wanted his penis, not a marriage proposal. It's not his fault my vagina and my heart are tethered together with an invisible string. I knew what I was getting myself into. Hell, I even knew, given half a chance, I could fall hard. And the thing about falling is that there's always a risk of getting hurt.

'I'm tired of sneaking around with you,' he admits in a husky tone.

'It's okay.' I slide my hand from his neck, but he catches it and places it on his sculpted chest. Beneath the smooth, hard muscle, the steady thrum of his heart flutters beneath my fingertips.

'I think we should come clean to Dermot.'

'What?' My head snaps up.

'You're mine, Ivy. Sneaking around feels wrong, like I'm ashamed of what we have. I'm not. You waltzed into my life and lit it up like Fourth of July fireworks. You made my house a home again.' The tortured look in his eyes switches to one of tenderness. 'You're not going anywhere at the end of the summer. You *will* come to James's wedding with me. I want to give this thing between us a real shot, if you're up for it, that is.' A rare flash of vulnerability ignites in his pupils.

My heart slams against my ribcage in an erratic rhythm. Emotion squeezes the air out of my lungs.

'If I'm up for it.' A breathy laugh floats from my lips. 'You could suggest we move to Antarctica, and I'd probably agree. I've been obsessed with you from the second you put your hands inside my lingerie in the bar.'

'It always comes back to sex with you, doesn't it?' His face dips closer to mine until our foreheads are touching. 'Horny brat,' he whispers.

'It does help that you're particularly skilled in that department, but truthfully, I like being with you. Your house is the first one where I've felt at home. I've always enjoyed my job, but minding your kids has never felt like work. I adore them.'

He presses a tender kiss to my temple. 'Which is why we should tell Dermot.'

'Not yet! Please. He'll freak out. I don't want anything to taint what we have. I don't want to cause a showdown. I don't want you to have to choose between me and him.'

Caelon huffs out a breath. 'It will be you, Ivy. Spoiler alert, I'm crazy about you. But he's my best friend, my only friend, other than my brothers. I hate lying to him. My brothers know. The staff know. He deserves to know.'

His words are a balm to my soul, but from behind his rose-tinted glasses, he's forgotten how protective my brother is of me. 'He does—just not yet.' Dermot *will* flip. I don't want the pressure of that on Caelon, on our new relationship. I'm not ready to test its strength yet. 'You're not lying to him. It's a tiny little omission–for now.'

'There's nothing tiny about it.' His hands skirt over my waist. 'I'd rather he heard it from me than saw it splashed all over the tabloids. We've already had one near miss.'

'Let's give ourselves a bit more time.' I trace the lines of his six-pack.

'Fine, but I'm going to plant the seed. That way, it'll be less of a shock when the time comes.'

I refuse to waste the remainder of the weekend discussing my brother. I reach inside his waistband again. 'The only seed you're planting should be between my legs.'

Chapter Thirty-Two

CAELON

August

Dermot whistles as he scans the Luxor Lounge −or more specifically, as he scans the nearly naked dancers on the podiums. Rian might be a jumped-up asshole who hits on my partner, but he's done a stellar job with the décor. Where this place was once all marble and chrome, it's now rustic and masculine. Dark wooden panelling lines the walls, ceilings and floors. Rich, red leather circular booths are dotted around the room, and a dark mahogany circular-shaped bar dominates the centre of the space. It looks like what it is—a gentlemen's club. Not a high-end knocking shop.

We're sitting in a booth adjacent to the main stage, with a bottle of Beckett's Gold on the table between us in a crystal Beckett decanter, a welcome present from Rian, who is busy greeting his new members.

'This is like being a kid with fistfuls of cash in a sweet-shop, only better.' Dermot wets his lips and strums a finger over his chin.

'I never did have a sweet tooth,' I mutter, taking a sip of whiskey.

'Maybe you haven't found the right candy yet.' He shoots me a wink and I shake my head.

I've found the right candy, alright, but he'd rather knock my teeth out than let me have my fill of it.

'What about her?' He nods at a dancer on the main stage. She's five-foot-nine with legs up to her armpits, and breasts that are too perfect to be anything but plastic. Her deep chocolate-coloured eyes are the same shade as her silky hair. Physically, she's beautiful, but she elicits zero response from my cock.

There's only one woman who can command its attention and she's sprawled out on my couch sipping a whiskey, watching Love Island.

'She's okay.' I shrug while Dermot's eyes almost pop out of his head.

'Okay?' He leans across the table 'She's fucking stunning with a body I'd pay a serious amount of money to bury myself in.'

'Want me to ask Rian who she is?' I glance at the bar where my little brother is man-hugging the new Irish president.

'No, I'll ask her myself when she's sitting on my lap in about ten minutes.' Dermot turns his attention back to the stage.

'What about her?' He points at a red head dancing on one of the smaller podiums. She has curves in all the right places. Creamy, flawless skin. An ass that could give J-Lo a run for her money. Yet I can't even muster a semi for her. It's official. Ivy Winters has ruined me. I'm falling hard for a short sassy blonde with a mouth as big as her baby blue eyes, and a fondness for my family's whiskey and my family jewels.

Ivy has got under my skin. Which is why I sleep in her bed every single night. Why I bring her coffee in the morning before hitting the gym. Why I feel unsettled any time she's not within three feet of me.

'I'll get you a private dance. Call it an early birthday present,' Dermot offers, tapping his finger against his glass.

'My birthday is six months away.'

'That's why I said it's an *early* birthday present.' Dermot rolls his eyes.

'Thanks, but no thanks.'

'What the fuck, man? Who even are you?' he tuts, refocusing on the brunette.

My phone lights up on the table.

I snatch it up before Dermot can see the screen and question why his sister is texting me at midnight on a Saturday night.

> Ivy: You can look, but don't even think about touching, or it'll be me tying you to the bedposts and I won't be nearly as generous with the orgasms.

My cheeks lift as a ridiculous smile cracks open my face. I force my lips straight, sneaking a glance to check Dermot is still occupied before typing out a reply.

Is that a promise?

Three dots appear instantly.

> Ivy: Try me...

Is that jealousy I detect?

> Ivy: No, it's a concern. I'm worried you won't be able to get it up again when you get home, old man, and I'm wet and waiting.

I've a good mind to bend you over the bed and smack your ass for your cheek.

Ivy: Is that a promise?

The sexy little wench.

What are you doing?

Ivy: Lying in bed...

Don't even think about touching yourself. Or you won't be tied to the bed post, you'll be tied to the kitchen table so the staff can see what happens to people who misbehave.

I smirk, taking another sip of whiskey. Ivy probably wouldn't care who saw if she got to come at the end of it. My woman is insatiable, and I love it.

'Okay, who the fuck put hearts in your eyes?' Dermot's staring at me like I've grown two heads and a pair of tits.

'What?' I stuff my phone into my pocket, ignoring as it vibrates with another message. My fingers itch to pluck it out and read Ivy's text, but if Dermot so much as suspects I'm flirting with his sister, he'll saw my cock off like a wronged Samurai.

'The woman texting you.' His cobalt eyes gleam with interest. 'Who is she?'

'No one.' A stab of guilt pierces my chest. Not because Ivy

is his sister, but because I said she was no one, and that's the biggest lie of all.

She's not no one.

She's the woman who's bringing me back to life. The woman whose smile stirs something in my chest that I never dared to dream I'd feel again. The woman who I see every time I close my eyes.

'No one you need to worry about,' I correct myself.

'Ah ha! I knew it.' His palm hits the table with a loud thwack. 'Is it someone you met in Monaco?'

'What makes you think that?'

'Because you looked tired and guilty the other week when I called in and you'd only been back a matter of hours.' He points an accusatory finger in my face, but he's grinning from ear to ear. 'Now stop deflecting and answer the question.'

'Look, it's still very new, but there is someone.' I shrug.

'That's amazing!' he says with genuine enthusiasm.

Rian chooses this moment to grace us with his presence.

'Hey, Baby Beckett, congratulations on the club,' Dermot stands and extends his hand in greeting.

'Baby Beckett?' Rian huffs. 'Please! I might be the youngest, but have more experience than the rest of my brothers put together.'

Rian accepts Dermot's hand and shakes it vigorously. I roll my eyes.

'The real baby of the family is our sister, Zara. You might have met her?' A devilish smirk lifts my little brother's lips. 'Don't you have a sister too?' He drops Dermot's hand and motions for him to sit back down.

'Yeah, Ivy. She's actually nannying for Caelon at the moment.'

Rian clicks his fingers like he's just remembered. The little fucking punk. 'Oh, that's right. I met her at the beach before with the kids.'

Yeah, then you took her out to lunch and asked her what her favourite sexual position was. A vein pulses in my temple as I shoot Rian a look deadly enough to kill.

None of my brothers would ever tell Dermot about Ivy and me. Our loyalty to each other runs deeper than the ocean, but that doesn't mean that they won't take pleasure in tormenting me.

'Lovely girl.' Rian bites back a smirk and slides into the booth beside Dermot. 'Caelon finds her very obliging.'

Thankfully, Dermot doesn't get the dig. 'Did you hear Caelon has a woman on the go?'

'He mentioned he's been buried balls deep in someone half his age. He reckons she's a real go-er.' Rian winks at me.

I will actually kill him. I squeeze my eyes closed and pinch the bridge of my nose, feeling my blood pressure rocket.

'Spill, motherfucker.' Dermot's attention whips to me as a gleeful expression inches over his face. Technically, sister-fucker would be more appropriate. He won't be nearly as chirpy if Rian doesn't shut his huge trap. 'And I thought I was your best friend, yet Baby Beckett knows everything, and I know nothing. So, who is she? And more importantly, has she got any friends?'

I imagine wrapping my hands around Rian's neck and choking him slowly. Maybe not to death, because that would be difficult to explain to our parents, but hard enough to ensure his throat is so bruised he won't be able to swallow, let alone talk, for a week.

'Have a bit of respect, you fucking moron.' I glare at Rian. 'Don't talk about my woman that way.'

'Oh, "my woman",' Dermot repeats. 'It's serious, then? When do we get to meet her?'

I inhale a breath, then blow it out slowly.

'Believe me, if it were up to me, we'd all have had dinner together by now, but it's not that simple.'

'Oh, is she married? Or the second secret daughter of your rival? No wait, don't tell me, she's a mafia princess!' Dermot slaps his thigh and laughs.

I could wipe the smile from his face with one three-letter word, but I promised Ivy I wouldn't tell him. I promised when the time was right, we'd tell him together—a promise I know I'm going to regret making.

'She's not married.' Not yet anyway. But the way things are escalating, it's a possibility I wouldn't rule out—one day.

Thankfully, my other brothers choose this second to stride into the club. James is in the centre, flanked by Killian and Sean. Killian surveys the premises in the same way he surveys every room he enters, sweeping each nook and cranny like he's searching for a hidden masked man who's planning to jump out at him with a machete. He definitely has a touch of post-traumatic stress from his time in the forces, but it's not something he's ever discussed. Not with me, anyway. He comes across as cold and aloof, but I don't doubt he'd take a bullet for any one of us.

'Ah, look, the whole family reunited.' Rian rises, motioning one of the topless waitresses over to bring more drinks.

'Not quite,' I mutter. Thankfully, Zara is away travelling, and my parents are still in Europe.

'Congratulations, Rian.' James sweeps a hand around the club. 'I like what you've done with the place.'

'You know, if Scarlett wants her old job back,' Rian teases. Man, my little brother really does have a death wish.

James's jaw tenses in a deadly grimace and his black eyes narrow to slits.

Rian raises his hands in surrender. 'Just joking, brother. Relax.'

Killian, Sean and James slide into the booth as the waitress brings another bottle of our family's most expensive whiskey and four more crystal tumblers.

Sean fills up everyone's glass, raises a toast to Rian's new business venture, and James's jaw eventually slackens.

'Remember that dancer, Candice? Hot as fuck and takes cock like a champ?' Rian sighs wistfully, like he's reliving a memory. 'I tried to get her back, but she's shacked up with some sugar daddy in France.'

'Never mind Candice. What about Avery? She's killing it in the UK,' James says, knocking back a double shot and holding his glass out for a refill.

Scarlett's best friend, Avery, started as a dancer at the Luxor Lounge five years ago to fund her way through university. Now she's one of the most sought-after glamour models in Europe.

Killian huffs out a breath and rolls his eyes skywards.

'Something wrong?' James's gaze weighs on our usually stoic brother.

Killian shakes his head but the way his fingers whiten around his glass tell a different story.

'Will Avery make the wedding?' Rian asks, oblivious to the tension rolling from our thunderous looking brother. Our baby brother's probably already trying to work out how he can get into Avery's panties.

'She's going to be a bridesmaid. She wouldn't miss it for the world.' James's gaze is focussed solely on Killian when he answers. At least he hasn't missed the weird animosity Killian clearly holds towards Avery.

'For fucks sake,' Killian's baritone voice cuts through the air like a knife.

'Is there a problem between you and Avery that I'm unaware of?' James hunches over the table towards Killian, 'Because she's my future-wife's best friend and I refuse to let anything spoil our big day. God knows we've waited long enough for it.'

'The only problem between me and Avery is that she's reckless, loud and incapable of staying out of trouble. Have you seen the British tabloids? My own personal favourite headline was "Wardrobe Whoops–Avery gives Paris Fashion Week an "Eye-full."

'Oh, I get it!' Rian snaps his fingers. 'Eye-full, instead of Eiffel.'

'How are we even related?' Killian mutters grimly. 'The point is, do you really want all her drama at your wedding? Avery is a PR nightmare.'

'She's Scarlett's best friend and that's the end of it,' James's tone is final.

Killian's mouth opens, then closes again. He's already said more tonight than he's said all month.

Something about Avery really grinds his balls.

Interesting.

'This used to be our favourite venue to meet,' Rian changes the subject, glancing around pensively.

Killian scoffs. 'Speaking of family meetings, we need to arrange one. I have news.'

My head whips up. 'News?' It occurs to me that I forgot to call him this week for an update on the O'Connor situation. It's the first week since Isabella died that I haven't hounded him for a report.

'Potentially.' He looks pointedly at Dermot. He might be my best friend, but he isn't family.

'Danny Bourke's latest neurological assessment showed increased brain activity,' Killian says solemnly. 'The doctors think he's showing signs of waking.'

A shot of adrenaline bursts through my body. I've waited years to find out what happened the night Isabella died. I tighten my hand into a fist to hide the tremor. 'But he's still in a coma?'

'They reckon they've seen him flexing his fingers, like he's trying to reach out. One of the nurses treating him swears he can hear her.'

'What about the money trail? Any news?' I demand.

'I'm working on it.' Killian looks pointedly at Dermot again. Dermot's gaze is fixed on the brunette, but I don't doubt his ears are firmly tuned in. My friend didn't make it as a self-made millionaire because he was caught napping. Still, I trust him to keep his mouth shut if anything unfortunate should happen to the O'Connors.

I take a huge mouthful of whiskey, revelling in the burn as it coats my throat.

This is it.

I'm so close to getting what I want—enough proof to legit-imately execute my revenge. To bleed the souls of those who've bled mine. I'm about to find out exactly how sweet revenge truly tastes.

Chapter Thirty-Three

IVY

The summer is drawing to a close and with only a couple of weeks until the kids go back to school, it's time to go shopping for their last few bits. Orla is about to start her second year at Dublin's most prestigious girls' school, St. Jude's. Owen is about to start at St. Michael's. Uniforms were ordered a long time ago, but the kids need books and stationery. Fortunately, Caelon's given me his credit card and I intend to use it.

'Will you pick them some new shoes, too?' Caelon hands me a coffee just the way I like, then leans against the kitchen counter, pulling me against him, hip to hip. He's topless and sweaty after his two morning workouts—first in the home gym and the other in the bedroom with me. These days, I no longer lurk in the doorway of his gym to leer. I do it openly, perching on a bench as he presses weights.

'Of course.' I eye him over the rim of my cup, resting my free hand on his pecs. He's leaving for Portugal later today and my stomach aches at the thought of him being away. We haven't slept separately since he returned from Monaco. I've become accustomed to having his hot body in the bed beside me.

'Get yourself something, too.' He points to the credit card on the window ledge.

'I don't need anything,' I say, tracing my finger over his slick skin.

'You must want something. Buy some jewellery. Or shoes. Dresses. Whatever you want.' He tucks a wispy strand of hair behind my ear.

'I already have everything I want.' I dig my teeth into my lower lip. It's almost true. I live with love and laughter, but I'm not sure I'll ever get the full package; the husband, the kids.

I'm falling in love with him.

I've been falling harder every day since he first took me in the hallway. Maybe even before. I haven't said it to him. I haven't wanted to terrify him. But there's no denying his hard edges have softened. There's a light in his eyes that wasn't there before.

'Buy yourself something, please. It'll make me feel better about leaving you.' He presses a fleeting kiss to my temple.

'Now I'm definitely not going to buy myself anything. I want you to feel so bad about leaving me that you race home the second you have the chance.'

He nuzzles into my neck. 'Do you think I want to be apart from my sexy, sassy girlfriend?'

'Girlfriend?' It's the first time he's used the word, and it turns my blood into molten lava.

'I know, I know, you're all woman,' he sighs. 'Do you prefer the term partner? Just so you know, I think of you as my equal in every way.'

'Call me whatever you like, as long as it's *yours*.'

'You were mine the second I touched you,' he purrs, running his lips along my jawline.

'Hmm, maybe I touch myself again and see how quickly that brings you home.' I buck against him, the low stirring of arousal building in my stomach.

'Don't even think about it,' he murmurs, slipping a hand between my legs. I'm wet for him. I'm always wet for him.

He groans, prises the coffee cup out of my hand and shoves it on the counter. 'I really don't have time for this, but you make it impossible to be anywhere on time. Until you moved in, I'd never been late for anything in my life.' He spins us around, hoists my bum up onto the counter, and spreads my legs. 'Now, my PA lies to me about my schedule because she expects me to be late. You're bad for business, Tranquil.'

'I'm good for your prostate, though.' I inch forwards and lift up my night dress. His eyes fall to my crotch and he hisses out his approval, then tugs down the waistband of his sweatpants and frees himself.

'This is going to have to be quick,' he warns. 'I need you to come hard and fast on my cock like a good girl, okay? Can you do what I say without defying me, just this once?' He pushes the tip against my entrance until I'm the one hissing.

'You know, just this once, I think I could do that for you.' Firm fingers grip my ass as he slides into me, filling me and stretching me before pulling out and driving in again and again. It takes less than four minutes for me to come and only a few more seconds for him to follow suit.

'I'm going to miss you.' His ragged heartbeat pounds against mine.

'Not as much as I'm going to miss you.'

The "l" word hovers in the air like a cloud between us, ready to be plucked from the sky. Or maybe it's just in my mind.

As he's finishing cleaning us both up, we hear footsteps on

the stairs. I hurriedly tug my night dress down and hop off the worktop, fluffing my hair.

Owen rounds the corner, rubbing his eyes, his dark hair spiked up where he's been lying on it. His face is creased with marks from his pillow, but notably, he doesn't have his favourite tatty teddy with him. Is this progress at long last?

'Morning buddy. How are you today?' Caelon squats to Owen's eye level.

'Daddy, I have a 'fession,' he says, but instead of his usual pained expression, he's sporting a smile like it's Christmas morning.

'It's okay, buddy, I'll take care of it.' Caelon ruffles his hair, then pulls him towards him for a hug.

'No, Daddy, this 'fession is different.' Owen resists Caelon's embrace, his big innocent eyes bouncing between his father and me as he puffs his chest out. 'I didn't have an accident.'

'You didn't?' Caelon's pride is audible. 'That is amazing! I'm so proud of you, big man!'

'Thanks, Daddy.' Owen looks at me again.

'That's amazing, sweetheart. You're such a big boy now.' Owen runs to me, burying his face in my chest as I stoop to catch him in my arms.

'I think we need to buy you something cool while we're shopping today,' I pretend to whisper, like it's our secret.

'Can I get something cool, too?' Orla appears in the kitchen doorway wearing a Barbie nightie and fluffy pink slippers.

'Sure.' Caelon lifts his little girl and twirls her around the kitchen. 'Anything you like. Make sure Ivy buys herself something, too. Samuel will drive you into the city when you're ready.'

'Can we go for ice cream?' Owen tugs my hand.

'Sure.'

After four painful hours of shoe and stationery shopping, we pull up outside Sweet Freeze, Dublin's quirkiest ice cream parlour. As I'm not driving, I decide my present from Caelon, other than his cock, should be a whiskey whirl, a rich, creamy milkshake blended with vanilla ice cream and the whiskey of your choice, topped with whipped cream and sprinkles.

I snap a quick picture of it and send it to him, along with one of the kids with their chocolate brownie sundaes. He replies instantly.

> Caelon: You can't get enough of the white stuff...

I snort and stuff the phone back in my pocket.

'You know Daddy said we could get something cool?' Orla says, with a mouthful of sundae.

'Yes, sweetie. What do you want?'

'I've been thinking about it all day and I want a dog.'

Uh-oh. Caelon will kill me if I take a dog home. Then again, now I'm staying, I could take care of it. Maybe a fur baby would be good for all of us.

'Please, Ivy. Daddy did say anything I like,' Orla reminds me with huge puppy dog eyes. I swear she has me wrapped around her little finger.

Samuel shakes his head subtly at me.

'Please, Ivy,' Owen begs. 'It'll be so cool. We can walk it, and train it, and play with it in the garden.'

Orla pipes up over her sundae, 'You know I overheard Liz telling Damon that a couple of dogs around the garden would save his legs a lot of work.'

Samuel snorts.

'And you know there are probably loads of dogs in the pound just waiting for a home. Imagine their big sad eyes.' Orla bats her eyelashes dramatically.

I swear these kids know exactly which buttons to press. I take a mouthful of my whiskey whirl as I contemplate. 'Fine, we'll look, okay, but I'm not saying yes or no until we get there and see what they have.'

Samuel tuts under his breath. 'I hope you're planning on picking up the shit in the garden.'

'I'm more worried if it shits on the sofa,' I whisper with a giggle.

'Mr Beckett will lose *his* shit with all of us if that happens.'

'Let me worry about him.' I offer him a wink.

'You do seem to have a way of softening him up.' Samuel quirks an eyebrow.

'Softening him?' I smirk. 'I wouldn't exactly say that.'

He raises a hand. 'Enough information, thank you. We're all just delighted he's finally found a bit of happiness again.'

'Happy people buy their kids dogs, right?' I shrug.

'It's your head, not mine.'

'I'll take care of it, don't worry.'

'You'd better. I'm security, not a dog-sitter.' He shakes his head, but the corner of his lip lifts. Maybe he's not as averse to the idea as he claims to be.

When we get to the local pound it's overflowing with cute little handbag-sized dogs, big shaggy dogs, and dogs that are too old for new tricks.

'Are you sure this is a good idea?' Samuel asks, restraining our new fur baby on a lead as I sign the paperwork. Roxy is a boisterous boxer bitch who was too much of a handful for her previous family.

Ha, I can relate.

Dermot has been texting me incessantly all week to ask if my love bite has healed, if I've thought any further about going back to college, and if I'm free to take our parents out to dinner for their ruby wedding anniversary next month. I'd rather bite my own hand off than sit through another family meal, or family intervention, as I prefer to call them.

'It's not a good idea. It's a brilliant idea, don't worry,' I reassure him as the receptionist fetches us a week's worth of dog food and some treats.

Roxy bounds around, nudging the kids playfully with her nose and whacking their backsides with her tail as she shakes her excited ass. If I wasn't convinced already, the kids' delighted squeals are enough to change anyone's mind, maybe even Caelon's.

And if he's not happy that I've bought them a dog, I welcome his punishment. If the last one was anything to go by, I'm in for a treat.

Chapter Thirty-Four

CAELON

'What the fuck is that on my couch?' I zoom in on the camera in the sitting room. My eyes must be deceiving me because it looks as if there's a sixty-kilogram, furry, drooling beast on my custom-made Italian couch.

'I wondered how long it would take for you to check up on me,' Ivy sing-songs.

I watch on my laptop as she flicks her head towards the camera above the eighty-inch TV screen and waves casually, like she isn't curled up with a slobbering dog on sixty-grand's worth of Italian leather.

'Answer the question, Ivy.' A vein throbs in my temple. 'What the fuck is that thing doing on my couch?'

'She's not a thing! This is Roxy, our new fur baby.'

'Is this some sort of fucking joke?'

'You told the kids they could buy something cool, and this is what they wanted. I'll take care of her, I promise. She's already house-trained. And she's great with the kids. They adore her. Boxers are great family dogs, you know. They also have longer life expectancies than goldfish, so there's that, too.'

'Send it back. Get rid of it. It can't stay.' I tug my hair in despair.

'Fine, but are you going to tell the kids?' Ivy beams at the camera and winks.

Orla and Owen race into the sitting room. 'Is that Daddy on the phone?' A worried look pinches Orla's face.

Ivy hands the phone over and my daughter's voice floods my ear.

'Please, Daddy, don't make us get rid of her. She's my best friend. I love her so much.'

I blow out a breath, rock back in my office chair, and plant my feet on the desk. 'Put Ivy back on the phone, please.'

'Love you, Daddy,' Orla says. She's good. She might be small, but she already knows how to pull my levers. Beckett genetics run strong. I'm torn between happiness and horror.

'Love you too, princess.'

By the time Ivy comes back on the line, I've come to a decision.

'Get that thing off my couch. Buy it a kennel, put it in the garden and make sure Jared cleans up its shit. Whatever you do, do not let it back in the house.'

'Does that mean we can keep her?' I watch the screen as Ivy pets the dog and kisses its head. For fuck's sake.

'Do I have a choice?' I growl. 'How can I get rid of it when Owen has finally stopped wetting the bed and Orla has finished mourning the last damn goldfish?'

'Having a dog will be good for them. Every child should have one.' Ivy beams at the camera. She's wearing a pair of tight skinny jeans and an off-the-shoulder t-shirt that reveals the strap of her ivory lace bra. 'Anyway, how are things going over there? Are you getting everything sorted?'

'Sadly, not. I'll be here another few days at least.' A sharp stabbing lances my chest. I miss her so much.

Ivy pouts and whispers, 'I miss you. But at least I have someone to curl up with later.' She snorts as she slides off the couch and leads the dog towards the French doors.

I should be hopping mad at her for letting a four-legged beast wreck my couch. But the truth is, I'm mad *about* her.

And if she wants ten dogs, I'd suck it up if it made her happy. Especially if it makes her *and* my kids happy.

She's going to have to change my nickname from Tortured to Thwarted.

I spend the next two days checking the cameras between meetings. The damn dog remains outside for most of the day, but despite a new kennel appearing at the back of the house, the spoiled mutt somehow ends up sleeping upstairs each night.

I don't know what annoys me more—that Ivy continues to defy me, or that the dog gets to sleep upstairs while I'm stuck here. I've taken residence in one of the smaller Beckett Boutiques in Carvoeiro. The hotel is one of our most luxurious, bolted onto the cliff overlooking Vale Covo, a small, stunning sandy beach. Every time I glimpse the golden stretch below, I'm reminded of the day I spent at the beach with Ivy. The day I began to unravel. Although, arguably, that happened the night I met her. She's in my head every damn second of every damn day and there's not a thing I can do about it.

I need to get home. The week is dragging. The days are endlessly long and the nights are even worse. Nothing beats my own bed. Well, Ivy's bed. She's yet to sleep in mine. I've always been protective of that space—up until now. The more joy Ivy brings to our lives, the more I'm coming around to the thought that if she makes me happy, it's what Isabella would want.

I need to tell Dermot I'm dating his sister, because I'm ready to shout it from the rooftops. When I do, she'll need twenty-four-seven security. I can't risk anything happening to her. The O'Connors may be behind bars, but the war between us is far from over, especially when I've yet to avenge Isabella. But that day is coming, and soon, if Killian's reports are anything to go by. A team of the best doctors in the country is working on Danny's recovery, and by all accounts, it's only a matter of days before he wakes. It's a day that can't come soon enough.

Which is why I need to deal with the mountain of shit accumulating here. Portuguese regulatory hurdles. The painfully slow pace of obtaining permits. And complications caused by unexpected structural issues. I've been round and round in circles and I'm no closer to coming up with a solution.

I'm sitting with my lead designer, head architect, and three members of the Portuguese council around a vast boardroom table, hashing out potential solutions. They keep slipping from English to Portuguese and my mind keeps slipping to Ivy.

For the hundredth time this week, I pull up my house cameras on my laptop. I've watched Ivy walk around in that fucking night dress, swaying her hips through the hallway as she goes to get her coffee every damn morning. She always pauses at the exact spot on the wall where I took her. Sometimes the little brat even looks up at the camera and winks like she knows I'm watching.

The men around the table debate the best way to resolve the permit issues while I perve on Ivy's bikini-clad body. She's in the pool with the kids. The sky looks overcast, the spell of good weather finally broken. We don't have that problem here. I'm sweating like a nun in a sex shop.

I note the damn mutt is at least in its kennel.

Two more clicks of my mouse and I have a close-up of Ivy

adjusting Orla's armbands while Owen rests on her hip. Something twists in my chest.

Lust and something stronger. It takes me a minute to pinpoint the sensation.

It's longing.

Ivy's bikini leaves little to the imagination. Her nipples are pointed beneath the red Lycra, her skin peppered with goosebumps. She's visibly shivering, yet she's still smiling at my kids. The woman was made to be a mother. For a second, an image of Ivy, heavily pregnant with my baby, bursts through my brain and, surprisingly, it doesn't terrify me.

It's clear she's trying to convince the kids it's time to get out of the water. Both Orla and Owen are shaking their heads in protest. Ivy's hands gesticulate wildly. She seems to be trying to make a deal with them. Good luck with that.

I watch as she lifts Owen to the edge of the pool and settles him on the ledge. Then she takes Orla's hand and pulls her to the edge too, before hoisting herself up, filling my screen with an image of her full, round ass for a hot minute. My dick strains in my pants.

'What do you think, Mr Beckett?' the architect says, clasping his hands on the table.

I think I need to sink myself inside my woman again, and the quicker the better.

'I pay you to deal with these complications, so deal with them,' I snap, refocusing on my laptop. Ivy takes Orla's and Owen's hands, and the three of them stand in a row. I read Ivy's lips as she counts down. Three. Two. One. Then they jump into the pool together. I hold my breath as they disappear under the water, panic clawing at my chest. It feels like minutes, but after a couple of seconds they burst up from beneath the turquoise surface.

I sigh with relief and grin as my children's beaming faces fill the screen. They're laughing and spluttering in a way which, until Ivy arrived, I hadn't seen since before Isabella's death.

Jared saunters over. The slippery fucker. Red rage clouds my vision. Is he seriously stupid enough to make a move on my woman while I'm away on business?

I pluck my phone from the table, push my chair back and stalk across the room towards the door.

'Mr Beckett,' someone calls. Every eye in the room is on me. I ignore them and motion for them to keep talking. I can't leave Portugal until every one of these issues is resolved, but that doesn't mean I have to sit here through every painful second of this debate.

I don't bother looking back. 'Don't waste my time until you've come up with viable solutions.'

In the air-conditioned corridor, I dial Samuel, who I left in charge of security at the house while Damon travelled with me.

'Mr Beckett?' Samuel answers on the first ring.

'Tell Jared if he takes one more step towards Ivy, he's fired. Tell her if he so much as looks at her, he's fired.' I stride towards the lift, heading for the penthouse suite.

Stunned silence greets me on the other end of the line.

'Samuel?' I bark.

'Yes, sir, absolutely. Is that all?'

'No, that's not all.' I step into the glass lift and stare at the beach below. 'Looks like I'm going to be stuck here for another few days. Ask Liz to pack a bag for the kids. Book the jet. I want them here tonight.'

'And Ivy, sir?'

'I want her too.'

I've never been on a private jet before. I certainly didn't expect to be on Caelon Beckett's jet, yet here I am, sipping champagne, with Orla and Owen watching Taylor Swift's Eras Tour on a sixty-inch cinema screen.

The flight to Faro takes a little over two hours. We breeze through security, the scent of summer lingering in the air. Caelon, with Damon at his side, is waiting for us in arrivals. He looks absolutely devastating in a crisp white shirt that complements his olive skin. His sleeves are rolled up to reveal tanned forearms covered with masculine veins that look like a map to my own personal treasure. His inky hair is slightly tousled as if he's been raking his fingers through it in frustration. Dark, dubious eyes light up as he spots us.

'Daddy!' Owen and Orla scream, running to him. It's a battle not to do the same. He's only been gone a few days, but it feels like an eternity. I've been missing him more than I have any right to. I have no idea where this thing between us is going. The only thing I do know is that my stomach flips uncontrollably every time his name appears on my phone.

Caelon lifts his kids up, one in each arm, kisses their foreheads tenderly, and squeezes them to his chest. My ovaries sing like a pair of sopranos.

Caelon's eyes lock on mine, then linger on my lips for a beat before dropping to my chest. He lifts an eyebrow, and I bite back my smirk. I deliberately chose a short white summer dress. One that's light and airy, and so low at the back, it's impossible to wear a bra.

'Ivy.' He places the kids on the ground and gives me his full attention. Damon watches on with a neutral expression, but a hint of curiosity lights his eyes. I'm guessing Caelon hasn't flown too many other women out to meet him on his business trips.

I expect Caelon to be cold, reserved and professional in front of Damon, but he stalks towards me and presses a tender kiss on my cheek. His lips sear my skin. The gesture is so chaste compared to what we've done, but it sets my soul alight.

'Welcome to Portugal,' he murmurs into my ear, and I get a lungful of his woodsy, masculine scent.

He takes Owen's hand and slips the other on the base of my back, guiding us out of the airport and into the bright Portuguese sunshine. Heat shoots up my spine, but it has nothing to do with the climate. Orla falls into step beside me, chattering about the flight, the sunset, the sweets the air stewardess gave her, and Roxy, who Liz and Samuel have promised to take care of.

All I can focus on is Caelon's palm. Specifically, the tremors it's sending through my body.

Throughout the forty-minute drive, Orla and Owen ask a million questions about Caelon's week, about the size of the hotel pool, and if they can buy a dolphin while they're here.

Caelon answers with the patience of a man who has genuinely missed his children, though the primal glances he keeps tossing at my breasts are anything but patient. I swear, if the kids weren't here, he'd have them in his mouth by now. I don't even think Damon's presence would stop him.

We pass a gigantic billboard for a waterpark and the kids press their noses against the glass in their desperation for a closer look. Taking full advantage of their distraction, Caelon leans across and traces his tongue over my lips in a slow, seductive gesture. I glance at Damon in the driver's seat, my eyes widening.

'You are in so much trouble,' Caelon murmurs in my ear.

'The dog?' I knew he'd be mad, but I don't regret my decision.

'Not the dog. What did I tell you about those damn dresses?' he growls, and my core clenches. When we finally reach the hotel, I'm not sure if I need a cold drink or a cold shower.

Damon drops us at the gleaming glass entrance. The front of the building comprises brilliant white marble, the name, Bliss, carved directly into the wall in a bold italic font with a gold leaf inlay that sparkles under the setting sun. "A Beckett Hotel" is written in a smaller font beneath it, and it hits me with a sudden clarity just how successful Caelon and his brothers are.

Caelon greets the immaculately dressed staff with a curt nod before ushering us through a bright, airy lobby and directly to a glass lift. 'We're in the penthouse. The porters will bring the bags up shortly,' he tells us.

As we start our ascent, I soak in the panoramic views below; a crystal-clear infinity pool overlooking a stunning sandy beach, rugged cliffs, and azure-glittering water as far as the eye can see. I can't believe I'm here. That this is real.

'Can we swim in the pool, Daddy?' Owen asks, pressing his hands and face against the glass.

'Tomorrow, buddy. You've had a big day travelling.' Caelon ruffles Owen's hair. 'It's almost bedtime.' The feral look he shoots me suggests I won't be getting any sleep, though. A burst of butterflies soar through my stomach as I clench my thighs together.

The penthouse is every bit as opulent as the rest of the hotel. A huge, open-plan living area with a wraparound terrace overlooks the sea. There are three bedrooms, each with their own enormous en suites, plus a master bathroom with a rainforest-type shower with mood lighting and a million different settings.

'And you call this work?' I tease Caelon as he gives us the tour.

He lets out a long, slow breath. 'Don't get me started on work. It's been a shitshow this week. One complication after another. I've got planning problems, and permits and paperwork coming out of my ears.'

'You sound like you need a distraction,' I whisper, brushing my body against his as I pass to help Orla take her sandals off.

'I'm permanently distracted watching the nanny cam, and that's half the problem,' he moans.

An hour later, both kids are asleep in one of the queen-sized beds, wrecked from the impromptu journey.

'Hungry?' Caelon asks, retrieving a bottle of Louis Roederer Cristal Brut from the fridge. He's changed into a pair of navy linen shorts and a white polo shirt that's every bit as appealing as his earlier outfit.

'I told you before, I never met a calorie I didn't like,' though the only thing I really want to eat is him. It must be apparent on my face because his lips part in a wolfish grin.

He pops the cork and pours the champagne into two long-stemmed glasses. 'Dirty girl.'

I shrug. 'My boyfriend—or is it "partner"—banned me from touching myself.'

'Damn right he did.' Caelon pulls me towards him, until we're chest-to-chest, hip-to-hip, and I can feel his arousal pressing against my pelvis. 'I want all of those orgasms detonating on my face, on my hand, or on my dick.'

I swallow hard at his filthy words; at the images they stir in my brain. 'Don't hold back or anything, hey?'

'Oh, believe me, baby, I don't plan to.' His voice is low and gruff. The way he calls me baby makes my insides melt. Given how I've been babied my entire life, it should feel irritating. Instead, it feels intimate.

'Promises, promises.' I run my tongue over my lower lip and take a sip of the champagne.

'Are you wet for me?' His hand reaches beneath my dress, cupping the junction between my legs.

'Obviously.' I roll my eyes.

His fingers snake inside my lingerie and slide over my seam. 'Up on the island. I need a closer look.'

'No,' I say, putting down my glass.

His black eyes blaze. 'What do you mean, no? Don't you want me to lick your delicious little cunt until you come all over my face?'

I inhale a sharp breath. His filthy mouth might just be the death of me. 'Of course I do, but first I'd like to wrap my mouth around your delicious big dick until you come in the back of my throat.'

It's his turn to inhale sharply. 'And I thought *I* had a filthy mouth. I think I may just have met my match.' Deft hands reach around my back and loosen the gigantic bow tying my dress. It slides to the floor, leaving me standing in nothing other than a white silk thong and silver-heeled sandals. His gaze roams hungrily over my body. 'I will never tire of looking at you like this.' He reaches for my already hard nipples and rolls them between his fingers. 'Do you know how distracting it's been, knowing you're in my house while I'm stuck here? You're like poison, Ivy. I've tasted you and now I'm ruined.'

'Let me taste you.' I breathe him in, drinking in his intoxicating cologne and pure masculine scent of his skin.

'Over there.' He points to a luxurious daybed with a thick mattress on the terrace, then picks up our glasses and tucks the champagne bottle under his toned arm.

I don't need telling twice. I practically run out of the door, desperate to feel his dick in my mouth, then in my centre. He follows languidly, a smile lifting his lips. 'The impatience of youth,' he tuts.

'The impatience of a woman who has been sexually starved.' I motion for him to lie on the bed.

'It was four days,' he reminds me.

'Exactly.'

He places the champagne on a small, circular glass table and lies down. I reach for his shorts and tug them off, along with his black boxer briefs. He's rock hard and my lips are around him within seconds.

'Not so fast.' His palms rest on my cheeks. 'Turn around and back your ass this way. I want you to ride my face.'

My moan reverberates over his shaft, and he laughs, actually laughs, as I spin my body round and shamelessly back up onto his face, yanking my thong to the side, all without taking my mouth from him.

'Good girl,' he purrs. He offers my slit a long languid lick before his tongue plunges into my centre. I take him deep into my throat before running my tongue back up to his tip as I rock back.

My hums of pleasure vibrate around his length and the taste of precum fills my mouth, leaving me desperate for more. Firm hands grip my ass, stilling me as he catches my clit in his mouth and hums out his own appreciative moans.

It's carnal.

I don't care that anyone with a drone or long-lens camera

could see us. All I care about is the magic he's working with his tongue, and making magic with mine.

My legs shake, my orgasm building with every passing second. I work him at an increasingly frantic pace. I'm so close to coming, and I'm determined to drag him into oblivion with me.

'Ivy,' his voice is guttural, low and weighted with warning.

I take him as deep as I can, and when the first rope-like spurt hits the back of my throat, white-hot primal pleasure pulses through me, carnal and consuming.

Looks like we've both been poisoned, because I'm officially ruined for anyone but him.

Chapter Thirty-Six

CAELON

Ivy knows exactly what to do to make me blow. I love how unashamed she is of her body and her sexuality. How she knows what she wants and takes it. I love the taste of her. The way she trembles when she comes. The way her fingers claw into my thighs as she bucks against my face.

She spins until she's straddling me, and despite having the most debilitating orgasm of my life, my dick is already stirring again.

'Ready for round two, old man?' She shimmies on top of me.

'You have a thing for old men, don't you?' My fingers grip her ass, guiding her onto me.

'Not, usually,' she admits. 'But I have a thing for you.'

Her words stir something in my soul.

I have a thing for her too. A thing that's growing every damn day. Instead of analysing it, analysing the future, I surrender to the inevitable and let her claim me, one life-affirming inch at a time.

When I've proved exactly how capable this "old man" is,

twice—I might add, I order room service. Ivy showers while I pad around the penthouse barefoot, a deep sense of contentment filling my chest.

It's been so long since I experienced it, I forgot what it felt like. I peek in at the kids, who are spread out like starfish across a queen-sized bed. Orla's glossy hair falls messily over her forehead and Owen's small hand rests on that tatty teddy, as usual. At least it smells better since Ivy washed it. I pull the door closed and head in search of a drink.

Ivy saunters in, hair damp, wearing one of her flimsy night dresses just as I'm opening a bottle of white wine from our own Provencal vineyards. I'm in the process of building a luxury spa retreat in the region, offering bespoke wine-tasting experiences.

'Food will be here any minute,' I say as I pour two glasses.

'I'm starving.' She accepts the wine gratefully and sips, a low appreciative moan melting into the glass.

'Riding a person's face, then their cock tends to have that effect,' I tease, feeling a smile stretch my lips. Smiling is something that's been happening more and more frequently lately. 'Shall we sit outside?'

'Sure, it's such a gorgeous night.' She strides out onto the terrace and rests her elbows on the glass balustrade as she gazes out over the sea. A myriad of stars decorate the sky. Moonlight cascades over the water, the soothing sounds of the waves providing the perfect soundtrack to what has been a perfect night. Away from Dublin, away from the house, I feel... lighter.

No, that's not right. It's not being away from the house.

I've been here all week, and between work and watching the cameras at home, the load was heavy.

It's Ivy's presence that makes me feel lighter. Ivy and the kids.

I step outside, drawn to her like a moth to a flame.

'This is the perfect temperature.' Ivy inhales the balmy evening air and breathes out a happy sigh.

'It's perfect now. Earlier, it was like a sauna.' Though it wasn't nearly as hot as her sitting on my face. 'How do you fancy a boat trip tomorrow? I have meetings all morning, but I can get away in the afternoon.' I can pretend it's for her sake, but really, it's for mine. I want to be with her every minute of the day and night, and the feeling is escalating. 'I can arrange a sitter for the kids.'

'I *am* the sitter.' She eyes me over the rim of her glass.

'We both know you're so much more than that.' Again, those three little words linger like heart-shaped balloons between us, yet I can't quite bring myself to say them.

A genuine smile touches her lips. 'Still, I think we should take the kids.'

I love how she puts my children's needs before her own.

'Be ready for two.' I force my voice into a gruff tone to hide how hard I'm falling for her.

A short, sharp knock at the front door alerts us to the arrival of dinner. Rui, a young waiter, wheels in a gleaming silver trolley loaded with delicious-smelling food.

'Good evening, Mr Beckett.' His voice trembles slightly as I direct him to the terrace.

'Good evening, Rui.' I make a point of knowing all my employees' name, where possible.

His head snaps up in shock, his face creasing in surprise. I fetch the bottle to top up our glasses while he sets the table. Ivy being Ivy is asking him if he likes working here. Ha, like he'd say no with me within earshot.

'This is the most luxurious hotel in Portugal,' he tells Ivy.

'Yeah, I heard the boss is a real dictator, though.' Ivy winks at me. Brat.

'Only to some of his staff,' I bite out. 'The ones who

should keep their mouths shut if they value their positions.' I eye her meaningfully.

'Oh, I value every position,' she snorts, and as much as I want to put her over my knee and smack her pert ass for her audacity, I laugh.

Rui's deep brown eyes dart between Ivy and me as he backs away. 'Can I get anything else for you, sir?'

'No, thank you.' I hand him a hundred euro note and motion for him to leave.

'You and your runaway mouth,' I tut, my eyes boring into Ivy's.

'You seemed to like it earlier,' she shrugs, taking a seat at the table, poring over the decadent spread.

This woman. So full of sass. My brain is overflowing with the sinful things I want to do to her. But more than that, I want to take her to my bed and hold her all night long. To feel her body curl around mine, her heart pressed against my chest. The comforting sound of her breathing beside me.

'What are you doing to me?' I blurt out, watching as her head whips up from the lobster salad she was eyeing.

'I know what I'd like to do to you.' She cocks a brow. 'Just let me eat first.' She pierces a chunk of lobster with her fork and pops it into her mouth.

'I didn't mean sexually, though I've never been one to look a gift horse in the mouth.' I wink as I fall into the chair at her side.

'So, what *did* you mean?' Her usual sass is replaced with a rare seriousness.

'You're in my head all the time. You steal my every waking thought and most of my sleeping ones, too. You fill my life with noise and mess and a fucking dog, and I'm still fucking crazy about you.'

She sucks on her lower lip, processing for a second. 'The feeling is mutual. You've turned me into one of these crazy bitches who checks her phone all day, every day, in case I miss a text from you. And as much as I love your body...' she pauses, and her eyes widen like she's waiting for me to freak out at the "l" word, but I don't. I'm slowly starting to accept that's what this is. So much so, I'm almost ready to tell her. But once I do, there will be no going back.

'You were saying...' I prompt, spearing a scallop dripping in lemon butter, and shove it into my mouth.

'As much as I love your body, I've missed your arms around me at night, and your snoring.'

'I don't snore.'

'You do, but I don't think we'll have to worry about that tonight.' She winks.

'What are you talking about?'

She waves a hand over the table. 'Am I supposed to believe you *accidentally* ordered every aphrodisiac on the menu? Come on, admit it, you planned to get me even hornier and keep us both up all night, right?' Her soft laugh permeates the air, weaving through the space between us to thaw the final remnant of ice surrounding my previously frozen heart.

'I wasn't planning anything,' I tell her honestly. 'Funnily enough, all my plans get forgotten when you're around.'

Which is why I need to tell Dermot I'm in love with his sister.

Chapter Thirty-Seven
IVY

I wake up to find Caelon's muscular arms wrapped around my waist, his taut torso pressed against my bare back, and his chin resting on my shoulder–the exact position we fell asleep in. I feel the gentle thud of his heart and hear his soft, deep breaths. His unique male scent encases me in a Caelon-shaped bubble I'd happily stay in forever.

I squint at my Apple watch. It's two minutes to five. Neither of us has moved for almost five hours straight.

As if sensing I'm awake, Caelon stirs. He presses his nose against my neck and inhales my skin before sprinkling tiny kisses across my shoulder blade.

He's always been A1 at the aftercare, but this, these sensual little kisses, and the way he's cuddling me, are on a whole-new level. Even after I bought a dog for his kids.

'I wish I could stay in bed with you,' he whispers.

'Yeah, yeah, but you have a six-pack to maintain and a billion-euro empire to run, I know.' I twist to face him, and our eyes lock. 'And I have a date with an adorable five- and six-year-old, a teddy that's in need of a wash, and a strong coffee.'

'Your job is way more important than mine.' Caelon presses his lips to mine and a heat stirs in my stomach and lower. I pull back before we start something we won't have time to finish.

'Oh, believe me, I know.' I shrug playfully, running my fingers through his hair.

'My kids love you.' His voice is rough with gratitude.

'I love them.' *And you.*

Thankfully, for once my mouth behaves and doesn't blurt the latter part of that statement out loud.

His hand glides over the back of my arm slowly, sending goosebumps scattering in its wake. 'I'll see you this afternoon.'

'We'll be ready.' I smile. I'm not sure I'll ever be ready for Caelon Beckett in any shape or form because the more time I spend with him, the more his tortured soul claims my tranquil one.

He untangles his limbs from mine, presses a kiss to my forehead, and drags himself from between the crisp white sheets. I roll over, staring at the wall, waiting for him to go so I can process everything that happened last night, last week, and last month, but instead of him slipping away quietly, he returns five minutes later with a cup of coffee, just the way I like it.

'Here. If you need anything else, just ask any of the staff. They'll take care of you.'

My eyes drift to the platinum wedding ring he still wears.

I sit up, propping the plump pillows behind my back while Caelon picks up a remote and points it at the blinds. They open electronically, revealing the morning sunrise over the sea.

'How's that for *tranquil?*' He smiles, something which has happened multiple times in the past twelve hours, even though we were asleep for five of them.

'It's perfection.'

He kisses me one more time before disappearing.

I spend the entire morning in the opulent infinity pool with the kids. Between the excitement, the heat, and the exercise, they're exhausted before midday. It doesn't bode well for the boat trip. Wrapping towels around them for the hundredth time, I prop them on a sun lounger under an umbrella and order ice creams from the waiter, Rui, who can't do enough for us.

I pull out my phone from my beach bag to check the time and find missed calls from both Dermot and Caelon. My heart sinks. I hope Caelon's not too bogged down with work that he's cancelling this afternoon.

I'm about to call Caelon back, but my phone rings before I have the chance.

'Sorry, I only just saw your missed calls.' I smile at Orla, who is reclining on a lounger rocking a pair of pink Barbie sunglasses. She's going to be one hell of a diva when she grows up. A pang strikes my sternum. I hope I'm around to see it. 'The kids are fine. Everything is fine.' Caelon worries about them, and I can't blame him.

'I know they are,' his smooth voice purrs into my ear. 'I'm watching you on the hotel's CCTV. That's my favourite bikini, by the way. I can't wait to peel it off you later.'

My head snaps, scanning for the hint of a camera.

'It's deliberately discreet.' Caelon barks out a laugh.

'Can't I go anywhere without you perving on me?' I whisper, but there's no denying the thrill that he's as into me as I am to him.

'Nope, it's my favourite pastime.'

'And did you ring specifically to tell me that? Or do you want something?'

Rui returns with two cones topped with whipped ice cream and sprinkles. He hands one to Orla and one to Owen.

'I want something, but that will have to wait until later.' I hear his smile, even though I can't see it. 'The boat won't be ready until three. Meet me in the restaurant for lunch at one.'

'Yes, boss.' I raise my hand in a salute and he snorts.

'I think we both know you're the one in charge.' He hangs up before I can respond.

The ice creams melt quicker than the kids can eat them and they're soon wearing more than they've swallowed. I take them up to the penthouse, shower them and dress them for lunch in their father's fancy hotel restaurant. Room service has changed all the sheets, but Owen's weren't the ones that were in need of replacing this morning. Whoops.

I pick out a blush pink playsuit from my wardrobe and team it with a pair of gold low-heeled wedges. In this heat, there's zero point in even trying to do anything with my hair or make-up, so I settle for a few squirts of Jo Malone perfume and a lick of mascara, and hope for the best.

When we reach the restaurant, Caelon is already waiting for us at a table by a window overlooking the cliffs. In a suit and tie, and wearing his serious game face, he looks positively powerful. His sheer presence sucks the oxygen from the room. Despite the air con, I am on fire.

His face breaks into a crooked smile as he spots us and his espresso-coloured eyes glint with an energetic spark. He stands as we approach. Orla and Owen run to him, hugging his legs and yelling over each other in their excitement to tell him about their morning.

Caelon answers with a convincing enthusiasm but his eyes are trained firmly on me, roving over my outfit before settling on my face. His crooked smile stretches into an almighty grin that makes my heart beat right out of my ribcage. Tortured has always been beautiful in that masculine way, but when he smiles, really smiles, he's fucking devastating.

But his face morphs into an expression of horror as I reach the table.

'What are you doing here?' he demands incredulously.

I'm about to remind him he invited me, when I note his gaze has shifted to over my right shoulder.

'Grandma!' Orla and Owen squeal, leaping into the air.

I spin on my heels and find myself face to face with an immaculately dressed woman wearing a necklace dripping in diamonds and a grin as wide as the sea. A man who can only be Caelon's father, given the striking resemblance, stands at her side.

'Well, well, well,' Caelon's mother says, not even attempting to mask her glee. 'Fancy meeting you here.'

Caelon drags his jaw from the floor and steps forwards so he's standing beside me. 'Ivy, I'd like you to meet my mother, Vivienne, and my father, Alexander.' His voice is crisp, sharp and sullen again.

'Ivy,' Vivienne coos, taking my hands. 'It's such a pleasure to meet you.' There's an unmistakable warmth in her voice and actual tears welling in the corner of her eyes.

Alexander has the same deep, brown, thoughtful eyes as Caelon, which dart between us with curiosity. It's clear to see where the Beckett boys got their looks from, even with the deep purple scar that's carved across Alexander's cheek. A shiver rips down my spine. The scar reminds me that the Becketts are dangerous. I should know. I've spent hours reading about the bitter feud between their family and their rivals, the O'Connors.

Vivienne launches herself at Caelon, wrapping her arms around him. He stands stiffly until I nudge him in the ribs with my elbow and he eventually reciprocates the hug, though not with nearly as much enthusiasm.

'It's so great to see you're dating again,' she whispers, none too discreetly, as she disentangles her arms from his back.

'Oh, I'm just the nanny.' I hold my palms up and take a step back, glancing at the kids pointedly. They have no idea about their daddy and me, and now is not the time to tell them.

Vivienne swats a slim, manicured hand in front of her face before leaning close enough that I can smell her expensive perfume. 'That grin certainly wasn't for me,' she whispers, cocking her head.

She turns to her son again, who is flushed in the face and tight-lipped. 'Do you mind if we join you for lunch?'

'Do I have any choice?' Caelon mutters, but Vivienne's attention is already refocussed on me.

'We've been touring Europe. We spent last month in the south of France and then we decided to come here. It's a special place for us as Alex proposed to me in Portugal many moons ago. I have a soft spot for Carveiro. Thought we'd check in for a night or two before moving on to Lisbon. I am so happy we did.'

Judging by the grim expression on Caelon's face, he's not quite as ecstatic about this turn of events.

Three waiters appear, pulling out seats and faffing with napkins. Caelon orders wine. I think we're going to need it.

'Tell me, Ivy, how long have you been working for Caelon?' Alexander doesn't beat around the bush.

'A couple of months.' I brush Orla's hair from her eyes, then turn my attention back to Caelon's parents.

Surprise flits across Alexander's eyes. 'And he hasn't terrified you yet?'

The only thing that's terrifying is how hard and fast I'm falling for him.

'He's not as big or as bad as everyone makes out,' I beam. Caelon coughs to hide his snort.

'Well, I'm so glad it's working out,' Vivienne clucks, leaning into my ear as Orla climbs onto my lap. 'Caelon deserves some happiness.'

I nod, but don't comment, all too aware of little ears listening. The waiter returns with the wine, and we order a selection of tapas.

'How long are you here for?' Vivienne asks.

'I'm stuck here for at least another week,' Caelon replies. 'Although you can go home before, if you want to?' he says to me.

'Hmmm, let me think about that,' I tease, 'Stay in this luxurious five-star hotel with my two favourite kiddos and my broody boss,' I tickle Orla's ribs, 'or go back to dreary Dublin with my two favourite kiddos and see if Uncle Rian calls in for a visit.'

Caelon growls, his nostrils flaring. Vivienne and Alex exchange a look of surprise.

Alex steers the conversation towards business, and Caelon launches into a long-winded, boring spiel about red tape, regulations, and structural repairs. I tune out, and drink more wine than I should as Vivienne keeps up a rapid stream of conversation which thankfully, requires little or no response. The woman is warm and so welcoming, but my God, she can talk.

'We go to the Eden spa every Friday; you simply must join us! Have you met my daughter, Zara?'

I shake my head. 'I met Scarlett, though.'

'Scarlett is such a doll. She's so good for James. And the kids are just adorable. I miss them all, but we'll be home in a couple of weeks. It's good for Alex to get away. Even though he's retired, he's a devil for "popping into the office" to check on the boys.' She rolls her eyes dramatically, 'Boys! They're all men now.'

That we can agree on.

By the time we've finished eating, the kids are practically asleep on the table.

'We might have to take a rain check on the boat trip.' I cradle Orla's head and reposition her on my chest. Her eyelids are fluttering closed, even as she protests that she's not tired.

'What's this about a boat trip?' Vivienne asks Caelon.

'I'd arranged some time off this afternoon to take them out.' Caelon lifts an equally exhausted looking Owen onto his lap. 'Looks like we might have to give it a miss. Pity.' His eyes stray to mine.

'You two go,' Vivienne says. 'Alex and I will take the kids for the afternoon. They're not the only ones who need a rest. We'll take them up to our suite and put a movie on for them, won't we, Grandad?' Vivienne stares pointedly at her husband. 'You two go have some fun.'

Alex's eyes glitter. 'Caelon is overdue some fun. He's always so serious.'

That's what he thinks. Caelon's been having a lot of fun lately. It's me who's been getting serious. Although, Caelon's decided he wants to tell Dermot about us, so perhaps I'm not the only one.

Chapter Thirty-Eight

IVY

The boat isn't just a boat, it's a multimillion-euro yacht, stretching an impressive one hundred and fifty feet from bow to stern. If I wasn't already well-acquainted with Caelon's beautiful big dick, I'd have to wonder if my darling boss was trying to make up for something. But no, he's the full package.

The Beckett logo is emblazoned on the yacht's bow in a gold italic font that matches the sign outside the hotel. It's gleaming white with sleek aerodynamic lines and large, tinted windows that wrap around the main salon and upper decks, providing panoramic views of the sea. The deck is lined with polished teak, and there's a spacious sunbathing area furnished with plush loungers and umbrellas.

A delicious warm breeze whips through my hair. I snap a hairband from my wrist and scrape my unruly beach waves into a ponytail on top of my head.

'Did you bring my favourite bikini?' Caelon asks, nodding towards the stern. He's changed into a pair of navy swimming shorts and a white polo shirt that complements his tanned skin and taut muscles. Raybans shield his eyes from the blistering sun.

'I'm wearing it under this.' I glance around, looking for the crew. They made themselves scarce as soon as we set off. The yacht glides gracefully through the azure water.

'Good, we'll anchor somewhere private in a while.' His suggestive tone leaves his intentions crystal clear. My stomach flips. No matter how many times I have this man, I doubt it'll ever be enough.

'My parents loved you,' Caelon says, taking my hand and guiding me towards one of the plush seating areas.

'I think they're just happy they caught you smiling.' I slide onto a seat and tuck my legs beneath a glass-topped table. I tilt my face up to the sun, revelling in the warmth kissing my cheekbones.

'*You* make me smile,' Caelon says in a low voice. '*You* drive me fucking crazy sometimes, strutting around in tiny outfits and dating my brother, but being with you makes me...' he pauses for a second and I tilt my face to meet his gaze, 'feel alive.'

Warmth blooms in my chest and heats my blood. 'You drive *me* fucking crazy strutting around in those sexy suits and looking all tortured, but being with you makes me...' I pause, trying to think of a meaningful word that captures how he makes me feel, without terrifying him. 'Being with you makes me feel strong.'

'You are strong.' He yanks the strap of my playsuit down, 'And sexy. And smart.'

'Shame my family didn't get the memo.'

'Fuck them.' His lips part and I get a flash of perfect white teeth. 'Take this off.'

I glance around the empty deck. 'What if someone sees?'

'What if they do?' he teases, tugging the other strap down. 'You never struck me as the shy type.'

'You know exactly what type I am,' I remind him, my mind wondering back to the first night we met.

'*My* type,' he says gruffly, like it's a curse instead of a compliment, but before I can overthink it, he grabs my waist and hoists me up onto the table. I shriek as my backside hits the hot glass and he rasps out a cruel laugh. 'It's about to get hotter,' he says, tugging my playsuit down to my stomach and wiggling it down my hips and over my shoes.

He's still fully dressed while I'm sitting in my bikini and heeled wedges for his pleasure. I'd love to get another look at his toned body and that tattoo. There's something so damn arousing about it. Why did he pick the phoenix? Maybe one day I'll get the chance to ask him, but not today.

'Take your bikini top off.' It's not a request.

I glance around once more before pulling at the small bow at the back. The Lycra falls to my lap, then slides to the floor. Caelon hisses out his approval.

'You're so fucking beautiful,' he says, as his greedy eyes drink in my body. 'I didn't want to want you, but I can't help it. Just like your name, you've grown tenacious roots beneath my skin. You've breached the walls of my house, and you've weaved your way into my heart.' He pauses and the air swirls thickly between us.

He pushes his sunglasses onto his head. Our eyes lock with an intensity more powerful than the sun. I swear I can see his soul through those giant, dark orbs. I suck in a breath, holding it like it might be my last.

Three little words hang like a guillotine about to slice through life as I know it. Anticipation hums in my veins.

I've fallen so hard for him. I can only pray he feels the same.

His fingers skim over my breasts, sending shockwaves rippling in every direction. 'I love you.' It's barely more than a whisper, but I hear it loud and clear. 'It fucking terrifies me,' he admits, 'but I do.'

He loves me. He loves me. He loves me.

As the significance of his words washes over me, my blood turns to hot molten lava and my whole body vibrates with pleasure. 'I love you, too.'

His lips capture mine, cementing our mutual confessions with a raw, primal carnality that sets shivers soaring over my spine. I lean into him, and he pulls me tighter until our torsos are flush. I need more. I need every inch of him against every inch of me. I need him inside of me. I need us to be one.

He breaks our kiss, his eyes boring into mine again. 'Your brother is going to murder me when he finds out I'm in love with his little sister, and we've been fucking our way through the Kama Sutra.'

'He doesn't need to know. Not yet.'

'He does.' He cocks his head. 'I hate lying to him. You're mine and I'm ready for the whole damn world to know it.'

I glance at Caelon's hands. 'Can we talk about this when I'm not nearly naked and wet? My boyfriend just told me he loves me, and I want him to show me. Actions speak louder than words, you know.'

Caelon's lips twist. 'You have an awful habit of distracting me from important issues.' He pinches my nipples between his fingers, inciting a moan of pleasure.

'The only important issue right now is making me come,' I pout.

He shakes his head, a low chuckle rumbling from his ribcage. 'Horny brat,' he tuts. 'Fine. But we have to talk about this later.'

I roll my eyes. 'After you make me come.'

'How exactly would you like me to make you come?' His tongue darts out over his lower lip and his palms fall to my thighs.

'Hard,' I answer, though with him, it's the only way.

He pulls the string tie at the side of my bikini bottoms and they fall to the floor with the top, laying me bare for him. His thumb grazes my throbbing clit, sending delicious shocks jolting in every direction.

I shimmy my ass towards the edge of the table.

'Your body was made to take mine.' He slides two fingers into my slippery core and my eyes roll into my head.

'Show me,' I beg unashamedly.

He tugs down his shorts with his free hand, working me with his fingers. I hiss, watching as he grips his cock and pumps. 'Come sit on my lap,' he purrs, sliding his fingers out. I launch myself onto him.

Our lips fuse, tongues dancing to a rhythm we've perfected. I lower myself onto his length, taking him inch by life-affirming inch until I'm full of him. His hands glide over the globes of my ass, fingers digging deliciously into my skin as he guides me into a slow and sensual pace. Even when I'm on top of him, he never fully relinquishes control. I love that about him. That and his eyes. They're so deep, I could drown in them. We've had sex seventy different ways, yet this time feels different. More intimate. Like we've only been playing around until now.

We grind and rock, swallowing each other's moans. My fingers rake through his hair, over the nape of his neck and down his back until I reach the hem of his shirt and pull it over his head, tossing it on the floor.

'I need your skin on my skin,' I say, pushing my breasts against his chest.

Fire flashes in his irises as my hands skim over his. Intensity builds low in my stomach. It's carnal but tender. Hot pleasure scorching me from the inside out. My nipples could cut glass. His hips jut upwards and into mine as I slam myself back down on top of them. His mouth moves to my jawline, peppering tiny kisses which set my spine shivering.

'Cold?' he asks, amusement lacing his words. His lips glide along my neck as he nips and sucks his way down to my breast. He knows just how to tease me. I need more. Now.

I rest my palms on the hard planes of his obliques. 'Caelon,' I pant.

'I need —' before I even get the words out, his hand reaches between our slick bodies and his thumb settles on my clit. I moan out my relief.

'Is this what you wanted?' He draws tiny, torturous circles before stroking my sweet spot again.

'Stop torturing me,' I plead, grinding harder against him.

'But it's so much fun.' His lips lift in a wolfish grin.

'I'll do anything.'

'Anything?' His dark eyes light up.

'Anything,' I confirm.

'I'm going to hold you to that.' His thumb glides back to where I need it and when my legs lock tight and my fingers dig into his skin, he doesn't tease me, and he doesn't take them away. Our mouths meld again as I ride him hard until I explode. Wave after wave of relief courses through me in the form of blinding, hot, hedonistic pleasure. My clenching core has him in a vice-like grip and he curses as he spills himself into me.

Chapter Thirty-Nine

CAELON

Ivy and the kids stay with me until I conclude my business in Portugal. It takes another eight days to resolve things, and while the days are sometimes long, drawn-out, and stressful, the nights are short, lust-fuelled, and tranquil.

Eight nights of waking up with her in my arms.

Eight nights of intense, soul-shattering sex.

Eight nights of whispered 'I love yous'.

I haven't slept as well in years. I feel rested, despite the tedious meetings and mountains of red tape.

We've been in our own beautiful bubble, but now it's time to go home and I'm about to cash in on Ivy's 'anything' promise.

The jet lands in Dublin just after five o'clock. It's Saturday, so the traffic is heavy. Damon drives while I respond to a couple of important emails that can't wait. Stephanie can deal with everything else.

Ivy sits in the back between the kids, who are watching a movie on their tablets.

'Are you looking forward to meeting our fur baby?' Ivy teases.

I roll my eyes. 'Feckin' dog.'

'You're going to love her.'

'Doubtful.' Though the damn mutt might come in handy for security purposes.

'Are you okay?' Ivy leans forward, whispering into my ear.

'I will be. You know the other day, on the boat, you said you'd do anything...' I stare at her intently. At the freckles dusting her nose. At her sun-kissed skin. I've caressed every inch of her beautiful body. I know how she feels from the inside out. I could tap out the rhythm of her heartbeat like a melody.

'That was in the heat of the moment.' She eyes me suspiciously. 'You're not seriously going to hold me to it?'

'I am.' I glance at the kids, checking they're still engrossed in their screens. 'And if you want me to make you come just as hard tonight, I need you to do two things for me.'

'Are you blackmailing me with sex?' She doesn't sound annoyed. If anything, she seems to like the idea. Kinky brat.

'I prefer the term "rewarding you".' I nip her left ear lobe, gently blowing on her skin. She visibly shivers.

'What do you want me to do?'

I pull back so I can look into her eyes. All teasing evaporates from my tone. 'You need protection now that we're back in Dublin. I have enemies and I refuse to let them get to you, like...'

I trail off, wincing. I still love Isabella. I always will, but my relationship with Ivy has given me a reason to go on. A reason to think past revenge. That's not to say I won't take it when the opportunity arises, but now I have something, someone, to live for afterwards.

Ivy reaches for my hand. 'It's okay. I mean, it's not really.' She scrunches up her nose. 'Do I want to be followed around twenty-four-seven? Do I want someone to wait outside the toilet for me every time I want a pee? Do I want someone following me round the lingerie department when I'm shopping? Honestly, not really, but I get it.'

I let out the breath I'd been holding. I thought she'd take it harder. Like I was babying her, the way her family does, but it's far from that.

She tilts her chin to meet my gaze. 'You've been watching me anyway, between the cameras and having Samuel escort me and the kids everywhere.'

'I love you.' I kiss the back of her hand. 'If anything happened to you, it would kill me.'

'I love you too.' Her expression softens. 'Nothing's going to happen to me.' Concern floods her eyes, but it's not for herself, it's for my feelings. She's so selfless. So perfect. 'What else do you want me to do?'

'It's time we came clean to Dermot,' I whisper grimly.

She shakes her head vigorously. 'No way. Not yet. You know he's going to explode. I can't deal with that right now.'

'It's one thing flaunting it around Portugal, but here, the press are all over my family. He *will* find out. It's better he hears it from us.'

Ivy groans, her face falling to her hands. 'This is going to cause a war.'

'It will.' There's no point in denying it. 'But I'm hoping I can make him understand. We're together. You're a grown woman. My woman. And I take care of what is mine. Dermot knows that. It'll take a while to get used to the idea, but you were always going to find someone one day. It just happens that someone is me.'

'You know that security we just talked about? You might want to double up on it. Yours, not mine. You're going to need it.' I'm not joking.

'He might not take it that badly. We could be brothers one day.'

Ivy's head whips around. 'Good luck with that.'

When we finally reach the house, there's a car in the driveway.

Dermot's BMW.

Oh fuck.

Did another sneaky pap get a shot of us?

My mind returns to the yacht. Jesus, anyone with a drone or a long lens could have photographed us together. It's one thing telling Dermot I'm with his sister, and another thing for him to see it in high definition.

Guilt snakes into my stomach. I had five missed calls from him over the last week. I couldn't bring myself to call him back. Couldn't be sure my voice wouldn't betray me. That I've been eating his kid sister like she's my favourite dessert and wearing her like she's my favourite fucking outfit.

Damon stops at the gate, glancing between Ivy and me in the rearview mirror. 'Would you prefer if we kept driving for a while? Samuel can arrange for Mr Winters to return tomorrow if it's easier.'

I flick my head round to meet Ivy's gaze. 'Are you ready?'

Dermot is pacing up and down the drive with a thunderous expression on his face.

She blows out a breath. 'Fuck it. Let's do this.' A horrified look crinkles the corners of her eyes. She clamps her hand over her mouth, glancing at the kids. They're still engrossed in their tablets, thankfully. Though, it's not the first time they've heard the F-bomb.

Damon drives up to the front of the house, parks next to Dermot's BMW, and ushers Orla and Owen into the house where Samuel is waiting for them. The slobbering, furry beast bounds from the house and charges towards the kids. My breath catches for a second as I wait for her to knock them over, but for a creature that size, she's surprisingly gentle with them, leaping around and licking their faces as they squeal out their delight.

If only Dermot would give us such a warm welcome. Judging from his pacing, he is furious.

I help Ivy out of the car while Damon covers my back, ready for anything.

'There you are!' Dermot shouts, glaring at Ivy.

'What's the problem?' I step in front of her, sheltering her from her brother's wrath.

'I've been trying to call you all week. I was worried sick.' His eyes sweep over her, like he's looking for scratches or bruises. He'd have better luck finding them on my back. My woman has a habit of digging her claws into me when she's close.

'She was working,' I tell him. 'You don't have to worry about her when she's with me. I'd never let anything happen to her.'

'*You thought that about Isabella too,*' an invisible devil on my shoulder reminds me. I swat it away. Lightning doesn't strike twice.

Declan and Jack O'Connor are behind bars. The other brothers fled the country. Their assets are still frozen, so they have no funds for retaliation. After Isabella's death, I doubled security around here as a precautionary measure for the children. Ivy is safe with me.

Dermot's shoulders visibly relax. 'I know I shouldn't worry about her when she's with you, but you seem to have forgotten how a phone works, too,' He looks at me pointedly for a long beat, but the anger has dissolved from his voice.

'I've been snowed under with work,' I tell him, motioning for him to go into the house. 'So much bureaucracy and legal bullshit. Thankfully, I found a mayor who wasn't averse to helping oil the wheels, for a price.'

'Glad to hear it.' Dermot wraps an arm over Ivy's shoulders, walking her up the steps. The dog and kids rush in ahead of us. 'How are you getting on? Did you enjoy Portugal? Is Caelon being good to you?'

'He's not being too bad.' She twists her head and winks slyly at me. 'Oh, Roxy, I've missed you!' she coos, rubbing the dog as she passes her in the hallway.

'Good, because I'd hate to have to fuck him up for not treating you right,' Dermot grunts.

Liz is in the kitchen preparing dinner. The kids settle on the couch with their tablets and the dog rushes towards me, slobber foaming from her mouth. Gross.

'Go away.' I shoo her with my hands.

'I thought you hated dogs.' Dermot frowns as Roxy ignores my attempts to dismiss her. She's as defiant as Ivy, but nowhere near as loveable.

I grab three beers from the fridge. 'Let's drink these on the patio,' I suggest, determined to get Dermot as far away from my kids as possible in preparation for the beating he's liable to give me before this evening is over.

Dermot sits on the outdoor sofa. Ivy sinks into the seat beside him, and I take the armchair opposite. I can't trust myself not to accidentally touch her the way I've grown accustomed to doing.

'How was Portugal?' Dermot asks Ivy.

The damn dog pads out, sniffs the air, then pees on the patio. I shake my head at Ivy, who lets out a laugh and a shrug.

'It was way more fun that I imagined.' She sips from her beer bottle and as she tilts her head back to swallow, I catch a glimpse of a shadow on her neck. Another fucking hickey. One I put there last night.

Oh fuck. Her hair mostly hides it. My eyes snap to her

wrist where she perpetually keeps a hair tie. I pray she doesn't decide to use it.

'Did you think any more about going back to college?' Dermot cocks his head towards me. 'Did you know Ivy's thinking about studying for a degree,' Dermot says, peeling the label from his beer bottle with his thumb nail.

'But I need her.' It's out before I think about it.

'She needs to settle on a proper career now she's home. Summer is almost over. It's time to think about what she wants to do with her life.'

'This is what she wants to do with her life.' I sweep a hand towards the door, motioning towards the kids in the living room.

Dermot scoffs. 'She's twenty-three. She's not going to want to be your nanny forever. She has so much potential.'

'Hello, I am here, you know.' Ivy waves sarcastically. 'Dermot, I told you, I don't want to go back to college.'

'You said you'd think about it.' He arches an eyebrow.

'No, you *told* me to think about, and I did. I don't want to.'

Dermot's jaw locks and he inhales deeply through his nose. 'I just want what's best for you.'

'What's best for me is doing a job I love. Look at me.' She points at herself. 'How many jobs do you know where I get paid to drink beer by a pool? To go on holiday with two of the coolest kids I've ever met?'

'You don't seriously plan on being a nanny forever?' he scoffs.

'Why does she have to have a plan? Why can't she just take things one day at a time?' I interject.

'Ha, says the man who always has a plan,' Dermot reminds me wryly.

'And look where that got me.'

Dermot's eyes narrow as he glances between Ivy and me. The breeze picks up, fanning her hair back, revealing her neck and the hickey I put there. Fuck. He leans forward, peering at it. 'Is that another love bite?' Horror hangs on his every word.

Ivy's hand flies to her throat. 'Oh, probably. I met this really hot single dad in Portugal, and we had crazy, intense, indecent sex every day. Multiple times.' She says it like she's joking. I hold my breath, waiting for Dermot's reaction.

His eyes narrow. 'You'd better be kidding.'

'I'm an adult woman with needs.' Ivy shrugs, deliberately brazen. Damon and Samuel step out from the house as if sensing a storm brewing.

'I don't need to know about your needs.' Dermot shakes his head, then turns to me. 'You were supposed to be keeping an eye on her.'

Ivy crosses one long leg over the other, drawing my focus to her silky tanned skin.

Dermot catches me looking. I avert my eyes rapidly, but not quickly enough.

'Motherfucker!' He leaps out of his seat, tossing his beer aside. The bottle smashes on the ground.

Samuel and Damon react instantly, grabbing him before he can launch himself at me. Roxy leaps forwards, a low growl rumbling in her throat.

'You!' Dermot's veins pulsate in his temple. 'Tell me you're not sleeping with my kid sister.'

I stand and motion for Damon and Samuel to let Dermot go. If he wants to hit me, I won't stop him.

They loosen their grip, but don't completely release him.

'Answer me, Caelon. Fucking answer me,' Dermot snarls, beet-red and panting. 'Are you sleeping with my sister? Is she the woman you were talking about in the club?'

Ivy stands and attempts to placate her brother, placing her palm on his bicep, but he shrugs her off. The dog positions herself between Ivy and Dermot. Maybe she's not so bad after all.

'Yes.' I nod for Damon to release Dermot. He pauses for a split second and waits for Ivy to step back. It gives me three seconds to prepare myself. When Dermot's fist hits my jaw, I barely even feel it. I grab his wrist tightly, despite his efforts to keep swinging punches. 'Dermot, I'm in love with your sister,' I announce, not caring that half my security team is witnessing my declaration.

'Love?' he splutters. 'Is that what you tell yourself so you can sleep at night? How would you feel if I was fucking your kid sister?'

I open my mouth to answer, but Ivy beats me to it. 'Dermot, I'm not a kid anymore. Caelon and I are in love. We're together, whether you like it or not.'

'Like it? I fucking hate it. I trusted you,' he spits. 'I trusted you with my sister. I told you her last boss came on to her, and you did the same thing. You took advantage of her while she was under your roof.'

'He didn't, Dermot.' Ivy waves her hands like a white flag, with Roxy at her side. Yep, the damn dog can stay, drool and all. 'If anything, I pursued *him*. I know what I'm doing. I know what I want. It's my life. Let me live it.'

'You know nothing. He's not the right man for you, Ivy. He's not good enough.'

I wince, but Dermot has a point. Ivy is so sunny, so selfless, so good, and I am tortured, after all.

'He's the best man I've ever met.' Ivy steps closer to me, folding her arms over her chest.

'He's still in love with Isabella.' Dermot's gaze blazes to the wedding ring on my finger, but I told myself I wouldn't take it off until I've had justice. 'You need to give him a wide berth. You have no idea what he's capable of.' Dermot's rage has him practically foaming at the mouth.

Ivy's jaw ticks. 'I know exactly what he's capable of.'

The fight evaporates slowly from Dermot. 'Fine. Do what you want. It's your life. Just don't expect me to sit around and watch you make a car crash out of it.' Dermot stalks away without looking back.

Of all the metaphors, he chose the one that strikes the hardest.

He's right. I'm not good enough for Ivy. But as long as she wants me, I'm hers.

I'm going to Hell. But I accepted that fact a long time ago.

Chapter Forty

IVY

I offer to fetch a dustpan and brush to clean up my brother's mess, but Samuel correctly points out my hands are shaking too hard to use them. Damon ushers us into the huge kitchen/dining area and pours us a neat whiskey. Thankfully, the kids are still crashed on the couch and missed the entire heated exchange.

Caelon shuts Roxy in the lounge with them, rubbing her head. 'I suppose you have your uses,' he mutters. 'But you're not sleeping upstairs.' He turns his attention back to me. 'Are you okay?'

'I'm not the one who got punched in the face. How's your jaw?' I trace my thumb over the bruise that's already forming.

'It's fine.' Caelon leans into my touch. 'I let him have that one. Hoped it might make him feel better.'

'It's going to take more than that.' I sip my whiskey and close my eyes as the burn slides down my throat.

I hate hurting my brother. Hate disappointing him. But I can't live my life the way he wants. His words play through my head like a CD stuck on repeat. 'He said something strange. What did he mean when he said I don't know what you're capable of?'

A shadow crosses Caelon's face. 'Let's talk about it later, after we get the kids to bed.'

An hour later, after the kids have crashed out with exhaustion and are safely tucked up, I head to the kitchen with a sense of dread building in my stomach. Everywhere I turn, family photos remind me of Caelon's past and reality smacks me in the face like a sledgehammer now we're back in Dublin. I'm not sure he's ready for a future with me.

Roxy lies on her back, paws up in the air, snoring like an ogre. Caelon shoots her a filthy look as he pads across the kitchen, but I can tell he's warming to her. 'Back to the real world with a bang, right?' He's changed into those low hanging grey sweats I love, and my gaze falls to his perfectly formed ass as he opens the fridge door and pulls out two cold beers.

'Not the kind of bang I was hoping for,' I joke, but I can't force a smile. Dread knots in my stomach like a ball of wool.

'It wasn't the friendliest welcome home, but at least it's out in the open,' Caelon concedes. He rests against the kitchen counter and beckons me over with a single finger.

As I close the distance between us, I turn the word "home" over on my tongue. It's his home. Yes, I live here. But so does the ghost of Isabella, and I'm not sure there's room for both of us. Especially when he still wears her ring. I wish he'd take it off, but I'd never ask him to.

'Are you sure I'm what you want?' He asks before taking a swig from his bottle and wrapping an arm around my lower back, pulling me close. 'I don't want to hold you back.'

'You're not,' I say truthfully, leaning into him, drinking in his scent, collapsing into his solid frame. 'Are you sure I'm what *you* want?' My eyes veer to the picture on the fireplace of Caelon with Isabella, Orla and Owen.

'I've never been surer of anything.' He presses a kiss to my temple. 'Dermot was right. I'm not a good man. I've done things I'm not proud of. And I can't guarantee I won't do more things I'm not proud of.'

'Like what?' the dread in my stomach intensifies. Of all the things Dermot said, one line stuck out more than everything else.

'You have no idea what he's capable of.'

A flashback of the night Scarlett and James were here sears through my mind.

'I live for two things. My kids and revenge. I have no intention of leaving this earth until I've taken care of all of them.'

It was just the drink talking.

Wasn't it?

I've always known Caelon has a darkness in him. Hell, it was half the attraction. But he wouldn't really act on it, would he? It's one thing to be with a hot billionaire vigilante in a fictional romance, and another entirely in real life. A shudder ripples down my spine.

'It's better if you don't know. All you need to know is that I love you.' He rests his chin on the top of my head as he cradles me in his arms.

'And I love you, but if we're a partnership, you need to be honest with me.' I swallow hard, raising my face to meet his gaze. 'Is this about avenging Isabella?'

His lips purse into a tight line. 'The less you know, the better.'

'Don't do something stupid. Don't put your past in front of our future.' I cup his face and angle his chin down, forcing him to meet my stare.

'Don't you see? I need to deal with the past in order to have a future. Danny Bourke killed Isabella and I have it on good authority that he's about to wake up from his coma. Killian's been doing some digging for me. He's found evidence that Danny was paid by the O'Connors to kill my wife.' The word *wife* stings like a bee. 'If that's true, the O'Connors are going to pay with their lives. That's a promise, not a threat.'

I pause for a beat, trying to steady my hammering heart and find the right words.

I can deal with tortured, dark and pained.

I can't deal with the man I love doing something so vindictive. No matter what Jack O'Connor, Danny Bourke, or anyone else did in the past, we don't get to decide who lives or dies. 'If you do this, if you choose revenge over redemption, it's over between us.'

His molars clank as they slam together. 'You don't mean that.'

'I do. I can't be with a man fixated on revenge rather than planning a future with the person they claim to love.'

Caelon's eyes close. 'Don't make me choose, Tranquil.'

'Even if I could get over you hurting, maybe even killing a man, I'll never get over it if you got hurt or sent to prison.'

'I won't,' Caelon's eyes snap open.

'You don't know that.' A crushing tiredness settles over my skin and seeps into my bones. A mental and emotional exhaustion. First, there was the drama with Dermot, and now this. It's too much.

'There's no way in Hell I'm giving you up'.' Caelon's eyes bore into mine with an intensity that sears into my soul. He sighs heavily. 'I love you.'

But does he love me enough?

'Take me to bed.' I can't talk about this anymore tonight. I can't begin to contemplate what he might be capable of. I just need to feel the Caelon I thought I knew hold me.

'With pleasure.' He swallows the last mouthful of beer and places the bottle on the marble counter, then slides his hand beneath my legs and swoops me into his arms like he's carrying me over the threshold.

'You're sleeping in my bed tonight,' he growls, carrying me up the stairs.

My heart expands in my chest.

He hasn't had another woman in his house, let alone in his bed. He's choosing me. This proves it. All the talk of revenge is just that. Talk. It has to be.

The remnants of dread roiling in my stomach wither and I bury my face into his chest.

Chapter Forty-One

IVY

Bright light penetrates the cracks on either side of the blinds, but no amount of sunshine spilling across the floor could fully eradicate the darkness of last night's conversation. It plays through my mind like a movie. In the light of day, it feels like it had to be a dream, but acid eating at the lining of my stomach assures me it wasn't.

While I don't *think* the man I love is capable of murder, I can't rule it out. All I can do is trust that Caelon will respect my feelings on the horrendous situation, trust that he won't give me up. Trust that the prospect of a future together is enough of an incentive to keep his past from destroying him. From destroying us both.

I rub the sleep from my eyes and soak in my surroundings. Caelon's room is nothing like I imagined. I'd expected it to be dark and masculine, but it's decorated in cool shades of silver and sage.

He stirs as I untangle myself from his arms.

'Good morning, Tortured,' I whisper, kissing his neck and inhaling his scent.

'I'd be far less tortured if you didn't have to sneak out,' he grumbles, interlinking his fingers with mine and squeezing.

'The kids have been through enough. They don't need to see us together yet.' Owen's only just accepted me. I don't want to undo all the good work by confusing him when this is still so new.

'I know, I know,' he sighs, blinking the sleep from his eyes. He's so gorgeously docile. It's hard to believe I'm looking at the same man who was threatening murder last night.

He arches up, resting his weight on one elbow, hand flat on top of the Egyptian cotton sheets. A beam of sunlight blazes a trail across his bare, muscular chest and the curve of his bicep, illuminating the masculine veins on his forearm and the platinum ring on his finger.

'Are you okay?' He cocks his head.

Translation–Are *we* okay?

'Yes,' I say, though the word doesn't come out as convincingly as I intended. 'I'll see you for breakfast in a couple of hours.' I back away from the bed and tiptoe out of the room. Roxy is snoring softly at the top of the staircase. Her ears prick as I approach. The soft thwack of her tail beats against the floorboards. Someone's happy to see me.

'Come on.' I beckon her downstairs with me, towards the kitchen, and out the back door. The early morning sun does little to take the chill from my bones.

Grabbing a coffee, I settle at the table with my Kindle, hoping my latest bad boy MMC will take my mind off the fact I have one of my own.

But it's no good. Last night's conversation won't stop playing on repeat in my head. After all, it's not every day your boyfriend confesses to plotting murder.

I'm halfway through my second caffeine fix when the kids jolt down the stairs. Owen races ahead of Orla, that damned tatty teddy under his arm.

'Ivy!' Excitement taints his tone, and my heart warms. He's progressed so far in a couple of months. 'What are we doing today?' he demands, his ebony hair mussed from sleep, his bright eyes full of wonder. He's the image of his father.

Will my child look like that one day?

'There's no way in Hell I'm giving you up.'

Never in my life have I planned so much as a year ahead, but now I'm looking five, ten, fifteen years into the future, to a life with Caelon and his two adorable children. The Caelon who kissed me on the lips on the pier. The Caelon who surprises me with his underlying tenderness. The Caelon who took me to his bed last night and held me in his arms until we drifted into our dreams.

Not Caelon the crazed, revenge-seeking vigilante.

'It's Sunday, doofus.' Orla climbs onto my lap. 'It's Ivy's day off.'

'Ah, what?' Owen grumbles, tugging my elbow.

'What do you want to do?' I put my Kindle down to give him my full attention, brushing my fingers through his hair and meeting his gaze.

'Swimming, ice cream, maybe the funfair.' Hope hangs on his every word.

'We'll need to ask Daddy about that.' I reposition Orla on my lap so her bony little butt isn't digging into my thigh. 'But I don't mind if he doesn't.'

'Don't you have a family of your own you're supposed to visit?' Orla peeps up at me from under long, dark lashes. She's going to break a lot of hearts when she's older.

Owen scoffs. 'Ivy's part of our family now, *doofus,*' he says, throwing her insult back.

My blood heats as I realise how much I want it to be true. I want to be part of this family. To be Caelon's wife. I want the ring he wears on his finger to be one *I* put there.

'I hope you stay forever,' Orla whispers, snuggling into my chest.

So do I.

Ten minutes later, Caelon strides into the room in a cloud of cologne and raw masculinity. He's dressed in smart shorts and another chest-hugging polo shirt. My mouth waters at the sight of him.

'Good morning.' His deep velvety voice floats across the kitchen.

The kids abandon their cereal and run to him. My ovaries weep on either side of my achingly empty uterus. I need to get a grip.

'Dad, can we go to the funfair today? Or the circus?' Owen demands, tugging his father's hand.

'We need to put flowers on Mammy's grave,' Caelon says, 'then we're going to see Uncle James and Aunty Scarlett.'

'We are?' Orla exclaims. 'Do you think Scarlett will let me hold the baby?'

Do you think she'll let *me* hold the baby?

The thought bombards me, followed shortly by another crushing realisation. No one's invited me. The kids don't even know Caelon and I are together.

'I don't see why not.' Caelon shrugs. 'Coffee?' His attention shifts to me, his eyes roaming appreciatively over my bare thighs before landing on my face. An involuntary shiver rips down my spine.

'Earth to Ivy,' Caelon teases. 'Coffee?'

'Yes, please.' It's not as if I have anything else planned. I texted Dermot last night, hoping he'd come to his senses and finally realise I'm an adult woman who can see and sleep with whomever I choose, but I've heard nothing. It's going to take him a while to get over this one.

I suppose I could visit my parents. It's been a while. Though I'm not sure I'm ready for another, '*What are you going to do with your life?'* speech, especially not when it's become crystal clear what I want to do; marry my hot tortured boss and have stinkingly cute babies.

Caelon makes the coffee while the kids return to the table to shovel in spoonfuls of Cheerios like they haven't eaten in years. Milk splatters in every direction with each flick of their spoons, much to Roxy's delight. She licks the floor until it's gleaming.

'We'll pick up some flowers and go to the graveyard, then circle back round for you just after one," Caelon says, over his shoulder.

'Sorry?' I startle, dragged from my daydreams.

'I want you to come to dinner at James and Scarlett's,' Caelon smirks. 'Rian, Killian and Sean will be there.'

I push my chair back and slink over to him. 'Isn't it a family event?'

'Yes.' Caelon glances at the kids, who are still engrossed in their breakfast, before fleetingly brushing his lips against mine, stealing the breath from my lungs.

'Are you taking me to rub it in Rian's face?' I quip. Little does Caelon know, Rian has it bad for someone else. I have no idea who, but he had no qualms admitting it on our date.

'I'm taking you because you're my girlfriend, and I hate being more than ten feet away from you. The only thing I'm rubbing is myself against you any chance I get,' he growls into my ear.

'About last night...' I keep my voice low so the kids can't hear.

'Don't.' Unspoken words hang between us like an assassin's axe. 'I told you, Ivy, there's no way I'm giving you up.'

It's not exactly, *'I've given up all thoughts of murder and revenge,'* but for now, it'll do.

'In that case, I'll go get showered.' I take the coffee he

offers, and I'm about to stride away when something occurs to me.

'Do you want me to come to the graveyard with you?' I suck on my lower lip. This is unknown territory for both of us.

'One day,' he says solemnly, catching my hand, 'but not today.'

I squeeze his hand back and drop it before the kids see. 'I'll go and check Owen's bedsheets.' He's been mostly dry the past ten days, but there's been the odd accident.

'No need.' Caelon's lips part in a genuine smile. 'They're dry.'

'Again?'

'Yep,' he brushes a hand over the ebony stubble dotting his jaw. 'And did you notice we haven't had a "remember the time Mammy..." story for a while? I'll never let him forget her but it's probably healthier that she's not at the forefront of his mind all day, every day. Perhaps we're all finally beginning to heal.'

I hope so, because if not, and if Caelon can't move on properly with me, it'll be me who is tortured.

Chapter Forty-Two

CAELON

Isabella's mother, Jocelyn, is already at the grave when we arrive. It's not surprising. Her visits are even more frequent and regular than ours. Naturally, she's ecstatic to see the kids.

'That looks sore,' she nods at my purple-tinged jaw, curtesy of my girlfriend's brother.

'I've had worse.'

Thankfully, she doesn't pry. While she's fussing over how Orla and Owen have grown, asking about their suntans, and generally lavishing attention on them, I rest my hand on my wife's marble headstone as gently as if I was touching her face. 'I'm sorry, Isabella,' I whisper. 'Sorry it's you lying here. Sorry I couldn't save you.' I hesitate, thinking of last night, of Ivy in our bed. A fresh ripple of guilt washes over me.

But Ivy is here, living and breathing, and she's bringing all of us back to life. Owen's dry sheets are proof of it. So as much as I swore I'd never let another in my bed, it wasn't just me I was depriving of the love of a woman—it was the kids too.

I told Ivy I wouldn't give her up. It's true. I won't. But I can't give up the idea of punishing Danny Bourke and the O'Connors, either. They're going to pay. All of them.

'What are your plans for the afternoon?' Jocelyn asks the kids.

'We're going to collect Ivy, then we're going to Uncle James's house for dinner. Dad said I can take my swimming shorts. James's pool is even bigger than ours,' Owen explains excitedly.

'Ivy?' Jocelyn repeats, her eyes flipping to mine. 'You mean your new nanny?'

'Yes. It's supposed to be her day off, but she comes everywhere with us now,' Owen blabs. 'I thought she'd leave like the others, but she seems to like us.'

'She adores you,' I say. And me, apparently. I never dared to imagine I'd find love again, yet Ivy's bulldozed that notion to the ground.

'I'm glad you've found someone to help,' Jocelyn quirks a brow.

'I wasn't looking for anything. She blazed into our lives like the first rays of sun after a long cold winter.' I say, stepping back from the headstone, staring at the glittering gold writing. *Isabella Beckett. Wife, Mother, Daughter.*

'I'd like to meet her,' Jocelyn says, patting my arm.

'One day.' I turn to the kids. 'Now, say goodbye to your grandmother. Uncle James is lighting the barbecue and if he burns the food, I don't want him to have anyone to blame but himself.' I place a hand on Owen's shoulder, steering him back towards the car.

Jocelyn follows, the gravel crunching beneath our feet. 'Would you like to take the kids next weekend?' If Danny Bourke wakes up, I want the kids as far away from Ivy and me as possible. If Danny takes "a sudden turn for the worse", Ivy is going to take a hell of a lot of convincing I had nothing to do with it.

I hate lying to her.

But I can't let Danny live. Or Jack.

Not just to avenge Isabella, but so they can't hurt Ivy, or anyone else I love.

She doesn't realise it, but I'm doing this for her. For us. I don't want anything or anybody threatening the ones I love ever again. I'm protecting her. I'm protecting all of us.

'It would be my pleasure.' Jocelyn's hand dips into the pocket of her shorts and she pulls out two miniature packets of Haribo. 'Here,' she slips them in the kid's hands, and they squeal.

'See you next week,' she pats my arm again.

I hesitate at the car park gates, shifting from foot to foot. 'You know I'll never forget her, don't you? I'll always love Isabella.'

'I know.' Jocelyn smiles, her blue eyes sparkling. 'And I'm happy for you. I'm certain Isabella is too.'

Rian's car is already parked on the drive at James's mansion, along with Sean's and Killian's. We're the last to arrive.

Orla and Owen bound around to the back of the house. I slip my hand into Ivy's and we follow close on their tails.

'You okay?' I brush my thumb over hers. She looks good enough to eat in a lemon-yellow strapless sundress that clings to her curves before kicking out at the waist, stopping a couple of inches above her knee. Is it any wonder I'm head over heels in love with her?

If Rian so much as looks at her, I'm going to drown him in James's pool. I still haven't forgiven him for moving in on my woman. Mind you, if he hadn't, would I have been brave enough to give into this thing between us?

Probably not.

'I'm fine, just bracing myself in case Rian asks me my favourite sexual position again.' Her fingers squeeze mine.

'I'll tell him you like it any way *I* give it to you,' I growl, slipping my arm around her waist. I can't keep my hands off her.

'Are we going public?' Her topaz eyes snap to mine.

I shrug. 'My mother-in-law has already guessed. My parents know. Dermot knows. And my brothers thought we were sleeping together long before we technically were.'

'That just leaves Orla and Owen.' Ivy twists her lips, pausing before we round the corner and face the music. The sound of my brothers greeting my kids carries on the gentle breeze.

'I know we said we'd wait to tell the kids, but if you're serious about this, about taking on me and my baggage, I think we should tell them. It'll save setting alarms and sneaking out of each other's rooms. They clearly adore you. I think they'll be over the moon.'

'Hmm.' Ivy bites on her lower lip, unconvinced.

'Are you getting cold feet?' I push her against the brick wall, pinning her with my hips. 'I know last night's conversation freaked you out, and I don't blame you, but I'm asking you to trust me.'

'I trust you,' she says shakily. Her teeth dig into her lower lip. 'And by the way, there's nothing cold about me when you're near.' Her chest heaves and my mouth crashes against hers, our tongues colliding. I savour the taste of her with a moan.

'Where's your dad?' Rian's voice travels round the corner over the sound of low music coming from the house.

'Probably smooching Ivy.' Orla howls with laughter. 'They smooched all holidays and they think we didn't see. It's gross, but it's kind of cute, too.'

I tear my lips from Ivy's and roll my eyes. 'Well, I guess that decision has just been taken out of our hands.'

'I don't want them to think I'm trying to replace their mother,' Ivy confesses.

'They won't. We're lucky to have you. Lucky you didn't turn on your heels and run right out the door when you realised your new boss is the guy you let in your lingerie in a packed bar.'

'You need to do that again sometime. The sheer badness of it had me coming in seconds.' She squirms against the bricks.

'The badness? Not my fingers?' I yank her dress up and brush a thumb over her silk thong. She gasps.

'Okay, both.' Her hips buck against my hand and I slide the material to the side, slipping my fingers through her wetness.

I run my tongue over her lips, tracing the perfect dip of her cupid's bow. Her head rolls backwards as she looks up at me.

I'd be a fool to risk this. To risk what we have. But we can't sleep safe at night until I've dealt with the O'Connors once and for all.

Rian rounds the corner, wearing a pair of luminous yellow swim shorts and no top. He's clutching a beer in one hand and a burger in the other. He stops abruptly when he sees me pinning Ivy against the wall, her dress around her waist and my hands between her legs. His eyes widen and his lips part in a crooked smile. 'Well, well, what do we have here? Don't stop on my behalf.' He raises his hands in the air. 'Maybe I can help.'

'She wants it done properly, dickhead.' I reluctantly remove my hands from my girlfriend's underwear, smooth her dress down over her thighs, and then suck my finger, ignoring Rian's jaw as it hits the floor.

'So, you guys are official?' Rian chuckles, then takes a sip of his beer.

'We are,' I confirm, and man, it feels fucking good to say it out loud.

'Did you tell your best friend you're fucking his little sister yet?' Rian's eyes glitter.

I twist my head, giving him a full view of my bruised jaw.

Rian slaps his thighs and guffaws. 'That looks sore.'

'If you so much as think about asking my woman about her sexual preferences again, you'll find out what sore is.' I take Ivy's hand again and guide her past Rian, towards James's extravagant outdoor living area.

Killian and Sean are lounging on plush sunbeds next to James's turquoise glittering pool. They're both clutching beer bottles. Sean sips intermittently, listening as Killian speaks in a low voice. They're talking shop. I'd bet my life on it.

Owen wasn't joking, James's pool is twice the size of ours. Perhaps my big brother is trying to make up for something, although judging by the grin on Scarlett's face, he's doing okay with whatever he's got.

'Ivy!' Scarlett beams, rushing towards us. She takes one look at our joined hands and squeals. 'Ahh! Welcome to the family!'

James turns to squint at us from the barbecue, swatting smoke away from his face. He puts down the cooking utensils and joins us, slapping my back before hugging Ivy.

'Great to see you,' he says, but what he really means is, "great to see you happy". And I am happy. Though, I'll be happier when our enemies are six feet under, and Dermot has accepted me as his future brother-in-law. Because I am. Even if Ivy doesn't know it yet.

Killian and Sean stand to greet us. Killian's gaze flits between Ivy and me, taking in every micro movement. Sean strolls languidly over. He's easily the most relaxed of my brothers. I've yet to see him with a woman, but I doubt he's short of them.

'Great to see you again, Ivy,' Sean says, pressing a polite peck on my girlfriend's cheek.

Killian nods but doesn't touch Ivy. He's never been big on PDAs and since he returned from his last military tour, he's been a man of few words. 'We need to talk,' he says grimly.

Chapter Forty-Three

IVY

James and Scarlett's house is like something from a glossy society magazine. So is Caelon's, but I've grown accustomed to its grandeur and I'm far more impressed with the owner than the interior.

Scarlett fetches me a glass of champagne then guides me towards a free sunlounger. 'Tell. Me. Everything. I need details,' she squeals, flicking her hair from her shoulders. 'Didn't I tell you we were going to be great friends? Who knows? We could even end up being sisters.' She glances at the enormous solitaire engagement ring on her left hand and beams.

'Woah, calm down.' Heat flushes my cheeks. I check to see if Caelon heard, but he's strolling back around the side of the house to speak with Killian in private about something. An ominous feeling slides into my stomach.

'Ivy, where's my swimming stuff?' Orla demands, eyeing the water gleefully as if she hasn't just returned from a holiday in the sun.

'It's in the car. I'll grab it now.' I hand Scarlett my glass. 'I'll be right back.'

'And then I need details.' Scarlett waggles her eyebrows.

'Are you going for a dip, Ivy?' Rian calls. 'It looked like you could do with cooling down.' He fires a wicked smile my way. It's a good job Caelon is out of earshot.

'Very funny,' I yell, traipsing back towards the car. I hear Caelon before I see him. He sounds like he stopped roughly where he had me pinned against the wall.

I don't mean to eavesdrop, but Caelon isn't exactly being discreet.

'I want blood, not money,' he growls.

A cold chill sweeps over my skin despite the summer sun.

He promised me.

He fucking promised he'd pick me.

'You don't need to involve yourself in this. I have men that can take care of it, discreetly.' Killian's voice is even deeper than Caelon's.

'This is personal,' Caelon insists in a tone I've never heard him use before and never want to hear again.

'You've got too much to lose if something goes wrong.'

'I've been waiting years. There's no way I'm going to let the opportunity pass by me now,' Caelon snaps.

'So, you're willing to risk your own life, seeing your children grow up and living happily ever after with your girlfriend?' Killian's tone is weighted with warning.

I slam to a halt at the corner of the building.

Killian's head snaps round. His sharp eyes land on mine.

'I'm just getting the swimming stuff out the car. Sorry, I didn't mean to interrupt.' I sidestep the two men and head for the Mercedes.

'It's okay, we were done anyway.' Killian purses his lips together tightly. 'As soon as he wakes, the doctor will give us the nod. Until then, we just have to wait.' He eyes Caelon meaningfully.

'I need to burn off some energy,' Caelon announces, his torso taut with tension. 'I'm going for a walk.'

'Go with him,' Killian says to me. 'We'll take care of the kids for a while.' He grabs Caelon's arm. 'Think about it. It doesn't have to be you.'

Caelon stalks away from the house, across a manicured lawn, and I have to run to catch up. Anger burns inside me. He lied to me. After everything, he lied. He has no intention of choosing me over his past.

I follow him through a secluded pathway leading to a lower level of the garden. The sound of laughter carries on the wind from the pool, but we can't be seen.

'Let's not talk about it, Ivy,' Caelon says sharply as I catch up with him. 'The less you know, the better.'

'You promised.' My voice cracks and the air feels as though it's being ripped from my chest.

'I promised I will always choose you. And that's what I'm doing.' He turns to face me. His hands catch mine, but I shrug him off.

The sun twinkles brightly over the sea on the horizon, yet Caelon is shrouded in darkness again, that tortured look back with a vengeance.

'You're choosing your dead wife.' I glare at his ring. 'You're choosing revenge. You're choosing your masochist pride. You're choosing to ruin everything we have and risking a future with your children.'

'I'm choosing to find out the truth. I'm choosing to eliminate anyone who threatens our future. I'm choosing a life with you and the kids where we don't have to keep looking over our shoulders.' His jaw is tense. 'You have no idea what these people are capable of.'

My eyes burn with unshed tears. 'I had no idea what *you* were capable of.'

He reaches for me again and I shove him away with enough force that he steps back.

'I love you. I love your children. But I can't live with a man who is so obsessed with the past that we'll never have a future. I'll stay until you find another nanny, but consider this my notice.'

I charge up across the lawn with one hand over my mouth to muffle my strangled sobs. My chest feels like it's caving. Every breath is a battle. Every step feels like a mile. Eventually, I reach the mansion and head for the car at the front. Damon's sitting in the driver's seat, scrolling on his phone. When he spots me approaching, he leaps out.

'What's wrong?'

'I'm not well. Take me home, please.' Although I don't have a home. Not anymore.

He hesitates for a split second, glancing over my shoulder. I follow his gaze and see Caelon standing fifty meters away, grim-faced, arms folded across his chest.

Damon looks at him with a questioning expression.

Caelon offers a single stoic nod, and Damon opens the car door for me.

Chapter Forty-Four

CAELON

When I arrive home, Ivy is in her room. I hover outside her door but don't knock. There's nothing I can say to make her feel better. She has no concept of our feud with the O'Connors. It's spanned generations. My father bears the scars of their violence on his face. I bear mine on my heart. I don't expect her to understand, but I had hoped she'd trust me to deal with things my way. It doesn't mean I'm not choosing her. On the contrary, I'm choosing to protect her.

I sleep with my bedroom door open in case she wants to talk, but I don't hear the click of her door until the next morning when the kids start making noise.

'Good morning, guys.' Her enthusiasm is so forced, she sounds borderline hysterical.

I rush into the corridor in time to see her take Owen and Orla by the hand and lead them down the stairs. The damn dog is wagging her tail like a whip as the kids fuss over her.

I inhale a deep breath, then follow them to the kitchen, checking my phone for the hundredth time, in anticipation of an update from Killian.

Nothing.

Liz is in the kitchen whisking batter for pancakes. 'Morning, kids. Nutella or syrup?'

'Nutella!' they both shriek, racing to the table.

Ivy heads straight for the coffee machine. Her hands tremble as she reaches for a cup.

'Let me do that.' I rush across the room, noticing her flinch at the sound of my voice.

'Daddy!' Orla and Owen exclaim, launching themselves from the table in a race to get to me. I only wish Ivy had a fraction of their enthusiasm.

I've well and truly fucked things up.

If only I could get her to see I'm trying to keep her, my children, and myself safe.

Ivy keeps her back to me, loads a capsule into the machine, and hits the start button. When she finally does turn around, her eyes are red-rimmed, her cheeks covered in strawberry-shaped blotches, and her eyebrows knitted together in a wariness I've never seen before.

'Good morning,' I say cautiously. Thankfully, the kids are too engrossed in Liz's pancake flipping to pay any attention to the tension between Ivy and me.

'Is it?' she scowls at me. 'Have you had a change of heart? Finally come to your senses? Chosen life over death? Realised that neither your dead wife nor your girlfriend would want you to act so violently?'

'I—'

I've been so consumed with my own desires, I hadn't stopped to think about what Isabella would want.

But she isn't here to stop me because they ripped her away from us. And while I've moved on, fallen in love again, I haven't forgotten.

'Spare me the bullshit,' Ivy whispers. 'The only reason I'm still here is because I would never walk out on your children.'

As she struts towards the open French doors, the sun bounces off her blonde beach waves.

'Ivy, please,' I follow her outside, brushing a hand over her waist. She jerks away like she's been shocked.

'I gave you a choice and you chose.' She shrugs. 'You know what I think?' she says in a hushed voice, swivelling to face me.

'Tell me,' I beg. Because while she's talking to me, at least there's a chance I can make her understand. If there was no hope, she wouldn't waste her breath, would she?

She places a hand on her hip. 'You've endured more than two years of the worst type of misery.' Her expression softens a fraction. 'And I think that now you're so close to finally finding happiness again, you're fighting it. Because deep down, there's a part of you that still doesn't feel that you deserve it.'

Her words hit my heart like a hammer.

'I told you from the start I'm a bad man.'

'You're only as bad as your behaviour.' A pained expression streaks across her face. 'It's not too late. Don't do this. Choose again. We could have it all.' She rests a palm on my chest and exhales a shaky breath. Electricity hums in the air between us.

'We *will* have it all.' I place a hand on the flat of her stomach. I want her so badly. I want a future with her. I want her to carry my babies. But I want all of that and the security of knowing that no one can take it away from me.

Her eyes fall to my hand. She pauses for a beat, the significance of what I'm offering slowly sinking in. Her eyes widen. Her chin rises and her gaze finally meets mine.

The shrill ring of my phone pierces the air and shatters the moment like a bomb detonating in a glass house.

I pluck it from my pocket. Ivy rips her hand from my

chest. Pain lances her features. She takes a slow step back, shakes her head in disgust, then stalks back into the kitchen.

It's Killian. I swipe to answer.

'He's awake.'

Damon has the Bentley ready for me outside the front of the house. Killian's already spoken to him and put him on standby. After all, he might be in my service, but ultimately, Killian is his boss.

'Ready?' His face is grim as he opens the door for me.

My stomach churns with bile.

'As I'll ever be.' I smooth a hand over the front of my suit and glance up at the front window. Ivy is nowhere to be seen, but Orla's little face appears, pressing against the glass. My heart flips in my chest. I wave goodbye, blow her a kiss and pray it won't be for the last time.

Killian has paid the hospital security staff to make themselves scarce. The cameras have conveniently gone down. There will be no trace of us ever being there.

I've been over it and over it in my head so many times.

Ask the questions.

Do whatever it takes to get the answers.

Put an end to Danny.

Put an end to the O'Connors.

Put an end to the incessant rage roiling beneath my skin.

Forty minutes later, we reach the Blackrock Clinic, Dublin's most expensive private hospital. I should know. I've been paying Danny's medical bills for the past two years to keep the fucker alive so I could kill him myself.

Killian, James, Sean and Rian are already in the carpark waiting for us, grim-faced and glowering. The slight swell beneath their suits assures me they're armed. I run a hand over my own weapon, a Walther PPK nestled discreetly in the inside pocket of my jacket. A sleek, sharp folding knife is concealed in the other.

I've never killed a man before.

I've done some questionable things over the years to protect my family and our businesses, but I've never taken a life. Now the time has come, the moment I've spent years waiting for is within reach, the revenge I've been relishing suddenly doesn't seem so sweet.

It seems tragic.

But I will do whatever it takes to uncover the truth and protect my family.

My brothers nod in a silent greeting. Even Rian doesn't open his trap. There are no words. Every cell in my body vibrates with nervous anticipation. I glance at my fingers. Despite my internal turmoil, they remain steady.

We stride in through the sliding doors and are met with white walls, white floors and spotlights so bright they're blinding. The reception desk and hallways are deserted.

'Third room on the right,' Killian says without any hint of emotion.

The sound of our shoes on the hard floor echoes off the sterile walls.

When we reach the door, James places a palm on my chest, halting me. I swear he must feel the pounding of my heart.

'You don't have to do this.' His eyes are so dark, it's impossible to distinguish his pupils from his irises. 'I'll do it. You don't have to have any part in this.'

'I do.' I reach for the handle before I change my mind.

Chapter Forty-Five

CAELON

I hear the gentle beeping of a life support monitor before I see the man it's attached to.

Man? Huh, coward, more like. O'Connor's dog. Henchman. Whatever. He'll be bleeding and pleading for his life any minute now.

I slip into the room with my brothers at my heels. Adrenaline courses through my blood, fizzing through every cell of my body. My pulse pounds in my head like a war drum.

Danny Bourke lies on a trolley bed, half reclined, with his eyes closed peacefully, as if he doesn't have a care in the world. His complexion is smooth and sallow, his skinny arms tucked tightly beneath the covers from the elbows down. His biceps have wasted away beneath his sagging skin. My eyes home in on the subtle rise and fall of his chest, watching as his heart beats sturdily, while mine has barely survived.

The Danny I remember was a mountain of a man, ripped and muscular, built like a brick shithouse.

The man who lies before me is weak, withered and built like a bird.

I kick the bed and it slams against the wall with a crack.

Danny's eyes jolt open, wide and white like a rabbit trapped in a snare. They dart wildly around the room, from me to my brothers, fear flashes over his features.

'Welcome back, Danny.' I prowl closer. 'You certainly kept us waiting.

'What do you want?' he whispers. His rancid breath wafts through the air between us.

My nose crinkles. 'What do I want?' I repeat, running a hand over the gun tucked in my suit. 'Let's see...' My palm grazes my jaw. 'I want my wife to still be alive. I want her to see our children grow up. I want to watch her grow old. But seeing as I can't have any of those things, because you took them away from me,' I whip the knife from my pocket pointedly and flip it open, its blade glinting beneath the hospital spotlights, 'I want to know what happened the night you killed her. I want to know who put you up to it. And I want to know how much they paid you. And then, when I've cut off every limb, I want to know if it was worth it.'

A low guttural gasp slips from his cracked lips. 'It was an accident.'

'Bullshit.' I rest the tip of the knife in the hollow of Danny's throat.

The weight of my brothers' eyes bores into me. The room is silent bar the beeping of the monitor and Danny's sharp, ragged breaths.

I press the blade harder, not hard enough to draw blood, but enough to blanch the skin. He flinches.

'Caelon,' Killian warns me.

'I was off my head. I barely remember what happened,' Danny spits.

'But you remember who gave the order. Who paid you. Who put you up to it.' My blade pierces his skin. Crimson liquid leaks from the incision, trickling down his neck. I spent so many nights lying awake thinking about this moment, yet it doesn't feel as satisfying as I'd imagined.

Danny swallows hard, his eyes homing in on each of my brothers. His mouth parts, then closes again.

'They all want to know as much as I do. Tick tock, Danny. We're all waiting.'

His eyelids close as he sucks in a breath.

'I needed the money.' His resigned sigh reeks of desperation.

'I didn't ask about your financial affairs. I asked who ordered a hit on my wife.' I remove the knife from his flesh and hold it in front of his face. He watches as his blood trickles over the blade.

This was supposed to satiate my rage, but only now do I realise it's already gone. It has been for a while. Since Ivy's light broke through my darkness. But I've fucked that up. Why is it that everything I touch I tarnish?

I don't know if she'll ever forgive me, but I can't afford to think about that right now.

'Who ordered the hit?' I repeat in a slow, low voice. 'We can do this the easy way or the hard way. It's up to you.'

Danny shifts beneath the bedsheets. 'It wasn't supposed to be her.'

'What are you talking about?' I hiss, leaning closer.

His eyes snap to James. 'It was supposed to be Scarlett.'

'What?' James booms incredulously. The air vibrates with his wrath.

'I couldn't get within a hair's breadth of her, though. You never left her side.' Danny's gaze remains focused on James. 'Cole wanted to hurt you Becketts and the best way to do that was through your women.'

'Cole?' Killian and James bellow in unison.

Cole was Scarlett's creepy boss, the previous owner of the Luxor Lounge, who mysteriously disappeared. I assumed

James had taken care of him, but clearly James has gone soft in his old age. Love changed him. The way it's changing me.

'I'd already taken the money, spent half of it, and I couldn't deliver on the job.' Danny shrugs, an evil smirk lifting the corner of his lips. 'So, I did the next best thing and took out his brother's wife.'

'You fucking bastard.' James lunges at him and wraps his hands around his neck and squeezes.

Danny's face turns pink, then purple.

I should feel a sense of satisfaction as the life drains from his body. Instead, all I feel is a deep sense of sadness.

And it's not Isabella's face I see at the forefront of my mind. It's Ivy's.

Danny took so much from me already. I refuse to let him take any more.

I choose redemption over revenge.

I choose the future over the past.

I choose Ivy.

'Let him go!' I yank James's hands away from Danny's throat. 'It's not worth it. He's not worth it. He's taken enough from us. Don't give him any more.'

The walls are closing in. The stench of Danny's scent seeps into my nostrils and crawls over my skin. I need to get out of here. I need to tell Ivy I choose her. And I will choose her over and over again.

James steps away from the bed, the disgust etched into every line of his face mirroring my own. The skin around Danny's throat is ringed with violet bruising.

Suddenly, Danny throws back the bedsheets. I register a small, silver blade in each of his hands a split second before I feel one slice my suit open.

I watch helplessly as the other knife sinks into James's chest.

The last thing I hear before I hit the ground is Killian's roar.

Chapter Forty-Six

IVY

I snatch my phone and dial Scarlett. Seconds tick by like hours until finally she picks up. 'You're up early.'

'Where's James? Can I talk to him?'

'He's at a family meeting. He left early this morning.'

'Did he say where? Or what it's about?' There's no point trying to hide the desperation in my tone.

'He didn't say. Are you okay, Ivy? What's up?' Scarlett's concern is audible.

I have no idea how much she knows or how much James has told her.

'I take it Danny Bourke woke up?' Me and my big mouth again.

Scarlett sighs. 'Ivy, I don't ask questions and it's better if you don't either.'

'Don't you care?'

'Of course I care, but I trust James. He tells me what I need to know and protects me from the things I don't.'

'Protect you?' It hits me like a sledgehammer. Caelon thinks he's protecting me, when in reality, all he's doing is babying me, the way my family has always done. Trying to stop me from making my own decisions. Treating me like I'm fragile, when I'm far from it.

'Yes, protect me and our family. There are some things we're better off not knowing. The Becketts have dangerous enemies. I should know.'

'What do you mean?'

'The O'Connors. They're brutal. Violent. Capable of murder.'

'Is that what James told you?'

She pauses for a beat. 'Jack O'Connor killed my mother.'

I almost choke on my gasp. 'What? I had no idea.'

'How could you?' Her voice cracks with emotion. 'Look, the Beckett boys are...' she scrambles for the right word, '... unique. They're possessive. I don't doubt Caelon would kill for you, the same as James would kill for me. Is it any wonder they want answers about what happened the night Isabella died? That they want to know who is responsible?'

'I gave him an ultimatum,' I whisper. 'I told him if he picked revenge over redemption, then that would be it for us.'

I cradle my forehead in my hands.

'Did it occur to you that he might need to take revenge to find redemption? That the two are intricately interwoven?'

'I hoped I would be enough.' I hang up before Scarlett can hear the sobs that wrack my body.

An hour passes with no word from anyone. I put on a brave face. Dress the kids, read to them, play with them in the garden. I plaster on a smile and blink back the tears threatening my eyes while I label every single item of stationery ready for school tomorrow, wondering if their father will return home to see them start the new term.

What if he does something stupid and the guards take him away?

What if Danny Bourke fights back?

What if he doesn't?

What if Caelon returns and pretends everything is okay, as if nothing has happened?

Will I follow through with my threat of ending it between us?

Can I live with someone capable of such vengeance and violence?

And if the answer is yes, then what does that say about me?

That I'm just as dark and tortured as the man I'm in love with?

Dread leaks into my limbs, making them as heavy as my heart.

'Are you okay?' Liz asks, as she cleans up the breakfast dishes.

I swallow the lump of emotion clogging my throat.

I spent the night praying to every god I don't believe in making my boyfriend—or is it ex-boyfriend—come to his senses. It's like living in one of my mafia romances, only the reality is nowhere near as sexy as the fantasy.

'No, Liz, I'm not.' I sink against the kitchen countertop, gripping it for support. I squint out of the huge windows overlooking the pristinely manicured lawn. The kids are outside bouncing around with Roxy, blissfully oblivious to the devastation their father is wreaking on all of us.

'Lover's tiff?' She cocks her head to the side in a rare show of sympathy.

'It's a bit more than that, unfortunately,' I confess.

She puts down a pan she's drying and tosses the tea towel to one side. 'Don't give up on him.'

Our eyes meet. Hers crinkled at the edges, mine wide and watery. 'I'm afraid it's him that's giving up on me.'

'I don't believe that.' She places a hand on my arm. 'These

past couple of months, he's burst back to life.' She pauses for a beat. '*You* brought him back to life.'

I shake my head. 'I think there's a part of him that's gone for good.'

'Isn't there a part of all of us like that?' She steps closer. 'Haven't you ever lost anyone you cared about? Are any of us the same afterwards?'

My mind flicks to Katie. Specifically, the weeks and months following her death. I was a child, but the weight of my grief still hangs heavy today. I've had the best part of twenty years to deal with it. Caelon's had two. And while Katie died of an illness, Isabella's death was violent and cruel. I can understand Caelon's desire for vengeance, but I can't understand him acting on it.

His grief doesn't give him the right to play God.

If only he'd see sense through his pain.

'He loves you, you know,' Liz says wistfully. 'I see the way he gravitates around you. Like you're his entire world. Don't let it slip through your fingers. Whatever he's done, it's not too late.'

Maybe it isn't. Maybe he hasn't done the unthinkable yet.

'Can you watch the kids for an hour?' I hate asking, but I need to find Caelon before he does something that will destroy everything.

'Of course.'

I grab the keys to the Merc and slip out the front door. Samuel is at the gate. 'Where are you going?' he asks with a pinched face.

'I'm hoping you can tell me.' There's no way Caelon's security team doesn't know exactly where he is.

'You can't be near this, Ivy.' Samuel purses his lips.

'I might be the only person who can stop him making the biggest mistake of his life.' I thrum my fingers on the leather steering wheel. 'Open the gate and tell me which hospital.'

He pauses, staring blankly ahead. 'Blackrock Clinic. I'll let Damon know you're on your way.'

Traffic is a bitch, between countless diversions and road-works, but I make it to the hospital in less than an hour, whisper a mantra in my head over and over for the entire journey.

Please don't let me be too late. Please don't let him have done something stupid.

I abandon the Mercedes at the hospital door and rush into reception. Damon is pacing the white, soulless corridor with a grim expression on his face.

Fuck.

I'm too late.

I run towards him. His head jerks up at the sound of my sneakers squeaking. 'Is he dead?' I whisper, grabbing the lapel of his jacket.

'It's touch and go. The surgeons are operating on him now.'

'Thank God.' I exhale. 'I know what Danny did, but he doesn't deserve to die.'

'It's not Danny they're operating on.' Damon's green eyes glow with sympathy. 'It's Caelon.'

Chapter Forty-Seven

IVY

'What?' I don't recognise the strangled voice that leaves my mouth. 'But I saw him this morning. He was fine.'

Shock seeps under my skin, chilling me to the bone until I'm shaking uncontrollably.

'He went to talk to Danny Bourke, but it seems he was expecting the visit. Danny was armed with two blades hidden beneath the sheets.' Damon exhales a pained breath. 'I blame myself.'

The blood drains from my face. 'Where is he? Can I see him?'

'In surgery. The doctor will let us know when they've finished operating.' Damon leads me through a door to a family waiting area. It's equally white, bright and clinical as the corridor, but twice as suffocating.

'Where was he stabbed?' An image of Alexander Beckett's scarred cheek fills my mind.

'His stomach. He has a lot of internal bleeding. I'm sorry.' Damon takes my hand and squeezes it reassuringly. 'James was luckier,' he adds as an afterthought.

'James?' I squawk as the door bursts open.

Scarlett's hair hangs wildly over her silver eyes. Her complexion is as white as the walls. 'What's going on? I want to speak to a doctor.'

'Oh, Scarlett.' I run to her and we collapse into each other's arms. Three security guards linger in the doorway. James clearly doesn't take any chances with his fiancée's protection.

'The doctors will be along as soon as they can. James's wounds aren't critical.'

Scarlett shakes her head. 'I can't believe this could happen. Where is Danny Bourke now?' Her eyes narrow.

Damon clears his throat. 'I believe Killian is dealing with him.' His gaze falls to the floor. 'I offered to take care of it, but the Beckett brothers like to deal with some matters personally.'

'Caelon will be okay. He's a fighter. They all are.' Scarlett takes my hand which I hadn't noticed was shaking until she stills it.

'What if he's not? What if he doesn't make it?' The prospect of a world without Caelon makes my stomach bottom out. I blink back the tears. I swear to God if anything happens to Caelon, if he doesn't make it, I'll find Danny Bourke and kill him slowly and painfully myself.

Finally, I can appreciate how Caelon felt for the past two years. The rage, the horror, the devastation of having someone you love ripped from your life.

Finally, I understand his motivation for coming here in the first place.

Fucking ironic.

Hysterical laughter bursts from my chest and once it starts, I can't stop, the sounds echoing round the room like a wild animal. Scarlett and the security guys watch on warily. I open my mouth to tell them what's so funny, but I can't get the words out. I pray to fuck I get to say them to Caelon one day. To tell him I understand.

My laughter morphs into huge hiccupping sobs that rack my ribcage. I crumple forwards in a heap, rocking back and forth in a rhythm that does nothing to soothe me.

Random thoughts drip into my brain like a tap.

What if Owen and Orla lose another parent?

How can one family who supposedly has it all experience so much pain?

A clock on the wall ticks in the background. Time stops for no one, but each minute feels like an hour.

A doctor appears in the door, and both Scarlett and I jump to our feet expectantly.

He's wearing dark green scrubs and a serious expression. 'Scarlett?' his jade-hued eyes dart between us.

'That's me,' she whispers, gripping my arm, her finger digging tightly into my skin.

'James is out of surgery. He's going to be fine. A few scars, but his wounds are superficial. He's asking for you.'

'Oh, thank God.' Her shoulders sag and the breath rushes from her mouth with a whoosh.

'And Caelon?' I swallow thickly.

The doctor's expression turns darker. 'He's still in surgery. I'll give you an update as soon as I know more.'

'Will you be okay?' Scarlett asks.

'I'll take care of her,' Damon declares, stepping forwards and ushering Scarlett out the room.

'Go to him.' I swat Scarlett away as the envy eats my insides alive. I wish it was my man asking for me.

I retake my seat, resting my head in my hands.

Damon slides into the chair next to me. 'He couldn't do it, you know.'

I tilt my face to meet his eyes. 'What do you mean?'

'Caelon. He wasn't going to hurt Danny. He got the answers he needed with minimal force. Sean told me he urged James not to hurt Danny, either. Said they should all choose the future over the past. I thought you should know.'

I cradle my head in my hands. He chose me. He got his answers, and he chose me. But look at the price he's paying for it. If I hadn't had intervened, opened my big mouth, maybe it would be Danny in surgery and not the man I'm in love with.

What have I done?

Three hours later, Alexander and Vivienne Beckett burst through the doors with stricken faces. Alexander's scar is another reminder of just how much the Becketts have been through.

'Any update?' Vivienne rushes to me, fingers clasping her diamond necklace. She's aged ten years since I saw her in Portugal.

'Not yet.'

Alexander beckons Damon into the corridor.

I catch scraps from their heated, hushed words.

Cole is responsible.

Who the fuck is Cole?

It's impossible to hear anything over Vivienne's nervous chatter. The woman could talk for Ireland. 'Where are the children? Where is Samuel? How many security staff are at the house?'

I do my best to answer while trying to eavesdrop.

Heavy footsteps thud along the corridor. My head yanks up expectantly. Please let this be the doctor with good news. Please.

But it's not the doctor.

'Dermot.' I jump up and rush towards him. His familiar cologne wraps around me like a security blanket.

'Ivy.' he pulls me against his chest. 'Any news?'

'Not yet.'

He steps back to scan me, probably searches for injuries, but all my hurt is on the inside.

Dermot exhales heavily. 'Rian called me,' he explains. He greets Vivienne with a peck on the cheek and murmurs a few words of comfort.

'I wouldn't have thought you'd care if he lives or dies,' I say.

'Of course I care. I love Caelon like a brother,' he snorts indignantly. 'I just didn't expect him to actually *become* my brother.'

'I hope he lives to get the chance.' I pinch the bridge of my nose.

'He will.' Dermot drapes his arm over my shoulders and pulls my head towards him. 'He has to. Because I will never forgive myself for being so damn hard on him about you if he doesn't. I just want what's best for you.'

'Caelon is what's best for me. I know you want me to have a high-flying career and do something with my life, but there's only one thing I've ever really wanted.'

'And that is?' Dermot lowers his face to mine.

'To be a mother.' I bite my lip. 'I want a family of my own. A husband who loves me. I know it's old-fashioned, and those women who burned their bras will be turning in their graves, but it's what I want. And I want all of that with Caelon, Orla and Owen.'

'Are you sure? You've always gravitated towards broken things, as if you could single-handedly fix them. Is that what this is?'

'No! And I've never been surer of anything in my life. I

want Caelon, whatever he's done. I just need him to live long enough for me to tell him.'

More footsteps approach. I leap to my feet, expectantly. 'Doctor,' I hear Alexander say. 'What's happening?'

'I have an update,' he says, but his tone doesn't leave a lot of room for hope. 'Where's Ivy?'

Chapter Forty-Eight

CAELON

I feel as if I've done twelve rounds with Conor McGregor in a boxing ring. Everything hurts. I have more tubes and wires than an electric switchboard. But the second I see Ivy's face, all that evaporates.

'Caelon.' She flies into the room and launches herself onto my bed. The familiar scent of pomegranate surrounds me like a blanket.

'Easy tiger,' I warn her with a wince.

She scans me intently, taking in the tubes and the white sterile dressing over my stitches.

'Thank God you're okay.' Her chest heaves out a sigh of relief. 'I've been worried sick.'

'You can't get rid of me that easily, Tranquil.' Her nickname is uncannily suitable because the second she's by my side, that's exactly how I feel. Her presence alone is enough to heal half my wounds, the ones on my heart, at least.

'Are you in pain? The doctors said it was touch and go for a while. You frightened the shite out of me.'

'I'm fine. I will be, anyway.' It's a battle to breathe and

every minute movement is agony, but thank God I'm alive to feel it. 'You came.'

'Of course I came. For a while there I thought you wouldn't make it.' She brushes her thumb over the side of my face. Her eyes dart over every inch of me, like she's still not convinced. 'And do you want to hear the funny thing? All I wanted was to murder someone.'

A deep burst of laughter bolts from my chest, followed by a sharp pain slicing through my abdomen. Fucking stitches.

'Finally, I get it.' Her hand falls to my chest, hovering over my heart. 'I get why you felt the need to punish the man who caused you so much pain.'

Killian beat her to it, according to Rian, but Ivy doesn't need to know that.

'And I get that obsessing over the past isn't going to help the future. When the blood was spilling out of me earlier, all I could think of was you. I thought I'd find comfort in retribution, but the only place I ever truly found comfort was in you.' I take her hand in mine, interlacing our fingers. 'You are my future, Ivy. I choose you and the kids, and hopefully two more kids. I will always choose you.'

'You want to have more babies?' she squeaks.

'I want you to have *my* babies. I want to watch your stomach swell with my children. You were born to be a mother. You brought me back to life, gave me hope when I had none. You give and give and give and give time and again, to me and to my kids. I'm going to give you everything you ever wanted and so much more.'

'I'll never force you to choose anything again. I'm yours.'

'There are things we'll encounter that you won't like, but we'll deal with them together. The threat is far from over, unfortunately. Danny was paid to take out Scarlett, but when he couldn't get to her, he went after Isabella instead.'

'Paid by the O'Connors?'

'No, by someone else. There are people who want to hurt my family. There will always be people who want to hurt my family. With a profile like ours, there's always someone who's going to want what we've got and if they can't have it, they don't want us to have it either. We're going to need to double security again. You don't go anywhere without Samuel, do you hear me?'

She nods. 'Who's Cole?' she asks

'What?'

'I heard Damon and your dad talking.'

'He's no one. A loose end I assumed James had taken care of. Killian is on the case.' God help him when he catches him.

'I'm not going to ask, but I trust you'll tell me if I need to know.'

'Of course.' My fingers brush over hers. She hasn't noticed yet.

I stare at our joined hands pointedly until she follows my line of sight. Confusion mists her eyes for a split second before they lift to mine.

'Where's your ring?' she asks, scanning the small table beside the bed.

The doctors cut it off when I had surgery, but I was going to take it off, anyway. 'I've decided not to wear it anymore.'

I watch as Ivy's throat bobs. 'Because you got answers?'

'Because I'm making room for the one you're going to put there.' My lips lift in a small smirk.

'Confident, aren't you?' she teases.

'Don't act cool now. I've been tortured enough,' I sigh.

'Let's just get you better first, so we can practise making those babies.' She kisses the back of my hand. 'Dermot's downstairs in the waiting room.'

'Oh fuck, don't let him up. He'll probably slice open my stitches and string me up by my intestines.'

'Actually, he was worried about you.' She quirks a brow.

'He said he thought of you like a brother, but didn't expect you to actually become his brother.'

'So, we're forgiven?'

'Not entirely, but after everything, we will be. Maybe if he has you to boss around, he'll finally stop babying me.'

'He'd better put on one hell of a stag do when the time comes,' I tease. 'Speaking of which, I need to organise James's.'

'Huh, one day at a time, Tortured. Let's just get you better first.'

'Lie with me.' I pat the bed. Ivy gently curls herself around my body, careful not to touch my torso. The soft purr of her slow soft breath is the perfect sleep soundtrack. 'This is the best medicine of all.'

'I love you, Caelon Beckett.'

'I love you Ivy Beckett-To-Be,' I murmur. The desire to sleep slithers over me.

'If that's your idea of a proposal, you may need to rethink it,' she tuts, nestling her face against my arm.

'I'll be the prince and you be the princess; it's a love story, baby, just say yes,' I croak.

'I knew you were a secret Swiftie, but you got the words wrong!' she exclaims, tears welling in her eyes.

'No, baby, I got them just right.'

My eyelids flutter closed and I drift off to the sound of her soft laughter.

EPILOGUE

November

Ivy

It's a balmy twenty-five degrees in St Barths and Caelon and I are basking in the sunshine on Flamands Bay. The kids are with their new nanny, Nikkita. I take care of them most of the time, but Caelon insisted we need time together, too. Especially given we've decided to try to expand our family sooner rather than later.

Scarlett and James got married here last week in the most beautiful, intimate ceremony. We decided to stay on for another week by ourselves when they left for their honeymoon.

'Do you think the dog's okay?' Caelon asks. He and Roxy bonded while he was recovering from his surgery at home. The two of them are joined at the hip, whether it's on the couch —Italian leather or not — or in the garden. Roxy follows him round like a lovesick puppy. I can't blame her. He's pretty fucking spectacular, even if I do say so myself.

'Liz and Samuel are probably spoiling her.' I swat a hand

in front of my face. 'Let me rub some cream on your back.' I roll up one of the hotel's plush daybeds and straddle my fiancé's backside. The sunlight glints off the enormous diamond ring on my left hand as I reach for the sunscreen.

Caelon proposed properly three weeks after he was discharged from the hospital, when he'd had the chance to meet my parents and ask their permission. I'm not sure they were utterly convinced it's the right move for me, but they've finally accepted I'm old enough to make my own decisions. And Dermot couldn't stay mad at Caelon after everything that had occurred, especially given that they're going to be brothers now. We've yet to set a date for the wedding, but we will, soon.

'Only if I can rub you down afterwards.' Caelon twists his head to face me. The sight of his burning eyes is enough to send a lightning bolt of desire flashing through my core.

'That's exactly what I was hoping you'd say.' I shimmy my hips, wiggling on top of him.

As I massage the sunscreen into his broad, strong shoulders, I trace the lines of the tattoo that turns me on so much. 'When did you get this ink?'

'A couple of years ago.'

'What's the significance of the phoenix and the flames?'

'At the time, it was the largest design the artist could offer,' he shrugs. 'I wanted to feel the pain of the needles everywhere. I wanted to hurt on the outside, like I did on the inside. But you know what the phoenix represents?' Caelon flips beneath me, so I'm resting on his pelvis instead of his ass cheeks. I squeal, but he steadies me with two strong hands.

'The Bennu bird that bursts into flames upon its death? I studied Egyptian mythology in high school, but that's as deep as my knowledge goes.'

'As the tattoo artist was inking me, he told me the story. In Greek mythology, the phoenix is a legendary bird that after its death is reborn from its ashes, signifying immortality and renewal. The phoenix rising represents the circle of life, death and rebirth. I didn't believe any of it, of course. Rebirth seemed like a load of bollocks until I met you.'

'And now?'

'Now I am the phoenix, reborn after death, overcoming adversity and beginning a new life. And you, Tranquil, are the hot flames forcing me upwards, licking my skin and scorching my soul, forcing me up from the darkness, pushing me out of my comfort zone. I was ice when we met. You were fire. Opposites attract, right?'

'They certainly do.' That darkness that attracted me in the beginning still lingers, but these days he's not afraid to let me shine a light on it and live it with him. 'I'm so glad that life is with me.' I lean down to kiss his lips.

'Me too.' He runs his hands over my waist as his cock stirs underneath me. 'Finally, I've stopped beating myself up about things. Finally, I feel like I've been through enough. No amount of torturing myself will change the past. Which is why I'm fully focused on the future. And I plan on making the most of every second of it.'

The sound of waves crashes invitingly in the distance while the scent of summer lingers on the warm breeze whipping through my hair and kissing my face. It's utter paradise.

'You know you deserve to be happy.' I cup his face with my hand.

'Thanks to you, I finally believe it.'

'Come on.' I leap up, reaching for his hand, lacing my fingers between his, tugging him from the day bed. 'Let's soak up this moment. We'll be back in Dublin before we know it.'

We're the only two on the small, secluded beach. The white sand seeps between my toes as we stride towards the turquoise glittering sea.

'It's been a crazy summer.' Caelon snakes his hands around

my waist, his black eyes boring into mine with that intensity that snared me in the first place. 'I found myself in you, Ivy, but God woman, I love losing myself in you too.' The air crackles with an invisible charge.

As much as I've loved seeing Caelon come back to life, seeing him smiling and laughing, his broody tortured look will always be my kryptonite.

I trace the hard planes of his six-pack as his lips crash onto mine in a blaze of heat and need. Our teeth clash as we claw at each other with an animalistic urgency. His hand reaches for my bikini and tears it from my body with two sharp tugs.

My moans fill his mouth as I fumble to undo his swimming shorts. 'Get on all fours.' He nudges me towards the warm sand.

I do as I'm told, with pleasure, baring my backside to him. I want this as much as he does.

He drops to his knees behind me and lets out a low growl as he devours me with his eyes. 'You're weeping for me.' I watch over my shoulder as he licks his lips like he's starving.

'Still like it rough?' he growls, folding himself over me and sinking his teeth into the back of my shoulder.

His face dips and he offers my slit one long, languid lick before plunging his cock into me so deep it hits my stomach.

I cry out in pain, but as he slides back and sinks himself inside me again, that pain quickly morphs into a decadent, depraved pleasure. Thick, strong fingers dig into my hips, hard enough to mark the skin as he pummels into me relentlessly.

'Harder,' I pant, thrusting against him. I love how he's not afraid of hurting me, love how he trusts my body can take him, the way it's made to. I've never felt more alive. I'm teetering on the delicate edge of that pain/pleasure threshold and when I fall, it's going to be catastrophic.

'I love how you take my cock,' he murmurs, licking the spot on my shoulder where his teeth nipped.

I pant, grinding back on him. As my orgasm builds, my clit throbs, begging for attention. 'I need your fingers, too.'

'So greedy.' He reaches round until his fingers find my sweet spot. I cry out in relief as he pinches, rolls and rubs. 'I need you to come, Ivy, because I am seconds away from filling you up. Maybe this time I'll put a baby in there.'

My eyelids squeeze tight as every muscle in my body goes taut. He pulls himself almost all the way out of me before slamming back into me, and I am gone, catapulting into the most devastating release of my life. My core clenches. Pure primal pleasure vibrates through every single cell in my body.

'Fuck,' he bites out before sinking his teeth into the skin of my shoulder as he spills himself into me. His hips still and his grip on my waist loosens. He rests his cheek on my back as he struggles to catch his breath. My knees are chafed from the sand, but a deep sense of satisfaction overrides all of my discomfort.

'Are you okay, sweetheart?' He asks through his own ragged breaths.

'I'm not okay. I'm destroyed, in the most decadent way,' I admit. Even though I've wanted a baby for a while now, I almost hope it doesn't happen right away. Trying is so much fun.

His lips blaze a trail of kisses across my exposed shoulders as he slides out of me. Come drips between my thighs and on to the sand. 'Let's go get you cleaned up.' He motions to the sea. 'Then we can do it all again.'

'You're a bad man, Caelon Beckett,' I tease, slipping my hand in his. 'Just not in the way you thought you were.'

'I'm *your* bad man, Tranquil.'

'You bet you are. Always and forever.' I kiss the back of his hand as the sun kisses us from above.

. . .

Click here for a special extended bonus of Caelon & Ivy's wedding.
https://dl.bookfunnel.com/j5lf0bbpo3

Want more of the Beckett Brothers?
Check out Killian Beckett's story, RUIN ME.
Ruin Me: A hot, forbidden, bodyguard romance (The Beckett Brothers Book 3)

RUIN ME BLURB:
AVERY:

I'm a psych graduate turned glamour model, but it's not as glamorous as it sounds when I've got a stalker leaving black calla lilies in my dressing room with little love notes that say, "I'm coming for you."

Cue my worst nightmare: needing a bodyguard. But not just any bodyguard—Killian Beckett, the infuriating CEO of a global security empire, former soldier, and certified grouch.

Killian's all hard muscle, military precision, and absolutely zero charm. He insists on hovering around like I'm some kind of fragile damsel in distress.

Newsflash: I'm not. And his 'no-nonsense' attitude drives me straight up the wall. The guy radiates disapproval—of my job, my dates, my wardrobe. You name it, he's judging it.

Unfortunately, Mr Control Freak also looks like he was sculpted by the gods, and smells like temptation itself.

The more time we spend sparring, the more I realise there's something buried under all that brooding. Something damaged. Something that just might ruin us both if I get too close.

Sleeping with my bodyguard?
Bad idea.
Falling for him?
Absolutely fatal.

KILLIAN:

Babysitting a spoiled celebrity wasn't how I planned on spending my days, but when Avery's name lands on my desk, I can't say no, even if she's trouble wrapped in taffeta.

Avery is everything I can't stand: reckless, loud, and she lives for attention. Day and night, her smart mouth tests my patience, and her curves increasingly test my control.

I don't even like the woman, but my God, do I want her. But I can't cross that line. Instead, I watch, I wait, and I fight —both the outside threats and the escalating pull between us.

But the battlefield I learned to survive on is nothing compared to the war Avery stirs up inside me.

Getting involved with a client is the ultimate risk in my world, but when it comes to her, I'll risk it all.

Even if it ruins me...

Get RUIN ME here...

Come hang out with my at my Facebook reader group, Lyndsey's Book Lushes... https://www.facebook.com/groups/530398645913222

ALSO BY L A GALLAGHER

WRECK ME

SCARLETT:

Pole dancing at the most exclusive 'Gentlemen's Club' in the country is lucrative, though the men are anything but gentle. They're all desperate to take the only significant possession I have–my virginity.

I've spent five years hiding in plain sight, burying my head in my books, courtesy of a scholarship at Dublin's most prestigious college. But now, for the first time in my life, I feel seen. Wanted. Desired. And I've awakened a need I never knew I had.

Enter James Beckett, a billionaire bachelor with a reputation as famous as his family's whiskey empire, and he wants *me* to be his fake girlfriend until he conquers the next part of his empire.

He'll even tutor me through my final exams... and anything else I require tuition in...

Our arrangement will either secure my future, or shatter my world...

JAMES:

Yet another sex scandal means I'm heartbeat away from being fired as CEO from my own family's whiskey distillery, unless I can prove to my father and The Board that I've shed my playboy reputation.

The last thing I want is a showpiece society wife.

Especially when I'm obsessed with The Luxor Lounge's newest pole dancer.

At only twenty-three, Scarlett radiates an innocence that drives me wild. Turns out, my little dancer is a virgin.

Fooling around with my fake girlfriend was *always* part of my plan.

Falling for her *wasn't*.

She's everything I crave, but everything my father forbids.

Even if I can convince him that Scarlett is the one for me, she's been keeping a secret.

One that could wreck me...

Get WRECK ME here...

RUIN ME

AVERY:

I'm a psych graduate turned glamour model, but it's not as glamorous as it sounds when I've got a stalker leaving black calla lilies in my dressing room with little love notes that say, "I'm coming for you."

Cue my worst nightmare: needing a bodyguard. But not just any bodyguard—Killian Beckett, the infuriating CEO of a global security empire, former soldier, and certified grouch.

Killian's all hard muscle, military precision, and absolutely zero charm. He insists on hovering around like I'm some kind of fragile damsel in distress.

Newsflash: I'm not. And his 'no-nonsense' attitude drives me straight up the wall. The guy radiates disapproval—of my job, my dates, my wardrobe. You name it, he's judging it.

Unfortunately, Mr Control Freak also looks like he was sculpted by the gods, and smells like temptation itself.

The more time we spend sparring, the more I realise there's something buried under all that brooding. Something damaged. Something that just might ruin us both if I get too close.

Sleeping with my bodyguard?

Bad idea.

Falling for him?

Absolutely fatal.

KILLIAN:

Babysitting a spoiled celebrity wasn't how I planned on spending my days, but when Avery's name lands on my desk, I can't say no, even if she's trouble wrapped in taffeta.

Avery is everything I can't stand: reckless, loud, and she lives for attention. Day and night, her smart mouth tests my patience, and her curves increasingly test my control.

I don't even like the woman, but my God, do I want her. But I can't cross that line. Instead, I watch, I wait, and I fight—both the outside threats and the escalating pull between us.

But the battlefield I learned to survive on is nothing compared to the war Avery stirs up inside me.

Getting involved with a client is the ultimate risk in my world, but when it comes to her, I'll risk it all.

Even if it ruins me...

Click here to learn more about RUIN ME.

Falling For The Rockstar At Christmas

THE COLDEST HOLIDAY OF THE YEAR IS ABOUT TO GET BLISTERINGLY HOT...

SASHA

Ten years ago, I inherited our family castle and sole care of my youngest sister. More Cinderella, than Sleeping Beauty, at the mere age of twenty-eight I have a teenager to raise and a hotel to run. If the hotel is to survive past Christmas, I need a lottery win, a miracle, or Prince Charming himself to sweep in with a humongous... wad of cash.

When my super successful middle sister announces she's coming home for the holiday season, I'm determined to put my problems aside and make this the most fabulous Christmas ever. Especially as it might just be the last one in our family home.

I didn't factor in the return of my first love, Ryan Cooper. Back then he was the boy next door. Now, he's a world famous singer/song writer. We were supposed to go the States together. He left without me. Now he's back. Rumour is he has writers block. Apparently this is a last-ditch attempt to find inspiration before his record label pulls the plug permanently.

And guess where he wants to stay? You have it in one- the most inspiring castle hotel in Dublin's fair city.

Every woman in the city wants to pull this Hollywood Christmas cracker. Except me.I'm going to avoid him at all costs.

Easier said than done when he's parading around under my roof, with enough heat exuding from his molten eyes to melt every square inch of snow from the peaks of the Dublin mountains...

Falling For The Rock Star At Christmas is an OPEN DOOR steamy, love conquers all, stand alone romance, with no cliff hanger- and a guaranteed happy ever after.

Get FALLING FOR THE ROCKSTAR AT CHRISTMAS here...

Falling For My Forbidden Fling

WHAT GOES ON TOUR STAYS ON TOUR, RIGHT?

CHLOE

Even the name **Jayden Cooper** sends a hot flush of irritation through my veins. His rockstar brother might be about to marry my darling sister, but that does **NOT** make us family.

Thankfully, there's a continent separating me from his ridiculously attractive but super-smug face. And his arrogant tongue.

I'm rapidly carving my name in the glittering world of celebrity event management... and what better event to manage than the final farewell tour of my sister's fiancé, Ryan Cooper.

It's the biggest gig of my career.

Eight cities.

Eight concerts.

Eight opportunities to propel my business to a global level.

I couldn't turn it down if I wanted to.

The catch?

It involves working with closely with Ryan's agent– his brother, Jayden-Super-Smug-Cooper.

Going on tour with Jayden is almost as inconvenient as the hate-fuelled lust that steals the air straight from my lungs every time he's near.

Someone somewhere is testing me, but I've survived worse. And I'll survive him.

As long as I don't melt under the intensity of his smug but admittedly smouldering stare ...or fall foul of the talents of the aforementioned arrogant tongue...

Especially when technically...like it or not, we're about to be related.

JAYDEN

I've been through hell to get to where I am today.

I'm *the* best agent in Hollywood's cut-throat industry because I clawed and dragged myself there inch by excruciating inch.

Which is why I refuse to be bossed around by a pushy, Prada-wearing princess when it comes to organising my Rockstar brother's farewell tour. I've got bigger fish to fry, starting with upholding a promise I made a lifetime ago...

But Chloe is about to find out the hard way, what goes on tour stays on tour.

Get FALLING FOR MY FORBIDDEN FLING here...

I'M TRYING TO PROTECT HER. SHE'S TRYING TO KILL ME- ONE INDECENT LITTLE BLACK DRESS AT A TIME.

VICTORIA

As a student doctor, I deal with bullet wounds on a regular basis, but one teeny nightclub shooting is all it takes for my sister and her rock star husband to send me a new bodyguard/ babysitter.

The last person I expect to turn up is Archie "can't-bear-to-look-you-in-the-eye" Mason.

Now we're roommates until graduation. I can't turn around without tripping over him. If only I could trip underneath him. Because he is every bit as alluring as he was five years ago. And equally as unavailable.

But when my night terrors result in us sharing the same bed, our situation sparks a brand new danger.

One that could hurt both of us irreparably...

ARCHIE

I've been *obsessed* with Victoria Sexton for years.

If my boss and friend, Ryan Cooper, had any idea how bad I have it for his wife's little sister, he'd sack me on the spot.

Living with her is testing every inch of willpower I possess.

How can I watch her back when I can't stop imagining her on it?

Falling For My Bodyguard

DATING IN THE DEEP END

Savannah:

When He-Who-Has-Never-Been-Named knocked me up and ceremoniously knocked me down with the revelation, "I'm actually married," I fled back to Dublin. There, I dusted off my big girl (maternity) pants and launched my blog, chronicling my life as "Single Sav."

Fast forward six years, and I've built a lucrative empire on that premise, which is precisely why I haven't so much as looked at the opposite sex for over half a decade.

Well, apart from slyly perving on my twin daughters' swimming coach, Ronan Rivers, a former Olympic gold medalist.

The man is ridiculously easy on the eyes. He's also a complete manwh*re who lives to torment me with his filthy mouth and decadent innuendos.

When Coral Chic, Ireland's hottest new swimwear brand, offers me a million euros to represent their new swimwear range, it's impossible to turn down. Becoming the face and body of that campaign has the potential to take my Single Sav brand global.

But there's one tiny problem... I can't swim and the photo shoots are in the sea.

When Ronan offers to give me a crash course in the deep end, the only thing I'm drowning in is his mesmerising baby blues.

I've built my entire brand on being single.

The one man who can save me is also the same man who can sink me...

Ronan:

I've been obsessed with Savannah Kingsley since she crashed into my Aston Martin two years ago, but Single Sav is the one woman I can never have.

Which is precisely why I spend Saturday mornings tormenting her with my tongue, and Saturday nights wishing I could tease her with it, instead of embarking on yet another meaningless, lackluster liaison.

When fate forces us together in the form of one-to-one swimming lessons, her skimpy yellow bikini betrays the extent of her body's baser needs and no amount of water can dampen the sizzling attraction between us.

But while she's floundering in the shallows, I'm already in deep.

Can I turn the tide and persuade her to shed her single status?

Click here for Dating In The Deep End

Dating In The Deep End: A hot, single parent romcom! (Dating In Dublin)

DATING THE DELINQUENT

Being with a bad boy never felt so good...

Ashley:

I've always played by the book. As the principal of a prestigious all-girls Catholic school, my life is as orderly as the plaid on my students' skirts. My future was perfectly planned—until a humiliating public proposal ended my decade-long relationship.

It turns out, playing it safe was the riskiest move of all...

Now it's time to let loose.

Which is precisely why I've decided to swap my notions of a ring for an orgasm-fueled fling...

Enter Damien, my younger, intoxicatingly handsome new mechanic. With his rough, oil-covered hands and dirty mouth, he's the perfect distraction—to the point he's ALL I can think about.

Our nights together are explosive, but the days we spend together are what could truly burn my future to the ground.

Because it turns out, Damien is even badder than I could have ever imagined...and it's not just my heart that's on the line—it's my entire world.

It's time to choose between my good girl reputation and the bad boy who's hijacked my heart...

Damien:

Falling for a saint was never in the cards for this sinner...

Life's taught me that sometimes you have to take the fall to protect what's important. I paid a price in the shadows for reasons only I know. Now, I keep to myself, avoiding complications—until Ashley walks into my garage with an overheating motor and an urgent pressure issue—in her panties...

She's everything I'm not—polished, composed, and completely out of my league. But her eyes tell me she's looking for an escape, and I'm reckless enough to offer her one.

But with each day that passes, the weight of my past grows heavier, threatening to pull us both under.

She thinks I'm just a bad boy, but if she knew the truth, it could unravel everything.

Now, I'm faced with the hardest choice: keep hiding the darkness within or let it come to light, risking the only connection that feels real...

My Book

Dating The Delinquent: A hot reverse-age-gap, opposites-attract romance. (Dating In Dublin)

DATING FOR DECEMBER

Ava:

My perpetually single status hardly serves as a shining advertisement for HeartSync, the dating agency I own. Nor is it likely to convince my incredibly successful movie star brother, Nate, to invest in my business. Which is precisely why I agree to fake-date Cillian "can't-crack-a-smile" Callaghan for the month of December.

Sure, his role as a stoically single father and a notoriously grumpy divorce lawyer is far from ideal, but his silver eyes, sculptured shoulders and sharp tongue tick all the right boxes.

Even boxes that are supposed to remain, ahem, unticked...

One mistletoe kiss sparks a lust that could melt Lapland, and frosty fake dates blaze into something feverishly real...

Cillian:

I'm the country's most successful divorce lawyer. It doesn't take a genius to figure out why I don't date. Add in the fact that I'm a full-time single dad, even if I had the inclination, I don't have the time. But when my cheating ex blows back into town, the only way I can convince her it's over for good is by fake-dating someone else...

Enter Ava Jackson, with her infectious laugh, long legs, and luscious lips.

Throughout December, her witty one-liners and effortless bond with my daughter thaw my every defence.

She's everything I never knew I needed.

I'm an expert at breakups... but perhaps this Christmas, it's time to master a love that lasts...

Click here for Dating For December

ACKNOWLEDGMENTS

Thank you so much for reading Redeem Me. Without you, dear readers, I wouldn't be able to dream up brooding billionaires and call it work! I'm beyond grateful to all of you that read my words. I hope you enjoyed Caelon & Ivy's story. I can't wait to bring you Killian & Avery.

I need to say a massive thank you to my beta readers, Jennifer Brooks-Brown, Kathy Mercure, and Katy Pyle. I really appreciate you!! 🩶 And to my exceptionally patient friend and helper, Lona McCombie!

Thanks to all the lovely members of my Facebook reader group, **Lyndsey's Book Lushes**. I appreciate your friendship and support, and I love our daily check-ins, the inappropriate memes, and just hanging out with you all.

If you'd like to hang out with us too, we'd love to have you. https://www.facebook.com/groups/530398645913222

A massive thank you to my bookish besties, Sara Madderson and Margaret Amatt. I don't know what I'd do without both of you.

Last but not least, thank you to my endlessly patient husband who listens to my ideas, supports my dreams, and helps with my research! 😏

If you enjoyed Redeem Me, please consider leaving review on Amazon, Goodreads & Book Bub.

ABOUT THE AUTHOR

L A Gallagher writes swoon-worth contemporary romance featuring billionaire bad-boys, blush-inducing steam, and copious amounts of glamour. She lives in the west of Ireland with her own book boyfriend (that accent—swoon!), two crazy kids, and an even crazier fur baby.

Come hang out at her Facebook reader group Lyndsey's Book Lushes to find out more! https://www.facebook.com/groups/530398645913222

Or check out her Lyndsey Gallagher books here...
https://www.amazon.com/Kindle-Store-Lyndsey-Gallagher/s?rh=n%3A133140011%2Cp_27%3ALyndsey+Gallagher

Printed in Dunstable, United Kingdom